Sentinel Peak

ISBN: 978-1-947578-36-4

Ink Smith Publishing
P.O. Box 361
Lakehurst, NJ 08733

SENTINEL PEAK

By Jay Chalk

Ink Smith Publishing
www.ink-smith.com

I dedicate this book to Rachel, who left me those notes in a CD that was wedged under the seat of a certain Jeep...

1

New Mexico Territory, 1853

A bright spring morning stretched over the Apache camp. Thin spires of smoke rose into clear air. A soft breeze blew, the air smelling of cedar and roasting horseflesh.

Several warriors milled about. One recited a few quiet words then turned, nodding to the four-corners of the Earth. Lighting his pipe, the warrior puffed thoughtfully. The long, cool shadows of morning retreated, giving way to the torturous, ever-present sun. The day began just as 10,000 others.

All shadows vanished with a blinding flash.

A light blazed overhead. A second burst low on the horizon. The fireballs bathed the landscape in ghostly white. Villagers cowered. Only stunted cries of fear broke the silence.

The intense glare dissipated and familiar morning shadows returned. The people remained face down in the sand, eerie stillness enveloping them. After several heartbeats the medicine man stood erect and chanted.

Everyone rose, glancing around tentatively. The shaman's chanting subsided; the tribe looked at him in silent expectation.

"Yi-na-yes-gon-i is displeased," he announced. "The lights herald the arrival of The Creator's consul." Surveying the camp, he took in the people's frightened glances. "They will demand an account of our bravery, and that of previous generations."

Men stared apprehensively to the azure sky. Boom-boom! A rolling shock wave jarred the camp, echoing off red sandstone cliffs. Several dropped again, covering their ears.

Searching the sky, the shaman's hand lifted. "Behold!"

A cylindrical object tracked silently overhead. Trailing it was a finger of smoke that stretched to the horizon. The craft disappeared behind low hills.

"It burns!" a lone warrior shouted.

"It is not a consul," another yelled. "It has been cast out of 'beyond-the-sky.' It is a demon!"

War-whoops went up. Several warriors demanded to find and slay it, to please The Creator.

The old medicine man shook his head, pointing in the craft's direction. "It is the 'silver eagle' of my vision; it has riders."

"We will test their bravery then slay them too!" a warrior cried.

"No! The riders have strong magic. They are deadly."

The chief, a powerfully built man, strode to the shaman and gazed at him with flat black eyes. "If that is true, how are we to fight this 'magic'?"

The medicine man's eyes narrowed. "Watch and listen," he said, turning toward a distant sound, "and you will witness their strength. We cannot oppose them—even their glance carries death!"

Hesitating, the chief's gaze followed the shaman's.

At first only a murmur, the sound grew to a rumble that pounded their chests. A cry rang out, and several warriors pointed to low hills to the west.

A dark cloud billowed from the horizon. A shiny object shot from within, burgeoning into a long silver wedge that sped toward them, whistling shrilly. Like a thousand winds screaming across the desert, a resonance blasted into the canyon. The people covered their ears. The craft accelerated, hugging the desert floor, a swirling sandstorm in its wake. Its quarter-mile long shadow ate the terrain.

Dogs barked and the tribe broke for cover. The craft shot over with an explosion. Cedars snapped. Rushing wind flattened crude shelters, showering the people with rocks and debris. Ionized air pricked their skin and hair stood on end as if lightening struck. A few horses broke free, scattering in terror down the narrow canyon.

With a high-pitched whine, the "silver eagle," trailing smoke, banked left and disappeared over a plateau several miles away. Thick black smoke rose from a mountain on the plateau's far end. Rolling thunder reverberated across the desert, then pounded the canyon, its echo dying in the distance. A silent pall settled over the countryside.

For two days the tribe argued about the flying object's meaning. Against the medicine man's wishes, the chief organized a half-dozen of the tribe's most courageous warriors to investigate. Dressed in war-paint, they headed for the plateau. They never returned.

Under the circling sun, moon and stars, the tribe soon moved on.

August, 1986.

Dressed in a faded, green T-shirt, jeans and work boots, Daniel McKntyre stood on the edge of a gravel road, gazing. The land was barren, sunbaked, and forlorn. Desert mountains in shades of gray, brown, and red reflected off his aviators; distant purple ones shimmered in midmorning sun. Whispers echoed in Dan's mind. Sagebrush cacti and creosote seemed to wither, die, and then re-sprout at a rapid pace.

His eyes were riveted on a plateau with an attached, isolated peak. The peak had haunted his dreams. Dan had loaded within sight of it several times and always felt like he was being watched.

A large dust devil swirled his way. Tumbleweeds and other debris spun around the tan funnel. It grew closer as if it were drawn to him. A tumbleweed skidded past. He thought he could hear a rasping sound—voices? He stood there, squinting through Ray-Bans.

Dark shapes moved inside the spinning sand. "What the hell?"

Inside the dust devil a man led a pack animal. Both man and animal seemed unfazed or unaware of the swirling sand. The column of sand hesitated, swirling in place only a few yards away. The man inside took several determined steps, halted and looked Dan's way. He beckoned for Dan to follow.

Sweat trickled down Dan's jaw, and he shivered, too stunned to move. I'm dreaming, he thought. The stranger was perhaps in his thirties, his long, dark hair held in a ponytail. He wore a white, waist-length tunic over a black, long-sleeve shirt with white designs around the wrists. Fatigue-type trousers were tucked into gray boots. The whole attire seemed to be a uniform of sorts, but bizarre and out of place—especially in the mid-summer Arizona desert.

"Who the hell are you?" Dan shouted.

Only the sound of chafing wind answered. The man pointed toward the plateau Dan had been gazing at, then gestured, inviting Dan to follow.

Dan's eyes widened in recognition; he knew this man.

And time stopped.

Something touched his shoulder. "Dan."

Dan shivered and blinked as if coming out of a trance.

"You okay?" came a voice behind him.

"I don't know…uh, yeah, I guess." Dan eyed the older man. Charles Fulton was taller than Dan's six-foot-two, his thin frame highlighting a slight beer-belly. The man's face was leathery and care-worn. Dan glanced once more to the desert and retreating dust devil. "Just thought I saw something in that—" He hesitated, nodding toward the desert. "There was someone out there—I think."

"You were gonna step into that dust devil, weren't you?"

"Why the hell would I do that?"

"The kid in you." Charlie shaded his brow with a brown, gnarled hand. "Could've swore I heard you talking. But I don't see a thing out there but that ol' sand devil—and it's pulling away." He turned to Dan. "You probably saw a deer. I've seen deer around these parts; big ol' mule deer the size of a horse come down from the mountains in the morning." He paused. "Come on, let's get our wagons loaded and get the hell outta here."

"You're right," Dan said, unconvinced. "Probably just a deer." He tried to recall some the local legends about dust devils—something about seeing people you knew in them? He damn sure didn't see a deer.

Dan sighed, rubbing his forehead. It had to be because of his lack of sleep. No way could that have been his great-grandfather.

Both turned, stepping across crushed caliche rocks toward two eighteen-wheelers, the sounds of idling diesel engines filling the air. Charlie headed to the rig in the rear, a red Peterbilt pulling a white trailer. Dan stepped to a blue Kenworth parked in front. He paused, stretched his lean, muscular frame, then climbed into the cab.

13

Thirty minutes later, Dan sat in the high-back driver's seat, his truck loaded and pointed downhill, waiting for Charlie to finish loading. The Caterpillar engine idled with a distinct, metallic rumble. Cool air blew from an air-conditioning vent, teasing the logbook in his lap. He kept glancing out the window to the distant horizon; that damn mountain in the distance and the episode with the dust devil kept him distracted. Dan gave a loud sigh and tossed the logbook on the passenger seat; no way could he focus. He scanned the desert, searching for more dust devils. Nothing, thankfully. His eyes went back to that lone, distant peak and nearby plateau.

Ignoring that little voice of caution, Daniel McKntyre slowly climbed from the cab of his rig, hopping down the last rung. He stepped around the Kenworth's large hood, staring out to the desert and rubbing the stubble on his strong jaw. There had to be some kind of tracks. The wind in that dust devil wasn't powerful enough to erase everything. A man and heavily loaded mule had to have left some kind of sign. He stepped around creosote and sage brush, pausing where he thought he saw the pair. "Shit!" The only foot prints were his own.

"You just can't leave this damn desert alone, can you?" Charlie shouted.

Dan turned. "You were right when you said you heard me talking. When that dust devil came past, there was some dude standing nearby—right about here where I'm standing. He just came out of nowhere."

Charlie gave an annoyed sigh, shaded his brow, and

scanned the brush. "Well he ain't here now." He paused, eyeing Dan for several seconds. "Did he say who he was or what he wanted?"

"No, he never said a word. And then you came sneaking up behind me and spooked him."

Heat waves danced over baked sand. "That was over thirty minutes ago. Only a fool would still be out there in this heat."

"This is bullshit! This guy stood right here. I asked him who he was and he wouldn't answer."

The older man shrugged, shaking his head.

"And, Charlie, get this: he wore some kind of uniform, military I think."

Charlie scratched his neck. "What would a soldier be doing out here?"

Dan stared back.

"Look, son, the desert can play all sorts of tricks on a person."

"Yeah, whatever." Dan searched the ground for footprints. Except for his own, the sand lay undisturbed. Goose bumps crept down his arms.

"Danny boy," Charlie shouted, "give it up. There ain't a soul out there, except the fool I'm looking at."

"Dammit, Charlie—I know what I saw!"

Sighing, the older man shrugged. "Come on, Dan," he said, nodding to their nearby rigs, "let's get the hell out of here before you totally flip. We have a thousand miles to go. And you said you wanted to stop and see Anna and your daughter on the way."

"Yeah, yeah." Sighing, Dan took a step, winced, and limped back to Charlie.

"Thought that knee had healed," Charlie said. "Better get it checked out again. Limping makes you look weak. Don't wanna look weak in front of Anna and Amy."

"Whatever." Dan removed his aviators and wiped them on a shirt sleeve. Every time Anna and Amy were brought up, his stomach churned. Every day he regretted leaving the army and it compounded daily. And his regrets for leaving Anna so long ago would fill a box store.

He had joined the army, hoping the discipline and stress of soldiering would force him to focus his thoughts away from Anna. But in the back of his mind, Anna was still there. Always. He had to get out, get away, and do something other than dwell on her. After five years of service, he reluctantly left the military, hoping for a new distraction. Perhaps trucking would work? Dan had prayed all his adult life that he could bury the guilt he carried about their past relationship. Living the life of a trucker had one big plus: it helped him shrug off personal responsibility, and he had hoped, along with it, guilt. He'd deliberately stuck himself behind the windshield of a big-rig to help prevent the possibility of his past—or his future—from overtaking him. But all trucking did was give him too much time to think. He was forced to conclude that the only way to rid himself of his memories of Anna and the resulting guilt was to confront both.

He had challenged their past. And now? Seems he may, indeed, get that second chance with Anna—if he didn't blow it.

Dan climbed into his rig. Settling in, he fastened the seatbelt, his thoughts shifting from Anna to the dust devil. Being constantly on the move in seventy feet of tractor-trailer still didn't prevent half-baked ideas from taking root. Ideas like, in spite of his quirkiness and seeming lack of responsibility, Anna still cared.

Moments later, the two trucks pulled away. Hands gripping the giant steering wheel, Dan slowly, carefully guided the heavily-loaded big rig down the hill, Charlie a tenth of a mile behind. Working through the gears, his mind focused on the reoccurring dream that had come to life inside that dust devil—and how all that bizarre stuff seemed tied to Anna Wildaer.

The dreams began in his senior year of high school. That was the year he'd first met Anna. He had lived in Las Vegas and Anna had just enrolled in his high school. Something had instantly clicked between them and they were constantly together.

A year passed. He was nineteen and had just finished his freshman year at the University of Texas. Anna, eighteen, had just graduated from high school. He drove to Las Vegas to be with her on her special day.

Dan instinctively scanned the cluster of gauges, then stared back out the grimy windshield. The day after her graduation they'd hiked to the summit of Mount Charleston. That was the first time he'd really noticed something strange about Anna.

He and Anna, winded from the altitude, had just

reached the almost 12,000 foot summit. Dan tossed his backpack near the navigation tower, stumbled and fell. Anna collapsed on top of him. Both gulped the thin air. He unfastened her pack, letting it fall to the side. They lay in each other's arms, recuperating. After a moment he rose and stepped over to a tiny American flag someone had thrust into a haphazard rock cairn. Stiff winds blew constantly at that elevation, the scent of pine and spruce filling the air.

Anna crept up behind him, slipping her hand into his. "Didn't think I could make it, huh?"

"I never said you couldn't.

"But you thought it."

"I'm not taking the bait." Dan faced her and did a double take. For a fleeting second, something in Anna's face seemed older. His gaze roved over her delicate nose and full lips. Her long, curly brown hair was fastened behind her, but a few strands had worked loose, blowing across her face. Smiling, Anna brushed wisps of hair from her eyes, and the look vanished.

An updraft blew his hat off and Anna dashed after it. Stepping to him she shoved it on his head, then snaked her arms around his waist, pulling him back from the trail. Both fell to the ground, silent. Anna rolled on top of him, the haunting look in her hazel eyes forever seared into his memory.

Unfastening her hair, Anna shook her head. Long, brown curls spilled over both their faces. She bent down, brushing her lips gently over his. "These precious moments in time are fleeting. But time is our friend, for now."

"'For now?' What in the hell are you talking about?"

"You and me, of course." Her eyes searched his. "On the way up here, you said this hike reminded you of these strange dreams you've been having: of your great-grandfather wearing a strange military uniform and hiking up a mountain, with you as a young boy at his side."

"I never said he wore a uniform."

"Did he?"

"Yeah, but—"

"You must have mentioned it. Otherwise, how would I have known?"

"The same way you seem to know a lot of shit about me that I never talk about."

Her eyes were like windows in time. Confused, he felt like a small child, witnessing something forbidden. "Anna, I," he stammered.

Anna touched his lips with a fingertip. "Shh…" Sliding her lithe body against his, she wrapped her arms around his neck, their lips meeting.

Dan sighed. The roar of the diesel filled his ears, snapping him into the present. Anna Wildaer was an addiction. She was his only connection to those strange dreams—a dream that had played out in a freaking dust devil earlier that morning.

Dan downshifted, steering his rig around a downhill, hairpin turn. The curve straightened and he shoved the gearstick back and to the right, picking up speed. He hadn't seen Anna in a couple of months, although they had talked since then. Her divorce was final. And her daughter, Amy, was ten by now. Dan sighed; Amy was always the point of contention. The last time he and Anna were together, they had bickered over the little girl. And it was his fault, which made it even worse.

What he needed to do was grow up and get over it. Yet all those years of silence on Anna's part was hard to ignore. He and Anna broke it off over ten years before Amy was born.

The two trucks eased down the dirt road, rooster tails of sand billowing from the tires. Dan tried to focus on driving, but found himself recalling that night, so long ago, when they'd called it quits. Their relationship had grown stormy, but that night it was different. He was demanding and made the mistake of giving Anna an ultimatum: either come live with him in Texas, or it was over between them.

Anna dropped a box at his feet full of keepsakes and gifts he'd given her over the years. He stood there dumbfounded as she fumed, her eyes fiery.

"'There, my lord,'" she had mocked, "'are remembrances that I've longed, long to redeliver. Rich gifts wax poor when givers prove unkind.'"

Eight months later, Anna gave birth to a little girl with dark hair and gray eyes. His eyes...

Whop! Dan jumped as something smacked the underside of the hood. "What the hell?" He scanned the cluster of gauges; all was normal. He glanced in the mirror, expecting to see rubber shredding from a peeled tire. Only a trailing dust cloud filled his vision. It was probably nothing but a rock.

The cab grew stuffy and Dan adjusted the air-conditioner. He was still scanning the gauges when it finally dawned on him what he heard. He moved his fingers to an A/C vent. Hot air hit his fingers.

"Son-of-a-bitch!" Dan reached for the CB mike. "Hey, Charlie Brown."

"Yeah, come on."

"I just threw both A/C belts. You wouldn't have a spare would you?"

"Nope."

Tossing the mike on the dash, Dan grumbled, rolling down the window. A searing blast of air hit him on the shoulder. Staring through the windshield, he moved his fingers to a toggle switch marked "RH window." The right window lowered; the swirling wind was like a blast-furnace. He cursed his luck; it was always something.

The two long-haulers followed the twisting dirt road another three miles where it dead-ended at the east-west highway. Dust drifted across the road, the two big trucks rolling to a stop. Dan eased the nose of the Kenworth out onto the two-lane blacktop. Charlie's rig mirrored Dan's. The two heavily loaded trucks sluggishly headed east on U.S. 70.

Dan glanced at his clothes. His faded tank top stuck to his sweat-soaked chest. Grime covered the tattoo of an inverted triangle on his right shoulder. It was a hell of a time for the A/C to conk-out—just as he was trying to make a good impression on Anna.

Laying a tan arm on the windowsill, he moved the transmission through the gears with the other hand. It was sixty miles to Stanton, where Anna lived. He reached for the radio mike. "Hey, Charlie Brown?"

"Come on."

"I need to stop somewhere and make a phone call."

The two eighteen-wheelers parked in front of a convenience store on the outskirts of Peridot, Arizona. Charlie went inside to get a couple of Cokes while Dan used the pay phone.

"*Hello?*" came the feminine voice.

Dan coughed and took a deep breath. "Hey, girl, it's me."

"*Danny. I was just thinking about you. Are you at home?*"

"No." He cleared his throat. "Actually, I'm in Peridot."

"*Peridot? You mean—*"

"Yeah," Dan interrupted, "I'm heading back to the house. I'll be passing through and thought I might drop by. See you and Amy." He hesitated. "That is, if—"

"*Amy and I were going to church tonight.*"

Dan stared at some initials scratched in a rail by his head. Sighing, he examined his boot laces.

"*But,*" Anna continued, "*I guess for one Wednesday evening the church can get along without us.*"

Dan lifted his head, gripping the receiver. "Anna."

"*Amy has been asking about you. I think she'd like to see you.*"

"What about you?"

"*If I didn't want to see you, you'd know it.*"

The line went silent. He fought down a snarky remark. Keys in hand, Dan scratched at the coin-holder.

"*So, when can you get here?*"

He paused, smiling in relief. "Maybe in an hour or so, but I've got another driver with me. Charlie Fulton, you've met him."

"*The guy who drives the red truck?*"

"Yeah. We emptied in Phoenix yesterday, then loaded near Globe this morning. Both loads are going to Dallas. We're running together."

"*Are you two in trouble again?*"

Dan chuckled. "We're behaving. Hey, can he stop in with me?"

"*Of course.*"

"I've missed you, baby," Dan murmured.

The line again grew silent. "*Just park in the drive like before.*"

"Got it. I'll see you in an a bit."

Saying good-bye, he replaced the receiver. His stomach knotted.

"Was she there?" Charlie asked, handing Dan a Coke.

Dan pulled the tab ring and took a long swallow. "Yep." He leaned over the phone, brow furrowing. "I just don't get it."

"Did Anna tell you to get lost?"

"That's just it. She didn't." He took another gulp, sighing. "She still seems a little cold, but I thought she would've been more pissed at me for the way I left last time. It wasn't a pretty scene."

"Maybe she's saving it 'til she sees you. Women do that crap, you know."

"Especially this one." Emptying his can, Dan tossed it into a nearby trash barrel. "What am I going to say to her?"

The older man shook his head. "Just don't be an asshole if she tells you it's over."

"Thanks for the help, man."

Both drivers headed to their idling rigs. "Give me a second to change," Dan shouted, nearing his truck.

Moments later, two rigs lumbered away from the convenience store. As Dan moved through the gears, he recalled what brought him to this moment.

Last Christmas, he'd taken a week off. While cleaning out a storage shed, he unexpectedly came across the box containing forgotten record albums and mementoes Anna had returned. Reaching for the top album, he unconsciously trailed fingers over the dusty cover. He gingerly examined Pink Floyd's *Dark Side of the Moon*, and a Lynyrd Skynyrd album. He worked out the album jacket— and there, taped to it, was a faded note. The tape holding it was yellow and brittle, and the moment he touched the note, it fell into his hand, a little paper time capsule. Holding his breath, he gently unfolded it.

The note was dated eleven years ago. It said, in part,

that no matter how much time had lapsed, he was to contact her or her parents when he found the note. Included in the note were several phone numbers in Arizona, Utah, and curiously, one number Dan later learned was in Belize.

It took him a couple of weeks to work up the nerve and call. On the second try, calling an Arizona number, he finally got through to Anna. She could hardly believe it was him. Dan's heart sank when he learned she was married, but he wasn't surprised. They talked for nearly an hour. Anna wanted a complete run-down of the last ten years of his life. She found it hard to believe he was driving a truck. Their conversation ended with her wanting to see him. Dan thought it curious that Anna failed to mention she had a daughter until he asked her about children.

And then she'd asked him if he was still having those dreams. He shook his head. Those bizarre dreams nagged at him and were now interfering in his waking life. If she knew anything about them, he knew he had to press her to get an answer.

The man was a granite statue. With sharply chiseled features and deep creases around his eyes, he seemed cut from stone. Those lines were his life: austere and intense. Seated at an old, steel desk, the man replaced the phone receiver and instinctively reached to his chest. He caught himself as fingers touched an empty shirt-pocket.

Chuckling, he shook his head. A smoker for as long as he could recall, he'd quit nine years ago upon his wife's death. She was killed in a car accident a week before their twenty-fifth wedding anniversary. That, alone, would drive most people to start, but not Simon Terrell. Terrell never did things conventionally.

Outwardly, Terrell seemed unaffected by the tragedy. As a former Marine officer, he had lived with death in Vietnam. But the connoisseur of darkness was always elsewhere, until now. The optimism he once held for life was another casualty. Spontaneity was replaced with cold, methodical cynicism.

Tapping a finger on the desk, he rose and sauntered

to a large living room window. He stared blankly across
the manicured lawn. When he and his wife bought this
home twenty-five years ago, they were in the desert.
Now the neighborhood was considered an upscale part of
suburban Tucson. Terrell hated how the city encroached
upon his little section of the world. With his wife dead, both
children grown and gone, there was no reason to stay in
Arizona. Well, he mused, he only had a few short years until
retirement from the FBI. Then they could all kiss his ass.
Afterwards, he'd sell and move. Then he could get back to
Katherine and Beth. Maybe he could finally leave this life
behind him. Yet something lay unfinished in his life: a case
he had been working on, erratically, for over thirteen years.
Always hanging in the back of his mind, it grated on him
like fingernails on a chalkboard.

It started with the kidnapping of a millionaire's
twenty-eight-year-old wife from her Beverly Hills home
back in the early 1960s. No ransom note was ever delivered;
the woman and kidnappers had simply vanished. The
case remained open. In 1972, the year he was assigned to
the case, an individual matching the kidnapped woman's
description surfaced in Utah. According to The Bureau,
this look-alike was connected to a Utah based right-wing
extremist group—a suspected terrorist organization The
Bureau had under surveillance. Without warning, the
extremists suddenly disbanded, its members evaporating,
including the "kidnapped victim." Terrell was about to
throw in the towel when he received a break. A year later the
woman surfaced in Las Vegas. By the time he was on her

trail, she had vanished again. That was twelve years ago.

Sighing, Terrell rubbed the gray stubble on his chin. He concluded she had staged her own kidnapping, probably to get away from her husband. The husband, a wealthy Beverly Hills land developer, was investigated and cleared.

Terrell stared out the window. The case grew more bizarre by the year. Time had slipped by for everyone except the kidnapped woman. The sketchy reports he recently received about the "young lady" were extraordinary. When chasing recent leads, he deliberately used old photos taken in 1960, a year before her disappearance. Yet current sightings still had her as a young woman. The last time he showed the old photos was two weeks ago at the Arizona State University registrar's office. They produced an expired faculty ID and 1984 yearbook photo. University records listed her as a former assistant professor. Anna Wildaer, Ph.D. Archeology. Almost twenty-five years after being "kidnapped," she had scarcely aged.

Surely there was a mistake? The woman he sought would now be in her early fifties. A daughter? As far as he knew, the kidnapped woman had no children.

The conundrum ballooned last week. While at a jeweler's on personal business, he came across the photo of an icon all Special Agents were ordered to investigate: an inverted triangle enclosing a sword flanked by lightning bolts. The jeweler said the design was engraved in a pendant brought in by an attorney a year earlier. The necklace had belonged to the attorney's wife. The lawyer was named

Jeffery Albright. His wife—now ex-wife—was Dr. Anna Wildaer.

The jeweler's photo stirred up a hornet's nest. The phone call he'd just received was from his boss. Terrell was told it was now a matter of national security. He was to drop everything and report to D.C. for a briefing. What the hell had he stumbled on?

The agent sighed, running a hand over stiff, crew-cut hair. He'd almost forgotten about the boyfriend. Seems Dr. Wildaer was involved with some nondescript truck driver. At least, that's what Agent Kirby in Stanton reported. Terrell frowned. With her credentials and circle of friends, why cavort with a guy so low on the food chain? Maybe the man was one of those survivalist friends of hers? Terrell strode back to the phone. He needed a description of this "boyfriend." The agent paused, receiver in hand. Maybe he should order all the Wildaers seized? He had the authority.

No. Not yet. The Wildaers had friends, and it could turn ugly. Then The Bureau's nemesis, the media, would begin sniffing around. The last thing The Bureau needed was publicity, especially on such a bizarre case. Discretion was needed. He would have the trucker investigated before making a move. The poor sucker would never know he'd been had.

Chuckling, Terrell punched in Agent Kirby's number.

4

The low, jagged peaks of the Gila Mountains merged with the sweeping heights of 11,000-foot Mount Graham, creating a panoramic backdrop to the Gila River valley. The two big-trucks rolled through the valley's center, now in the heart of the San Carlos Apache reservation.

Dan took in the surroundings; the poverty was horrendous. The reservation reminded him of a shantytown in a third world country. Dotting the landscape were rundown wood-frame and stucco shacks, bed sheets for curtains. Squalor soon gave way to well-ordered cotton and hay fields as the truckers sped off the reservation, heading east.

Dan made a right onto a narrow farm road. Charlie followed suit. The Wildaers were a half-mile down on the left. Dan's heart pounded. How would Anna receive him? His rig idled up to the Wildaer home and Dan spotted Anna's father signaling for them to back in. Dan sighed, disappointed; everyone had stayed home from church. Easing the big-truck past the driveway, Dan glanced over to the long gray farmhouse, doing a double take. A young woman descended the front porch steps. Arms folded, she smiled, gazing Dan's way. A dark-haired girl shot past her and the woman grabbed the girl by the shoulder, jerking her back.

The two-way crackled. "There she is Danny-boy, waiting on you. Both of them. Yessir, that Anna is a real cutie."

The two big rigs, four-ways flashing, slowly backed into the wide gravel drive, halting next to a large John Deere tractor. Killing the engine, Dan glanced out the windshield, eyeing the woman walking toward his truck. Arms still folded, she stopped by the fuel tank on his side.

Nervous, Dan scrambled out of the truck.

Taller than average at over five-seven, Anna seemed to fill her shorts out a little more than he remembered. A light blue cotton blouse hung loose about her waist. Cut-offs and white Reeboks accented smooth, tan legs. Anna's naturally curly hair moved in the breeze; two silver studs sparkled in each ear. Her small nose and full lips were so delicate as to be almost aristocratic. To Dan, Anna seemed as young and fresh as ever. Yet he thought she carried herself differently; there seemed a quiet reserve about her he'd never noticed. Stepping closer, Dan held her gaze, searching the triangle of light in her hazel eyes.

"Wondered if you'd ever find your way here again," Anna said, eyes narrowing.

He cleared his throat and kicked at the gravel. "Hey." *That's all you can manage? How freaking lame.*

"So help me, McKntyre, if you ever—"

Dan pulled her to him, almost crushing her.

She hesitated. Her arms encircled his neck. "Danny…" Holding each other tightly, their lips brushed.

"I've missed you, baby," Dan whispered.

"Oh, sorry—don't let me interrupt," Charlie blurted, coming from around Dan's truck.

Blushing, Anna quickly pulled away. "You didn't."

"The hell he didn't," Dan grumbled. "It's your timing, Charlie. You're just like an old hen."

Laughing, Anna grabbed Dan's hand, pulling him toward the house. "Come on, Mom and Dad are waiting for you." She glanced at Charlie. "You, too, 'old hen.'" Anna turned to Dan. "Are you guys hungry?"

"I am," Charlie shot back. "I could definitely use some home cooking."

The couple, followed by Charlie, headed to the front porch. Dan glanced back to his friend. "He's the perfect guest. You feed him and he leaves."

The three walked up the porch steps. Anna paused, letting Charlie slide past and into the house. Stepping closer to Dan, she gazed up at him, hesitating.

"What?"

"We need to have a heart-to-heart."

"Now?"

Anna eyed him, silent.

Dan winced. "Here we go again. Let's play that wonderful game called, 'mind reading.'"

"After dinner."

Dan's jaw tightened. He turned, grabbing the screendoor handle. Anna remained on the steps.

The Wildaer's house was ranch style, like most of the large homes in the region. To Dan, who had paid several visits, it was a homey type of home.

Anna's father greeted them. "Come in, come in!" He grabbed their hands, one by one.

Completely bald, Wildaer looked to be only in his early fifties, yet Dan knew he was at least twenty years older—and he still wore no glasses. Wildaer flew B-17s in World War II, then F-86 Sabers in Korea. He was shot down twice—once in each war. Well respected in the community, Wildaer was now a successful farmer and rancher.

Joan patted Dan's arm, smiling.

To Dan, Joan Wildaer seemed almost an enigma. Joan's appearance had scarcely changed since he had first met her, over fifteen years ago. Joan had to be in her late sixties, and like her husband, she appeared at least twenty years younger. She wore her long, gray-streaked hair in a braid. And, like Anna, there was something about Joan's eyes.

"How are you doing, boy?" Joan said, giving him a warm hug.

Small arms encircled his waist: Amy.

"Hi, Danny! How long can you stay?" Before Dan could reply, she began chattering. "Would you like to see my rabbits? Mom and I named them. But there's a bad one and I can't tell you his name. Mom can," the little girl shot a quick glance to her grandmother, "but not in here."

Dan dropped his arms around the girl, giving Joan a quizzical look. "A bad rabbit? How can a rabbit be bad?"

"You don't want to know," Anna said, approaching them.

Joan laughed. "If you guys are hungry, follow me." Joan and Ben, with Charlie following, headed for the kitchen.

Anna placed a hand on Amy's shoulder. "Sweety, Danny will see the rabbits later, okay?" Amy turned to leave. Dan pulled her back. Kneeling, he studied her. Large, gray eyes returned his gaze. Amy suddenly threw herself into his arms. Dan kissed her softly on the cheek, squeezing her to him.

Anna laid a hand on Dan's shoulder, her eyes glistening.

▽▽▽

Thirty minutes later Anna, with help from her mother and Amy, cleared the kitchen table. The two truckers, not having to deliver until day after tomorrow, were invited to stay the night.

Charlie excused himself first. A few minutes later Dan followed. He met Charlie coming up the steps.

"Those folks think a lot of you, Dan. They'd make great in-laws." Pausing, he studied the younger man. "Don't screw it up this time. Do the *right* thing for a change."

Dan smiled, continuing down the steps. "What? And give up the most disjointed, warped lifestyle ever known?"

The summer sun dropped behind Mt. Graham. A lone cricket chirped. Hands in his pockets, Dan strolled to his truck. The Wildaers had always been odd, from their perpetual inability to age, to their strange knowledge of his dreams. When he looked at Anna's parents, he felt a sadness like he'd felt this morning while gazing at that mountain. It was as if he and they were already family. He closed his eyes for a moment, feeling the mysterious melancholy that covered the Wildaers' home like a blanket. A peculiar sensation gripped him, similar to earlier out in the desert.

A swirl of dust blew across the gravel drive, vanishing as quickly as it appeared. He studied the mailbox. It was as if time stopped there, right where civilization met the Wildaers' home.

Dan's thoughts returned to the stranger in the desert. He hadn't yet told Anna of him, still trying to digest it himself. He'd heard of dead relatives coming back to give warning of impending tragedy. He chuckled at the ridiculousness.

Dan continued walking, wondering what Anna wanted to talk about. She seemed worried. Could it be about her divorce? Perhaps Anna wasn't ready to be close to him yet. In any case, Anna and he definitely had to clear the air, learn where they stood with each other. Dan's jaw tightened and he shook his head.

Reaching his truck, Dan gripped a handhold, hesitating. He felt like a doomed astronaut out of a Bradbury novel. He imagined he was climbing into his spaceship, his only way back to sanity. Sighing, he scrambled up the steps.

"You need a reality check, McKntyre."

Dan tossed an overnight bag out of the rig. Footsteps came from the other side of the John Deere. Hopping down the last step, he turned. Ben Wildaer stood, staring at him. In the older man's hands were two brown bottles of Coors.

Ben winked. "If you don't like cold beer, leave it there." He pointed with a bottle to the fuel tank behind Dan. "I'll drink it later."

Dan reached for the offered drink. "No, sir, it's not that I don't like a cold one, it's just that…Mr. Wildaer, I didn't think you—"

"It's Ben. And you didn't think a God-fearing Mormon like me could enjoy an occasional brewsky?" The old man chuckled, taking a long pull from his bottle. "I've done a lot worse than this in my day, boy. And I don't plan on burning in hell either. Now drink up!"

Leaning against the truck steps, Dan hooked a foot on the lower rung. Raising his bottle, he took a long swallow. It was like rain on a sweltering summer afternoon. Taking another drink, Dan noticed old Ben eyeing the full length of the tractor-trailer. An expectant silence filled the air.

Dan examined his beer bottle, feeling the older man's gaze.

"How much diesel she carry?"

"Three-hundred gallons." Dan tapped the tank with his bottle. "Twin One-fifties."

Ben stepped toward the front of the truck. Halting, he glanced back to Dan. "She yours yet?"

"In five months."

"Then what?"

"Then I'd like to drop a grenade in the fuel tank, push it off a cliff, and pray I never see the son-of-a-bitch again."

Ben looked on, silent.

Dan's eyes flicked to the truck. "If it wasn't for the driving, being away from home, and having to deal with morons, trucking would be a great vocation."

Chuckling, Ben took another pull. "Did you leave anything out?"

"No, that about sums it." Dan titled his bottle. "Every time I crawl behind the wheel, more precious sand slips through the hourglass. The bottom half is almost full, Ben, and I have nothing to show for the emptiness above." Dan sighed in disgust. "The list of things I never thought would happen grows everyday. To me, that truck represents my latest in a long series of failures."

"Seems to me you need to take a chance. Make a commitment, Dan, and follow through. We all take chances. The secret is making the payoff worth it." He paused. "You don't know how fortunate you are at this moment."

"Yeah, I'm alive, with a cold beer in my hand."

"Son, you know what I mean. You've been given a rare opportunity to go back and correct one of those 'what ifs.'"

Dan looked away.

Ben cleared his throat. "Anna's divorce was final a few months back. At least on paper. But if you ask me, it was over long before then." He paused, tilting his bottle.

"I still can't believe my own daughter would marry such a lout. There are times 'Doctor' Wildaer just sets herself up for failure. Like someone else I know." Ben eyed the younger man. "Know what I mean?"

Dan studied his boots.

"Yessir," Ben continued, "Anna could've had anybody. For the life of me, I could never figure out what she saw in Albright."

Dan frowned. "I thought he was a filthy rich lawyer? Why, I couldn't even—"

"He is 'filthy'—like a snake. Son, you're cut from different cloth." Ben paused. "Have you ever met him?"

"Yeah, once," Dan said. "Earlier in the year. He struck me as a strange dude. But then again, how do you expect a guy to act when his wife is meeting a long-lost boyfriend? And, that old boyfriend happens to be the paternal father of his daughter?"

Ben muttered something about, "Doing the right thing."

Taking a quick swallow of beer, Dan recalled his first and only meeting with Jeffery Albright.

It was just after Christmas and only a couple of weeks since he had re-established contact with Anna. She was anxious to see him. He had called her, telling her he would be passing through Phoenix in a few days. Anna insisted Dan stop and meet her somewhere. Dan chose a shopping mall; he could park his rig there. He recalled his nervousness when she told him to look for a silver Mercedes

450 SE. He almost told her to forget it.

His insides turned to Jell-O when the Mercedes pulled up alongside his parked rig. A slender woman emerged from the front passenger side of the car. Wearing heels and a calf-length flowery dress, she headed his way.

Anna was no longer the cute, young co-ed he had left in tears so long ago. She was now a breathtakingly beautiful woman. He glanced down to his worn jeans and work boots. No way was he in her league. Anna halted a few feet from him, smiling. Her hair was held back with a lace ribbon, and an expensive necklace circled her neck.

Removing her sunglasses, Anna smiled. "Danny?"

He choked, nodding. "Yeah, girl, it's me."

Anna gave him a quick hug, pecked his cheek, and then quickly pushed away.

They stood gazing at one another for several seconds, each not quite knowing what to do or say. Anna stepped closer, eyes glistening.

The driver's door on the Mercedes opened. A tall man stepped out, clearing his throat.

"Oh, how shameful of me." Anna glanced apologetically to the man. "Danny, this is my husband, Jeffery."

Jeffery Albright was slightly taller than Dan, but slender, with short, blond hair and brown eyes. The expensive polo shirt and Armani slacks only added to Albright's handsome Neiman's looks.

"Glad to meet you," Dan said, shaking the attorney's limp hand. Albright eyed him, silent.

Dan recognized the look. He knew that to the attorney, he was nothing but a low-life, blue-collar laborer, someone to be brushed off, despised and exploited. Dan knew the only reason Albright even tolerated his presence was because it was important to his wife. Heading back to the Mercedes, Albright kept glancing back to him. Dan's jaw tightened.

A dark-haired girl of perhaps nine approached Anna, stealing his attention. He recognized something in the shape of her nose and chin. His throat tightened.
Anna stepped aside. "Danny, this is Amy, your...our," she averted her eyes, "our daughter."

"'Our' daughter," Dan repeated, "as in yours and mine?"
Anna nodded.

He held his breath, his gaze fixed on the child. Amy had large, gray eyes—his eyes. "Anna. You're kidding, right?"

Anna stepped closer and touched his arm, the scent of lilacs drifting around him. "Not now, Danny. Please, not now. We'll talk later. I promise."

Dan was speechless. He felt like he'd been slugged in the gut with an iron bat. He stepped stiffly back to his truck, trying to collect himself. Dan recalled the soft breeze, the air smelling of sagebrush. He rubbed his right palm on his pants, trying to wipe off Albright's touch.

Dan felt a hand on his shoulder. "You okay, boy?"

"Yeah." Downing his beer, he rested the bottle on a fuel tank. "Just thinking."

Setting his empty beer bottle next to Dan's, Ben rubbed his bald dome. "Albright cleaned her out. They'd been married for nine years, and Anna got nothing out of it except a hard lesson. When she told him she was leaving him, Albright went berserk. Even beat her. To get away from him, she signed things that she normally wouldn't have."

"What?" Dan shot back. "He hit her and she never told me? If I'd have known, I would have—"

"Got yourself thrown in jail. Or killed. That's why Anna never explained what was really going on. She knew what you would do."

"Yeah. I'd take care of the guy."

"Oh, no doubt. But that's just it. It would never be 'one on one' with him. Jeffery Albright is a coward. He doesn't settle things like you or I would. He could order yours or Anna's death on a whim, then sleep very well that night."

Dan shook his head, his jaw tightening.

"You have to understand, son, that to someone like Albright, we're powerless."

"Because we don't have money?"

"Because we have a conscience."

Dan dug at the gravel with a booted heel.

"Dan, there is something you can do."

"And that would be?"

"We want our daughter and grandchild out of harm's way. The sooner the better. Texas would be good."

Dan was about to reply when the old man raised a hand. "Now, I know you and Anna have things to iron out.

But it's nothing that the two of you can't patch up, if you'll just sit down and talk."

"Sir, I—"

"Take Anna and the little one with you." The older man gazed at the younger. "For God's sake, the two will be safe with you."

"But—"

"Son, it's not just Albright I'm worried about. There are others." Ben rubbed his eyes, hesitating. "Anna—"

"Danny, are you out here?" Anna, breathless, came around the corner of the tractor. "So, there you two are." She eyed her father. "What have you been talking about?"

Dan stared hard at Ben. "You."

"I bet." Sighing, Anna touched Dan's arm. "I thought you wanted a shower? Or would you rather gossip?"

Anna's father nodded at Dan, grabbed the empty beer bottles and headed toward the garage, leaving the two alone.

Reaching for his overnight bag, he slung it over a shoulder and started for the house. "Your shower's big enough for two," Dan murmured.

"Charlie's had his."

"Smart-ass."

The two kept walking. "One day, perhaps, when we're alone," Anna whispered.

"What did you say?"

Anna looked away. "Umm, nothing."

The couple slowed as they neared the front steps. Letting the overnight bag slide from his shoulder, Dan gazed at her, savoring each second. "Anna…"

Anna stepped closer. Her eyes slowly closed, her lips parting.

Their lips brushed. The screen-door popped open. "Mom! Phone!"

Warm water struck Dan's shoulders. He turned, facing the shower nozzle. Steamy water hit him full in the face and he gasped, enjoying the feeling of privacy and being clean.

With reluctance, Dan turned off the shower and dried himself. Gazing in the mirror, he was shocked at how rough he really looked. Gray eyes stood out starkly in his deeply tanned face. Yet the two-day growth of beard couldn't hide his boyish looks. Trucking had not yet taken its toll. Not physically, at least. He combed his short, dark hair, shaved, then quickly dressed.

Within minutes Dan was standing on the screened-in back porch, a close darkness settling. Faint red streaks reached like ghostly fingers into the dark, star-filled east, fading into memories. The mingled scent of freshly plowed fields, ocotillo, and ponderosa filled his nostrils.

Anna sat alone on a porch swing. Casually rocking back and forth, she studied Dan as he gazed into the darkness.

Ben lounged in a nearby recliner. Joan sat in an old wooden rocker next to him, Amy curled in her lap.

"Where's Charlie?"

"He said you two would have a long day tomorrow," Joan replied. "He decided to turn in."

"And he told me," Ben added, "to tell you not to stay up too late. Said he didn't want to hear you griping all the way to Dallas about not getting any sleep."

"Oh, he did, did he?" Dan laughed, knowing God had never made a bigger cry baby than Charlie Fulton. Anna scooted over. Dan crossed the porch and dropped next to her.

They made small talk. Amy fell asleep in her grandmother's lap. Anna snuggled closer to Dan. The wind carried a cool, earthy smell and Dan closed his eyes, feeling it move through his memory. The single moon split into two. He blinked several times, the world around him feeling somehow less stable. He stood.

Dan walked slowly to the edge of the porch, as if in a trance. A bright, wide swath of the Milky Way tore across the blackness, and he was struck with a sudden sense of loss. Forgetting where he was, he spoke out loud:

> 'Tis not too late to seek a newer world.
> Push of, and
> sitting well in order, smite the sounding furrows; for my purpose holds.
> To sail beyond the sunset, and the baths of the western stars, until I die.
> It may be we shall touch the Happy Isles. And see the great Achilles, whom we knew.

Suddenly he was in the present. Even in the gloom

he felt their eyes on him. Swallowing hard, he turned and faced them, thankful for the darkness.

Ben stared at him. "Where did you get that?"

"It's Tennyson," Anna said before Dan could reply. "How curious."

"It's titled Ulysses," Dan said, leaning against a post. "'But who mourns for Tithonus'? I once had an English professor who, after we read a tragedy, always asked that." "Tithonus?" Anna queried.

"Tithonus is another of Tennyson's works. Tithonus was the son of the King of Troy, and the epitome of irony. He married Aurora, goddess of the dawn. She asked the gods to grant him immortality, which they did."

Anna frowned. "I don't understand. He got what he wanted, didn't he?"

"Remember the old saying, 'be careful what you ask for'? She failed to ask for his eternal youth. He became so old and shriveled she finally turned him into a grasshopper." Dan chuckled. "That's my kind of luck."

"How awful," Anna murmured. "Danny, what made you think of that now?"

"I don't know. Looking at the stars, sometimes I get this odd feeling."

Ben snorted. "A trucker who spouts Tennyson— that's as weird as a football bat. Do they teach that in truck-driving school?"

"Yeah. I hold a Ph.D. in trucking with a minor in English. After midnight, I quote Shakespeare over the CB." "Dad," Anna interrupted, "Danny wasn't always a trucker.

You know he's a college graduate and was an army officer—"

"Yeah, yeah," Ben murmured, "whatever. Dan, if your goal was to wander, you should've stayed in the army. At least that was a career."

Dan nodded, silent.

Ben eyed Dan in the dimness. "Do you remember our visit this afternoon?"

"Yes, sir."

"It's good that you do."

Joan rose from her seat, half-carrying a sleeping Amy. "Okay everyone—I think we can call it a night." She shot Ben a glance. "Help me tuck in your granddaughter." Ben gave Dan and Anna a last glance and rose, stepping toward his wife.

Dan felt he needed to say something, a word, a comment, but remained silent. He felt Anna's eyes on him and fidgeted, tapping the floor with the toe of her boot.

"Come on, Papa, give me a hand," Joan said, shifting Amy in her arms. "This little girl isn't so little anymore."

Ben gently lifted Amy from Joan's arms. "We won't be doing this much longer."

Amy mumbled but never woke. The Wildaers said goodnight and headed inside.

Dan sighed, his eyes again flicking to the star-filled sky, his thoughts on Tennyson's poem.

Suddenly the fragrance of scented body lotion filled his nostrils. He felt a warm breath on his neck, slender arms snaking around his waist. Anna pressed against his back, her arms moving up his broad chest and shoulders.

"You don't know how long I've wanted to do this," she whispered.

Dan turned, his arms curling around her waist. Anna's arms encircled his neck, the gold bracelet on her delicate wrist sliding against his cheek. Their gazes locked, time halting. "And you don't know how long I've wanted to do this," he whispered, his eyes closing, his lips sensuously touching hers.

Their lips touched again and they kissed passionately. Anna yielded and her body arched to Dan's, molding against him as he pulled her deeper into his arms.

Dan moved his lips over her soft neck. "I love you, Annie."

Fraught with desire, Anna could scarcely breathe. "And I love you, Danny, but...." Gently pushing him away, she looked up with wet eyes. "Sometimes I wonder about how you found those notes I wrote you. I'm even more surprised you had the guts to contact me."

"That thought has also entered my mind. But probably not for the same reason as yours."

Anna wiped an eye with a finger, gazing at him. "I thought that, maybe, you actually wanted to be with me. But when you're here, you seem distracted, like you'd rather be somewhere else."

"I didn't mean to project that."

"But you do, whether you know it or not."

Dan sighed, shaking his head. Oh, God. What a mine field. "Annie, it's...I don't know, it's like you're something I can't have. It's as if you know how things…our lives, are going to unfold."

Anna stared at Dan in the soft darkness, her eyes glowing. "No. You mistake my wants for some kind of special power. You're scared to take on the responsibility for someone else's feelings. You know what you should do, as do I, but you keep pulling back: back from me, from, us, and from what's inside of you."

Dan raised a brow.

Anna paused. "Something's going to have to give."

Dan's heart stopped. "Annie, I…"

Anna shook her head, tears streaking her cheeks. "Don't you know what I'm trying to say?"

He swallowed, averting his eyes.

"Look at me!"

Reluctantly, Dan looked up. "I don't want to lose you. Just give me more time."

"You're scared, aren't you?" Anna's eyes narrowed. "What are you running from, Danny? What is it that you think is chasing you?"

Dan reached out and silently touched Anna's cheek, catching a tear.

"Well," Anna brushed tears from her eyes, "I'm not waiting on you any longer. Time is running out, mister. I'm not living with a part-time husband." She paused, sniffing. "I received a job offer at the local junior college. They've given me until next Tuesday to sign a contract. But the way it's looking, I won't need that long. Either you get out of trucking or—"

"Now look who's giving ultimatums? Let's go back to the part about being a part-time husband."

Anna glared at him.

"I haven't even asked you."

"Don't bother!" Anna snapped. "I should've known better." She stood, fists clenched at her sides, her lips trembling. "Can't anybody reach you—Lord knows I've tried! And I'm not talking about trucking. That's nothing but an enabler—"

"What are you talking about?"

"You know the answer to that. Your dreams." Anna paused, gauging him. "And we—as in you and I, Danny—are part of what's happening to you. You sense it but you won't address it."

Dan shut his eyes, trying to force his thoughts elsewhere.

Anna grabbed his arm, shaking him. "You know I'm right!"

Dan stared in stunned silence.

"McKntyre, sometimes you are so blind!" Anna turned to leave.

"No, you don't. Not this time!" Dan grabbed her by the elbow, spinning her around. "I got the shot across the bow—but don't get sanctimonious with me, little missy. I'm not the one who kept my daughter from me all these years."

Anna's hand lifted. Dan caught her wrist. Looking into her eyes, he suddenly pulled her to him. She struggled for a moment. Their lips met again, and Anna melted into his arms.

Anna pushed away, her face flush, her breath coming in short gasps. "It's always a sex thing with you isn't it?"

"I'm sorry."

"No, you're not. You know exactly what you're doing." Anna turned and stepped across the porch for the house. Pausing inside the door, she looked back. "This isn't over." She disappeared inside.

Dan kicked at the ground, swearing. Couldn't they just reach a middle ground without getting into it? He sighed, feeling ashamed for bringing up Amy. That was a low blow and he knew it. Shaking his head, he headed inside.

He had the guest room at the far end of the house. Dan settled himself into the soft double bed. Drowsiness crept over him. He'd forgotten to talk to Anna about the man in the desert. Tomorrow, he told himself. As sleep finally overtook him, Dan again saw the bright stars in the Arizona sky and Tennyson's Tithonus drifted through his conscious:

Immortal age beside immortal youth,
And all I was in ashes…
Of April, I could hear the lips that kissed,
Whispering I knew not what of wild and sweet,
Like that strange song I heard Apollo sing…

He woke with a start, a soft hand over his mouth.

"Shh," Anna breathed in his ear. Stepping from her robe, she pulled back the covers, quietly crawling into bed with him.

Dan felt the warmth of her nude body as Anna

snuggled. Turning, he pulled her to him.

"I don't know why I'm even here," she whispered.

"It's just a sex thing."

Anna playfully slapped Dan then crawled on top of him. He felt her wetness on his thigh as she moved across him, the warm fullness of her breasts brushing his face. Capturing a nipple in his lips, his tongue sensuously circled around it. Anna moaned softly, pulling away. She rolled onto her back, Dan rolling with her and the two intertwined.

▽▽▽

Lying on his side, Dan opened a blurry eye and squinted at the fuzzy red numbers. Three A.M. Anna pressed against his back, her arms wrapped around his waist, her breath flowing in a soft steady cadence. Dan moved a leg and Anna stirred, her hold tightening.

"Danny?"

"Yeah?"

"I never meant to keep Amy from you."

Dan rolled over and Anna curled up in his arms. Her heart thumped against his chest. "If I had been more of a man back then, I could've spared you a lot of heartbreak."

"I don't think it would've worked back then."

"And now?"

"Now, here we are. Let's not question it." She paused, dragging a finger over his skin. "When I married Jeffery, I knew it was wrong. I guess I just wanted to get back at you, make you jealous or something. Make you see what you were losing."

"It took ten years, but it worked."

"I love you, Danny. I never stopped loving you. If you only knew." She laid her head on his chest, her curly hair spreading across his shoulders.

"Annie?"

"Umm," she sighed, snuggling deeper in his arms.

"Something odd happened to me yesterday. I would've told you earlier, but I was afraid you'd think I was weird."

"It's too late for that." Anna paused. "So, what happened?"

"Yesterday morning I was just killing time, waiting to get loaded. Then this dust devil appears." Dan hesitated.

"And?"

"This is gonna sound wacky."

"Out with it."

"There was a guy pulling a pack-mule inside the dust devil."

"Next you're going to say it was a long-dead relative."

Dan's breath left him. "Yeah. As a matter of fact, it was. The person I saw was my great-grand father. How did you know?"

"There are Indian legends about long-dead relatives returning inside dust devils." Anna shifted around, facing Dan. "It's supposed to be a warning that something tragic is on the horizon."

Goosebumps crawled down Dan's arms. "Of course,

you don't believe it. Those old Indian myths have—"

"Have a habit of coming true."

He stared at her in the dim light.

Anna reached out and stroked Dan's face. "Do you believe what you saw?"

Dan sighed. "I don't know what to believe. These days my minds a freaking mess."

Anna withdrew her hand and gazed at Dan. "A while back, you told me those bizarre dreams had returned."

"With a vengeance. These days they even haunt my waking life. I must be going crazy." Dan paused, touching Anna's shoulder. "Annie, what's happening to me?"

"One thing you're not, Danny, is crazy." Anna curled up in Dan's arms. "Something must've triggered it. What were you doing when you saw the dust devil?"

Dan wrapped his arms around her. "I was staring at this strange-looking mountain. It has a plateau on one side."

"Sounds like Sentinel Peak."

"You know about it?"

"It's pretty prominent in the region. Apaches say it's haunted."

"Well, it's haunting the hell outta me!"

"Shh…" Anna snuggled deeper. "Could it be that something in your past is tied to that mountain?"

"In my dreams, I'm a young boy. My great-grandfather, dressed in a strange uniform—like the guy I saw yesterday—leads me up to the top of that mountain. He says there's something very important up there that I would need later in life." Dan sighed. "And get this, baby: he spoke in a strange language I've never heard—and I answered him in the same language." Dan paused, feeling Anna quiver in his arms. "What is it? Why are you shaking?"

Anna ignored his question. "Did you make it to the top?"

"No. I've never made it to the top. Don't know if I want to."

Expectant silence ensued. Dan held Anna even closer, her warmth reassuring, easing his troubled thoughts.

Anna broke the silence. "You know you'll have to do it."

"I know."

Anna patted Dan's arm. "How 'bout you and I take a little trip?"

"Are you serious?"

"You need to deliver your load, take some time off, and return here. We'll tackle the mountain together."

Dan released Anna and rolled onto his stomach. "No way."

Anna rolled over. "Danny," Anna whispered, caressing his shoulders, "I can help if you'll trust me."

"Yeah, right."

"I know what causes those dreams."

"No, you don't," Dan grumbled. "And I don't need your pseudo-psychology. I'm disconnected enough already."

"Those dreams have a definite meaning. Take a little trip with me and I'll show you."

"God, I don't like what I'm feeling. Annie, did something happen up there?"

"Maybe we ought to check it out."

"What's up there, Annie?"

"I don't know, but I'll go if you will."

Dan paused, considering it. He knew he would tackle the mountain. He had to. It was as if every odd sensation emanated from there. "So, you'll really hike up there with me?"

"As soon as you can return—but if you're in a semi, keep driving."

"Jesus," Dan groaned, burying his face deeply in to the pillow. "Let's not get into that again."

"Okay. We'll work on that later."

"We'll work on a lot of things," came his muffled reply.

Chirping sparrows filled the early morning air. Anna stood on the front porch steps, watching the two drivers head for their trucks. Glancing at her watch, concern furrowed her brow. Dan and Charlie must rush to meet their delivery schedule. Sighing, Anna eased down on a cement step, head hanging. A screened door creaked, jarring her thoughts.

"I haven't said goodbye to Danny yet," Amy said. She released the door. Whack. Amy plopped down beside her mother. "Mom, are we moving to Texas?"

Anna's arm went around her. "Where did you get an idea like that?"

Amy hung her head. "I heard Papa tell Grandma that you and me should go to Texas with Danny."

"Would you like to move to Texas?"

"Yes!" The girl perked up, smiling. "I love Danny, don't you?"

Anna nodded. "Yes, honey, I love Danny, even though sometimes he makes it hard. But you must understand, Danny and I would have to be married first. We couldn't just—"

Diesel engines roared. Black puffs of smoke shot from chrome exhaust stacks. Anna rose, stepping into the house, Amy at her heels.

Wedged sideways behind the huge steering wheel, Dan faced the passenger seat. The metallic rumble of the Caterpillar reverberated through his pen. *Breakdown* drifted from stereo speakers. Pausing, he shook his head, forcing himself to concentrate.

The passenger door opened. Anna breathlessly scrambled in. She slumped into the high-back seat. "I brought you this." She set a thermos on the floor. "Coffee— black, the way you like it."

"Coffee? I didn't know Mormons drank coffee."

"Didn't know they drank beer either, did you?" Anna winked. "It's from my private stash."

Dan chuckled. "Thanks." He turned back to the logbook.

Here Comes My Girl flowed from stereo speakers. Anna turned up the volume, swaying. "I see you like Tom Petty, too."

Dan nodded.

She sang a few lines, glancing around. "So, this is home, huh?"

Dan glanced over his glasses. "Not hardly."

Kicking off her shoes, she placed socked feet on the

padded dash. "Haven't seen you wear your glasses much. Afraid they'll make you look old?"

"No."

"Good, because you don't know what old is."

"So, you've given up psychology to practice geriatrics."

Anna smiled.

Dan closed his logbook, attached it to the clipboard, then tossed both into the sleeper.

A warm breeze blew through open windows, stirring the sleeper curtain. Anna brushed a strand of hair from her eyes; the bracelet on her wrist shimmered. Dan swallowed, mesmerized. Anna's ponytail blew about and, without thinking, Dan caught it. His fingers slid from her hair, drifting sensuously over her neck and along her cheek.

Anna closed her eyes. Like a feline, she moved her head against his gentle caress. After a moment, she reached for his hand. "Don't start something you can't finish."

He gazed at her, silent.

"Danny, you never answered my question last evening. I ask you again: what are you running from? It's more than just responsibility."

Dan swallowed. "Not now, Annie. Please."

Reaching for Dan's other hand, she looked softly at the man sitting across from her.

Dan inhaled the delicate scent of perfumed body wash. His heart pounded. A huge chunk of the brick wall protecting his innermost self now lay smoldering at Anna's feet. "Annie," he wavered, "I, I don't feel I can ever live up to your expectations. I'm not the man you think I am."

"You're making excuses again."

"Anna, you'd become bored with me. You're a rich girl, used to the good life. You've been all over the world, eaten in the best restaurants, worn the best clothes, driven the best cars, rubbed elbows with VIPs and God knows what all." Dan shook his head. "I'm worried that your idea of what matters in life and my idea of what matters would never mix."

"How little you know of me."

Dan took a deep breath. "Oh, God, Annie girl, I love you so much it hurts."

"Then do something about it," Anna whispered, her lips brushing Dan's fingers. "There's strength in you—and a streak of wildness that takes my breath away."
Blushing again, Dan looked away.

"I wouldn't trade you for a thousand Jeffery Albrights. You, Daniel McKntyre, are a *man*." Anna smiled demurely. "Can you blame a woman for wanting a gentleman?"

"Annie, you're playing me like a fiddle."
"And?"

Dan rose and tenderly kissed Anna, his lips lingering. He moved back into his seat, feeling Anna's gaze on him. He began fidgeting with the gear stick. "Anna…I… uh…"

Anna pulled Dan's hands away from the gearstick, her eyes shining.

Her hands quivered in his. Butterflies rolled in his

stomach; he swallowed hard. "I don't know how to say it."

"Talk to me, Danny," she breathed, her gaze riveted on him.

"I want to be part of your life, baby—forever." Dan glanced at Anna nervously. "I can't picture life without you."

"Why, Mr. McKntyre, that sounds like a proposal."

"It is," Dan replied shyly. "Would you marry me, Annie? Would you be my wife?"

She stared silently at Dan for a long moment, then bolted out of her seat, landing in his lap, her arms around his neck. The seat hissed from the added weight. "Forgive my angry words last night," Anna said. "And yes, I do want to marry you."

"Sounds like there might be a 'but' in there."

Anna sighed and returned to her seat.

"Anna?"

Anna buried her face in her hands. "It's just that everything is happening at once."

Dan eyed her, his insides shaking. It took great effort to steady his words. "We can wait."

"No!"

"Then what is it, Annie, girl?"

Anna hesitated, and faced Dan. "There are other things going on and I'm just afraid to drag you in on it. But…"

"But what?"

"Guess it doesn't matter." Anna sighed again and looked away. "You're part of it—whether you want to be or not."

"Annie, you're speaking in freaking riddles. What am I 'part of?'"

The passenger window framed Charlie's head. "Son, I hate to interrupt, but conjugal visitation is over. In case you forgot, we have a seven A.M. appointment in Dallas. We need to rock and roll. Can't afford to get stopped. Our logbooks?"

"Yeah, yeah, I know."

Charlie muttered and disappeared.

Anna tugged on her shoes. "I can't believe you asked me to marry you. I didn't think you had the nerve." She paused. "I hate that you're leaving, but I know you must."

"You never answered my question. What am I part of?"

Anna grabbed his hand, her eyes searching his. "You're about to be part of my life, okay? I just hope you're ready for the avalanche bearing down on both of us."

Dan was about to press her, but thought better of it. There would be time for that later. Hell, he should be worried for Anna becoming part of *his* convoluted life. He cleared his throat. "Annie, this is the last time I'll leave. After today, 'goodbye' won't be part of my vocabulary."

"I'm holding you to that promise."

The two climbed out of the truck and, arm in arm, walked slowly toward the house. Charlie and the Wildaers stood on the front porch, talking.

"So, you want to tell me what's *really* bothering you?"

"I don't think you know what you're in for."

"Why do I have this sudden feeling I'm about to get shit on?"

"Would you stop it?" Anna sighed impatiently. Several seconds passed. "I'm pregnant."

"Say what?"

"You heard me."

Dan, stunned, gazed at her. "Pregnant? You're kidding."

"Nope."

"But, but," Dan stammered. "Oh my God."

"My sentiments exactly."

"Are you sure you're—"

"Yes, Dan, I'm sure." Her voice grew terse. "And let's clear the air right now—I haven't been with Jeffery in over two years. Only you."

Dan remained silent.

"I can't believe you haven't noticed," Anna continued. "Especially after last night."

"I just thought maybe it was the homemade ice cream or something."

"Are you trying to be funny?"

"No." Still seconds passed. Dan looked Anna up and down. "How far along?"

"Twelve weeks."

"Three months! And you're just now telling me?"

"I didn't want you to feel trapped."

"Trapped? You're shitting me."

"It took me by surprise, too," Anna said, ignoring the

remark. "After Amy, doctors told me I probably would never have children again. It's been over ten years." Anna touched his hand. "Danny, I know the timing really sucks, but I'm excited about it. As you should be."

"The problems and dollars keep mounting."

"I've saved a little. We can—"

"Keep it. We'll get by without it."

"Afraid to accept help from a woman?"

"No." Dan ran a hand through his hair. "I'll be back in a week or so. We can figure things out and start planning then."

"Make it quick. I couldn't put my parents through this again." Reaching behind her neck, Anna unfastened a thin, gold necklace that was concealed under her top. "Before you go, I want you to have this." She placed the necklace in his palm.

Dan stared at the gold chain dangling from his hand. "And this is?"

"It's yours."

"I don't remember it." He held up the necklace. "Why are you just now giving it to me?"

Anna shrugged. "Maybe it's safer with you."

"'Safer?' Safe from who?"

"It's just an old family heirloom. There's nothing like it on earth." She paused, gauging his reaction. "It's been passed down through generations. It's connected to both your family and mine, but it rightfully belongs to *you*. I've only been its steward."

"Me?" Dan frowned. "If it belonged to me, how did

you end up—"

"It's an amazing story, Danny, that we don't have time for now. I'll explain it all when you get back." Anna paused. "It is yours."

The necklace pulled Dan like a magnet, but he was strangely hesitant to examine it.

"Well," Anna said, "check it out."

Dan reluctantly inspected the gold necklace. The fine chain felt strange to the touch, seeming to move as if it were alive. Attached to it was a small diamond-shaped pendant. He held up the pendant with sudden reverence. It swung like a pendulum, an iridescent silver, blue, and gold. Etched on one side was an inverted triangle with a sword flanked with lightening bolts. Goose bumps pricked his arm.

"I see you recognize it."

He turned the pendant over. On the reverse side were cuneiform-like characters. Dan's brow furrowed; he'd seen the writing before. Tracing a finger over the fine cursive lines, bizarre memories flooded his consciousness like water from a breached dam.

He saw a night sky with two moons, and then an emerald sea, its waves whispering a strange melody. A woman in a shining robe stood in a doorway, calling to him. He worked the controls of a spacecraft, the instruments as familiar to him as his own arms.

"Danny!" Anna shook his arm. "It's okay—snap out of it!"

The memories dissolved into an image of Anna's worried face. He touched her cheek and realized his hands were shaking. "What the hell?" Dan shook his head and took several deep breaths.

"It's awakened," she whispered. She ran her fingers through his hair. "Are you sure you're okay?"

Dan nodded, casting a glance to the empty porch. "What did you say, Anna?"

"Nothing." She paused. "I gather you've seen the pendant before?"

"No. I mean, yes, but..." Dan swallowed. "How did you get this?"

"I told you, it was a family heirloom."

Dan rolled up the right sleeve of his T-shirt. "How do you explain this?" He eyed the inverted triangle tattoo on shoulder—it was identical to the pendent.

Their eyes met. Dan let go of his sleeve and faced Anna. "You knew my tattoo had the same design as the pendant, yet you never mentioned it. Why?"

"Because I wanted you to remember things on your own."

"Remember what, Anna?"

She seemed to consider this. "Your dreams. Have you ever considered that, perhaps, they're memories of our ancestors?"

"Anna, what-in-the-hell are you talking about?"

Biting a lip, Anna looked away.

"Here we go again."

"You've probably seen the design of that pendant in your dreams. It means something to you, doesn't it? Hell, you've even got it tattooed on your shoulder." Anna paused.

"I'm just saying that you couldn't have gotten the design idea from the pendant itself. That pendant has been with me for over sixty years—"

"Sixty years?" Dan interrupted. He noticed the color leaving Anna's face. "Anna, now come on."

"I mean," Anna stammered. "I mean, it's been in my family for over sixty years. And it's good that you saw the design in your dreams. I think you'll be seeing a lot more."

Dan's jaw tightened. "Anna, I'm sick and tired of all this secretive crap! What the hell happened to you since I was last here?"

"Stop shouting."

"I'm not shouting!"

"Look, baby," Anna said, "just go deliver your load. When you get back, I'll lay *everything* out for you, I promise. Okay?"

"Annie—yes, I've seen this symbol in my dreams, with my great-grandfather. And now they're affecting me when I'm awake." He shook the pendant at her. "I ask again: how did *you* come by the necklace?"

"It was given to my grandfather for safe keeping."

"It was given to my grandfather for safe keeping."

Dan stared in disbelief.

"Danny, your great-grandfather received it as a gift from his first wife. It's a long story, but his best friend ended up with it. That best friend was *my* grandfather. It was to be passed on to your great-grandfather's descendants. Eventually it was put aside, forgotten, until recently."

"Hey, Dan, we gotta go!"

Both looked to the porch. Charlie began ambling toward his truck.

Dan nodded, then turned back to Anna, his eyes searching hers.

Anna touched his hand.

"Annie, I don't know how I supposed to feel."

"When you get back, we'll tackle things together, one at a time." Moving into his arms, Anna rested her head against his chest. "I'm looking forward to us taking care of each other."

The small, gray, pentagon-shaped box lay undisturbed in the bright sunlight. Two short, metal rods, one tipped with a crystal sphere, protruded from the top. The whole device was barely distinguishable from the surrounding landscape.

The box had lain undisturbed for a century. It replaced a larger box that had sat in the same spot for one hundred years. And that one had replaced another that had replaced another. For centuries there had been a watcher in that spot. Its builders could witness in great detail the last five hundred years of human history. Now it waited for its owners to return.

Suddenly, the crystal sphere sparked, turning cobalt. Its insides began spinning. Something had awakened it.

A tapered-rod telescoped out. As it rose, large metal arms extended from its sides like a spoke-wheel. Halting twenty-five feet above the ground, it rotated then stopped. The once-simple metal rod was now an antenna array, aimed thirty degrees above the horizon. Nearby, solar panels—hidden underground—instantly emerged.

The small pentagon-shaped box also underwent transformation. A clear lens with multiple characters materialized on top. Next to the lens was a large symbol; an inverted triangle enclosed a sword and lightning bolts.

The device was totally silent. Sound needs air. And there is no air on the moon.

7

A day and a half after leaving Anna's, Dan stood alone outside his home, the darkness a soft blanket. The mixed fragrance of gardenia, magnolia, and pine breathed sweetly in the warm, humid air. A whippoorwill in a nearby treetop called for a mate, its whistle echoing through the forest. In the distance was an answering cry.

Tilting a beer, Dan leaned against a nearby pine. The full moon rose over the treetops. Taking another swallow, he closed his eyes, thinking about the day's events.

After delivering his load, he pulled into the terminal and quit. His boss, Sammy, was livid. When he realized Dan was serious, he tried cajoling Dan to stay a while longer. Not wanting to burn bridges, Dan compromised. He allowed them to work his truck until it could be sold. They would supply the driver and receive a percentage of the truck's profit. In return, they'd help him sell the truck, maybe even buy it. It was like a ball-and-chain lifted from his neck. If it hadn't been for one piece of disturbing news, Dan would've felt elated.

Sammy told him the FBI had called the day before, wanting to know names of drivers the company had that were passing through Arizona. They also asked for a description of the equipment, particularly a truck that matched Dan's. Sammy stalled them until he could question Dan. Naturally that got nowhere. Dan recalled Ben Wildaer's words: *"Son, it's not just Albright I'm worried about. There are others."*

At any rate, Dan was too exhausted to worry further about it that evening. He'd spent all afternoon catching up on the mowing and other chores around the house. Now, the heat and humidity of the East Texas summer had taken its toll. Factor in the 1,000-mile trip and he was wiped-out. His shirt was still dark with sweat, hair matted to his forehead.

Opening his eyes, Dan glanced to the travel-trailer—his home—making sure the screen-door was shut. He was in no mood to battle mosquitoes tonight. He leaned back against the tree. *Amanda* drifted from the trailer's open windows. Pulling a cordless phone from his back pocket, he walked to the patio steps and slumped down. He'd just hung-up from Anna.

They decided that in two weeks, he'd return to Arizona, they would marry, and move here to Texas. It would be crowded, but only for a short while. Using the money from the sale of his truck, Dan would have a home built in no time. Once his family was secure, he would probably return to the army. He'd contacted a recruiter that morning. Still in the Inactive Reserves, he could get his commission back, but he must decide quickly. Dan would discuss it with Anna. As a soldier, it possibly meant a whole new set of "goodbyes." Yet, with no war looming, his family could travel with him to most foreign assignments. And, no matter what happened to him, Anna and Amy would be taken care of.

Rising, he stretched. There was so much to do he didn't know where to begin. Dan placed the phone and beer just inside. Turning, he walked out to an open area for one last glance at the full moon.

He leaned against a tree trunk. The combination of alcohol, physical work, and lack of sleep was overwhelming. Dan closed his eyes, enjoying the cacophony of sounds in the summer evening. He staggered, catching himself. "That's it." Dan headed inside to shower, and then to bed.

The bedroom curtains stirred, bringing the honey scent of gardenias. The soothing sound of windchimes drifted as Dan lay staring into darkness. His eyes fluttered. Suddenly he was outside again, gazing into the night sky. "What the?"

A gargantuan blue-silver disk hung just above the horizon, filling half the sky. Just behind it was another, slightly smaller moon. The first cast a shadow on the one behind. Wisps of clouds streaked the larger moon: it was so close that Dan could make out cities on its surface. "Dear God."

"Kalyn?" came a familiar feminine voice. "Come in before you pass out. Please?" She spoke a strange language, yet Dan understood her. Turning, he froze. Standing in the doorway of a round dwelling was Anna—or someone like her. Giving an annoyed sigh, she headed toward him.

"Anna, what are doing here?" Before she could reply Dan pointed up to the sky. "Look—two moons!"

"Kalyn, what are you saying? I cannot understand you."

Anna—or whoever she was—was clothed in a pale blue gown. Long hair was braided with silver, and one hand rested on her pregnant stomach.

The woman stood facing him, her brow furrowed. "What is it?"

"Anna?" he whispered. He caught sight of the gold pendant around her neck, identical to the one given to him a couple of days back. "That necklace."

"What about it? It was our anniversary present to each other. We exchanged a matching set, remember?"

He was dreaming. He had to be.

"You have had a long, hard journey, my love. Come inside and sleep." She hooked an arm around Dan's, leading him into the dwelling. "Lord Captain tTisae told me what happened out there. Said your quick thinking saved lives."

"I don't know what you're talking about."

They entered what looked like a bedroom. Pushing Dan onto the bed, the woman began unsnapping his boots. Abruptly he noticed he was clothed in some kind of uniform. His eyes focused on an insignia on his sleeve: an inverted triangle enclosed a sword and lightning bolts.

"Oh, stop being modest, 'Lieutenant Kalyn mMyre,'" the woman said, tugging off the boot. Tossing it, she fumbled with the other. "The Lord Captain told me he recommended you for promotion." She looked up, apprehension filling her eyes. "I understand he also wants you as part of his crew on a new assignment."

Dan had no clue what she was talking about, nor did he care. He felt so at home. He *was home*. "Something is wrong," Dan said, the alien words rolling naturally off his tongue. The woman tossed the second boot near the other.

"I will tell you what is wrong. Your Lord Captain tTisae is a risk-taker, Kalyn. It is rubbing off on you." Dan stared.

The young woman rose, pulling Dan with her. She slipped a white jerkin over his head then pulled off his dark, long-sleeved undershirt. She unfastened a leather clasp and long, dark hair spilled over his shoulders. "What the hell?"

"What did you say?"

"Uh, nothing."

She ran her fingers over his bare shoulders. "I want to remember what you feel like, Kalyn, because if you take the promotion, I understand the new assignment goes with it." She pushed Dan onto the bed. "I see little enough of you now. I will never see much of you at all if—"

Dan kissed her. It was like kissing Anna. This was more than just a vivid dream. He recalled Anna telling him that the answer to what bothered him was in his dreams. This now seemed as reality; a reality of what might have been.

And suddenly Dan knew the name of the woman in his arms. She was Alisa, his wife.

Alisa worked her lips down his chest, pausing. "Kalyn?"

"Yes?"

"What was that language you spoke earlier?"

"What language? When?"

"Do not play games with me. When you were outside and I called to you, you answered back in a strange tongue. Can you talk about where you have been? It scares me, Kalyn. Why do you take such risks?"

"Alisa, I am a warrior. You knew that when you married me. Our civilization faces extinction. And where have I been? I have been holding the line against evil."

"Kalyn, you said the *Epsalyan* was only going on routine patrol near the demilitarized zone."

"Calm deceives. It breeds complacency. We are still at war."

Alisa rolled off him. "I saw the *Epsalyan* when she docked at Space Port Twelve. That was no 'routine patrol'!"

Dan rose to an elbow. "How did you see that?"

"It was on the monitor at Flight Control when I walked in. They tried rushing me out but I would have none of it. I wanted to see for myself." Her voice wavered. "It was a miracle you returned. The entire starboard side was charred. It looked like—"

"I know what it looked like!" Dan snapped. "And not all of us made it back. We lost seventeen crewmen."

Alisa pulled him down. "But you made it back," she whispered, "this time." Her eyes searched his. "Just hold me, Kalyn."

"I will take that assignment with Lord Captain tTisae." Dan cradled her. "Though I will be gone a bit more, the risk is less."

"I wish you were a shuttle pilot again," Alisa said. "We did not have as much, but you were home everyday. We were happier then. I," Alisa's voice broke, "I just want you here with me, please? I cannot bear the thought of…of…"

"You worry too much," Dan said, groggy. "I shall always come back."

There was a long pause. "What is the name of your new ship, my love?"

"The *Halaena*. It is a deep-space recon vessel, new Quasar class." He yawned. "For a change, I will be out of harm's way."

Alisa gazed at her young man. His eyes closed. "I love you, Kalyn." Laying her head on his chest, she wept softly.

"Alisa, no—come back! Alisa!" The words faded into an echo. Dan opened a blurry eye to daylight. He lay in his own bed

Staring at the ceiling, he touched the pendant around his neck. It was the one Anna—no, Alisa—had given him. No, Alisa gave it to Kalyn. Who the hell was Kalyn? Who was Alisa? As usual, the dream melted away. "No!" But it was no use. The visions dissolved. Dan punched a pillow then buried his face in it. "Sweet Jesus, why?"

He reached for the pendant again. He didn't recall putting it on. Slipping it over his head, he placed it under a pillow.

"Hey, Dan! Dano! You lazy ass! You gonna sleep your life away?"

The voice came from the walls.

"You awake?" the voice asked.

"I am now." Dan craned his neck.

Charlie grinned from an open window. "Howdy."

"Go away," Dan groaned. Grabbing a pillow, he

covered his head.

The bed jerked.

"Son, it's high-noon," Charlie said. "Rise and shine." He kicked the bed again.

"Just what in-the-hell are you doing here?"

Charlie smiled, sipping coffee from one of Dan's favorite mugs. "I think you need to flip that mattress over."

"Huh?"

"Maybe you'll get up on the right damn side next time."

"Don't jack with me today, okay?" Throwing off the covers, he slumped over the edge of the bed. His hands jerked to his temples. "Geesus."

"Serves you right. Did you tie one on again?"

"What do you mean, 'again?'" Dan replied in agony. He limped toward the bathroom.

"The knee still bothering you?"

Dan leaned against the bathroom doorway, nodding.

"Better take care of it now, son."

"Thanks for the words of inspiration. What are you doing here, anyway?"

"Hell, man, you wouldn't answer your phone."

Dan hobbled into the bathroom. "You didn't take the hint?" he shouted through the half-closed door.

"Carolyn was worried and sent me over to see if you were still in the country."

Carolyn was Charlie's wife. She watched over Dan like an overprotective mother, and it drove him crazy. And Charlie? At times, Charlie was a mentor, other times, a father. Now, he was just plain annoying.

"I made some coffee," Charlie said.

Dan relieved himself and hobbled from the bathroom. "I guess I'll have to drink some or it'll hurt your feelings." He limped to the kitchen.

Charlie followed.

Leaning over, Dan scrutinized the coffeepot. The decanter held a light-brown liquid the color of weak tea. "You call that coffee? That's squirrel-piss."

"Can't remember the last time I was here," Charlie said. He gazed out, sipping. "Looks like you've done quite a bit of work."

"Yeah," Dan said, heading to the bedroom, a mug in his hand, "and now I have all the time in the world."

"I heard. So, what line of work you going into?"

"I'll be carrying an M-Sixteen again."

"The army? You're crazy. That's worse than truck-driving! I bet Anna loved that."

Dan returned dressed in shorts, a T-shirt, and tennis shoes. "She doesn't know yet—and don't you tell her."

Charlie remained silent, his gaze focused on a small blemish near the door. "You know," the older man drawled, picking at the small splintered hole, "the only thing missing is a beach." Pausing, he gazed outside, then turned back to Dan. "Yessir, a beach."

"A beach? If I wanted a beach, I'd live in South Padre."

"If you had a beach, I could call you 'Sonny.'"

Dan sighed.

"Or would you rather be called, 'Jimmy?'"

Dan set his coffee mug on a nearby end table. "Charlie, I'm in no mood to hear your preaching today."

"This place reminds me of Rockford Files. Even down to the bullet holes."

"Hole," Dan added quickly, holding up one finger. "A hole—one hole."

"I wondered why you left that other place in such a hurry," Charlie added, taking a sip from his mug.

"I was late with my rent, okay, 'Rocky?'" Dan headed for the door. "I'm going for a run. You can hang around if you want."

Laughing, Charlie shoved the younger man onto the covered patio.

"When I quit yesterday, you thought I'd split, huh?"

Charlie was about to reply when something caught his attention. He strode over to a nearby cement foundation. "Damn, son, when did you pour that?"

"Three weeks ago."

"And here I thought you were moving to Arizona."

"Never said anything about moving. Charlie, this is my home." Dan rubbed a foot over a rough spot. Feeling Charlie's eyes on him, he looked up. "What?"

"You mean Anna is…?"

"Yeah, she's moving here. And I know I have a lot to do, so spare me the lecture."

"I don't believe it." Charlie snorted. "How the hell did you talk someone like Anna into moving down here? I mean," he waved an arm around, "there's nothing out here!

No malls, no restaurants, all the junk women like to do."

"I'm here."

"But," Charlie sputtered, "but? Is Amy coming?"

"Of course. They're a packaged deal."

"Do you have to become Mormon?"

Dan laughed. "Anna already had her temple wedding."

"Now, son, you two aren't going to live in sin in front of your daughter, are you?"

"Charlie, you know me better than that."

"Damn right I do. That's why I asked."

Dan wanted to get off the subject of Anna. "A crew will be out here next week to begin framing."

"You're just full of surprises, but I'm going to let you in on something. If you're intent on bringing Anna and Amy down here, you better do it quick—not wait for this house to go up. And don't make any noise about it either."

"Why?"

"Didn't you talk to Ben?"

"Yeah, we talked for a few minutes. What of it?"

"Did he mention Albright?"

"Not you too." Dan sighed. "What about Albright? He's nothing."

"Watch your back, Danny-boy. I was told Albright accused you of wrecking his marriage. Said he would make it up to you."

"What's that pin-head going to do? If he wants to know who wrecked his marriage, he needs to look in the mirror." Dan chuckled nonchalantly. "He's *persona non gratas.*"

"That may be so, you cocky son of a bitch, but from what Ben told me about this guy, he's nasty." Charlie tossed his coffee, setting the mug on the foundation. "You better take him seriously."

Dan cast an annoyed glance at Charlie. Now was a good time for that run. He turned back to the foundation, placing a foot on the highest part. He leaned forward, stretching a hamstring.

"Now that I cheered you up, guess I'll leave." The older man lingered, hesitating.

Switching legs, Dan stretched again. The more Dan thought of Albright and the way he abused Anna, the angrier he grew. How could she not have seen through him?

Jeffery Albright had come from a wealthy California family. Albright had promised Anna the world. Dan recalled Anna telling him about her honeymoon in New Zealand. Dan winced. And what did he, Dan McKntyre, have to offer? His and Anna's honeymoon would probably be spent in the sweltering heat, fighting off mosquitoes and deer flies while they roofed a house. How pathetic. He stood up, chuckling.

"What's so funny?" Charlie asked.

"I can't believe someone like Anna even gave me a second glance."

"Neither can I."

"We're getting married in two weeks."

"Well, congratulations!" He slapped Dan on the back. "It's about time you did the right thing."

"Yeah," Dan said, "I reckon it is."

Charlie glanced at his watch. "I've got to run. Carolyn wants me to drive her to Lufkin. I'm off the next few days. Come over tomorrow. I'll ice down some beer and smoke a brisket. You can explain how you're going to accomplish everything."

Dan barely heard Charlie. A gentle breeze stirred his hair. He smiled inside, thinking of Anna's gentle arms.

"There you go, blinking out again."

"Huh? What?"

"I said," Charlie repeated, as if addressing a son, "don't forget what I told you about Albright. Don't brush him off." Charlie headed to the driveway. He was almost to his truck when he spotted a motorcycle parked nearby. He eyed the Harley-Davidson low-rider. "Got that thing running yet?"

"Of course. I drove it over from Nacogdoches last month when I bought it. All it needs is a headlight."

"Well, be on it tomorrow. Carolyn's dying for a ride."

Nodding, Dan began jogging backwards, then turned and sprinted for the road. Ducking under a tree limb, he shouted back to Charlie. "That is, if it doesn't rain!"

"You big weenie!" Charlie shouted back.

His home behind him, Dan jogged down the dirt road, dodging occasional chug-holes. A pickup bounced beside him.

Charlie's arm and head dangled out the driver's open window. "Be over at noon," he snorted, "but only if it doesn't rain—you pussy!" Laughing, Charlie spun off in a cloud of dirt and gravel.

Dan kept running. He puffed loudly. While running, he thought about his and Charlie's conversation. Maybe he should take his big-truck, drive to Arizona and move Anna and Amy ASAP? He banished the thought; he'd move them in a wheelbarrow before climbing back into an eighteen-wheeler.

Sweat streaked his face. He played over the last few days. Was the government interested in Anna? If so, why? Maybe he needed to check her out.

He sighed. It was too late for that. Dan couldn't picture life without her. Still, she seemed so evasive.

Well, that was going to change. Before they married, Anna would tell all. Dan circled a large tree in the road and headed home. Maybe Anna was too paranoid? But then why had the FBI contacted his employer? A coincidence? Dan concluded it was all about her ex. What else could it be?

Seconds passed. In addition to buying a headlight for the Harley, he'd also pick up some extra ammunition. Just in case.

Jeffery Albright was propped against the counter at the city clerk's office, scanning records, when two deputies entered. Nodding, he resumed thumbing through the folder. They approached. One asked, "Are you Jeffery Albright?"

He thought that odd; they all knew one another. "No, I'm Al Capone. Come on guys, you know who I am. Of course, I'm Jeffery Albright—at your service."

Without warning, one of them handed him a folded document. Instinctively he reached for it, then jerked back, letting the paper flutter to the floor.

A deputy reached down, retrieving it. Opening Albright's coat, he shoved the document in an inner pocket. "You've been issued a protective order, Mr. Albright." Suppressing a smirk, the other deputy stepped up. "If you will please sign here…"

As the deputies turned to leave, Albright shot a glance at the clerks. Two were huddled together, snickering. To make matters worse, one of his colleagues was standing at the counter watching the spectacle unfold. It was that do-gooder Greenfeld. He always lightened Greenfeld's wallet on the greens. No doubt the scene just made the man's day.

Whack! Jeffery Albright was snapped into the present as the leather-bound chair bounced off the wall, scooting across thick carpet. He stood rigid behind the rich, teakwood desk. He strode across the plush office and halted, gazing out the fourth-floor window of his business complex. Scottsdale, Arizona sprawled before him. Dominating the vista was the greenery of the nearby golf course. He'd chosen this suite specifically for that view. Today, however, there was no thought of golf. The man's tan, handsome face grew taut. "I still can't believe she did this to me," Albright said, grimacing. "This is just un-frigging-believable."

A burly man sat draped in a nearby padded chair. Johnny Bentien was paid to smooth-over ruffled feathers caused by the attorney's excesses. He fixed things when a court of law could not. "Excuse me, Mr. Albright," he began, sitting up, "but I think you ought to reconsider. Anna—"

"I don't want to hear it."

"Yes, sir."

Albright cast an angry glance at the big man, then stomped back to his desk. Picking up a nearby folded document, he re-read the first line of the first paragraph: You are hereby ordered to immediately cease contact with said complainant Anna Wildaer, daughter Amy McKntyre, and any of the complainant's immediate family…

So, the break was complete. Yes, his overtures of reconciliation such as offering to return her Mercedes might have been shallow, but he hadn't expected the back-stabbing.

To Albright, the restraining order represented just that. Then Anna twisted the knife by having Amy's last name changed. Albright took little comfort in knowing McKntyre was now responsible for child support.

Albright seethed. Damn her—and that truckdriver! He knew colleagues snickered behind his back. Why couldn't she have been sneaking around with a doctor, a professor or even another attorney? He could at least shrug between holes, saying, "These things happen, you know." Or, play macho with a, "good riddance." No one would have thought much of it. But the way it all came down...how humiliating!

Well, it was irrelevant. McKntyre was just as responsible. It wasn't accidental that this McKntyre fellow just happened on the scene. More than likely Anna had contacted him before their legal separation. How did she know where to find him? Albright's neck muscles tightened. She probably was having an affair with McKntyre all along, even though he failed to prove it in court. Fearing his own infidelity would be exposed, Albright never pushed it.

Re-folding the document, the attorney casually tossed it on the desk. Sighing, he ran a hand over the back of his neck. Well, by God, he'd show Anna what he thought of her pitiful attempt at revenge. He walked around the back of his desk and punched a button on the intercom. "Shelia, step in here for a moment."

A pause. The door opened, and a petite blond of twenty-five stood in the doorway. "Yes, sir?"

"Would you get the Wildaers on the phone, please?"

"But," she hesitated, "do you think that's wise, Mr. Albright?"

"Why is everyone suddenly questioning my judgment?"

"I'm sorry, sir. I didn't mean to—"

"Never mind, Shelia," Albright said calmly. "You're right. I can't violate the law nor should I ask others to." Bullshit. He'd call them himself, later. Right now, he needed to get a grip.

Albright nodded to the young woman. "That will be all."

"Yes, sir." Shelia left.

Albright eyed Bentien. "I want you to round up The Indian and meet me at home tonight."

"A little 'OT,' Mr. Albright?"

"Yes, a little 'overtime.' Eight o'clock straight-up. Got it?"

"Yes, sir." Bentien rose from the chair. In his late forties, his shiny bald head contrasted with his dark, scarred face. "We'll be there, Mr. Albright."

The silver Mercedes 450 SL shot left at the green arrow. Albright nailed the gas, heading east on Indian School Road. Turning left on State Route 87, Beeline Highway, he drove northeast. His rancho was located some twenty miles out of town. Albright glanced in the mirror. He was already well-established at the law firm he now owned when he first met Anna. Girls always flocked to him. Of course, the fact that his father was a multi-million-dollar land developer in California and Arizona helped. Yet he knew *that* never impressed Anna.

Anna began disappearing into the desert during the last two years of their marriage. She claimed she was working at the archeological digs in the Salt River Canyon. Checking up on her, he found she hadn't been there in over a year. His always-suspicious nature morphed into full-blown paranoia. Believing Anna was rendezvousing with a lover, he had her followed. To his surprise, Anna always headed to the same place: a plateau with a high peak on one side. He couldn't recall the name. When Anna hiked down, she was always filthy, exhausted. That shot the lover theory all to hell. He'd thought of having her followed to the summit, but that would've given away the tail. Albright made a mental note to inspect that plateau again. At any rate, it was always well after dark when she returned home. When asked what she was doing, Anna would turn those fiery eyes on him.

"You want to know what I was doing?" she would snap. "Why don't you come with me? The desert is beautiful at night. You really ought to try it."

"And this, my dear," he would mock, waving his glass of Chevas Regal, "is something *you* really ought to try." He recalled how she stood there glaring at him. Albright shuddered. It was as if she were looking through him. That look gave him the creeps.

The Mercedes turned left onto a small asphalt road. Albright drove another tenth of a mile until he came to a wrought-iron gate. He aimed a remote-control. The huge

JAY CHALK

gate swung open and the Mercedes shot through. A small closed-circuit camera followed his progress down the hot, black ribbon until he disappeared over a barren hill a half-mile away.

This was his vast empire, although vast was a relative term. Compared to his parents' 4,000-acre hacienda, his measly 500 acres of saguaro-dotted domain was nothing.

The lawyer swept past the circle drive in front of his sprawling, two-story Spanish villa, heading to the east-side of the home. The car halted in front of the garage. Another mounted camera was aimed at the garage entrance. The door raised and the sleek, silver car quickly entered.

"Lance!" Albright shouted, emerging from the Mercedes. "I want that damn door-opener fixed!" He held up the remote. "I've been punching this thing for the last quarter-mile and the door just now opened!"

A tall, athletic, young man with sandy hair trotted to the lawyer's car. "Yes, sir, Mr. Albright. I'll get on it right away." Lance Perryman was the yardman, maintenance man, pool man, chauffeur, and whatever else Albright could dump on him. Lance had been a football star at the University of Arizona but failed to make the pros. As soon as his football eligibility expired, he dropped out. As the son of U.S. Senator George Perryman—an important client—Albright agreed to hire him.

"No. It'll end up an all-night clusterfuck. Do it tomorrow."

Lance nodded, inspecting the garage door mechanism.

"A bad day, Jeffery?" came a feminine voice. A slender, red-haired young woman stood in the doorway, a towel draped around her Barbie-doll figure. She threw her arms around the lawyer as he stepped inside.

Tossing his coat on a bar stool, Albright dropped his briefcase and shoved her away. "Damn you, Tiffany. You're soaking wet!"

The young woman pouted.

Albright pointed back to the garage. "What's that *prima donna* been doing all day? There's work to be done around here. The shrubbery looks like hell."
"I haven't the foggiest, darling. I was in the pool and saw you drive by, then I—"

"Forget it," Albright said gruffly, snatching up his coat and briefcase. "And bring me a brandy. The bar's empty in the study."

"Can I change first?"

"Sweet-cheeks, I don't care if you jump the Grand Canyon, as long as in ten minutes I have my brandy."

Tiffany scampered away, leaving wet footprints on the pavestone floor.

Albright grudgingly stared after her, admiring her curves. A twenty-four-year-old sweet peach, he mused, with nothing between the ears. Sighing, he turned away; she kept his bed warm, at least for now. His throat tightened. Is this what he was reduced to? A trophy girlfriend? What he wanted was a *real* woman, someone with depth, with substance, like—. He walked stiffly down the hall.

Slamming the study door, he tossed the coat and

briefcase onto a nearby sofa. Walking to the window, the lawyer jerked open the drapes and stared at the heat-soaked desertscape. The sun was low, his house casting a large shadow over russet sand. His gaze moved past the oleanders and palms that lined his wooden privacy fence. And there they stood, as always: giant saguaro cacti. Rolling up from the horizon, the colossuses halted at the fence. And there they lingered, waiting for when everything would again be theirs.

Albright suddenly hated them.

To the lawyer, the tall saguaros were like lonely sentinels. One after another, they stood, disappearing over a distant ridge. He stared, hypnotized. They were marching, forever ceaseless in their vigil, their pursuit of life. The saguaros seemed poised to storm his fence and plant themselves in his living room, reclaiming all for an unknown kingdom or god that existed eons ago. The saguaros were eternity. Forever watching, waiting, and laughing.

Albright shuddered. At times, Anna gave him the same feeling the saguaros did: smallness, helpless while in her presence. To Albright, Anna radiated the haughtiness of an immortal. There were times she appeared almost aristocratic, making his world seem petty, insignificant.

He had that same feeling around Daniel McKntyre. The moment he met the man, he knew Anna was gone. Albright stood rigid, eyeing a cactus. Was that a whisper? Maybe Bentien was right. Maybe he should let it be.

The attorney's lips twisted. He raised a balled fist

and struck at the window, stopping just short of smashing the glass.

Everything will fade.

Less than a half-day's drive from Albright's villa
lay a windswept, desert plateau with a tree-covered peak
on one end. The plateau was like a moonscape, remote and
forbidden. Few had visited it. According to Apache legend,
phantoms wandered the region, their imperceptible sighs
drifting across the lonely, surreal terrain. The manifestations
originated from the mountain, emanating from a large object
half-embedded in a hillside. Once a leviathan of the sky,
the object was now a forgotten mausoleum. The light of a
thousand suns had once glistened off her polished skin. Now,
only sand and tumbleweeds blew against a scorched hull.
The remains of the spacecraft appeared cold, lifeless.

Yet deep in its bowels a few circuits still whirred,
bending outside light and creating a screen of invisibility
around the wreckage. An automated program flashed a signal
twice a year. It would beam a five-minute message then fall
silent. Two hundred and eighty times it had practiced this
routine. But its calls for help always went unheeded.

Suddenly control panels burst to life. Flashing

programs created a kaleidoscope of lights. The antenna array on the lunar surface had detected a familiar signal. It was wakening its companion on Earth.

The white, four-mile-long vessel moved silently through the cold, black void of interstellar space. On its hull was a small insignia of an inverted triangle enclosing a sword flanked by lightening bolts.

The *Mnaerias* had once been a proud warship, but with the cession of hostilities a hundred years earlier, most of her weaponry had long since been removed. Refitted with cargo holds, *Mnaerias* was now an intergalactic freighter with a crew of eighty. She was on the return leg of her first run between the far away mining colony on Casaira and her home world. Six-hundred light years from her homeport to Casaira, the round trip took four months and was usually uneventful.

"Sir, long-range scanners detect a priority-one distress beacon. An obsolete frequency…bearing…sector five." A dark-haired young man stationed at a communications console moved a hand over several displays. His eyes widened. "Lord Captain, it is from the *Halaena*."

"What?" An older man rose. "The *Halaena*—are you sure?"

"Yes, my lord."

"That cannot be. The *Halaena's* disappearance was

three hundred parsecs from our present position, and one-hundred-forty years ago. Lieutenant, did you cross-check?"

"Yes, sir." The young man glanced at the console. "There is no mistake, my lord. The signal originates from sector five—the Soladine System. It is very weak, but it definitely is the *Halaena's* signature."

The lord captain glanced at a young, blond-haired man seated next to the lieutenant. "Ensign, distance to the Soladine System?"

"Eight light years, Lord Captain."

The older man surveyed the small elliptical bridge. All eyes were on him.

Lord Captain Ason mMyre was a tall, distinguished-looking man. Approaching middle age, he was still trim and athletic. His brown hair, streaked with gray, was worn in a long ponytail as is customary of a *Mataer* warrior. A thick but neatly trimmed mustache only accented his strong jaw. His long-sleeved dark shirt was covered by an officer's white jerkin, secured at the waist with a blue sash. Another blue sash hung from his left shoulder, the bottom half white with red emblems, indicating rank. Black fatigue pants were tucked and bloused into brown, calf-length, snap-up boots. Still a striking figure, the long years were now telling on his noble face. Nevertheless, Lord Captain Ason mMyre had a commanding presence that demanded attention and respect.

Though holding the highest battle-rank—that of Lord Captain—his superiors regarded him as a renegade. Had he not been a highly decorated warrior from the Brazaryan War, he would have been driven from The Fleet.

Of course, all the scorn heaped upon him by his superiors—
the High Council of Serena—did nothing but endear him
to his crew. A born leader, Lord Captain mMyre was now
despised by the High Council. They looked upon him as an
antique, a relic from another era. The Lord Captain's ideas
of individualism and personal responsibility clashed with the
socialist *Fasaline* culture sweeping his home world, Serena,
and accompanying star system.

The Fasaline race of Satari now made up 60% of
Serena's population and was rapidly increasing. Yet 95%
of the High Council was Fasaline and they succeeded in
imposing their political and cultural will on Serena and
its spheres of influence. Although the Matair and Fasaline
were both native to Serena and physically identical, the
Fasalines had long been envious of the Mataer's longer life
span. Over the centuries, the Fasalines grew resentful of the
Mataer's success in ruling a powerful nation, a world, then a
star system and, finally, a quadrant of the galaxy. Under the
Mataers, Satari culture and democratic principles grew and
flourished, spreading to several star systems. Yet their low
birthrate, along with other complex issues, such as cloning,
reduced Mataers to minority status. The Fasalines, who
came to power at the end of the Brazaryan War, could finally
push their agenda. They believed every citizen was part of
the whole, therefore they must surrender their individuality
to the whole. But men like Ason mMyre blocked Fasaline
ambitions. He was an anachronism to the pre-war society
that the Fasaline Council wanted purged. A freethinker, they
feared mMyre could corrupt the younger Satari, remind

them of pre-war individualism. The High Council believed mMyer the antithesis of all the ideals that befit an advanced civilization. He had served a purpose; now, mMyre needed to go away.

But the Lord Captain refused to cooperate.

The High Council had to move subtly; mMyre still had powerful friends. The Council's latest scheme was assigning him to a freighter that traveled to a far, obscure end of the quadrant. They hoped he would consider the assignment beneath him and retire. But the High Council, as usual, misjudged Lord Captain mMyre.

"Hard about, Lieutenant. I want the exact source of that beacon!"

"It will be done, my lord."

Ason glanced to the other young man. "Ensign, plot a course to sector five—maximum speed."

"Yes, sir!"

"Ensign, estimated time to the Soladine System?"

"At maximum speed, twelve hours, my lord."

An older, dark-haired man with a sallow look stepped forward. "Lord Captain, may I respectfully remind you that the Soladine System has been quarantined as of—"

"Commander Arnols, your protest has been dutifully noted and logged."

"But—"

"May I remind *you*, Commander," Ason turned cold eyes on Arnols, "that upon reception of a priority-one distress beacon, regulations still require the nearest vessel to respond."

98

"But, sir, the *Pristina* is closer. They are only—"

"The *Pristina* carries medical supplies. She cannot be diverted. Moreover, with their old coil-drive engines they could not outrun an Arrillian tortoise." Ason paused. "Any more questions?"

Commander Arnols' jaw tightened. "No, sir." Gritting his teeth, he stiffly turned away.

The lord captain's eyes narrowed as he watched the commander recede. Arnols was, Ason believed, living proof that bootlicking yes-men were always promoted to their highest level of incompetence. Arnols represented the times; the New Fleet was teeming with his type. Typical Fasaline.

The lord captain shook his head. Why should he, Ason mMyre, continue jeopardizing his life and others for a society now so shallow and sanitary? Where did things go wrong? Whatever happened to *pride, honor, and character*? They were nothing but mere words to the Fasaline.

Well, Ason mused, The Council better pray war never breaks out again. Thanks to that bunch of hand-wringing, excuse making bed-wetters, the once powerful Fleet was now eviscerated. And all the while the Brazaryans—mortal enemies of the Satari—were laughing and scheming. The captain sighed. He had two years left until mandatory retirement. Then he would tell The High Council how he *really* felt.

"Lord Captain," the ensign said, yanking Ason from his thoughts. "The distress signal has ceased."

"Did you triangulate the repeaters?"

"Yes, sir. The signal originated from the third planet

in the Soladine System."

"Them, again? That's impossible! They have barely achieved orbital flight." Ason stepped toward the science station. "The *Antaries* intercepted one of their probes last year. They are a humanoid race very similar to our own, which raises more questions than answers. However, there are significant differences; they are still in pre-techno-development. Their probe was extremely primitive. It was amazing it traveled so far." The captain cast a glance around. "A plus-light t-mag oscillation is decades, perhaps centuries beyond their current technology. They could not have transmitted the signal. At least let us hope not." The captain turned to a young, dark-haired woman seated at the science station. "Lieutenant Faelian, what is the *Padian* level of *Illysia-three*?"

"Level two, my lord."

"Just entering manned space flight, nuclear-fusion, maybe ion-drive." Ason nodded, contemplative. "They probably have not left the orbit of their own moon. Their naïveté could be disastrous."

"Lord Captain," Faelian began.

Gazing at her, Ason smiled inside. Lieutenant Tyona Faelian was young but highly intelligent. Although strong-willed and ambitious, Faelian was an excellent officer. He valued her opinion. "Yes, Lieutenant, what is your assessment?"

"Sir, it was after the *Antaries* intercepted the *Illysian* probe that the Soladine System was quarantined."

"Correct, but that is routine when a non-contact

civilization achieves space flight. We give it a 'wait and see' period before proceeding."

"But, sir," Tyona continued, "the signal is undeniably the *Halaena's*. Either the *Halaena* visited that world and for reasons unknown left a distress beacon, or…" Tyona looked around, hesitating.

"Yes, Lieutenant?"

"Or the *Halaena*, or what is left of her, is on the surface of *Illysia-three*."

Ason scrutinized the young woman. "Your suggestions are dangerous; some could perceive them as treasonous."

"Only by those who are themselves treasonous." Tyona paused. "There were rumors the *Halaena's* true mission was to unravel an old mystery. This enigma lies in the Soladine System, specifically centered around *Illysia-three*."

The crew looked at one another, speaking in quick whispers. They all knew she was referring to The Lost Colonists.

Centuries ago, during the Colonial War, Satarian civilization was on the brink of annihilation. A neighboring planet colonized by the Satari had rebelled. A planetary war ensued; a third of Serena was destroyed. It was a dark period in Satarian history; few records remain. However, according to legend, a small group of scientists and their families commandeered a starship. They set out to the area now known as the Soladine System. Plus-light power was still experimental. They were never heard from again.

"Lieutenant Faelian," commander Arnols said, "if you are referring to 'The Legend of the Lost Colonists,' nothing was ever substantiated to prove that it was more than myth."

"Why, Commander," Ason said, "have you no imagination? Has the High Council declared a moratorium on that also?"

Snickers drifted through the bridge. Arnols sighed, his demeanor even more sour.

Repressing a smile, Tyona glanced first at the commander, then to the captain. "That the distress beacon is the *Halaena's*, there is no doubt. The question we must ask is why the signal was not previously detected. Or, was it *recently* activated?"

Glancing around, the lord captain spoke to no one in particular. "If the native inhabitants, who prove intelligent, found the *Halaena* and cracked its technology—whew!" Ason rubbed his chin. "They could open a door that, for them, best remain closed. The consequences of kinetic-molecular technology falling into the hands of a level two civilization... For their own safety they would be declared a protectorate, and our defenses are already spread thin." Ason sighed. "I find it hard to believe the Brazaryans have not yet plundered that world. Those scaly-skinned demons have lacked natural resources for centuries. Illysia-three is loaded with mineral wealth. I shudder to think what would happen if the Brazaryans intercepted that signal."

"Sir," Tyona said, "for the Brazaryans to enter this sector would be in direct violation of the Treaty of

Windaqar."

"Treaties mean nothing to those bastards!" Ason sneered. "I know the 'Braz.' To them, treaties are discerned as weakness. Treaties do nothing but give the Braz time to regroup."

"Maybe they struck a bargain with the Illysians," the young ensign offered. "Technology for mineral rights?"

"No," the captain replied, "the Brazaryans do not bargain with technologically inferior worlds. They rape them, taking what they want, annihilating resistance. If the Illysians developed t-mag technology, the Brazaryans would perceive them a threat. The Illysians must lay low. And them being *human*, the lizard scum would need no excuse to enslave or obliterate them. Illysia would not have a 'prayer of six sisters' against the Brazaryan Sovereignty."

A long silence ensued.

Noticing their looks, Ason quickly changed focus. "Who else may have activated the beacon?" He looked at Tyona expectantly.

"Surviving crewmembers, my lord."

The captain raised a brow. "Survivors? After one hundred forty years? It may be possible but, if I recall my history, Lord Captain tTisae was the mission commander. He was over two hundred years old when the ship departed."

"Sir, there were younger crewmen aboard," Tyona said. She suddenly bowed her head. "I am sorry. I did not mean to—"

The captain raised a hand. "No apology necessary." He turned to commander Arnols, standing nearby. "Notify

Fleet-com of a few days delay in our return to port."

"Yes, sir," Arnols replied. He paused. "With your permission, I would like to check on Engineering. I can notify Fleet-com from there."

Ason studied Arnols, then raised a hand. "Go."

The commander nodded and left the bridge.

An hour passed. Ason sat in the Captain's chair, his eyes unable to focus on a monitor in the chair's arm. Was it only luck that *Haleana's* beacon transmitted while, he just happened to be in the vicinity?

"Lord Captain."

His thoughts broken, he glanced to the man at the communications station. "What is it, Lieutenant?"

"Fleet-com is recalling us."

Ason marched to the communications station and glanced at a monitor. After a moment, he stepped back, swearing softly. "We are not to approach the Soladine system. We are to resume our previous heading to Serena. The orders come straight from the High Council."

"The High Council?" Tyona asked. "The High Council does not usually trouble itself in routine Fleet affairs."

"Apparently they do now." Ason glanced around the bridge. "I am certain it has to do with me."

Tyona gazed at the lord captain. "Sir, would *Haleana's* crew manifest have anything to do with the High Council's decision?"

Ason stared at Tyona. "You know."

Tyona nodded.

The crew gazed at Ason in expectant silence. He cleared his throat. "The *Haleana's* navigator was Kalyn mMyer," he announced. "My father."

Gasps and whispers moved through the bridge.

He glanced to the young man seated at the helm. "Ensign D'roe, you have the bridge. I shall be in my quarters." Turning, the lord captain marched through an opening that materialized in front of him.

Replacing his wineglass, Ason paced back and forth across his stateroom. Rubbing the back of his neck, he gave an annoyed sigh. A loud beep came from the walls, startling him.

"Yes?"

"Lieutenant Faelian, my lord."

"Enter."

An opening materialized in the wall. A dark-haired woman in a Fleet Officer's uniform stepped hesitantly through. Pausing just inside, she surveyed the surroundings, the opening behind her solidifying.

Ason studied the young woman. Of average height and slender build, her long dark hair was secured above her collar according to regulations. A beautiful woman, Tyona's cool, professional manner belied her femininity. Yet to the captain, Tyona appeared almost as a naïve girl-child even though she was in her late twenties. He smiled inside; at 142, virtually his whole crew appeared as children. Yet he knew

Tyona was an Academy graduate and had served in The Fleet six years. Her tours included several deep-space missions; she was no rookie.

"How may I help you, Lieutenant?"

"Sir, I wish to express my—and the crew's— disappointment that the High Council recalled us." Tyona paused, gauging his reaction. "I know it was important to you."

"Thank you. And, yes, it was."

Tyona was about to speak when she noticed several holocubes on a shelf across the room. She trailed to the bookcase.

Ason smiled, watching the young woman, who seemed mesmerized. "Tyona—may I address you as such?"

Tyona stiffened and spun around. Blushing at the unaccustomed use of her first name, she lowered her eyes. "Yes, sir."

"Tell me, Tyona," Ason began, "and this will remain confidential. Who sent the message to the High Council informing them of our destination?"

"If you order me," Tyona hesitated, "I will—"

"I will not order you to betray your fellow officers. No regulations were broken, although protocol was violated."

Tyona stepped closer to the captain. "However, my lord, if you were to guess?"

Ason eyed her. "Commander Arnols."

Tyona looked away.

"I see," Ason said, chuckling.

Tyona smiled then turned, enticed by the bookcase. "May I?" she asked, pointing to the holocubes.

"Certainly."

A half-dozen or so clear cubes were arranged on a small shelf, each cube containing a hologram. Tyona picked up a three-D cube and it emitted music. The music stopped when the cube was replaced on the shelf. Lifting each cube, she turned them reverently in her hand. Tyona stared at the holograms, fascinated. "Your family?"

"Yes."

"Who is this?" Tyona asked, holding up a holocube of a dark-haired, pretty woman.

"Her name was Lyra. My wife." A spasm crossed Ason's face. "She, my oldest son, and my mother were killed in the last Brazaryan raid on Maynite-two."

Tyona swallowed. "Lord Captain, I am sorry. I did not know."

"It is quite all right, Tyona. It was a long time ago. Ninety-nine years to be exact. But I still miss her." Ason sighed. "I still miss them all."

Tyona replaced the cube. Suddenly catching her breath, she reached for another. "Who is this?"

"That, young lady, is my father, Kalyn mMyre. It was his fate I had hoped to settle."

She stared at the facsimile in the cube several moments, then slowly replaced it on the shelf.

"I was told he affected my mother the same way."

Her face crimson, Tyona quickly turned away. Nervously adjusting her uniform, her gaze fell on a portrait of a woman on the far wall. Tyona wandered over to it, her mouth agape. She glanced at the captain then back to the portrait. "She is beautiful. Your daughter?"

"No," Ason said, stepping next to the lieutenant. "My mother. It was painted the year I was born. Her name was Alisa. She and my father were very much in love. She never accepted his fate—or hers." Ason sighed. "As a child, I remember her in the cool of the evening, standing outside, forever watching the heavens. Occasionally she would spy a star-vessel returning from parts unknown and dash inside to contact Fleet-Com." The captain glanced at Tyona. "I did not have to ask what they told her."

Silence enveloped them. The young lieutenant finally spoke. "That signal…your father?"

"I would like to think so, but it is highly unlikely." Ason sighed. "No, Tyona, I believe him dead. Strange that, though he was a Matair warrior, I feel nothing from his passing."

"All Matair are born with *ishara*." Tyona gazed at the lord captain. "He left you no living memory of events?"

"No. As you know, *ishara*—living memories—can only be passed down to a single individual. My father has left no *ishara* for me or anyone I know." Ason sighed. "All my instincts tell me he met his destiny on Illysia. But he was my father. I must learn his fate."

"Sir, maybe the signal was automated and began transmitting on impact."

"No. We were at war. An automated signal would have been suicide. If the signal were indeed the *Halaena's*, they were far behind enemy lines."

"Was *Halaena* equipped with a T-Pan transponder?" Tyona asked.

"The T-Pan locator did not exist when the *Halaena* sailed." Ason's brow furrowed. "*Halaena's* distress beacon is manually activated only by voice authorization." He sighed in confusion. "What was she doing almost seven hundred light years from where records show her vanishing—if indeed that signal is the *Halaena's*?"

"Sir, maybe that is why we were ordered back. The High Council is concealing something—and not for the first time." Tyona paused. "What was the *Halaena's* mission? Records only reveal she was a Quasar-Class recon vessel with a crew of thirty-seven and was on nothing more than routine patrol in sector two."

"Mission details are *still* classified," Ason said. "Tyona, you know the only thing we are fed is the sewage that spews from the High Council. And now here we are, less than a day away from solving this...this enigma, and strangely, we are ordered to stand down."

Ason began pacing back and forth again, finally halting in front of Tyona. "I shall learn what happened to the *Halaena*, and to my father."

Tyona's eyes widened. "Lord Captain, I cannot believe you would disobey a direct order from the High Council! That would be—"

"I will disobey nothing. Upon reaching port, I shall retire. Then I may take a little 'vacation.'"

"If the Lord Captain would permit, I would be

honored to accompany him." Tyona stepped closer to the captain. "Please, take me with you."

Smiling softly, Ason reached and touched Tyona's delicate chin. "Thank you." Dropping his hand, he shook his head. "Thank you, Tyona, for your kind offer, but no. This is something only a fool would attempt. It is much, much too dangerous to consider—"

"I am an excellent pilot, and my last assignment was navigator aboard the—"

"No."

Folding her arms, Tyona stomped a foot, turning her back to the captain.

"Tyona, you must understand," Ason began, "I would not want such a fine Fleet officer jeopardizing her career on the whims of a middle-age man chasing after ghosts."

"I acknowledge and accept the danger. My navigation skills are unapproachable."

"Indeed, they are. But," the captain eyed the holocubes, "if my father is alive, he certainly would not look like that. His age would show."

"Sir, that has no factor in my request."

The captain suppressed a smile. "I see."

"Lord Captain," Tyona persisted, "I want to help you solve this 'mystery.' I wish to visit Illysia-three myself. Just to see if the old legends are true, of course."

"Of course." Ason chuckled, giving the woman a fatherly pat. "Tyona, you need to forget about him, and find a nice young Fleet officer. Why, I know of at least a dozen men who would—"

"My Lord," Tyona interrupted, "You insult me. 'Finding a nice young Fleet officer' is not why I joined Her Majesty's Fleet." She eyed the older man. "I longed for adventure, mystery, to feed my sense of history and where our place, as Satari, fit in to what seems as chaos." Her shoulders sagged. "However, I grow more disappointed with each passing year. Today's leadership has no spirit." Ason nodded; he could not argue her last point.

"I feel I am just biding time here."

"Tyona, you are much too young to 'bide time.'"

"Sir, things have become too tame for me. I am ready for *real* adventure." Tyona looked at the older man, her eyes large and brown. "My Lord, if you undertake a journey to that far away world, I wish to accompany you. I could be of great help." She paused. "I have nothing here, really. Even the Fleet—"

Ason raised a hand. "Enough."

"I am sorry."

"That is quite all right, young lady. You voice your sentiments well." The captain studied the woman in front of him. "When we arrive at port, we shall talk more of this matter. Until then, this conversation never occurred. Is that clear, Lieutenant?"

"Perfectly, sir," Tyona replied, grinning.

"That will be all."

Tyona bowed, turned, and headed for the door.

"Tyona."

"My Lord?"

"Be careful what you ask for."

Tyona eyed the captain, silent.

Ason nodded, his gaze softening. "Thank you for stopping by. Good evening."

"Good evening, sir." The lieutenant turned, leaving the room.

11

The cement patio floor shook from the resonant thumping of the Harley-Davidson. The big bike, with an ear-splitting roar, shot across the middle of the patio, scattering everyone. The bike circled back, stopping.

The biker wore a black, battle-scarred helmet and aviator sunglasses. Steadying the vehicle with one leg he eased it over onto the kick-stand. "Hey!"

"Hey?" Charlie sneered, giving the biker an annoyed look. He flipped up the lid of a BBQ grill. "That's all you can say?"

"No," Dan said, pulling off his helmet. "I have a wet ass."

"What'd you do, scare the piss out of yourself like you did us?"

"Rode through a little rain. Then everything got blow-dried—except my ass." Grinning boyishly, Dan hooked a leg over the gas tank. "How about a beer?"

"After the way you came tearing in here?"

"Charlie, you liked it and you know it. Besides, you

told me to ride my bike, so stop griping."

A woman's voice said, "Charlie, you leave that boy alone. Dan, ignore him."

Charlie lowered his voice. "Looks like Momma saved your ass, Danny-boy."

An attractive woman of perhaps fifty breezed onto the patio. She wore glasses, her dark hair short. In spite of her casual, countrified demeanor, Carolyn Fulton had a distinguished air about her. She held an MBA and until recently was a high-powered financial advisor for a Houston oil company. Now, except for keeping books on her husband and Dan's trucks, she was semi-retired. Carolyn said she preferred a quiet, country life with her husband and two grandchildren rather than the constant turmoil and grind of making lots of money. Dan wondered how one could consider living with Charlie and two small children a quiet life. Her previous job must have been a nightmare.

"Come here, Dan," she said, stepping up to him. "You look good." She gave him a long hug. "You need to stop by more often."

Dan tossed his sunglasses in his helmet and returned her hug. "I'm sorry, Carolyn. I've been meaning to come by. It's just that—"

"It's just that you've been so busy. The usual stuff. I know, I know." Carolyn led Dan to a lawn chair. "So, what's this about you getting married?"

Dan settled into the web chair.

Charlie walked over, handing the younger man a beer. "This is it until after you take the old lady for a ride."

He glanced at the bike. "And I wish you'd get that son of a bitch off my patio before it falls on one of the kids."

Dan popped the top on the can, taking a swallow. "They'll probably get burned from the exhaust first. Besides, the kids are out there." He nodded to the yard behind him. Grumbling something about a "smart-ass," Charlie moved back to the grill.

"Okay, okay, just let me let me finish the beer first."

Carolyn pulled a chair next to Dan. "So, when is the big day?"

Dan stared blankly. "Oh. Uh, probably in a couple of weeks."

"A couple of weeks?" Carolyn gave Dan a puzzled look. "Why the rush?"

"Hell, we waited for over ten years," Dan replied, tilting the can.

Hovering over the nearby grill, Charlie snickered. "Carolyn, I'll tell you about it later."

"What are you going to tell her, Charlie? Huh? And you're right. I do need to get them away from there."

"There're other reasons and you know it."

"I don't want to discuss it. Just drop it."

Carolyn looked first at Dan, then to her husband. "What am I missing here?"

"Carolyn," Charlie said, "do we still have that old crib of Davy's? If we do, give it to Dan."

Carolyn's eyes widened. "Dan!" She glanced at her husband. "Charlie—you don't mean it!"

"Oh, but I do."

"Anyway," Dan began before Carolyn could speak, "better plan a trip to Vegas if you're coming to the wedding."

"Vegas?" Carolyn asked. "So you're getting married in Las Vegas?"

"Yeah," Charlie added. "Why Vegas? That doesn't sound like Anna. What do you want to do, see some old buddies? If so, you better set up an appointment with the Department of Corrections."

Dan shot him the finger, took a swallow from the can, then turned to Carolyn. "Vegas is the only way we can get married quickly. Either that or lie. And *that's* no way to start a marriage." He paused. "I'd have to be a resident of Arizona for six months before I could get a marriage license there. It's the same for Anna in Texas. So," Dan said, shrugging, "to avoid all the BS, we decided to fly to Vegas, get married, spend a few days with friends and then fly back."

"I thought you were going to drive there and move Anna back here," Charlie said.

"I am." Dan looked at Carolyn, then to Charlie. "I'm heading up there in a few days. After we get married, we'll load a few things into her pickup and my Jeep, then haul ass back here. Movers will handle the rest."

"Sounds like you've got it all worked out," Carolyn said.

"I talked to Anna last night. We decided it was best this way."

"Dan, if you need a place to store her things, you can use our garage. We don't mind, do we Charlie?"

Charlie sighed. "Somehow, I knew this would happen."

"He doesn't mind," Carolyn said.

"I appreciate the offer, but we'll just stick to our plans." Dan eyed Charlie. "So, don't put yourself out."

Grumbling, Charlie lifted the top of the smoker. Thick gray smoke completely enveloped him. The acrid, sweet scent of mesquite and beef brisket drifted across the patio. Dan's stomach growled.

Tilting the beer can, Dan eyed the rusted, black smoker. A lot of memories were wrapped around that old piece of junk. It was nothing but a fifty-five gallon drum that was cut in half. It had a hinged lid and angle-iron legs. A cinder block now held up the bottom. The years had taken its toll on it, but Charlie wouldn't let it go. Dan remembered helping Charlie build it.

Dan's biological mother died of cancer when he was twelve. His father, a helicopter pilot based at Nellis, remarried. Dan was sixteen when his father, piloting a Huey gunship, was shot down over South Vietnam. Charlie, a door gunner, was the only survivor. He was with Dan's father when the pilot took his last breath. Dan's stepmother and stepsister all but abandoned him. Charlie and Carolyn had looked after Dan ever since. The couple relocated to old family land in East Texas after Dan graduated from high school, and Dan followed, attending the University of Texas.

As a junior in college, he'd driven up from Austin to Charlie and Carolyn's homestead in his old '67 Impala SS while on spring break. Most of his buddies had spent the week on Padre Island, staggering around in a drunken stupor trying to impress the girls. Dan had spent the entire week with Carolyn and Charlie.

Most said he had wasted a week. All Dan knew was that he had a good time. Besides helping build the smoker, Dan had stacked hay, helped deliver a calf, ran fence-line, and drank a lot of beer on hot afternoons. With Charlie's help, he even over-hauled that old Holley double-pumper on his hotrod.

The Fulton's home was only twenty miles east of Dan's, practically next door in rural Texas terms. To Dan, it seemed like Charlie had lived here forever. The last few years, this was as close to a real *home* as Dan had.

Dan was shaken from his thoughts by screaming children at play. Davy and Nicki were the Fultons' grandchildren. Their mother had died from a drug over-dose and their father had abandoned them. They now belonged to Charlie and Carolyn.

Another child ran with the Fultons' grandkids. She was a dark-haired, gangly girl Dan had never seen. She caught Dan watching her, then whispered something to Nicki, who giggled. The two girls ran over to Dan.

"Take us for a ride," Nicki pleaded, pulling on Dan's arm.

Nicki, twelve, was the oldest of the grandchildren. Dan would tease her unmercifully, asking her how she got all that long brown hair, when her hair was blonde, or hide, then scare her when she came around a corner. Recently Dan learned the name of a boy she liked, and used that as more ammo to incite her wrath.

"Ride will cost five dollars—apiece."

"Five dollars!" the girls screamed.

"Nicki, I'm sure *Nathan* will loan it to you—that is if he hasn't spent it on that other girl I saw him with at the mall last week."

"Da-ann-y!" Nicki shouted, turning four shades of red. "He wasn't with any girl—and you owe me a ride for saying that."

"Dan," came a voice near his motorcycle. Carolyn unstrapped a helmet. "I've never been on a Harley," she said, fumbling with it, "and you *did* promise me."

Groaning, Dan rose. He looked at the two girls and winked.

"Please, Dan, just a little ride," Nicki begged. "After you take Grandma?"

"No. I don't have a helmet that'll fit you. Maybe next time."

"How about just around here?" the other girl said, indicating the yard. She held Dan's gaze for a moment, smiling.

His brow furrowed; the girl had a strange accent. He'd heard it before, but couldn't place it.

"Let's go, Dan, before it rains!"

"Okay, okay." He headed for the motorcycle. Dan eyed the dark, cumulus clouds gathering on the western horizon; they had billowed up in just the last few minutes. The storm he'd driven through was heading this way.

Charlie dropped the smoker's lid, scanning the sky. "We could sure use the moisture."

Dan fastened his helmet and watched the two girls. Nicki had run back into the yard, but the dark-haired girl remained by the empty lawn chair, staring. The girl was a strange one, he thought, climbing onto the bike.

He turned the key and the V-Twin rumbled. Hopping on behind him, Carolyn slapped his back. "Let's get outta' here."

It was almost dark when the rain came. It whipped around in great wind-blown sheets that could drench a person in seconds. Standing near the edge of the covered patio, Charlie shoved his hands in his pockets, staring nervously into the gathering darkness. Where were Carolyn and Dan?

There was a bright flash, and he tensed for the follow-up. It began as a long, low rumble in the west, reaching an A-bomb crescendo that shook the ground. Charlie glanced at the uncovered portion of the patio. Wind-driven wavelets lapped at the one step that separated him from the forming lake in the yard.

Dan said they would only be gone a few minutes. That was an hour and a half ago. "Damn that boy."

Stepping back into the house, Charlie picked up the phone. He swore under his breath; the line was still dead. He glanced to the living room where the kids were watching TV. Thankfully, they seemed oblivious to the danger their grandmother and Dan were in. He turned to go back outside when the kitchen lights flickered. A blast of thunder cracked, and they were in total darkness. The children rushed into the kitchen.

"What happened to the lights?" Nicki hollered.

"Grandma's not back yet?" Davy asked.

"You don't see her, do you, stupid?" Nicki replied.

"That's enough!" Charlie snapped.

The other girl gazed at Charlie. "I'm sure they're okay. Dan would never let anything happen to her."

Charlie paused then waved an arm. "Ya' all go back to the living room, see if any headlights are coming, but don't get too close to the windows."

The children dashed noisily out of the kitchen. Charlie returned to the patio. The girl was right. If there was anyone on earth Charlie could trust with his family, it would be Dan McKntyre. He and Carolyn had agreed that if something were to happen to himself, she was to turn to Dan. Charlie stared into the solid curtain of rain, breathing a little easier. He had to have faith in the younger man.

About to head inside, he halted, catching the familiar *whumpta-whump* of a Harley. The kids burst onto the patio. "They're back! They're back!"

Charlie's smile vanished as the motorcycle weaved toward him. He stared in shock at the smashed headlight and dented gas tank. Dan was bleeding—and alone.

Swinging under the patio awning, Dan killed the engine, setting the bike down hard on the kickstand. Fumbling with the helmet strap, he wiped blood from his eyes. Its coppery taste filled his mouth.

"Where's Carolyn?" Charlie screamed.

"She's okay, Charlie!" Dan shouted, struggling to free the helmet-strap. The strap was soaked and wouldn't loosen. "Charlie, Carolyn is fine—just chill. I've got her stashed at the old Drummond place. If you'll let me use the pickup—and help me with this damn helmet—I'll go back for her."

Relief moved across Charlie's face. He glanced at the blood streaming from Dan's nose and turned to the kids. "Someone get a towel—a clean one—and hurry!" Reaching over, he helped Dan remove the helmet. "I'm sorry, son."

Dan stumbled, catching himself with the handlebars. Charlie grabbed Dan's arm, helping him to a nearby chair. A deep gash on the bridge of Dan's nose bled profusely. Stripping off his wet T-shirt, Dan pressed it between his eyes.

"Shit!" he swore in disgust. "I'll look like I've been in a bar fight. Here I am, trying to make a good impression on Anna's parents—"

"It's too late for that," Charlie interrupted, leaning over the younger man. "Let's have a look." Easing the shirt away from Dan's nose, he winced, pushing it back. "Where's that towel?"

"That bad?"

"You'll live. What happened?"

"Hail. We were coming back," Dan gestured behind him, "up there on the main drag when it hit. I've never seen anything like it, Charlie. Hail stones the size of softballs. Just look at my friggin' bike—look at the tank! We didn't have a prayer out in the open." Dan looked at the older man over the wadded-up shirt. "Carolyn doesn't have a scratch—I took it all."

Holding the shirt to his nose, Dan leaned back, closing his eyes. Gentle hands moved the shirt aside, and a towel carefully dabbed the gash. He sat quietly for a moment, too exhausted to move.

The towel brushed his eyes. He jumped.

The strange dark-haired girl stood with a bloody towel in her hand, a frightened look on her face. "I'm sorry. I, I didn't mean to hurt you."

"You didn't—and thanks. I really mean it." Reaching out, Dan eased the towel from her. "You knew exactly what to do."

Embarrassed, the girl moved away. Dan noticed her large brown eyes kept moving to the tattoo on his bare shoulder. He glanced to his shoulder, then back to her. She seemed confused, uncertain. Without warning, she turned and bolted for the house, slamming the kitchen door behind her.

"What the hell?" Dan murmured.

Charlie knelt by Dan. "What'd you say to her?"

"Nothing. She just glanced at—"

"Don't worry about it. She belongs to those foreigners that moved in down the road. They're from South

Africa. A strange bunch."

"South Africa? What the hell are they doing here?"

"The girl has leukemia," Charlie replied. "They brought her to the States for treatment. The girl and her family are living with some distant cousins down the road."

"Jesus. And we think we have problems."
Charlie turned his attention to Dan. "Hail did this to you?"

"Yeah, we took some bad hits, but like I said, Carolyn is fine. She's waiting for one of us to pick her up. Lucky we were near the old Drummond farm."

"I need to go," Charlie said. "The old lady is probably having a heart attack." He glanced at the darkening sky. The rain had eased. "Stay with the kids. I should be back in less than thirty minutes."

Twenty minutes later, Charlie returned with a wet, but otherwise unscathed Carolyn. She was more concerned with Dan's injuries than anything else. Within minutes she had Dan's head over the bathroom sink, dumping peroxide on his wound.

"There," she said, gently rubbing the edges of a bandage. "Now, don't pick at it." Carolyn began putting away the first-aid kit. "It may leave a tiny scar, but not enough for Anna to dump you." She eyed him, a hint of amusement in her eyes. "It'll just give you more character."

Looking at his reflection in the mirror, Dan gingerly touched the small butterfly bandage.

"I said don't mess with it!"

His hand jerked. "Yes, ma'am."

Charlie shoved himself into the bathroom and tossed

Dan an old work shirt. "Don't get blood on it."

Carolyn yanked the shirt out of Dan's hands, throwing it back at her husband. "Jesus, Charlie, I can't believe you. Get this boy a *clean* shirt!"

A few minutes later Charlie stepped into the kitchen. Carolyn and Dan sat at the kitchen table, Dan nursing a beer. "First you steal my old lady," Charlie said, tossing Dan a blue T-shirt, "by getting her to feel sorry for you, and now here you sit, drinking my beer after I gave you the shirt off my back."

Carolyn looked over her glasses. "Shut up and sit down."

Charlie opened a beer and joined. The conversation wound down after a couple of hours. The Fultons insisted Dan stay the night. As a matter of fact, they had anticipated it. And at the moment, Dan had little choice. He had drunk too much, he hurt too much, and once again, he had no headlight on his motorcycle.

At seven-thirty the next morning, Dan, helmet in hand, strode to the Harley with Charlie and Carolyn at his side. It was a quiet, peaceful Sunday morning. Dan recalled similar mornings, sitting out on his patio, enjoying the silence, feeling the cool breeze touching his skin, watching hummingbirds fight over a feeder. Soon he'd share those small pleasures with another.

"Sure you don't want me to go to Arizona with you?" Charlie asked.

"Not necessary," Dan replied. "Things will be fine. I,

we, should be back in a week or so."

The trio stopped at the motorcycle. Dan checked it over, shaking his head. It had taken a real beating. His nose throbbed just looking at it. Sighing with disgust, he tugged on his helmet.

Charlie patted his back. "For once, try staying out of trouble."

Carolyn grabbed Dan's neck, giving him a quick hug. "Be careful, okay?"

He nodded, silent.

As the Fultons headed back to the house, Nicki's friend, the little dark-haired girl, shot past them. She halted in front of Dan just as he was climbing onto the bike.

"Danny?" she said, breathless, brown eyes wide.

Dan raised a brow. Climbing back off the bike, he worked off his helmet. "You know my name, so what's yours?"

"Elizabeth," she said, smiling.

"Elizabeth. Now that's a pretty name." Dan returned her smile.

She blushed. "This is for you." She handed him a small rock. "It's my good luck charm. I want you to have it."

Dan started to protest but saw the sincerity in the girl's face. Apparently, the rock meant a lot to her. Smiling, he reached for it, turning it around in his hand. It was a chunk of what appeared to be gray granite that sparkled when held to the light. It felt strange to the touch, like it was manmade. "Why, thank you, Elizabeth. I'll treasure it." Dan stuffed it in a shirt pocket.

"You're welcome. After what happened yesterday, I thought you could use it."

Dan laughed, not knowing what to say. "How old are you?"

"Twelve."

"I have a daughter almost your age. Her name is Amy. She and her mother will be living with me soon. Maybe you and Amy will go to the same school?"

"Maybe," she replied, averting her eyes.

"I've got to go." Dan tugged on his helmet. "We'll see each other again."

"I'm sure we will." Elizabeth lingered, hesitating. Finally, she turned, trudging to the house.

Dan climbed onto the bike and turned the key. The ground vibrated from the V-twin. "Later," he shouted to the girl.

Elizabeth turned and waved. "Bye! Be careful. Don't forget me!"

Dan took off, shifting gears. The way she looked at him was strange; it was like she knew him. And last night, why did she suddenly run into the house? Dan sighed. Girls…geesus, would his own daughter be that weird?

Dan walked in the front door. The answering machine was flashing. He punched a button and Anna's voice blared, distraught. Dan returned her call.

"*Jeffery contacted me early yesterday morning,*"

Anna said.

"I thought you had a restraining order against him?" Dan replied. "Man, what a head-case. He's a lawyer, he should know the repercussions—"

"Danny, he doesn't care. That protective order is nothing but a piece of paper." Anna paused. *"To press charges and see it through, I'd have to stay here and that's not an option. I just want to get away from here, baby. How soon can you get here?"*

"I'll leave early tomorrow morning."

"Make it quick. I'm all alone. Mom, Dad and Amy left for Utah this morning. A close friend of the family is ill. They won't return until later in the week. I'm staying at a friend's house until you arrive. I'll give you the number. You can call me from Lordsburg, then I'll meet you here at home."

"Anna, I think you're too paranoid. I've never known you to be this…this—"

"Scared? Hell yes, I'm scared. And I'm not paranoid, just cautious. Danny, you don't know what Jeffery has done—to me and to others. When you get here, I'll share the horror stories."

"I can hardly wait."

"I didn't tell Jeffery anything about us. We only talked for a moment. Get this: he had the unmitigated gall to offer me the Mercedes, and transfer the vacation home in Costa Rica to me if I would meet with him and—"

"Vacation home…in Costa Rica." Dan repeated slowly. He sighed, knowing he had a long way to go to match a "vacation home" like that. Dan had spent time in Central America, but not on vacation. He was part of a covert military operation there, the CO in an Army unit that officially never existed. They had trained Nicaraguan contras in some of the nastiest kinds of warfare.

"*Danny, are you still there?*"

"Yeah."

"*Well,*" Anna continued, "*to buy us a few days of peace, I told him I'd consider his offer and get back to him in a couple of weeks. By that time, you and I will be married and out of here.*"

"Have you pulled his invitation?"

"*Don't joke. You need to take him seriously. Jeffery is dangerous.*"

Dan's grip tightened around the receiver. "I'm tired of hearing *that*. First your father insinuates I can't handle myself, then Charlie tells me to watch out, the sky is falling, and now—"

"*Someone has a bruised ego.*"

Dan swore to himself. "Anna, it's just that I—"

"*Danny, I'm worried about our safety, that's all. Can we save this discussion for later? Please?*" There was a long pause. "*I love you, Danny.*"

"And I love you, Annie girl."

Saying their good-byes, Dan held the receiver in his hand, staring out the screen door. The incessant droning of cicadas drifted from an open window. Replacing the receiver, he tapped thoughtfully on the kitchen bar, still hearing the anxiety in Anna's voice. Dan decided to leave for Stanton immediately. Reaching for the phone, he called her back.

The air was a sauna as Dan headed to the CJ-7 Jeep. In one hand was a 9mm pistol; the other held a shotgun. He shook his head. And to think he called Anna paranoid. He recalled a photo of a Serbian wedding: the Orthodox Church looked like an armory.

Opening the Jeep's canvas door, he stuffed the pistol in the center console, then gently laid the twelve-gauge-pump shotgun on the back seat. It was a nine-shot Winchester *Defender*, the very gun his father had kept in his gunship in Vietnam. He glanced at it, shaking his head.

It was early afternoon when Dan pulled out of the driveway. Suddenly slamming on the brakes, he bolted from the vehicle, sprinting to the house. Moments later, he emerged, a small ring box in his hand. He'd almost blown it again.

Albright stared at the receiver in his hand, then slammed it down. *Anna won't even reason with me. Damn her!* Shaking his head in disgust, he made his way to curtains.

Gleaming shafts of sunlight crept over far desert hills. Rays from an unrisen sun reflected off high cirrus clouds, turning them a fiery magenta.

Jeffery Albright peered through the drapes then glanced to the clock near the bed—5:45. He eyed the sleeping, supine outline of Tiffany lying under silk sheets. She was beginning to bore him. No passion, no fire. He never realized he would miss it. Releasing the curtains, Albright stepped into slippers, tightening the robe's sash and heading for the door.

The cool tinkling of water drifted from a nearby fountain as Albright sat on the covered veranda. Taking a sip of almond cappuccino, he stared blankly past the immense hanging ferns. The distant whine of a hedge-trimmer drifted. Taking another sip, his eyes focused on a date palm, its fronds whispering from an early morning breeze. A bird fluttered in a nearby orange tree. Anna would know what kind of bird that was. She always knew about those things.

The veranda was built for Anna, and she personally landscaped it. Albright sighed. No matter where he went, he couldn't escape her. Closing his eyes, he leaned back in the lounger, letting the morning coolness seep in. Now, all that tenderness belonged to another.

"No!" He bolted upright, cursing himself for lapsing into a moment of regret. Sentimentality was for the weak; he breathed for power. Yet Anna Wildaer was an obsession that threw him into a downward spiral, plunging with a splat into the pit of self-pity.

To Albright, rejection was incomprehensible, unfathomable and perceived as failure. Naturally others were to blame. Anna was a blemish on his otherwise near- perfect character. Her loss festered as an open wound; it drove him insane.

Minutes later the ringing phone on a deck table shook him from a deep loathing. The lawyer snatched up the receiver. "Yeah?"

"*Mr. Albright? I'm sorry to bother you,*" Sheila said.

"Didn't Bentien tell you I wasn't coming in today?"

"*Yes, sir, but something just happened that I think needs your attention.*"

"And that is?"

"*The FBI just left.*"

Albright stood. "What did they want?"

"*It was only one guy, Mr. Albright. I had just arrived*

when this nicely dressed man walked in and flashed a badge. Said his name was—just a minute, let me get his card—says here his name is Simon Terrell. Special Agent Simon Terrell, FBI. Do you know him?"

"Never heard of him. Did he have a subpoena, or warrant?"

"I don't think so. All he had was a brown business envelope under his arm. Said it was a private matter."

The attorney swore. Was it about his last phone call? Talk about fast and having contacts. Yet the FBI ignores family disputes—unless federal laws are violated. Albright sighed. The local constabulary frequently visited his office. Some for information, others as clients. Even those rottwielers at the IRS dropped by now and then. But the FBI? The Feds were more tenacious than a rottwieler or pit bull: a dog had to let go sometime.

"Shelia, did he say anything else?"

"When I told him you wouldn't be in today, he looked really put-out. Said his business with you was brief, but important."

That's the way it always started, Albright mused. It usually ended with a ride downtown. "Did he go into my office?"

"No, sir. He stayed right in front of me."

"Did he have any comments?"

"No. He just left his card and said for you to call him."

"How long ago did he leave?"

"Maybe ten minutes. I think he's heading out to your

place."

"So do I. Listen, Shelia, if he comes back, make sure you let me know. And one more thing: keep his visit to yourself, okay?"

"You can trust me, Mr. Albright."

"I'm sure I can."

Albright tossed the cordless phone on the lounger. It appeared today would be a rerun of yesterday. Running fingers through his hair, he forced himself to think clearly. What did the FBI want with him? When it came to CYA, he was meticulous, making sure every "t" was crossed, every "i" dotted. The IRS had taught him that.

Albright glanced around. The surrounding countryside would soon be baking in 115-degree heat. He chuckled, heading for the house. As he approached the kitchen door a giant man stepped through, halting in the doorway.

"Say, boss, do you still need Bentien and me to hang around?"

Albright eyed the large man. Benjamin "Indian" Morgan stood six-foot six and weighed well over 300 pounds. Long, black hair was permed and lay loose on his shoulders. Morgan's tattoo-covered arms were bigger than most men's legs. He had the dark eyes and high cheekbones that were characteristic of his people, the Apache. Morgan had been a professional wrestler, but something happened and he was blacklisted. Albright never asked why, nor did he care. His "associates" were handsomely rewarded for keeping their mouths shut and doing what they were told.

The lawyer paused before answering. "Yes. Yes, I want you and Bentien to stay close for a few hours. However, I'm expecting a visitor soon, and I want both of you out of sight—especially you."

"Mr. Albright," Lance said, walking up behind the lawyer, "I got those hedges trimmed like you wanted. Is there anything else you want done before I start on the garage door?"

"As a matter of fact there is. Turn off all the air-conditioning in the house."

"Boss!" Morgan protested. "Do you know how frigging hot it's gonna get?"

"Hot enough to melt Tiffany's silicone."

"But," Lance sputtered, "but why turn off the a/c? I mean, like—"

"Guys," Albright interrupted, "stop bitching—it's temporary." He glanced at his Rolex. "Hopefully we can get the a/c 'repaired' by this afternoon."

"But there's nothing wrong with it?" Lance said.

"Lance," Albright began, "it's too bad you live out here with me."

"Why's that, Mr. Albright?"

"Because you're denying some nice little village of an idiot."

"Five years of college," Morgan said, laughing, heading back into the house.

"Hey—screw you, Indian! Come back here!"

Morgan shot him the finger then stepped inside.

"You two, knock it off," Albright shouted. "Lance,

just do as I say."

Mumbling, Lance followed the other men into the house.

Two hours later a white Crown Victoria pulled up to the heavy iron gate near the highway.

"There's our guest," Albright said, tapping the video monitor. He dabbed his forehead with a handkerchief. "Let him in, Lance."

Lance punched a button. The car crept through the entrance, slowly picking up speed. The two men watched as the car moved from screen to screen at a leisurely pace. Albright licked his lips. "I'll be pool-side," he said, turning to leave. "Have Tiffany show him out."

Ice tea in hand, Albright made his way outside, taking a seat sat at a wrought-iron deck table. A nearby ceiling fan creaked, its blades circling lazily. Several similar tables were randomly scattered in the covered shade of the large pool-patio. A slight breeze stirred the collar of Albright's yellow polo shirt.

Hearing the sliding glass door open, Albright waited a few seconds before turning. Tiffany led a man to the attorney's table. The man, dressed in a light-brown business suit, was of medium height and build. He cradled a large brown envelope under an arm.

"Mr. Albright," Tiffany said, "this is Simon Terrell, with the FBI. Mr. Terrell, this is Jeffery Albright."

The two shook. Terrell dropped the envelope on the table and fished out a badge.

Albright nodded. The lawyer indicated for Terrell to

have a seat. Tiffany hovered nearby.

"Thank you," the agent said in a gravely voice. Tugging off his coat, he tossed it over a nearby chair and sat down.

Albright's eyes were fixed on the .45 strapped around the agent's left shoulder.

Terrell caught the lawyer staring at the pistol. "Surely, counselor, being around the courthouse, you've seen weapons before."

"Absolutely. It's just that I don't usually have armed guests."

"Then why all the hidden cameras?"

Albright raised a brow, smiling. Appearing to be in his fifties, Terrell wore a military style crew-cut. His features were sharp and well-defined, deep-set blue eyes scrutinizing everything. The agent reminded Albright of a former client, an army colonel. That guy was tough as nails.

"Iced tea?" Albright asked.

"Sure."

Tiffany looked at the agent. "Sweetened, unsweet—"

"Sweetened, please."

"I'll take a refill also," Albright said, handing Tiffany his glass.

As the young woman disappeared, Albright looked at the agent expectantly.

"Nice home, Mr. Albright. Seems as if you were expecting me?"

Albright tensed. "Thank you. And I wasn't expecting anyone, just escaping the heat. My home does have its quirks. Hottest day of the year and the a/c conks out." He shrugged. "This is the coolest place around."

The agent eyed the lawyer, measuring him. "I guess this will do, as long as we have a few minutes of privacy. I'll be brief, Mr. Albright. I came across something a while back and thought, perchance, you could shed some light on it."

Albright was about to speak when Tiffany returned with two iced-teas.

"Thanks," Terrell winked at her and smiled, revealing perfect white teeth.

Blushing, Tiffany returned his smile. "You're welcome."

"Yes, Tiffany," Albright added, "thank you. And hold all my calls, please."

"Yes, sir." Tiffany turned, glanced at the agent, then walked back into the house with a little more bounce than usual.

"Well," the lawyer began, "what brings you here? It's not everyday I have the pleasure of entertaining the FBI. Have I done something?"

"Mr. Albright, we've *all* done something. Only some have a few more skeletons than others."

The attorney gave a look of mock surprise. "And I suppose it's your job to expose them? Well, well, where's your lantern, Diogenes?"

"Are you telling me to keep going?"

Albright shrugged. "Do what you want."

"Actually," Terrell reached for the brown envelope, "I need an answer to an enigma. I believe you can provide clues."

"Did you say enigma or enema?"

Terrell sat stone-faced.

Albright took a deep breath. "I'll cooperate all I can, Agent Terrell, but 'enigmas' are not my specialty."

"We'll see." Terrell removed a small stack of photos from the envelope. Picking through them, he handed Albright an 8x10 glossy. "Take a look at that."

Giving an annoyed sigh, Albright spun the glossy around. "I'm telling you, I don't see…how…" His voice trailed off, his gaze fixed on a photo of Anna's pendant. In the photo was the inverted triangle necklace with its strange writing. Even the worn, gold chain was plainly seen. His jaw tightened; he should've known the agent's visit concerned her.

How *had* she come by that pendant? He had found it hidden in an old leather-bound book with the same kind of writing. Were they both stolen treasures? And to think he once had the necklace completely in his possession while getting it appraised, unbeknownst to her. The jeweler tossed the pendant back, saying it needed to be checked by a metallurgist; he'd never seen anything like it. Albright returned it to where he had found it. The necklace had felt strange; its allure still lingered. Why did she keep it hidden?

Albright's attention returned to the photo. His stomach knotted, yet years of acting in front of a crowded courtroom now served him. He showed no emotion, handing the glossy back to the agent.

Terrell eyed Albright. "It would go well with your

wife's, would it not?"

"If you are referring to my ex-wife, Anna."
Albright's eyes narrowed. "What are you driving at, Agent
Terrell?"

"We both know it's her necklace."

The lawyer picked up the photo again. "I do believe
she may have something similar—that is, if she hasn't yet
sold it." Albright dropped the photo, sighing. "Poor girl. \
She's badly strapped for cash."

"Do you recall where she got it?"

"No. And what's the big deal?"

Terrell shoved Albright another glossy. It was a
painting of a medieval knight.

"Do I look like an art critic?" Albright said,
glancing at it. "I've seen better artwork sprayed on the
Nineteenth-Street underpass in Phoenix."

"Check the bottom right corner of the shield, just
under the coat-of-arms."

Albright's breath caught. There it was—the inverted
triangle with the sword flanked by lightening bolts. Albright
handed it back. "So Anna's pendant looks similar. So what?"

"That design was overlooked until recent computer
enhancements. And it just so happens your ex-wife has a
piece of jewelry with an identical motif. How did she learn
of it? Or, is that necklace an artifact? These are just a few of
the questions we have, Mr. Albright."

"Why is the FBI interested in medieval emblems?"

"We have our reasons."

Albright sighed. "I'm sure she noticed the little

badge and found it interesting, herself. You know she holds a Ph.D. in archeology—a real ticket to wealth, huh? Do you know what she's been doing the past year?"

Terrell straightened.

Pausing, Albright reached for a cigar in his shirt pocket. He offered one to Terrell, who declined. "All that education—that I paid for—and she teaches music at a junior high school." Albright's eyes narrowed. "What did Anna do, make off with a museum piece, or steal a national treasure?" Laughing, he clipped the end off the cigar, shoved it in his mouth and lit it. "So, 'little miss can't be wrong' found something." Taking a long draw, Albright exhaled. Smoke swirled between them. Chuckling to himself, the lawyer puffed nonchalantly. "So what?"

Terrell remained quiet.

"Tell me, why the interest in her necklace?" Albright continued. "Why is the FBI suddenly fascinated with a coat-of-arms? What's so special about it?"

"Mr. Albright, don't you think it odd that your wife has a pendant with a design that hasn't been seen for over a thousand years?" Terrell sipped his tea. "In fact, nobody knew such a design, or the pendant, existed until a few months ago."

Realization hit Albright with an iron fist: Anna was being watched. His own plans where now in jeopardy. Playing along with Terrell became his only option.

And that 'writing,'" Terrell continued. "There's nothing on *Earth* like it. Computer analyses determined the language may be related to an ancient Gaelic dialect, but we're not certain."

"All those goddamn computers you guys brag about, and you can't decipher a few frigging lines of writing?" Albright laughed around his cigar. "Taxpayer's money at work."

"A computer only knows what's been programmed in." Terrell eyed the nearby glossy of Anna's pendant. "That stuff is bizarre."

"Well," Albright sighed, "you still haven't said why you're out here. Pray tell, Agent Terrell, why is the government—the FBI—involved with," he waved at the glossies scattered on the deck table, "all this? Do you believe my ex stole that necklace?"

"Stole?" Terrell repeated. "No, 'stole' is not a word I would use."

"What do you want from me, Agent Terrell?"

Terrell hesitated before reaching into the manila envelope, working out several more 8x10s.

Albright noticed the agent wavering. More alarms went off. What could be so different from what he'd already seen?

"This is why I'm here, Mr. Albright," Terrell said, handing the attorney the photos. "Those are from NASA. They were taken last year. It was the last thing received from *Voyager One* before they abruptly lost contact with it a billion miles beyond our solar system."

Shoving the cigar in his mouth, Albright reached for the photos. He gazed at the first one and his eyes widened. "My God." He jerked the cigar from his mouth, stunned.

A large vessel—a spacecraft—filled a third of the picture. The craft was oblong with four appendages on one end. At the end of each appendage was a cylinder which was at least half as long as the ship itself. The cylinders were brighter than the rest of the craft and blurred. Albright's attention focused on something in the center of the vessel. He dropped the glossy.

"Those are time-lapse shots taken as Voyager flew closer," Terrell said. "The one you just dropped was taken at a hundred thousand meters. NASA estimates the length of the vessel at approximately five kilometers."

"A three mile-long spaceship—good, God! How did we build such a thing without—"

"We?"

Albright stared at Terrell. Hands quivering, he reached for another photo. "That…that insignia—it's… it's…" He looked up. "I don't understand."

"Neither do we."

In the center of the vessel was an emblem identical to Anna's pendant.

Terrell reached across the table and snatched a cigar out of the lawyer's shirt pocket. Leaning back in his chair, he removed the wrapper, clipped off the end and lit it. He took a long drag and sighed, smoke escaping his lips. "Of course, those photos are highly classified," Terrell said. "Consider yourself privileged—and under oath. Officially they don't exist, got it?"

Nodding, the lawyer pored over the remaining glossies. The next photo was of the emblem itself. Several characters flanked the triangle. Each successive photo was the same shot, but taken closer as *Voyager* hurled toward the craft on an apparent collision course. The last photo was nothing but a silver-white blur taken moments before impact.

Terrell puffed thoughtfully. Albright sat in stunned silence. The agent's eyes darted to the glossies. "The *Voyager* mystery is solved, but a much larger one took its place."

The attorney examined the first photo again. "What country could construct such a monstrosity, and in secret?"

Terrell shook his head. "You don't get it, do you? No nation on Earth could build that." He paused, flicking ash into a nearby ashtray. "Comparing our technology to the ones who built that…hell, it's like comparing a donkey cart to the space shuttle." He stared at Albright through a haze of cigar smoke. "Kind of humbling, isn't it?"

Shaking his head, Albright gazed blankly across the patio, the whirring of the ceiling fan magnified in the silence. That vessel had to have originated from Earth. It just *had* to. Albright's mind would not accept the alternative. His thoughts went to Anna. Could she possibly have known about that giant ship, or who constructed it? Before Albright could gather his thoughts, Terrell was speaking. In the agent's hand were a note pad, a pen, and a small recorder.

"We think Dr. Wildaer can unravel a few things," Terrell began, "if she's not spooked. I'm here to make sure that doesn't happen." Terrell pushed the recorder in front of the attorney. "When and where did you first meet Anna Lynn Wildaer?"

"Now wait just a damn minute!" Albright protested. "I don't have to—"

"You're right, but I don't think you'd like the alternative."

"We both know I don't have to agree to this." Albright shot Terrell a hard look. "I haven't been charged with anything."

Sighing, Terrell ran a hand over close-cropped hair. "Mr. Albright, we can do this the easy way or we can do it the hard way." Taking a quick puff off his cigar, he placed it in the ashtray. "Now, you can answer a few questions in the comfort of your home, or we can go somewhere where the air-conditioning works. It's your call."

"And what are you going to charge me with? Divorcing my wife?"

"I could start by having you *officially* sworn in as a material witness. Of course, it could easily be changed to an accomplice."

"An accomplice to what," Albright sneered, "being married to a whacko?"

"How about possible terrorist activities, espionage, subversion, possession of illegal weapons?" Terrell paused, eyeing the lawyer. "I'm sure I can think of more before we get into town."

"You're crazy, Terrell! I have never participated—"

"I didn't say you, Mr. Albright. However, you were married to Anna Wildaer, correct?"

"Anna? My ex is a lot of things, but a spy? I don't believe you."

"Then tell me what to believe, Mr. Albright."

The attorney felt like he was in a bad dream. How well had he *really* known Anna? What was she doing on that plateau? Shaking his head, he stared at the agent. "You suspect Anna of terrorist activities because of a strange looking necklace? This is absurd! Why don't you drive out to Stanton and ask her about it? I'll give you the address."

"We intend to."

"I have no revelations."

"We'll see." Terrell picked up the notepad. "When did you first meet Dr. Wildaer?"

Albright feigned resignation. "It was back in Seventy-five. She was a senior at Arizona State and worked at the Museum of Natural History. That's where we first met."

"You don't strike me as the museum type."

"They employed the law firm I now own," Albright snapped.

The agent nodded, glancing at his note pad. He asked a few more general questions, which the lawyer knew Terrell had the answers to. The lawyer smiled inside at Terrell's vain attempts to bait him. Surely the agent could do better. After a few minutes, Terrell gathered up the glossies and stuffed them back in the envelope. It appeared the interview was over.

Albright waited for Terrell to pick up the recorder. To the attorney's dismay, the agent shoved it closer. "Tell me, Mr. Albright, why did you release parental rights to your daughter? It wasn't because you couldn't afford child support. A man of your means, surely—"

"It's personal, thank you," Albright shot back.

"Was it because you're not the girl's paternal father?"

Albright turned red. "I don't see where you're heading, Agent Terrell, except to deliberately provoke me."

"I apologize," Terrell said casually. "Perhaps I was out of line. When one uncovers a spouse's affair, especially one that produced a child, I understand how one could be sensitive."

"There was never any 'affair.'" Albright immediately regretted the words, cursing himself for falling for an old lawyer trick. Having done the same to others, he knew Terrell's next question.

"But you claimed that in the divorce decree?"

"What I meant was," Albright said through gritted teeth, "that there was no affair that produced a child."

Terrell cocked eye. "So, you knew Amy wasn't yours when she was born?"

Albright gave a start at the girl's name. "I didn't know Anna was pregnant when we married. I had assumed the child was mine. It was years later when I learned the truth." Albright stared with hostile eyes. "I'm through answering questions. If you want to take me in, let's go. Then you can talk to me with an attorney present. I'm through playing your little game, Agent Terrell."

Terrell sighed. "Look, Mr. Albright, I'm sorry if I hit a sore spot. Just a few more questions, then I'll leave, okay?" Albright was silent.

After scanning his notepad, Terrell glanced back to the lawyer. "Does the name 'Daniel McKntyre' mean anything to you?"

So, the agent was just fishing. Albright thought of telling all he knew of McKntyre, which was little enough, but that could jeopardize his own plans. "Just an old acquaintance of Anna's."

"Having his child hardly makes him 'just an acquaintance.'"

Albright showed no emotion, but inside a rage and resentment that had simmered for years reached the boiling point. He gripped the arms of the deck chair, his knuckles white. How could Anna have deceived him? She knew she was pregnant when they began dating—and said nothing. He never suspected anything until Amy was over a year old. By then, her dark-brown hair and gray eyes made it obvious. Even his parents began whispering behind his back. Yet Anna ignored the whispers and kept playing the game.

When Amy was seven he secretly had a paternity test done and it confirmed what he'd feared; he was not the biological father. He confronted Anna with it and she told him it shouldn't make any difference. He was the only father that Amy knew. Drunk and not wanting to hear it, he beat Anna unconscious. Then when he saw McKntyre, everything suddenly fit. He concluded Anna was only using him, Jeffery Albright, to further herself.

"Mr. Albright, are you okay?"

The lawyer nodded, eyes narrowing.

"So," Terrell continued, "what do you know about

Daniel McKntyre?"

"Not fucking enough."

Terrell sighed, shaking his head. He pointed toward the packet of photos on the table. "Do you think he'd know anything about those?"

"Him?" Albright sneered. "He's just a truckdriver. His world doesn't exist beyond the hood of his truck."

"Have you met him?"

"Yes." Albright glanced at the recorder. It was still running. "But only once, last winter."

"Can you describe him?"

"Agent Terrell," Albright sighed, "we met only once. He was passing through town and stopped to see Anna." Terrell frowned. "He never wanted to see his daughter? I find that odd."

"The guy's a drifter."

"Can you describe him?" Terrell repeated.

"Around my height. Athletic. Short, dark hair, clean shaven."

"That's all?" Terrell asked.

"I told you I only met him once," Albright repeated. "A lot of Saturday nights have passed since then."

Terrell scribbled something on a notepad. "You, perchance, wouldn't have his address or know where he lives or who he drives for?"

Albright suspected the agent already knew. "No."

"I see." The agent sighed, closed his notepad, and then took a long drink of iced-tea. He turned off the recorder. "Is there anything you'd like to add to all this?"

"Yes—you can leave now."

The agent eyed Albright for a moment, then reached for his coat. "Just doing my job, counselor." He picked up the brown envelope. "Thanks for the tea, and the cigar."

Albright rose, staring hard at the agent.

"I can find my own way out. Let me know if you hear from your ex."

"That's not likely."

Terrell eyed the lawyer a moment longer, then turned, heading inside.

Albright watched Terrell walk away. Lifting his iced tea glass, he tilted it. An idea he'd been mulling over just came to fruition. He'd noticed the agent never mentioned Anna's book with all that strange writing. Good. That book could figure in his plans. As soon as the agent left, he'd meet with Bentien and Indian Morgan.

The Crown Vic made a right and headed southwest toward Phoenix. Terrell's jaw tightened; what a wasted trip. He had hoped to gain insight on Anna Wildaer and/or her acquaintances. The agent had very little on the woman and even less on the father of her child. Sighing with disgust, he stared blankly out the windshield.

Maybe this was nothing but a witchhunt. Yet the fact he uncovered *nothing* on the Wildaer girl prior to the early 1970s said otherwise. And that boyfriend of hers, McKntyre. Judging by Albright's reaction, there was more to the guy than just being Wildaer's lover. At any rate, the agent had requested an extensive background on McKntyre and the Wildaers using the new computers The Bureau had just installed. Soon he'd have everything known about them, even down to shoe sizes.

As Terrell drove, he reflected on his visit with Albright. The lawyer couldn't be trusted. What had someone like Anna Wildaer seen in the attorney? Was it money? Terrell sighed, disappointed. He had begun feeling a grudging respect for Dr. Wildaer.

The agent wondered if it had been a mistake to show those classified photos to the lawyer. Yet, except for the pendant, the photos were seen by the general public six months earlier, having been leaked to the tabloids. Of course, NASA and the FBI denied any knowledge of them. The government had simply brushed off the tabloids. Doing more would give credence to the photos; then the real press would come sniffing. Apparently, it worked; the tabloids were no longer interested. Seen as only another "Elvis sighting," the fickle public moved on.

Terrell reflected on McKntyre and his illegitimate daughter, Amy. It reminded him of his own failings as a father. He couldn't throw rocks at McKntyre; Terrell lived in his own glass house. He felt locked out of the life of his own young daughter. At least McKntyre had made a move in life that he, Terrell, had struggled with in his own arena. He shook his head in disgust and regret.

The agent stared out the windshield, his thoughts returning to Anna Wildaer. Where did Wildaer's pendant come from? What was the meaning of that inverted triangle? Terrell slapped the steering wheel in frustration. One thing was certain: the pendant and spacecraft had a common origin, and he'd bet a case of Jose Curevo that Anna Wildaer knew where. It was definitely time to look up Dr. Wildaer—or whoever she was.

Pacing back and forth by the pool, Albright shot an impatient glance at Bentien and The Indian. The two stood in tentative silence. The attorney paused in front of Bentien. "Do you remember where the Wildaers live?"

Bentien nodded.

"I want you and Lance to drive out there. Stay at the same hotel as last time. Make sure you get a room that has a good view of that cut-off to their home."

Bentien began to protest but the lawyer held up a hand. "You and Lance will share a room. I want a twenty-four-seven on that place. Anyone comes or goes I want to know about it. I'll join you in a couple of days." Albright glanced around. "Speaking of Lance, has anyone seen him? He was supposed to—"

"He's in the kitchen," Morgan interrupted. "I couldn't pry him away from Tiffany."

Albright sighed. "Those two deserve each other. God help us if they ever breed. Maybe I'll just give him to her on the condition they both get lost." He turned to Bentien. "Would you go tell that moron to get his ass out here?"

Chuckling, Bentien headed for the kitchen.

Morgan fished out a pocket-knife and began cleaning his nails. "What about me, boss?"

Albright turned to the giant man. "You're with me."

The lawyer's jaw tightened. Anna dumping him for scum like McKntyre…his loathing for the two swelled, devouring him like cancer. Biting a lip, he forced the hatred down.

Bentien returned with the younger man. Albright explained the plan to all three. Within minutes they began preparations.

Albright nodded, watching the three men recede. Anna would listen to him this time; she would have no choice. He recalled all those notes and writings Anna had guarded so secretly. There was no doubt she'd found something. But if he could get to it first, maybe he could even get his respect back.

Without warning, Albright turned and viciously kicked at a deck table. It slammed into another, both crashing. Grabbing a chair, he flung it into the pool. With a blood-curdling scream, he trashed the entire patio.

13

Johnny Bentien tossed a bag on a hotel bed. "We need to set-up, ASAP. You finish unloading; I'll call Mr. Albright and let him know we're here."

Glancing at Bentien, Lance threw a suitcase on the other bed. "Man, I'm getting hungry. When can we eat?"

Bentien walked to the window, briefcase in hand, and peeked out the curtains. "Eating and screwing, that's all you think of."

"What else is there?"

Shaking his head, Bentien placed the black case on the floor, and popped it open, removing a small telescope. "You know, Lance," Bentien said, assembling the telescope, "being stupid and predictable is not all it's cracked-up to be. One of these days life is going to punch you right square in the face, and I hope I'm there to see it."

"Bite me, Johnny," Lance said, sneering. "Jealousy will kill you."

"Whatever," Bentien mumbled, adjusting the telescope's legs. "Just unload the damn car, then go get us something to eat."

Thirty minutes later Bentien was sitting by the window, the telescope trained down the dead-end road that ran in front of the Wildaer home. The house was a half-mile down on the left. Any traffic to the Wildaers' must pass in front of the hotel room window. Bentien was careful to adjust the drapes to conceal the scope. Rubbing a hand over his bald head, he sighed. He'd just gotten off the phone with his boss. Albright remained tight-lipped about their objective. Stake-outs weren't new to Bentien, but this one was different.

Jeffery Albright usually had clear, concise plans with definitive goals. Now the attorney was being uncharacteristically elusive about his final intentions. That visit by the FBI must've really rattled him. Albright said it was of no concern, yet afterwards, he was in a sudden frenzy to learn what Anna was doing.

What was she involved in? Anna was the last person Bentien expected to be under investigation.

Well, if Albright would take his advice—and he seldom did—they'd all steer clear of Anna. With that protective order issued, they were treading on thin ice. Even being seen in this town could land them in jail. Glancing through the telescope, Bentien paused, recalling a recent conversation with his brother-in-law up in Portland. He owned several nightclubs and had extended a job offer. That job offer looked more attractive all the time.

Bentien glanced at his watch and swore. Where was that damn Lance? He wished Indian Morgan had come along instead of that punk kid. Indian was a real professional. Bentien could count on him. But Lance? The guy was unreliable. If Lance Perryman's father wasn't a U.S. Senator, he knew the kid wouldn't have a job.

Albright's firm had insulated the kid's father from, well, a lot of stuff. Kickbacks, payoffs, extramarital affairs, even a pregnancy. Bentien winced when he thought of whom the public had elected to office.

Bentien turned at the sound of the door opening. "Where the hell have you been?"

"Just checkin' out the sights," Lance replied, tossing the older man a small paper bag. "Man, what a dead town, but those Mormon girls are fine! I'm telling you—"

"And I'm telling you," Bentien interrupted, pulling a hamburger from the sack, "don't mess with the locals. Keep your frigging pants zipped. We're not supposed to be here, pinhead."

"You're too paranoid, Johnny." Lance picked up the TV remote. "You need to chill-out."

"No," Bentien replied, "what you need to do is get your puppy-ass over here and keep an eye on things while I eat."

Grumbling, Lance replaced the remote and took a seat by the window.

Bentien plopped on the bed. "I may be too paranoid," he said, kicking off shoes, "but I'm not in jail." And, he added to himself, still alive.

Lance woke Bentien in the early afternoon. "There she goes. Bentien, get up. The bosses' ex just pulled out and headed east." Lance paused as he followed her with binoculars. "Damn, she's fine—I could watch that all day long! No wonder Mr. Albright wants her back. What I wouldn't give to—"

Bentien yawned. "Shut the fuck up."

Lance ignored the remark. "Should we drive by the Wildaers,' check it out?"

Bentien glanced at his watch. "Not yet. We'll give it few hours. Was anyone with her?"

"No, she was alone."

"What was she driving?"

"An old Chevy pick-up."

Bentien raised a brow, scratching. "Are you sure it was her?"

Lance nodded, holding up a small photo. "Yeah. But this picture doesn't do her justice—she's even hotter in the flesh." He shook his head. "I can't believe a babe like that drives around in a beat-up old truck."

"You've never met Anna?" Bentien asked, tugging on a shoe.

"No, but I'd like to. I was hired a month after she left."

Bentien nodded. Anna was *different*. She'd roam the desert and mountains at night as if she were checking on something. Albright wanted her followed but Bentien always found an excuse not to. That voice of caution spoke to him and he was relieved when Albright hired someone else as a tail. At times her gaze caused a chill, as if she knew your thoughts. Then there were times she seemed as an angel, pure and innocent. Bentien suspected it was only a façade. There was something deep and *deadly* about Anna he wanted no part of. Lance and he had better be very, very careful. It wasn't just the authorities that worried him.

Three hours later they drove a blue Ford Taurus by the Wildaers' home. They continued to the end of the road, and circled back. Lance eased off the gas and the car slowed. Leaning over the steering wheel, Lance scrutinized the house. "Doesn't look like a soul's home."

Bentien nodded, pointing to the driveway. "Pull in there. I want you to go up and knock on the door."

"Why me?"

"They know me. They've never seen you."

"What do I say?"

"Just tell them exactly who you are, where we're staying and that we're watching their every move."

"Don't be a smart ass, Johnny."

"Well, use your damn head—just don't overload yourself."

The Taurus came to a stop in the gravel drive. Both men glanced around, half expecting someone to emerge from the porch.

Reluctantly, Lance climbed from the car and strode up to the front porch. He stopped and cast a nervous glance around. Except for the low hum of their car engine, all was silent. His tongue touched dry lips. This place gave him the creeps. Lance fought down the urge to run. He knew Bentien was watching. If he didn't at least knock, he'd be facing the older man's wrath.

He rapped on the screen-door. All was quiet. He tried the door—locked. He looked back to the car and shrugged. Bentien signaled for him to return.

He practically sprinted to the car. "Nobody home," he said, winded. "I move we get out of here and tell the boss about it."

Bentien nodded. "Wonder where everyone's at?"

"Maybe they're on vacation or something. I really don't care. All I know is there's nobody home. Let's leave."

The older man glanced around. What if it was a set-up and *they* were being watched? An eerie feeling crept over him.

"Johnny," Lance pleaded, "let's leave. Anna's been gone too long. She may have seen us and gone to the cops."

"For once, you may be right." Bentien paused, furrowing his brow. "She could be staying with that boyfriend of hers. When the cat's away the mouse will play."

"Didn't the boss say he lived in Texas?"

"Yeah. But he's supposed to be a trucker or something. She could've gone to meet him." He glanced at the house again. It seemed as if *it* were watching them. "I don't like this either. Let's get the hell outta here."

Lance threw the car in reverse. They shot backwards then sped up the road. After a moment, Lance glanced over to Bentien. "What do you think the boss is *really* after? I can't believe he'd risk doing hard time just to get back at his ex."

"*We'd* do the hard time," Bentien said. "Mr. Albright would have a trump card, guarantee you."

"I mean," Lance began, "like Anna could care less about him, hates his guts I hear. Especially after her getting hosed in the divorce."

Bentien shot Lance a surprised look. "How did you know about *that*?"

"Duh? Living at Albright's, I hear and see a lot. I pretend like I don't—but I do."

"You mean, you being stupid is just an act?"

"Fuck you, Bentien. What I'm saying is, there's something weird going on." He paused. "You should've been in the room when that FBI guy showed up."

Bentien raised a brow.

"Tiffany and me watched them through the kitchen window," Lance said, nodding. "I told Tiffany I bet it has to do with his ex. Then that FBI agent asked me when I'd last seen Anna Wildaer."

"He asked about Anna?"

"Yeah. I told the dude I'd only worked there a few months and didn't personally know her."

Bentien sighed nervously. The more he sized things up, the farther away he wanted to be.

Within minutes, the two men were back in the hotel room. Lance punched the TV remote. Bentien, telephone in hand, sat by the window, looking down the way they had just come. Replacing the receiver, he glanced at his partner.

"So, when can we leave?"

"We don't. We stay put. Mr. Albright will be here in the morning." He turned back to the window. "Looks like it's going to be a long week."

Asphalt baked in the hot afternoon sun as Anna's pickup made a left onto the road in front of the hotel. Hotel curtains ruffled and the phone in the room hummed. Albright told the two men to relax and reaffirmed he'd see them in the morning.

An hour went by, then another. Lance stared out the window, watching the cross- traffic. Bentien napped nearby. Lance swore under his breath, his knees bumping together. He needed to take a leak, but it would be another hour before Bentien's turn at the window. He needed relief now. Lance thought of waking the older man but decided against it. He glanced down the road once more. Nothing. To hell with it. Nobody had come or gone on that road in over an hour. What were one or two minutes? Rising, he quietly tiptoed to the bathroom.

A couple of minutes passed and the toilet flushed. Lance opened the bathroom door.

Bentien stirred. "Lance."

Lance paused. "Yeah?"

"Why isn't your ass at the window?'

"I had to piss, okay?"

"You shoulda woke me."

"I didn't want to hear you bitchin.' Guess I get to, anyways."

Ring.

Both men stare at the receiver. Bentien reached for it. "Hello?"

Lance hurried past, resuming his position at the window. Glancing once outside, he thought he saw dust coming from the Wildaers' driveway. Ignoring it, he turned his attention to Bentien. The older man said little, only nodding into the receiver.

"Yes, sir," Bentien said into the receiver. "It's been quiet. Nothin' going on."

Bentien nodded again. Lance focused on the older man, trying to read his body language.

"We'll be waiting and watching, Mister Albright." Bentien replaced the receiver and pointed at Lance. "Focus on the goddamn road! A freight train could've gone by and you would've missed it."

"Chill, Johnny. Geesus…" Lance lifted binoculars. Nothing. The dust was gone. He lowered them. "So, what did the boss say?"

"He'll be here this evening."

"Good. Hopefully we can get this shit wrapped up soon."

Bentien glanced at him. "I wouldn't count it."

Setting the binoculars on a nearby table, Lance peered through the telescope. Only heat waves percolated up from pavement. He sighed and flopped back in the chair, popping his knuckles. God, he thought, Anna doesn't have much of a life. What that chick needed was someone like himself. He smiled. That could be arranged.

Dan stood outside the open canvas door, stretching. He was bone tired but the excitement of seeing Anna drove it away. Huge cottonwoods shimmered in the afternoon sun.

Anna walked toward him.

Alisa approached him, two suns hanging in the background. "McKntyre." She glanced at her watch. "You're fifteen minutes late."

Dan blinked, stumbled and caught himself.

"Danny, you okay?"

"Yeah. Just tired."

She gingerly touched his chin. "What happened to your nose?"

"Nothing serious. I'll tell you later."

He swept her into his arms. She clung to him. Dan buried his face in her hair, feeling guilty. He hadn't yet told her he wanted to return to the army.

The couple held each other for several seconds. Finally, Anna stepped away. "That was a hard drive. I bet you're exhausted."

"I'm used to it."

"Well get 'un-used' to it. You're not a trucker anymore; you never were." She stroked his face. "You're mine now, mister. Whether you like it or not, I'm taking care of you."

The two turned and, hand in hand, strolled to the house. A sense of déjà vu hit Dan. "Anna," he said, hesitating.

"What is it?"

"Those crazy dreams I told you about? They're getting stronger—more life-like." Dan worked a booted toe in the ground. "Fact is, they're scaring the hell out of me. I mean, just now—"

"Things will be fine." Her eyes searched his. "It's nothing to worry about."

"What's happening to me?" Dan ran his fingers through his hair. "I've got these crazy thoughts. That we met before, before you came to Vegas. But that can't be. Am I going crazy or what? At times I feel as if I'm in a waking dream, watching life through someone else's eyes."

Anna turned, leading him up the porch steps. "You're not going crazy. It's called *ishara*—living memory."

"A what?"

Anna stopped and Dan ran into her, almost knocking her over. She threw her arms around his neck, catching herself. "Listen, I'll tell you everything you want to know—but later." She let go, looking to him. "I have good news."

"Good news? Oh no." He winced. "I hate 'good news.' Good news for me is never 'good.' 'Good news' usually means more worry, heartache and sorrow. Give me bad news any day. Bad news and I are old friends."

"McKntyre, sometimes you can be such a bastard. Are you through feeling sorry for yourself?"

"For now."

"As I was saying, there's good news." Anna paused. "We discussed our change in plans on the phone this morning. You still good with getting married day-after-tomorrow?"

"The more I think about it, the sooner the better."

"Good. A friend of mine here in town said that, as a wedding gift, he would fly us straight to Vegas in his own plane, then in a few days, fly us back."

"Anna," Dan said, looking sheepish, "I, I'm sorry. That is good news."

"There's more."

"I knew it."

Anna slapped him playfully. "I had my monthly checkup yesterday. There are two heartbeats—we're having twins."

Dan enjoyed the warm water on his face, rubbing shampoo into his hair. So, Anna was having twins. And he would be a father again—times two. He felt giddy knowing he was on the verge of a whole new life. But twins? Oh well, he'd asked for it.

He held his head under the shower nozzle. What

really nagged him was how he had momentarily blinked out this afternoon. God, his mind was a mess. Anna had called it something, but he couldn't remember the word.

The radio played faintly in the background. Grinning, he recognized the song: I Can't Tell You Why. Anna stepped into the shower and embraced him. Water streamed down her face, her eyes closing as she moved against him slowly, sensuously, in rhythm with the music. The song ended. Her eyes remained closed, rivulets of water leaving wet trails over her upturned face, full lips open and inviting.

Dan gently moved his fingertips over them; a soft sigh escaped her. She melted into him and the two clung to each other as warm water covered them like a blanket.

Morning light peeked through closed curtains. Anna scrambled back into bed. Dan rolled onto his back and she crawled under the covers, snuggling. The room was bright, feminine, and radiated life—just like Anna. Years from now, he would think fondly back on these days. He'd lived enough of the rough side to relish the good. *Now* were the 'good old days.'

"Are you rested?" Anna asked, pulling Dan from his thoughts.

Dan yawned. "Yeah, but I bet you aren't. I couldn't help but hear you throwing up in the bathroom."

"Don't remind me; I'm still queasy. I won't be

wearing my old clothes much longer, thanks to you."

"So now we play the blame game?"

Both laughed. The phone rang, startling them. Giving Dan a worried glance, Anna reached across him to the nightstand. Her hand hesitated over the receiver.

"Maybe I should answer it," Dan said.

"What if it's my parents?" Sighing, she lifted the receiver. "Hello?"

Silence.

"Hello?" Anna repeated.

Click.

Anna slowly replaced the phone. "It was Jeffery. He just won't leave me alone." She crawled back into Dan's arms. "And I'm glad you're with me, Danny. As long as you're here, he won't come around. He won't face someone who'll fight back."

"Next time the phone rings," Dan said, "I answer it."

"Yes, sir." Rolling on top of him, Anna stared at the almost healed cut on the bridge of his nose. "So, what happened?"

"Hailstone hit me."

Her eyes widened. "What kind of hail are we talking about?"

"The kind that goes with tornadoes."

"What!"

"And hurricanes."

"Cut it out!"

"But in the winter," Dan continued, "you don't worry about hail. Only ice-storms that can knock the power out for days."

"You enjoy torturing me, don't you?"

"But the good thing about the ice is, it drives the fire ants underground and kills *misquotes gargantuas*."

"Misquotes gargantuas?" Anna laughed. "McKntyre, you're crazy!"

Dan spread his hands. "Darlin' those mothers are so big that their shadow weighs ten pounds. You don't swat them with a hand—you use a shovel. It's like hitting a ripe tomato."

Anna jumped off Dan, but he grabbed her, pulling her back down.

Two hours later Dan stood in front of his Jeep, holding up the hood. He let go. *Clang*. Wiping hands with a shop towel, he stepped back, wincing at the growing puddle of green underneath. He swore softly; they weren't going anywhere until the Jeep was repaired.

Anna handed him a plastic coffee-mug. "Radiator hose?"

"Water-pump."

"I know a good garage," Anna began. "They'll come get it. Or, you can wait until Dad gets home and—"

"I'll fix it myself."

"Oh? And I guess you'll want to do it before we leave for Vegas?"

"I know you wanted to introduce me to your friends today, but—"

"We can use my pick-up."

"No. I wouldn't be good company. I'll be fixated on

the damn Jeep until I get it repaired."

"So help me, McKntyre, if you're trying to weasel out of meeting my friends—"

"This shouldn't take more than a couple of hours, maybe less. That is, if I can find the right tools."

"Dad practically has a tool factory in the tractor barn. And don't waste time. We have a lot to do before the 'big day.' There are some special people who want to meet you."

"I can hardly wait."

Within minutes Dan had the Jeep parked in a corner of the garage. The tractor-barn was more like an airplane hanger. He spotted a large red *Snap-On* tool chest against a far wall and quickly wheeled it over. As he worked, he thought about how happy—and lucky—he was to have someone like Anna. He was anxious to get the wedding over with and have Anna as his bride. He loved her as much as any man could love a woman, but there was more. Turning a wrench, he paused; there was a kind of supernatural connection. Hopefully, Anna would fill in the blank spots etched across his memory. She had better, for sanity's sake.

Twenty minutes later Dan held up the old water-pump, and he hadn't even skinned a knuckle. Anna would be happy. He'd have the new one on in no time.

A blood-curdling scream pierced the air. He bolted outside.

"Danny!" Anna screamed. Glass shattered. "Get away from me!" came her muffled shout. A man swore in pain.

Dan sprinted across the backyard. Please, dear God, he prayed, please let the back door be unlocked. Bounding up the steps, he grabbed the door handle. It turned. Dan flew into the kitchen.

A man's voice came from the nearby dining room. "You goddamn whore! You were nothing—NOTHING— until I took you in. I made you what you were. And this is how you repay me? By getting knocked-up—by white trash, no less!" A pause. "I'm not leaving until I get that pendant and old book."

Dan rushed through the doorway. "What the hell?"

Jeffery Albright held Anna by the hair, poised to strike her. Bloody scratches lined his face.

"So, you're here," Albright sneered. He shoved Anna away. She fell, shaking.

In a flash Dan was at Albright. Albright swung. Dan effortlessly caught the fist, jerked it behind the lawyer's back, and punched him viciously in the face. The attorney went limp. Dan grabbed him by the throat and shoved him into the kitchen. The attorney sprawled across the floor, choking.

Dan rushed to Anna. "Easy, girl—it's okay. He won't hurt you again."

"I'm…I'm fine," she croaked, her hands trembling. "He just walked in like he lived here. Oh, God, Danny, I'm sorry to drag you into this!"

Anna's right eye was swelling and blood oozed from a split lip. Infuriated, Dan turned, intent on finishing Albright.

Anna held his arm. "He's not alone. Morgan—his bodyguard—is around somewhere."

Jerking free, Dan ran back to the kitchen, stopping just inside the doorway.

Albright wobbled against a counter top. Dabbing blood from the corner of his mouth, he gazed at Dan with contempt. "How long have you been screwing her?" Swaying, he nodded toward the dining room. "You don't know what kind of woman you're dealing with. Are you sure that's your kid she's carrying?" He took a step toward Dan.

A strange awareness stirred Dan's psyche. It was as if another entity were inside him, struggling to push his own consciousness aside. Dan took a deep breath. "Albright, you're lucky I've mellowed. A few years back and a coroner would already be looking you over." Dan took a step toward the man. "We're getting married tomorrow, and you know what? There's not damn thing you can do about it."

Albright shook with lethal rage. He reached for the small of his back and came up empty. He flashed Dan a seething glare. Edging backward toward the open kitchen door, he turned and bolted.

"I'm not through." Dan's hand lifted.

Albright froze mid-stride.

Dan pointed to the kitchen door. It budged hesitantly then slammed shut, the door-window exploding from the force. Dan slowly curled his fingers and the lawyer, as if being turned with unseen hands, was forced to face him. "You think you can just slink away?" Dan's voice reverberated with an eerie, hollow ring; the world seemed ringed with a faint glow.

Albright stood rigid, eyes wide, gazing at unseen horror. "No," he pleaded, "stop—please!" Albright's expression suddenly went blank. A muted shriek gurgled from his throat.

Dan's eyes blazed as he focused on the attorney. He felt he could crush Albright with a single thought. He was vaguely aware of another's thoughts gently but firmly surrounding his own. It was as if Dan McKntyre's thoughts were replaced by a stronger will. His mind swirled and he felt if he let go, his own thoughts would be lost forever.

Then, as if a switch were turned off, the light left Dan's eyes and they returned to cold gray. Dan swallowed, taking a deep breath; he felt totally drained. What the hell had just happened to him? He was conscious of the invader who had snatched his thoughts but could do little to stop him. *Him*?

Albright stirred. Avoiding Dan's eyes, he cast a fearful glance around, seeking an escape.

Dan felt woozy, his thoughts clouded as he struggled to regained his composure. "You're so brave—hitting a woman."

"Danny, no!" Anna screamed.

Dan hesitated, then stepped to the door, glass crunching under his shoes. Confusion wracked him. The kitchen spun. Something hindered his movements and settled heavily over his shoulders.

He lifted part of the bulkhead, struggling to free a trapped crewmen. The crewman was a woman.

Anna?

Anna!

He was back in the present. He caught his breath, disoriented, he yanked open the door, grabbed the lawyer by the collar and shoved him outside. Albright cartwheeled down the porch steps and landed on his back.

Dan slowly descended the steps, still trying to shake off the vision. He was almost to Albright when someone rushed his side. He spun and kicked. His foot collided with something solid. Blood and teeth showered the grass. The body hit the ground like a sack of dirty laundry. The man lay motionless, his head twisted at an odd angle.

Anna shot past Dan, heading for the tractor barn. She looked back and her eyes widened. "Danny—behind you!"

Strong arms encircled him from behind. "Run, Anna—get away!" He fought to move his arms, but the crushing grip was too strong. His own physical strength seemed sapped—his thoughts scrambled. The foreign thoughts and feelings drained away. He went limp and he was lifted off the ground.

"I got him, boss," came the deep, booming voice. "He ain't going nowhere."

Albright staggered, shaking his head. He limped to Dan. "Where the hell does your type come from?"

Dan's thoughts cleared slowly. He blinked several times and tried to take stock on his situation. The hold on him eased ever so slightly.

Taking out a handkerchief, Albright wiped blood

from the corner of his mouth. "I can't believe someone like you is allowed to roam free. You need to be caged—chained like the animal you are."

"You haven't seen the animal yet."

Albright swung at his face.

Dan jerked his head and the blow glanced off his chin. The big man holding him staggered. Dan's mind worked. If he could get the lawyer to throw another roundhouse like the last, the guy holding him may lose his balance.

Albright glanced at Morgan. "Take him back to the car. I'll find Anna. Then we'll all take a little ride. And don't look in his eyes."

The big man gave Albright a puzzled look.

"Something strange just happened to me." The lawyer pointed to Dan. "And it has to do with his eyes. We'll sort it out later. I know people who would be very interested in the two of them." Albright paused, looking around. "I thought I saw that little bitch out here?"

Morgan nodded toward the tractor barn. "She ran that way."

Albright turned to leave.

Dan fought down panic. "Anna really messed you up, man—or were you just born that way?"

Albright halted.

"She's the one you better worry about—not me."

"I can handle her," Albright snapped, "just like I handled you."

Dan forced a laugh. "Yeah, we all know how you

'handle her.' I heard how you'd beat, then rape her because that was the only way you could have sex with her."

Albright rushed back to him. "Shut up."

"Bitterness over your inadequacies in the bedroom?" Dan continued. "Although I wouldn't say that's your greatest shortcoming—oh, poor choice of words—because you have so many." His words were a left hook. "Anna told me how she laughed at you."

The big man holding Dan chuckled, his grip loosening even more.

"I said, shut up!" The lawyer lunged.

The big man stumbled. Dan pushed, breaking the big man's hold. He stomped with all his weight on the instep of a huge foot. His heel dug in. An agonizing howl filled the air.

Dan spun around. Morgan reached for a sheathed hunting knife. Dan knocked it away and the knife went sailing. The Apache lunged. Dan stepped inside his grasp and landed a fusillade of punches to Morgan's stomach, then viciously kicked him in the groin. Dan stepped away and spun on one foot. His other leg came around, knocking the feet out from under the big man. Morgan hit the ground hard, holding his crotch, groaning.

Dan felt a shocking blow in his back. He staggered, twisting around.

Albright stood gripping Morgan's hunting knife, the blade stuck in Dan's back. Withdrawing the knife, he savagely stabbed at Dan's chest.

Dan tried to sidestep the lunge but was too slow and caught the knife in his right shoulder. Dazed, Dan stared dumbly at the knife handle. Albright yanked on it but Dan grabbed the lawyer's wrist and twisted.

Albright yelped, dropping to his knees.

Dan's jaw tightened; he increased the pressure on his wrist.

Albright screamed.

He backhanded the lawyer, then again, then a third time. Dan's rage suddenly satiated, he shoved Albright backwards.

The attorney tumbled, then slowly wobbled onto a knee. Rubbing his wrist, he studied Dan through puffy narrow slits. "Your trouble is only beginning, McKntyre, I promise you. You'll find out that being with Anna is quicksand." Albright paused, nursing his wrist. "As long as you're with that woman, you'll never have peace. And it won't be just me hounding you."

"Don't push it," Dan shouted, pointing a warning finger at Albright, "or I'll finish the job."

"Get me this certain pendant, and that old book of hers, and I'll see to it the two of you never have to work again. Even get you new identities. You and her can live a life of luxury and peace. All I need is—"

"What you need to do, is shut up."

Dan caught movement on his right. The giant man he had flattened was up and hobbling toward him. The man was almost a head taller than his own six-two, and at least 150 pounds heavier. Morgan's .45 was aimed at Dan's chest.

Dan swallowed, forcing calmness. "You want another part of me, big boy?" Dan stood with his arms innocently outstretched. "Well, come on—let it fly! And this time I'll really spank you, unless you're going to hide behind that gun."

The Indian hesitated, licking his lips. "Nobody knocks me down. I don't need no gun." He shoved the pistol in his waistband. "I'm going to snap you like a dry twig with my bare hands." Morgan took a menacing step.

"You dumb fuck!" Albright screamed. "Just shoot him so we can get the hell out of here!"

Chink-chink. The sound froze everyone.

"Morgan, just keep coming," Anna taunted, standing twenty feet behind Dan. She had Dan's twelve-gauge aimed at the Apache. "Cough and I'll blow a hole in you big enough to drive that John Deere through."

The big man never twitched.

"Danny, get away."

Dan stepped backwards to Anna. She stood just outside the open barn door, the riot-gun trained on Morgan. Her gaze was cold, penetrating.

"I've got it," Dan said, reaching for the gun.

Anna stepped back. "No! I'm taking him out."

"Anna—don't! A moment ago you tried to stop me. Now give me the gun."

Anna took aim at Albright's head.

The lawyer glanced at Dan. "McKntyre—do something!"

"Annie!" Dan reached for the shotgun. "Let me have it."

Anna switched her aim to Morgan. "You," she

pointed with the gunbarrel, "toss the pistol over here, then face down, hands behind your neck. I'm sure you know the position."

The big man obeyed.

Anna glanced at Dan and did a double-take. "Oh-my-God, Danny—your back!" She stared at the large bloody spot on his torn shirt. "He shot you!"

Dan turned his right shoulder to Anna. "It was this." Anna's eyes widened. Choking back tears, she reached for the knife handle but Dan stopped her.

"Don't touch it. It's too deep—and it's evidence."

Dan caught sight of the body at the corner of the house. He'd forgotten him in the melee. He turned to Albright. "Get up and see to him."

Rising, Albright staggered over to the man.

"Well?" Dan called out.

The lawyer kneeled. "He's dead. You killed him."

Anna stifled a cry. Dan stared in apathy as sirens blared in the distance.

Albright rose, facing Dan. "His parents are wealthy and very influential. They won't go away." He pointed to the body. "You murdered the son of U.S. Senator George Perryman. I'd hate to be in your shoes, buddy. You can add another to the growing list of people coming after you." Albright gave a bloody grin. "Should've accepted my offer." Dan gave the lawyer an icy stare.

Ann fired the shotgun over the attorney's head. The heavy boom echoed off nearby buildings. "I've heard enough of your whiny voice, Jeffery."

"She's going to kill us all!" Morgan screamed, covering his head.

Anna racked the shotgun and a spent shell sailed ominously. Aiming at Albright's head, she glared at her ex-husband.

Albright glanced at Dan nervously. "McKntyre, she's gone berserk!"

Tears streaked Anna's cheeks. "He's ruining everything."

"Anna, no. He's not worth the ammo." Dan gently lifted the shotgun from Anna's trembling hands. "The cavalry is coming. Go meet them."

Ignoring him, Anna stepped toward the lawyer, screaming. "I will live to see you suffer!" Anna turned, then whipped back around. "It was self-defense and you know it. When—if—you make it out of prison, you'll be lucky having a job flagging traffic."

"Anna," Dan shouted, "go meet the police!"

Anna stood rigid, glaring at Albright.

"Anna," Dan repeated, "would you please run out and meet the cops? Tell them who the good guys are."

Anna seethed.

"Annie!" Dan yelled. "They're pulling in the driveway. I can just picture them with guns drawn and here I am holding a shotgun!"

Anna turned, dashing toward the driveway.

Holding binoculars to his eyes, Bentien peered out the hotel window. It had been quiet since Albright and Lance left, twenty minutes earlier. Lowering the binoculars, he cocked his head. Dread gripped him—sirens. The wailing grew closer and Bentien felt nauseous. He pictured his mugshot.

Suddenly he heard a gunshot. That little voice inside him whispered again. He glanced out the window just as three city police cars, lights flashing and sirens screaming, shot by, making a left. A few moments later a sheriff's deputy followed. From the other direction came another deputy, followed by a state-trooper. Turning, they fishtailed down the road, red lights blinking. Then came an ambulance, then another. Two minutes later a white Crown Victoria made its way down the road.

Bentien had seen enough. He knew whom the Crown Vic belonged to.

Johnny Bentien was two hundred miles from Stanton when he stopped and called his brother-in-law in Portland, asking if that job offer still stood.

Dan leaned against the fender of a deputy's cruiser, a paramedic tending his shoulder. He glanced to the chaotically organized squad cars. A kaleidoscope of red and blue lights flashed. Anna spoke to a state trooper and two city cops. Dan winced as another medic, wearing latex gloves, pulled the buck-knife from his arm. Blood spurted but the medic quickly slapped a compress over the wound, handing the knife to a nearby deputy. The deputy dropped it in a zip-lock plastic bag.

"Mr. McKntyre?"

"Yes?"

"I'm Detective Sergeant Brandt. I need a few words with you." The detective glanced at Anna, who stood nearby. "We think we know what happened here. It looks obvious, in spite of what Albright claimed. But I need statements from both of you."

"Mark," Anna said, addressing the detective, "can't it wait? Dan needs to get to the hospital."

The detective nodded. "We'll see you there." He

turned to Anna. "You and I need to talk."

Dan started to protest but Anna quieted him. "I'll be okay." She kissed his cheek. "I'll meet you at the hospital."

Another paramedic hastily treated Dan's back, then helped him into the rear of an ambulance. Dan stared out the window as the vehicle left the driveway.

Three hours later, Dan slid off the examination table. The bed paper crinkled loudly. A doctor stood by a sink, peeling off latex gloves. The distinguished looking black man of perhaps fifty glanced at Dan. "You're a lucky guy," he said. "That back wound isn't as serious as it could've been. But that shoulder injury is a different story."

He wrote prescriptions as a nurse bandaged Dan's shoulder. The doctor handed him two slips. "Smart thing, leaving the knife in." He glanced at the tattoo just below the reddened, swollen wound. "Interesting artwork. Military signet?"

"Yeah." Dan examined his shoulder. Just above the small inverted triangle were nine tiny, black sutures.

"He almost got it," the doctor said, "and that would've been a shame." He paused, examining his handy work. "That wound is serious. I thought for a while you would need surgery." The doctor looked over his glasses at Dan. "Keep it immobile for several days. I'll see you in my office in a week." After speaking to the nurse, he turned, leaving the room.

Dan had no intentions of returning. He'd remove his own stitches. It was no big deal—he'd done it several times.

The nurse helped Dan place his arm in a sling then pointed to some folded clothes. "Your wife brought those for you. Do you need help?"

Dan simply stared, relishing the word 'wife.'

"I guess not. There're two policemen waiting for you. I'll tell them you'll be right out."

Dan dressed and left the emergency room, carrying his torn, bloody clothes in a plastic bag. Anna ran to him, touching his good arm. "You okay?"

"Yeah."

She pointed to two approaching men. "I know you're not in the mood, but they're going to ask you a few questions." She leaned closer, lowering her voice. "Just tell them *exactly* what happened and everything will be fine."

Before Dan could reply, two plainclothes policeman appeared behind Anna and stopped. One of them was the detective Dan had met earlier.

"I hate to ask you this, but we need you to come downtown with us. Self-defense or not, the son of a United States Senator was killed today. The sooner we sort out the details, the quicker you two can get on with your lives."

"Do I need a lawyer?" Dan asked.

"An attorney friend of mine is waiting there," Anna said.

It was late afternoon when Anna's old pickup pulled away from the courthouse. Anna drove as Dan stared sullenly out a window. Anna sighed, breaking the silence.

"Danny, don't let that son-of-a-bitch Jeffery sabotage us. What you did was self-defense."

"But I killed someone."

"If my ex had had his way, we would've been added to the list."

Dan nodded silently. After a few minutes he began grinning.

Anna glanced at him, doing a double take. "What is it?"

Dan chuckled, shaking his head. "We'll present a real sight day-after-tomorrow—poster children for the 'Council on Prevention of Domestic Violence.'"

Anna laughed. "Well, look at some of the people who get married in those Vegas chapels."

"A bad casting call for a cheap horror flick."

"Then we ought to fit right in," Anna replied. "I'm not excited with the idea of getting married in Vegas, but I don't see any other way. I can move to Texas and lie, or get an apartment or something while I establish residency."

"Anna, you know it would be the 'or something.' For once, let's do things the right way." Dan paused. "I was going to keep this a surprise."

She glanced over her sunglasses at him. "I hate surprises as much as you hate 'good news.'"

Dan grinned. "But I think you'll like this—and keep your eyes on the road."

"So what is it? What's the surprise?"

"Do you remember my old friend, Tom?"

"Tom Logan? He's the one we're staying with in

Vegas, isn't he?"

"How do you feel about getting married in Tom's home, with a real ordained minister?"

"Danny, that's wonderful!"

Their conversation, momentarily lively, soon wound down.Quiet and contemplative, Dan's thoughts returned to the man who died. He kept reminding himself what would've happened had he, Dan, not been there. Albright and Morgan were now behind bars, awaiting a bond hearing. The death would not be referred to a grand jury, but Dan was warned he could expect a civil suit.

Anna stepped on the gas and they pulled away from the last traffic light west of town. Dan was thrown back in the seat. "Ouch! Easy, Annie!"

"I'm sorry," she looked at Dan apologetically. "We'll be home in a few minutes, then I can baby you."

"I need a beer."

A few minutes later the old brown pickup pulled away from a convenience store, a twelve-pack on the floor. They neared the farm road by the hotel and Anna's eyes narrowed. "You know he'll post bail. This isn't over."

Dan sighed, looking away. After several contemplative moments, he broke the silence. "The pendant Albright was asking about. Is that the one you gave me? And what about this book he kept referring to?"

"It's nothing."

"Anna," Dan said, "what the hell is going on? A guy doesn't break-in and beat you up over 'nothing.'"

The two drove in silence. Contemplative minutes

passed. Dan gazed out the window, shaking his head. He suspected the episode this morning only scratched the surface. "What a freaking nightmare."

"It'll be over soon, honey."

Dan touched the pendant under his shirt, his jaw tightening. "Why is the FBI watching you?"

"Who said anything about the FBI?"

Dan shifted, wincing. "The FBI called my former job, asking about trucks in Arizona. And this morning, a white car drove up after the others—an unmarked cop car—but nobody got out. Guarantee you it was the Feds."

Anna didn't answer for several moments. "So maybe it was." Anna sighed. "It's nothing I can't deal with."

"But what about me, Annie?"

"Calm down. You're in pain and only making it worse."

"Are they after you for the same reason your ex is?"

Anna hesitated. "Yes and no."

"There you go again!" Dan shouted, waving his good arm. "Anna, I want to know why the government is after you. What's so damn special about that pendant and book?"

"Now is not the time."

"The hell it's not!" Dan grabbed his shoulder. The throbbing only aggravated his frustration. "There's never been a better time." He glanced to the side of the road. "Pull over there, now!"

"Don't order me around."

"I'm not ordering you around."

"Yes, you are."

"No, I'm not."

"You are too."

"Okay. I'm sorry. Would you PLEEEASE pull over?"

Anna whipped the truck to the right, seemingly oblivious to Dan's injuries. They bounced across the shoulder, halting in the gravel just off the blacktop. Slapping the transmission into *Park*, she glared at him. "Why the sudden attitude?"

Her voice almost seemed older. "Being stabbed with a hunting knife will do that. And thanks for the smooth landing."

Anna looked away. "I'm sorry. But it would take the rest of the evening to explain. We're almost home. Can't it wait 'til then?"

There it was again. For a moment, he felt he was a child talking to his mother. "I can live with a brief synopsis."

Anna yanked off sunglasses, swearing silently. Sighing loudly, she killed the engine, tossed her sunglasses on the dash, then twisted around, facing him. "Remember that plateau and mountain you see in your dreams?"
Dan nodded.

"Well, I've been there. I found something up there. It's unbelievable. After you heal, we'll go there."

"That's right, just drag me into it."

"You're already in it."

Dan exhaled. "I'm assuming your 'find' also hooked Albright and the government? Did you find something, like that pendent, up there? Is it an artifact that belongs to—"

"That pendant belongs to *you*, Danny, and so does that book Jeffery asked about." She hesitated. "I…I found the remains of…of a spacecraft on Sentinel Peak. No one knows it's there, at least not yet. Only recently did the government become suspicious that maybe I found something out of the ordinary."

"Duh? Annie, one just doesn't *misplace* a spacecraft. Why don't you just tell NASA what you found, get the government off our back? Surely—"

"It's not NASA's."

Dan raised a brow. "Soviet? And our government's been looking for it, but you stumbled on it instead, right?"

"It crashed last century."

Dan laughed. "Last century? What happened, did it go through a freaking time warp or something? You've watched too much sci-fi."

"It's extraterrestrial."

"Say again?"

"You heard me."

Dan looked at her skeptically. "You're joking, right?"

She shook her head.

"Annie, stop jackin' with me! I'm in no mood for this fantasy crap!"

"Daniel, I'm not joking."

"Last century? Alien?" He scrutinized her. "How do you know?"

"You'll learn soon enough." She eyed him, her gaze

foreboding. "Do you not understand the seriousness of this, and how it's ripping *me* apart? It's the find of humanity, yet I can't come forth with it. There's too much at stake."

"Anna, why hasn't the government found it? They—"

"Can't learn of it," Anna interrupted, her eyes searching his. "There were survivors. Revealing my find would jeopardize their safety."

"Survivors?" Dan choked. "My, God. Survivors— and they're still alive? Where are they? What do they look like?"

Anna swallowed. "They live...let's just say, 'around.' All they want is to be left alone. Lead a normal life. That pendant I gave you belonged to one of them."

Dan's brow furrowed. "Wait a minute. You said that pendant belonged to my great-grandfather?"

"The pendant," Anna began, "along with a journal of what happened was given to me by one of the 'extraterrestrials' before he died."

"You met one?" Dan shouted. "Jesus. But you said this spacecraft came down *last* century, and the pendant belonged to my great-grandfather?" He paused. "Anna, what do these so-called 'extraterrestrials' look like?"

She slid across the bench-seat, pressing against him. "Are you sure you can handle seeing them?"

Dan nodded. "I bet you have a doctored photo."

Anna reached as if for her purse but instead twisted the rearview mirror around. "There are your aliens."

Dan gazed at their reflections. He could only blink.

"You're looking at the survivors."

Dan reeled. His skin crawled, hair rising on the nape of his neck, as he digested what Anna just revealed. As though a fog were lifted, he recalled the dream that eluded him: a snapshot of an alien world. *Their* world.

"There were eighteen survivors," Anna began, "your great-grandfather among them. That pendant, along with a journal, belonged to him." She gazed at Dan for a long, quiet moment. "The journal, pendant, and the wreckage on the mountain could be one of the greatest discoveries in all Earth's history. I haven't yet explored it. It's only fair that the two of us share in *our* history together before—"

"Back up a second," Dan said. "What do you mean *our* history?"

"My grandfather was also a crewmember," Anna said, touching his arm. "He survived, and for a very long time. As I mentioned earlier, he was your great-grandfather's best friend. My grandfather is the one that gave me the necklace and the journal."

"Holy crap." Dan breathed. "How old was…?" He glanced at Anna. "If my great-grandfather is dead, why did I see him in the desert?"

"There are differences between us and…and…" she averted her eyes. "It's called *ishara*—living memory of an ancestor. I'll explain more when we get home. Can we go now?"

"Just like that! After what you just told me?"

"What do you suggest we do, deary?"

Dan glanced around. "I don't believe you! Aliens—

bullshit!"

"How do you explain the kitchen door this morning, and those strange people in your dreams?"

"This-is-not-happening. What a freakin joke." He focused on the floorboard, shaking his head.

Anna slid back behind the steering wheel, her chin tight.

Minutes later they pulled into the driveway. Dan expected to see yellow crime-scene tape, but saw none. The kitchen and dining rooms were clean. Anna, indeed, had friends in high places.

That evening found Dan alone at the dinning table. Anna sat cross-legged on a countertop across the kitchen, cradling a phone. He stared at the beer bottle in front of him. No wonder Anna and he were always on the same page. All those strange dreams made sense, in a convoluted sort of way. Maybe everything happening to him was normal for his *species*. The word caused a chill. Examining his hands, he half-expected them to 'morph into wart-covered, clawed tentacles. He tilted up the beer bottle.

"Danny, come over here and speak to your daughter," Anna shouted. "Reassure her you're okay."

Dan gripped the receiver. "Amy?"

"*Dad, are you okay?*"

"Yeah, sweety, just fine."

"*You don't sound 'fine.'*"

"I'll be alright. Mom is taking care of me."

"*Mom does a good job at that. She says you guys are getting married in a couple of days! How cool! Wish I could be there!*"

After a few minutes Dan handed the phone back to Anna and wandered back over to the table, in no mood to talk. Anna soon joined him.

"The family will be back in a few days," she said. "They apologize for missing the wedding." Sipping Kool-aid, Anna stared at him. "Danny, it's not like you think. Life won't change much. You get used to it."

He gave her a somber look.

Anna touched his hand, hinting a smile. "This morning, the kitchen door. What do you do for an encore?" Dan tilted his bottle, then looked away.

The blast-furnace heat almost sucked the breath from them the next day as they stepped off the small plane at North Las Vegas Airport. Late that afternoon, on an old friend's patio, Dan and Anna exchanged wedding vows.

Noon, three days later, the twin engine Cessna cruised at 10,000 feet, returning to Stanton. Staring out the window from the rear passenger seat, Dan's attention focused on something below.

Anna leaned across him, touching the window. "My 'find' can't be seen from up here." She paused. "Are you up to taking another trip in a week or so?"

"Down there?"

"We can camp out, just the two of us, like old times."

"Isn't it a little dangerous around that plateau?"

"Now look who's wimping out?"

"You know what I mean, Anna. That place could be watched."

"I doubt it, at least not yet. Sentinel Peak is in the middle of the San Carlos reservation." Anna glanced at her husband. "Apaches take care of trespassers."

"And we wouldn't be?"

"Let's just say that I know what buttons to push."

"I won't argue with that." He continued looking out the window. "I'd like to see what you've found. As a matter of fact, I insist on it."

Anna glanced back to her mother. "If you don't hear from us in a couple of days, you've got my map."

"If you think we're coming out there after you," came Joan's voice from inside the house, "you'll have a long wait."

Laughing, Anna turned and headed for the Jeep where Dan waited. Ben had repaired it while the couple was in Las Vegas.

Dan stood by the fender, talking to Amy. "Make sure you pack only your important stuff, so when Mom and I get back, we can all leave for Texas. We'll send for the rest of yours and Mom's things later."

"But it's *all* important, Danny—I mean, Dad." Dan chuckled at the word *Dad*. Both would have to work on that.

He glanced into the Jeep. All their gear was in order. A sense of uneasiness filled him; he felt like he was being watched. He jerked around, but the feeling passed. Anna's paranoia was beginning to rub off.

The blue-and-white Jeep made its way to the main east-west highway. They turned left in front of the hotel, heading west. A minute later a white Ford pickup cruised from around the corner of the hotel and casually headed in the same direction.

Wind whistled through the open windows of the CJ-7, rattling the canvas top. Moving the gearstick into high, Dan glanced at his wife. Anna's hair was in a thick braid that trailed down her back. She looked very tomboyish in her baseball cap and sunglasses. She wore a loose fitting, light-blue T-shirt, khaki shorts and brown lace-up hiking boots.

"You know," Dan began, "a pregnant woman has no business wandering around in the desert, especially in one-hundred-ten-degree heat."

"That's okay. She'll be protected by a crazed wounded man."

Dan smiled, staring out the windshield. Traffic was light. Both remained unusually quiet. "Anna," Dan began, finally breaking the silence. "How did you find that wreckage? Surely you didn't just 'stumble' on it."

She hesitated. "Actually, I did. Sort of."

"You've avoided going into details for weeks. Now is an excellent time. So, from the beginning?" He paused. "Where was that ship from? What was it doing here?"

Anna sighed. "They were on a reconnaissance mission. The vessel was sabotaged and forced down. Believe me, Danny, they weren't here by choice." She paused. "They're humans known as *Satari*. Their home world is called *Serena*. It's located in a binary star-system that lies in the Orion region. Serena is surprisingly Earth-like. Similar length of day, year—"

"Whoa! How do you know all this?"

"Remember our grandparents? And I have the journal."

Disquieting moments passed. Dan was no longer interested in aliens, fearing what he may uncover about his own heritage. Yet years of reading Bradbury, Heinlein, and Norton had left indelible prints. Growing up on *Star Trek* and *Star Wars* only enhanced the fantasy. As a kid, many a summer evening he had lain in the grass, looking up to the stars, wondering. Now he'd give anything to not know.

"So," Dan began, "how far away is—"

"About eighty-eight light-years."

"Whoa. The technology for interstellar travel—"

"With our current technology, impossible. It takes us six months just to get an unmanned craft to Mars." Anna chuckled. "Eighty-eight *light-years* and they were only on a thirty-day mission."

The Jeep worked up a long grade. "And you say the wreckage is intact?" Dan queried. "Why isn't it already discovered?"

"I didn't say it was intact," Anna replied. "I saw what looked like a fuselage sticking out from the forest on Sentinel Peak."

"How do you know what you saw was a spacecraft, much less an alien spacecraft? It could be nothing more than old airplane wreckage."

"You keep forgetting about the journal." Unfastening her seatbelt, Anna rose and squeezed between the bucket seats. "Not only do I know that it was a Satarian starship," she shouted over the wind, "but I also know its name. The starship was called the *Halaena*." She scrambled back up front. "This is the journal I was talking about," she said, holding a plastic folder full of bound papers.

Dan eyed it doubtfully.

"You didn't think I'd bring the original, did you? It's much too fragile. I have it safely packed away."

"How do I know you didn't invent that?"

"Why would I?"

"I'm sorry, baby. What I meant was, that journal could be a fake, unbeknownst to you."

"Don't 'baby' me." Anna fell heavily back in her seat. "Mister, you just insulted me. Do you doubt my professionalism? *I* recall a time when multi-million-dollar research grants were based on whether I could tell an artifact from a fake." She glanced sullenly out her side window. "It's been awhile since I've been addressed as 'Doctor.'"

Dan felt stupid; he'd forgotten Anna was a former college professor. She had accomplished things he only dreamt of. "I'm sorry, Anna. I didn't mean to question your expertise."

"Forget it."

They entered a canyon, the road twisting and climbing. The air turned cooler, breathing cedar and ponderosa. The throaty sound of the Jeep's V-8 resonated off granite canyon walls as they sailed around one curve after another.

"So, did you ever get to poke around the crash site?" Dan asked.

"I never had the chance. It disappeared on me."

"It disappeared? What do you mean, 'it disappeared?'"

"Just that," Anna said, shrugging. "I was standing there, looking out across this small mountain meadow when suddenly there was this giant hull sticking out of the forest." Pulling off her sunglasses, she turned to him. "God, Danny, it was huge! I was about to head for it when it disappeared. It was as if it wasn't there. Then it suddenly reappeared, then vanished again!"

"What did you do?"

Anna replaced her sunglasses. "I got the hell out of there."

"Didn't that journal tell you what it was?"

"I didn't have the journal then."

"Then how did you know where to look?"

"Rumors. Old legends among the local Apaches. They tell of a large 'silver eagle' that swooped in with the sound of thunder, spewing flames and smoke. Legend had it that it came down on Sentinel Peak last century." Anna paused, glancing at him. "I already knew of the downed spacecraft from family history, but I wasn't sure of its location. Then when I heard about this 'silver eagle', well, naturally I checked it out. From the air, I saw this charred area, but no wreckage. On foot, I reached the top of the plateau, where I found this scorched trail. I followed it up the mountain." She shook her head. "Whatever it was came down hard and with tremendous heat. That trail was fused obsidian. Then when I received the journal a few years later, everything fell into place. It's the *Halaena*, all right."

"Have you been back since you got the journal?"

"No." Anna turned to him, touching his arm. "I've

been waiting for you. *You*, Danny, are the final piece of the puzzle."

Dan ignored her last comments; he'd get to those later. "Do you know what caused the wreckage to disappear? Where does it go?"

"It goes nowhere. According to the journal, the ship has some kind of shielding system that makes it invisible."

Dan chewed a lip. "Our satellites—can't they detect a power source, heat or something?"

"Apparently not." Unfastening her seatbelt, Anna scooted to the edge of her seat. She gazed bright-eyed at Dan. "We're going to explore it tomorrow!"

"What if it goes invisible again? How are we—"

"Doesn't matter," Anna interrupted. "Once we get close enough—inside the shielded area—then there it is. At least it should be." Anna sank back into her seat. "And there it's been, since eighteen fifty-three, alone and forgotten." She smiled at her husband. "We're going to walk into history tomorrow. Earth's and *our own*. If we're lucky, we'll get a glimpse of how our ancestors lived."

"It's scary to think that there's equipment on board that's still operational." Dan paused. "There could be a reason it's been untouched all these years. Maybe there's some kind of high-tech booby-trap."

"We have to take a chance."

Anna sighed, then rose and squeezed between the bucket seats. After replacing the journal in a backpack, she climbed back up front and settled in. "There's more," she began nonchalantly.

"Naturally."

"According to the journal, the Satari were in the middle of an intergalactic war with this cruel, reptilian race." Anna paused for a moment. "Earth was behind enemy lines, at least when the *Halaena* met her fate." She gave Dan a hard look. "I don't think that lizard-race has given us a second thought so far. But if they discovered a Satarian starship here all bets are off. Any way you slice it, if our government gets its hands on that wreckage, Earth's days of flying under the radar—and ours—are over. We must beat the government to the ship. *Our* lives, maybe the entire world, depend on it."

"Anna, from what you said, it's been there for over one-hundred-thirty years." Dan glanced in the rearview mirror. "Why the hurry? If the government had any clue of what was there, they'd be crawling over that mountain like fire ants."

"That may occur sooner than we think," Anna said. "Something freakish happened and the government is on to me."

"The whole damn thing is freakish," Dan muttered.

"I believe Jeffery inadvertently tipped them off," Anna continued. "For now, the government is hanging back, waiting for me to stumble."

"Sharks at a feeding frenzy, that's what we're getting caught in." Dan rubbed a hand over the back of his neck. "I'm in a bad episode of the *Twilight Zone*." He looked at Anna. "So, what are we supposed to do?"

"We save *ourselves*, McKntyre."

"What about the rest of the world?"

"How apocalyptic shall I be?"

Dan's jaw tightened.

"Look, I'll fill you in this evening. I promise." Reaching for Dan's hand, Anna placed it on her abdomen. "Feel that?"

Her shorts were unfastened at the top, the zipper part-way down. Dan rubbed her swollen belly.

"That's life, Danny. But it's Satarian life—full-blooded Satarian—as is Amy." Anna's gaze leveled on her husband. "There are difference between us and the people here. I shouldn't have to tell you that. If the government finds that wreckage before we do…"

Cresting the grade at the top of the canyon, they came off the hill, heading for the distant, desert floor. Pine gave way to cedar, which was soon replaced by the thorny brush of the low desert. The road flattened; it grew hot, stifling.

The Jeep approached the rear of a slow-moving eighteen-wheeler. At the bottom of the right door was a large bumper sticker that read: *How is my driving? If this vehicle is operating in an unsafe manner call 1-800-EAT SHIT.*

Dan pointed to the bumper sticker. "A billboard for morons. He's advertising for an inspection. He better hope he doesn't go through Banning, California; they'll knock the monetary snot out of him, then make him scrape off the sticker."

"It's the idiot element," Anna said. "I can't believe the driver thinks that bumper sticker's cute. He's trying to be offensive, but it's so sophomorically stupid he doesn't get it." She glanced at Dan. "If I were trying to piss someone off with a bumper sticker, it would at least be funny. Some guys have no class."

Dan eased the Jeep out from behind the truck. Seeing the road was clear, he nailed it. Suddenly he chuckled.

"What's with you?"

He pointed to the driver.

Anna glanced up to the cab as they raced by. Behind the wheel was a very petite-looking woman.

"Oh, well," Anna said, laughing. After a moment, she asked, "Do you miss driving?"

"Yeah," Dan replied, checking the rearview mirror, "about as much as I miss bathing in a barbed-wire bathtub."

Anna grinned. Her gaze tightened. "Danny, if you ever get behind the wheel of a truck again, I swear I'll leave you. I'll take Amy, the twins, and I'll be gone."

And Dan knew she would. What the hell was she going to say about him wanting to rejoin the Army? It appeared he also had a revelation he'd save for later.

He glanced in the mirror again, watching the big-rig recede. Suddenly a white pickup shot out from behind it and began passing. "That guy better make it quick."

"What?"

Dan hooked a thumb back. "Some half-wit's trying to pass that truck." He pointed to a line of cars whizzing by in the opposite direction. "I don't think he's going to make it."

Anna turned to watch. Brake lights flashed just as the pickup shot in front of the big truck.

"Whew. Talk about stupid," Anna said, sinking back in her seat. "That guy must have a death wish."

They passed several vehicles as they sped across the flat, desert floor. The white pickup mirrored their every move, always hanging back. Dan deliberately slowed, watching the truck in the mirror. The pickup pulled closer, then receded. Dan sped up. The truck followed suit, never getting nearer than an eigth-mile.

Anna turned to Dan. "What are you doing?"

"We have company."

"The white truck that almost caused the head-on?"

"Yeah. Stay cool."

"Oh, God, I bet it's Jeffery!" She leaned forward, gazing into the outside mirror.

Dan glanced at her. "Do you know anyone who drives a new Ford pickup?"

"No." She searched the mirror. "Can you make out who it is?"

"No, it's too far back. Could be a cop. Maybe the Feds."

"You brought the shotgun, didn't you?"

"What are going to do, Annie, lure him closer, then blow him away?"

Her eyes narrowed. "I'm sure it's Jeffery. You should've let me finish him."

"You can't be serious? But to answer your question: yes, I brought both the shotgun and pistol."

"Are they loaded?"

He eyed his wife. Anna suddenly bolted toward the backseat, but Dan was ready and jerked her back. "And just where are you going?"

"Let me go. I'm going to load the shotgun."

"No, you're not. Suppose that *is* a cop?"

"I'll take my chances."

"Look, baby, just sit down. Nothing's going to happen. When we get into those mountains up ahead, I'll lose him."

Anna hesitated, then flopped back into her seat, folding her arms.

Climbing a short, straight grade, they came up on another big-rig. A passing lane appeared and Dan stepped on it, flying by the truck.

Anna was thrown back in her seat. "Hey—careful!"

"Fasten your seatbelt and hold on."

"Danny," Anna warned, "don't even think it."

"Just hold on."

"Don't you dare. Not with me in here!"

The Jeep approached the summit. On the other side were several miles of twisting canyon, making it almost impossible to pass. But the road was also punctuated with turnouts—just what he wanted. He glanced in the mirror. The white pickup copied his moves, closing in behind them. The summit loomed. Near the top was another semi, lumbering over the crest. He knew he'd never make it around the truck before the passing lane disappeared. He slowed as they approached the back of the eighteen-wheeler, seemingly resigned to follow behind while topping the hill.

Dan eased out from behind the big-rig and was met with a rush of oncoming traffic. Pulling back behind the truck, he glanced in the mirror. The pickup was gaining. It appeared the pickup would be behind them for quite a while; inside was a lone, male driver.

Seatbelt fastened, Anna checked the outside mirror. "Well, Einstein, so much for your idea. There's Jeffery, right on our tail."

"Isn't this what you wanted? A good close shot?" Before Anna could reply, he downshifted, whipped the Jeep to the right shoulder and floored it. Fishtailing, they blew around the right side of the big-rig. Air horns bellowed angrily as they shot in front of the behemoth, just missing a guardrail. They were clear with nothing but open road in front of them.

The white pickup followed. The shoulder suddenly vanished. The truck skidded sideways, clipped a guardrail and in a cloud of dust, shot like a missile backward into the desert.

Dan glanced calmly at Anna. "Neat fake, huh?"

"Damn you, McKntyre!" she screamed, her face ashen. Throwing off her seatbelt, she bolted from her seat. "Are you crazy?"

"You just noticed?"

"We could've been killed!"

"Naw," Dan said, gripping the steering wheel, "I'm good at this stuff."

"You're not out here qualifying for NASCAR!"

Anna glared at him, then flopped back in her seat.

Dan checked the mirror; the highway behind was empty. They sped effortlessly through curves in the road. "You've forgotten those hot summer nights in Vegas. How we'd shut 'em up, then shut 'em down."

"I've tried to forget, believe me."

"Aw, Annie girl," Dan said, winking, "you liked it, admit it. Just like old times."

Anna looked away, suppressing a smile. "Just shut up and drive."

The road climbed steadily, the air turning cooler. The highway was a series of hairpin turns. Dan searched the side of the road. He made a quick right into a wide, sandy turnout between two low hills. They parked behind a hill. Dust drifted through the open windows, slowly coating everything. Although completely hidden, they still had a view of the road.

"This ought to do for a while," Dan said, killing the engine.

"How long is 'a while'?" Anna asked.

"Maybe thirty minutes or so, or until that white pickup goes by." He unfastened his seat belt. "If you need to stretch, now's the time."

"I need to pee."

A few minutes later Anna walked out from behind a large boulder. Dan took his turn, then the two climbed back in the Jeep. He fiddled with the radio, knowing reception in the mountains was sorry at best. Pink Floyd's Comfortably Numb blared. Turning it down, Dan leaned an elbow on the windowsill. "Let's say we get to the wreckage before it's discovered."

"We will."

"And then what? Pray tell, how are we going to keep it from being found?"

"We destroy it."

"Forgive me, but did you say we *destroy* it?"

Anna yanked off her sunglasses. "The spacecraft was equipped with a self-destruct device—"

"Jesus Christ."

"Would you let me finish?" Anna said. "Even if we manage to activate the self-destruct, we couldn't use it."

Tapping a finger on the steering wheel, Dan watched traffic whiz by. "Lord, I've just got to ask it." Shaking his head, he faced her. "Why not use the 'self-destruct?'"

"Sentinel Peak would become flat, glassy, and glow in the dark." Before Dan could react, Anna moved closer. "There is another way. According to the journal, there is this 'distress beacon' that can be set to overload. But instead of exploding it would implode, taking everything in a given area with it. Very nice and neat, no trace. Everything would just vanish."

"Wait. Wait. How large is this 'given area?'"

Anna stared past Dan.

"Who did I piss-off in another life?" Dan muttered, starting the Jeep. He looped the seat belt over his shoulder. "Some honeymoon."

Anna glanced down. "I'm sorry."

"And please stop apologizing." Dan eyed her, then

moved the gearstick around. "I didn't see that white pickup go by. Did you?"

"No." She looped the seat belt across her chest. "We couldn't have missed him. There hasn't been that much traffic. But Jeffery won't give up."

"Well," Dan let off the clutch and the Jeep crept forward, "I guess he's stuck back there." They slowly pulled onto the empty highway. "We should've kept going. Damn!"

They entered a high canyon, the cool mountain air refreshing after the oppressive heat of the desert floor. The throaty sound of the jeep's dual exhaust echoed off rock walls as they held to the twisting road. They were at their highest elevation yet—7,000 feet. Dan constantly checked the rearview mirror. It seemed they'd lost the pickup. The highway leveled and a canyon yawned before them. They found themselves on a long, narrow bridge spanning a deep gorge, the Gila River below.

A sudden gust of wind blew through the open windows, almost blowing Anna's hat off. "Isn't this wild?" she laughed, hand mashing her hat down. "I love it! It's like being on a motorcycle. I can hardly wait to ride on yours!"

"What?" Dan shouted over the wind.

"I said, I love you!"

"I love you, too!"

Crossing the bridge, they entered a dark, narrow tunnel. Inside, the road curved to the right in a downgrade. They shot out of the tunnel, a sweeping vista opening before them.

Thousands of feet below gleamed a patchwork of

brown and green; a valley ringed with purple mountains. Both had seen the valley before, but were still shook by its wild beauty nonetheless.

Anna pointed to a plateau with a peak at one end, maybe twenty miles to the southwest. "There it is, baby. Sentinel Peak!"

A chill shook him; he felt he was rushing headlong to an unknown fate. He had walked on that plateau and mountain before, but not in waking life. The valley disappeared from view as they descended the mountain in a series of short switchbacks.

"Do you think Albright siced the government on you?" Dan asked.

"No. At least not intentionally." Anna shot Dan a quick look. "The only thing Jeffery Albright is concerned with is Jeffery Albright. But there is something all of us have in common: mutual distrust for the authorities."

"That's an understatement," Dan added dryly. "Give me Albright, any day."

Their glances met in silence.

17

A white Ford-150 emerged from the tunnel, pulling into a wide gravel turnout. The driver's door opened. One booted foot, then another touched the rock-strewn ground. Agent Simon Terrell focused binoculars on the CJ-7 as it disappeared around a downhill curve. His obsession had almost cost him and he cursed his stupidity. Now they were spooked.

He waited for the Jeep to emerge from a bend, knowing McKntyre was driving. The guy was good. Underestimating McKntyre could prove fatal.

The Jeep popped into view.

Wearing Wranglers, work boots and a blue golf shirt with "Walker Construction" stenciled above the shirt pocket, Terrell climbed back into the truck. Jerking the transmission in gear, he headed downhill.

His thoughts went to the dossiers he received last week. Too busy to give them his full attention, he now mulled over them. Daniel McKntyre's file was the most complete, due to his military service.

McKntyre was born in San Antonio. His father, Artumus McKntyre, was from Dallas. Artumus was a highly decorated chopper pilot who died a war hero in Vietnam. McKntyre's mother, Louise Baliol, was born in Scotland but died when McKntyre was a young child. His grandparents were deceased. Seemed most of McKntyre's family had immigrated from Scotland and Ireland in the past century. Now all were either dead or couldn't be located. For a brief period McKntyre had lived with a stepmother and stepsister in Las Vegas. According to Terrell's sources, that's where McKntyre met Anna Wildaer. Terrell scribbled something on a nearby notepad.

Staring out the windshield, Terrell pondered on the type of man he was following. He was wrong to have taken McKntyre superficially, especially given the company he now kept. The agent negotiated a curve, sipping coffee from a thermos mug. McKntyre definitely was not what he had expected.

Not only was McKntyre educated, he'd also been an army officer. He'd served five years, attaining the rank of captain. What really impressed Terrell was that McKntyre was an Army Ranger, a CO of an elite company of Rangers serving in a Special Forces unit. Those Rangers were tough *hombres* and could be extremely dangerous. Survivors—or loose cannons—they were prideful and if crossed, would not hesitate to *do unto others*. McKntyre was not going away. Terrell swallowed; sooner or later he'd have to face him.

The agent thought back to his jailhouse interrogation of Albright and that big goon. McKntyre had cleaned their

clocks. The lawyer still showed the effects of the encounter.
He claimed McKntyre was insane and should be locked up.
The big Indian called McKntyre a "trained killer." Terrell
had chuckled. Still skeptical, the agent visited the morgue,
glimpsing the body of the Senator's son. A chill moved
through him; a professional job.

According to classified documents, McKntyre had
worked with the CIA in Special Ops in Central America.
Wicked things happen down there in the late '70s, early 80s,
during McKntyre's tour. Terrell's jaw tightened; so much for
the flag waving bullshit.

The pickup wound down the mountain. Terrell
turned to Ben Wildaer's file. The old man was born in
Cedar City, Utah, 1919. He flew B-17s from England during
World War II, then Saber jets in Korea. Shot down twice,
he received numerous commendations. Wildaer reached
the rank of bird colonel then suddenly resigned in 1954. He
moved back to Utah, where he apparently met his wife Joan,
married, and began farming and ranching. Ben Wildaer's
parents, like McKntyre's, were also from Scotland. A
connection? Probably not, Terrell mused. A lot of Americans
had ancestors from The United Kingdom.

Terrell stared at baked desert landscape. Tall, green
saguaros dotted the countryside. Reaching over, he cranked
up the a/c, mulling over the dossiers of Joan Wildaer and her
daughter, Anna.

Those files were weird. Joan Wildaer was from
Germany; most of her earlier records were either lost or
destroyed by the Gestapo. But what the Bureau had on her

was staggering. Running a hand through close-cropped hair, Terrell glanced out the side window. The dates just had to be wrong.

Topping a rise, he spotted the Jeep two miles ahead. Terrell slowed, letting several vehicles get between him and the Jeep. According to sketchy, reconstructed records, Joan was born on or around 1883 as Joanna Leigh Keihl. Place of birth was a small burg in northwestern Germany. Her mother, Sarah McKbryde, was from Scotland. Her father, Wilhelt Keihl, was a medical doctor. Shortly after Joanna's birth, the family dropped from sight. The records picked up again in 1915, when Joanna Keihl gave birth—out of wedlock—to a daughter named Katrin. The girl was born in Iverness, Scotland, no father listed.

Two years later, Joanna and her young daughter returned to Germany. In 1920 she married a German Jew by the name of Josef Rubenholt, occupation unknown. Her daughter, Katrin, took his last name.

That marriage produced two sons and another daughter. Then in 1943, Joanna's husband, a son, and her youngest daughter were arrested, shipped off to Auschwitz and never heard from again. Her oldest son was a lieutenant in the Wehrmacht. By late 1943, Hitler was in such dire need of warm male bodies and competent leaders that the son's Jewish blood was probably overlooked. The son was killed in action in the Ardennes in 1944. Joanna, along with her oldest daughter, Katrin, evaded arrest and fled the country.

According to records, Joanna and Katrin made their way through a ravaged, war-torn Europe to the relative safety of England. Joanna, because of her fluency in German, became employed as a civilian interpreter with the OSS for the remainder of the war. She was assigned to one of the many U.S. airfields scattered throughout the country at the time.

In 1946, Joanna and Katrin immigrated to the United States, settling in San Antonio and dropping from sight. The names of Joanna and Katrin Keihl never appeared again. San Antonio was home to several military bases. Maybe Joanna hoped for a civilian job with the military? Yet Joanna never worked for the U.S. government again. Gripping the steering wheel with one hand, the agent scribbled on the notepad. Terrell recalled seeing old IRS records from 1947, showing a Joanna Kyle employed as a librarian in the San Antonio school district. According to school records, she had a daughter named Katrina, who was a student there. No father or other relative was found. The girl gave her age as seventeen, then enrolled in high school. If it was Katrin, why not give her correct age and enroll in college?

If the birth dates were right, Katrin—Katrina would be around thirty-two at that time. Surely one could recognize a seventeen-year-old girl from a thirty-two-year-old woman? Terrell shook his head. It probably wasn't the same woman, but another family with similar background and names. Yet if the records weren't wrong and the girl *really* was Katrin Keihl...

Staring out the windshield, his jaw tightened. Someone screwed-up. The two in San Antonio spelled their names differently, yet anti-German sentiment had forced many with German surnames to change their spellings. Terrell sighed, convinced the two Joannas were one and the same. He had hoped for pictures of the two during that time period, but as of yet, none were forthcoming.

"Damn!" Terrell shouted, suddenly remembering the large sealed envelope agent Kirby handed him that morning. And there it was, sitting on the front seat with him, wedged against the passenger door, just beyond his fingertips. The agent scanned the side of the road for a place to pull over. He hit a dip in the road and all traffic in front of him disappeared. When he came out of the low spot he faced the rear of a semi. He cautiously eased out from behind the big-truck. All was clear and he stepped on it, shooting by.

His thoughts returned to the dossiers. It was 1948. Joanna and Katrina had moved to southern California. Joanna had taken a job as an elementary school teacher in suburban Los Angeles. Katrina attended UCLA and graduated in 1951 with a BA. Joanna moved to St. George, Utah in 1952. Katrina stayed in LA and attended graduate school, receiving a double Masters in History and Archeology in 1953. That same year she married a thirty-nine-year-old Beverly Hills' Realtor named Douglas Phillips. The couple lived in Beverly Hills until 1962 when Katrina filed for divorce. They had no children. Phillips was now a millionaire several times over. Katrina could've had half of Phillips' assets in the divorce, but settled for far less, a mere three million dollars. She deposited a million in a Swiss bank account under the name of *Anna Wildaer*. Rumor had it the remaining money went to Central America, but that was never substantiated.

Who was this Anna Wildaer? Terrell doubted the Anna Wildaer in the Jeep was actually Ben Wildaer's biological daughter. Maybe she was an out-of-wedlock daughter of Katrina's using Wildaer's name? Yet there were no records of Katrina ever having a child, at least not under Katrina Kyle, or Phillips. Could it be a relative in Europe? Terrell sighed. The Bureau's records were incomplete; glaring gaps magnified his frustration. So much was lost during the war. It appears 1962 was the first recorded use of the name Anna Wildaer.

Terrell nodded; this is where he came into the story. Days after her divorce, Katrina was kidnapped while moving out of Phillips' mansion and never heard from again. Except for unconfirmed sightings years later in Utah, then Nevada. Her disappearance remained a mystery.

Records show a Joan Kyle marrying Benjamin Wildaer in Cedar City, Utah in 1953. It had to be the same woman, Terrell mused. Yet if it were *the* Joanna Keihl from Germany, she would've been *seventy-two* by that time.

Terrell's brow wrinkled. Could that be possible? If there was a mistake on her original birth date, it could throw everything about her life in Germany out of kilter. If she were born much later, what about the rest of the records?

Terrell approached a slow moving, dilapidated pickup truck with several men in back. Stepping on it, he shot around, glancing at the occupants: Apaches. Terrell nodded, giving a friendly wave.

They gave him a go-to-hell look.

He smiled, nodding.

He spotted the Jeep two miles ahead. Who was *really* in that Jeep? Were they actually a threat? Terrell's jaw tightened. Whoever was in that vehicle was different—that was enough.

The Jeep slowed and Terrell backed off. He sighed, thinking back to the Wildaer girl. There was one startling anomaly about Anna Wildaer: The Bureau had absolutely nothing on her before 1971. Anna Wildaer seemed born at the age of seventeen.

Terrell always hit the school records first; they were easiest to trace. The earliest records he could verify on Anna Wildaer only dated back to 1971, her junior year of high school. According to those records, she lived with friends while attending high school in Las Vegas. Those "friends" had also conveniently disappeared. At any rate, he believed Las Vegas is where the Wildaer girl first met Daniel McKntyre. McKntyre's father had been TDY at nearby Nellis Air Force base before he was killed in action in SouthVietnam.

According to records, an Anna Lynn Wildaer enrolled at Ponderosa High School, the same school McKntyre attended, in late August of 1971. She gave her birth date as August 2, 1956, in St. George, Utah. Yet neither St. George nor Washington County had any records of an Anna Wildaer. Ditto for the state.

Terrell also checked with vital statistics of California and Texas. Nothing. It was as if Anna Wildaer didn't exist prior to 1971, except for the Swiss bank account opened in that name in the early 60s. Terrell stared through the windshield. He'd paid a personal visit to Ponderosa High School two months ago. Showing his credentials, Terrell asked to see both McKntyre and Wildaer's transcripts. The year 1971 was missing from both records.

After a few frustrating minutes he tossed the files back on the secretary's desk. "Those were no help," Terrell said. "Don't you have a copy of Wildaer's birth certificate or previous school transcripts?"

The gray-haired, wiry lady behind the desk looked up. "We did, but they were lost in a fire a few years back. Very strange, though. Only that year was destroyed."

"Yeah, just un-frigging-real."

"If you want records on the young lady prior to seventy-one, you'll have to try her previous school."

"They've never heard of her!" Terrell shouted. "That's why I'm here!"

The registrar stared at him over her glasses. "Sorry, that's not our problem."

He was forced to make do with what he had.

Wildaer graduated from high school in 1973, then from Arizona State in '76 with a BS in Archeology. She married Albright and gave birth to a daughter, all in the same year.

Wildaer received a Master's in Archeology in 1978, then a Doctorate in 1980. She held the position of Associate Professor at Arizona State until last year when she filed for divorce from Albright. Wildaer and her daughter then moved in with her parents in Stanton. Dr. Wildaer taught music at the local junior high until this summer, when she resigned. Then last week she suddenly married Daniel McKntyre. That brought things to the present.

The agent scratched his head. Why would a woman with such impressive credentials toss away a career in the ivory towers only to teach junior high, and then marry a man like McKntyre? Talk about a lifestyle change.

Terrell sighed. Who really were Joan and Anna Wildaer? Everything pointed to Joan as being Joanna Keihl, but that was impossible. Keihl would be dead by now, or over 100 years old, if records were correct. Yet Terrell never saw a death-certificate. And Keihl—Kyle's last reported location was in Cedar City, Utah. Joan Wildaer?

Terrell deliberately bumped into Joan Wildaer at the local supermarket last week. She couldn't yet be fifty. Was she a younger sister or another daughter of Joanna? And what happened to Joanna's daughter Katrin Keihl, or Katrina Kyle-Phillips?

The more he dug, the more screwed-up things got. Where did the Wildaer girl get that pendant? What was its connection with that *thing* in the NASA photos? Terrell surmised that the pendant and the vessel in the photos originated from the same place, and it wasn't on Earth.

Hair rose on the back of his neck. He was suddenly hit with a huge urge to turn and flee. His passport was up to date. Destination: South Africa. There, Kathrine and his young daughter awaited him. He would start over, live the normal life that always eluded him. Kathrine had almost begged him to take early retirement but he refused. He still had unfinished business here.

Terrell looked out the window, fighting with his instincts, the will to survive, to start new. It was so tempting. He could still see Kathrine's curves in the dim light as she disrobed…

The pickup hit a dip in the road, startling him from his thoughts. Glancing around, he saw what he was looking for—a wide turn out. Whipping off the road, he stopped, reached over, and snatched the envelope.

Terrell was a mile down the road when, with shaking hands, he ripped the envelope open, dumping its contents on the passenger seat. Several small stacks of photos, both black-and-white and color, spilled out. A rubber band bound each stack. Terrell rifled through them, pulling out a five-by-seven color glossy. Steering with an elbow, he dug through the remaining stacks, coming up with two more photos. He placed all three on a leg, then grabbed the steering wheel as he entered a curve.

The highway straightened and he tentatively picked up a photo, his heart racing. Terrell eyed the faded black-and-white passport photo of a young, light-haired woman. In the background was a swastika. The ID underneath was in German. Terrell flipped it over. On the back was written: *Joanna Leigh Keihl, German passport, 1944.*

Terrell carefully placed it on the seat near his leg, picking up a slightly larger photo. It showed a dark-haired, pretty woman standing with a group of children outside a school. He flipped the picture over; *Class 6B, Stewart Elementary, Pico Rivera, Ca. 1949. Miss. Joanna Kyle, teacher.* The agent placed it next to the passport photo, comparing them. He shook his head; except for the dark hair, the women were identical.

With growing dread, he picked up a third photo. It was a copy of Joanna Wildaer's current driver's license. It was the same woman in the two previous photos, yet the date of birth on the driver's license was 1925. "Whew, no way, man," he whispered out loud. "Late forties, fifty, tops." Yet according to the driver's license, she was sixty-one years old. The agent knew the license was wrong. Joan Wildaer was an attractive woman for *102.*

Goose bumps rose on his arms. My God, what had he stumbled on? Laying the three pictures of Joan Wildaer on the dash, he dug through the stacks of photos. He felt like he was reaching into a raffle bowl and that his next draw would be the winning ticket.

That little voice of warning began screaming. It told him to let things be. But the photos and what they implied were like watching a car wreck, or reliving a bad dream. His hand came up with a recent, familiar photo. It was from a 1983 university yearbook. The caption read, *Anna Wildaer-Albright, Ph.D., Archeology.* Setting it aside, he reached for an old black-and-white photo of a teenage girl standing by the landing gear of a B-17 bomber. Next to her was a young man in World War II flight gear. He appeared to be in his mid-twenties; both were smiling. Terrell's breath left him. Flipping it over, he read the faded ink: *Katrin Keihl, Major Benjamin Wildaer. Effingham Air Field, England. 1944.*

Terrell laid the picture on his leg, glanced to the

road, then back to the small stack of photos. His shaking hand fumbled through the pictures until he found what he was looking for: a senior year book photo. Underneath was printed, *Katrina Kyle, Senior class, 1949, Pico Rivera High School*. Terrell set it next to the World War II photo of Katrin Keihl. His jaw tightened—they were identical. He fished out a picture from his shirt pocket. It was of Katrina Kyle-Phillips, taken in 1962. Terrell laid it next to the others. Except for being slightly older, it was the same girl.

Staring out the windshield, he licked dry lips before lifting up another photo. It was another high school picture, but more recent. *Anna Lynn Wildaer, Senior, Ponderosa High School, 1973*, the caption read.

It was the same girl in the previous photos; she still *appeared* around eighteen to twenty. How could that be?

Katrina must've had a daughter. Maybe an affair with Wildaer during the war? A cold sweat beaded his brow. He'd seen enough.

The pickup began climbing. Terrell glanced out the side window, then back to the stack of photos. The corner of a large, colored eight-by-ten glossy stuck out from the pile, calling to him. The agent gazed back to the road, fighting the temptation. "Shit!" Slamming a hand on the steering wheel, he yanked the glossy out of the stack.

Attached to the bottom was a sticky-note from agent Kirby.

Simon, I shot this on 17-8-86. It's Anna Wildaer coming out of the mall in Stanton. Hope it helps.
Kirby

That was only two weeks ago. She appeared to be in her late twenties, perhaps thirty, yet Katrin—he was convinced that's who she was—had aged well for a *seventy-year-old* woman. Now known as Anna Wildaer, the woman was hauntingly beautiful.

Yet the years showed in her eyes. Even in the photo, they seemed to be gazing at him. Terrell caught his breath. If he let himself, he could fall in love with her. He now understood Albright's obsession.

The agent glanced out the windshield, then back to the photo, his blood afire. He felt he was looking at something veiled, forbidden. Terrell dropped the photo as if it burned. He shook his head, trying to clear his thoughts.

His pager went off and he jumped. Tugging it out, he glanced at the number. It was from DC. Terrell grabbed a nearby map. The nearest phone was in Peridot, fifteen miles past his turnoff. He thought of ignoring the page, but that would be disastrous. Agents would be swarming the area within a day, and that's the last thing he wanted. Glancing at his watch, he shook his head and swore.

Terrell pulled into a convenience store in a shit-for-nothing town. Within minutes he was arguing into the receiver. His supervisor apologized and agreed with him that it didn't make any sense. She said she was forced to remove him from the Wildaer Case; the orders came directly from FBI Director, Harlan Fairchild. Terrell was to return home. Colleagues would visit him in the morning to collect all data on the Wildaers.

Terrell slammed down the receiver, almost ripping

the phone off the wall. He stormed out of the store, all eyes on him. Scattering gravel, he tore off down the highway.

A creeping dread slowly engulfed him. Terrell gave a tentative glance at the jumbled stack of photos, then looked again. A white envelope with Agent Kirby's handwriting had fallen on the floor.

Seeing a wide spot in the road, Terrell pulled over. Grabbing the sealed envelope, he ripped it open and found a hand written note:

Terrell, Senator Perryman is spending a lot of time with the boss.

Watch your back.

- Kirby

Folding up the note, he stuck it back in the envelope, then shoved the envelope in a back pocket. Glancing around, he pulled back onto the road in the direction of Tucson. So, the Senator was involved. He wanted to throw-up. All his hard work and planning was slipping away. He couldn't let that happen. But if he stayed, it could cost him his career. Hell, it could cost him his life.

18

The blue-and-white Jeep sailed down the dirt fire road, a plume of dust billowing from the rear.

"Danny, slow down!"

Easing off the gas, Dan surveyed their surroundings. On all sides were ocotillo and saguaro cacti. Intermingled were short clumps of barrel and cholla cactus, with occasional groves of pungent smelling desert willows. The road twisted and turned; its surface rutted. The breeze through the open windows gave little relief. They began climbing and the heat broke.

Anna sat straight in her seat, looking young and pert. After a quick survey of the road, Dan's gaze returned to her. He frowned; she did look young. Earlier in the month, both had celebrated their birthdays. Anna had just turned thirty-one; two days later he turned thirty-three. Yet she *seemed* older, more so than he ever remembered. He stared back out the windshield, not knowing why he was suddenly uncomfortable. Was there more to their heritage than Anna related? He swore silently, feeling guilty for his suspicions.

The road ascended steeply. The Sonoran desertscape gave way to thick stands of fragrant juniper, cedar, and Arizona oak. The wind picked up; small swirls of sand skipped across the rough, deeply rutted trail.

Dan couldn't shake the thought that Anna was hiding even more than he originally thought. He glanced at her again. An almost impossible concept took seed. His heart pounded. He licked dust-coated lips.

The woman in the other seat called herself Anna Wildaer, but that wasn't her real name. He was sure of it. Yes, she was the same woman he fell in love with in high school, but that was just it; Anna wasn't a teenager even back then. He'd always sensed that, but until now, couldn't grasp it. He'd married a woman older than he cared to think. Who was she? And why the charade? Dan bit a lip, knowing it was tied to their ancestry. Taking a deep breath, he eyed her over sunglasses.

"What's with you?"

"Anna, how old are you, really?"

She stiffened. "We just celebrated our birthdays."

"Annie, you're avoiding the question. I asked—"

"I heard you! What a ridiculous question. I won't even dignify it with an answer."

Dan swallowed; he just learned all he cared to know.

They drove in silence. The Jeep topped a hill and the road widened, becoming smoother. They began climbing a series of cedar-topped hills, each hill higher than the last. A cooling breeze carried the scent of pine.

"Just over the next rise we can stop and take a

break," Anna said. "Maybe have a sandwich."

Dan glanced at Anna. She seemed her normal self. Any animosity she had at Dan's questions seemed to have evaporated.

The Jeep crested the last tree-topped hill. They drove slowly, staring at huge, ancient cedars, their gnarled limbs twisted grotesquely. Time and wind had taken their toll on the gatekeepers to the high country.

At the summit, two giant ponderosas straddled the trail. Their limbs formed a dense, shady canopy, under which Dan pulled up and parked. Both climbed out, stretching.

Anna glanced back down the trail. "I haven't seen anyone behind us since we turned off the highway. Do you think we lost him?"

"No." Dan's gaze followed Anna's. "Whoever was in that pickup is still there. I can feel it."

"Who do you think it was?"

"Don't think it was you're ex. He wouldn't be that stupid. No, I think it's the government. Maybe the FBI. If I was a cop, and had even an inkling of what you and I know, I wouldn't let a little spin-out stop me."

Anna went to the Jeep and came back with binoculars. She scanned the horizon. "No dust, nothing." She lowered the binoculars. "I hope you're wrong."

The two ate a quick meal in the shade of the two, huge ponderosas. "It's already late afternoon," Dan said between bites. "Do you think we'll get to the mountain tonight?"

"No. I thought we'd camp at the base of the plateau

so we won't be rushed going up in the morning."

"You have it all worked out."

They came off the hill and the road leveled. The horizon seemed closer. The road abruptly ended at the edge of an escarpment.

Killing the engine, Dan clambered out of the Jeep. Anna remained inside, watching him. Dan marched to the precipice's edge, the wind tugging at his floppy hat.

A thousand feet below was a hidden desert valley maybe three miles wide, barren except for spotty sagebrush. A wash carved a white gash across the brown valley floor before disappearing into far-off hills. At the other side of the valley the desert swept up to a craggy, rough-hewn wall of faulted rock. The rock wall formed the side of a large plateau. Rising from the far end was a steep, tree-covered mountain: Sentinel Peak.

A breeze brushed Dan's face. It turned the collar of his khaki vest and ruffled the Jeep's canvas top. Dan closed his eyes, the scent of history in his nostrils, melancholy in his soul.

"Daniel."

Startled, he jerked around, seeing only empty desert. He sighed; only the wind. Glancing to the Jeep, he noticed Anna eyeing him. Dan's gaze returned to the valley. Everything seemed forlorn, deserted. Then he spotted a small dust cloud on the valley floor, hardly moving. "What the?" He focused the binoculars. "Jesus. No way."

"What is it, Danny?" Anna said, suddenly next to him. "What do you see?"

"You won't believe this, but there's a guy out there on horseback, and he's leading a pack-mule—the same guy I saw in that dust devil a few days back! And he's heading toward the plateau."

"Where?" Anna said, shading her brow.

"Right where that dust is." Unlooping the binoculars, he handed them to her.

Anna focused them. "Nothing. I don't see a thing but swirling sand."

Yanking the binoculars back, Dan shoved them to his eyes. Dust and tumbleweeds danced in a circle; there was no sign of human or animals. Handing the binoculars back to Anna, he turned away in disgust. "Here we go again."

"Seems that legend about dust-devils has paid you another visit," Anna said. She studied Dan from under her hat-brim. "I believe you, Daniel. Kalyn's ishara is calling you, just like last month. You brought him back."

"Anna, who exactly is *Kalyn*?"

"Kalyn was the Satarian name of your great-grandfather," Anna began. "Danny, Kalyn's *ishara*, his living memory, is in you. He left unfinished business that you must finish."

"His ghost is haunting me? What a crock of shit." "Then I guess you *are* going crazy." Anna's features tightened. "Get over it, because you'll have to call on it again."

"Whatever happened to written instructions," Dan mumbled. Quiet seconds passed. "I never heard how my great-grandfather died."

"No one knows. It's a family mystery, though I suspect by this time tomorrow, we'll have an answer."

"A *family* mystery? Please tell me we're not related."

"What if we were?"

"Oh, Jesus, no—Annie! Don't do this to me. Why, all along you knew we—"

"We're not related. At least not by blood."

"Damn you!" He sighed in relief. "So, how do we get down there?"

She pointed to a group of rocks on the right. "The trail picks up there."

Both climbed back in the Jeep. With a rock wall on either side, they descended in a series of switchbacks. The path was rough and full of washouts.

The Jeep rolled to a stop in the wash on the desert floor. Dan looked at Anna. "There's only about two hours of daylight left." He moved the gear stick around. "Does this gully take us to the other plateau?"

Anna nodded. "It's a straight shot from here, but I'm worried about this part."

Dan glanced to the surrounding mountains. The Jeep would be in the open for miles. "We have no choice; let's get it over with." Shoving the gearstick forward, he popped the clutch and raced across the desert floor.

Anna glanced back to the swirling rooster-tail of dust, shaking her head.

In less than ten minutes they were across the valley. The wash turned into a gravel road that snaked between low hills. Within minutes they were hidden from the rear. The plateau loomed imposingly in front of them.

Anna tapped Dan's arm. "A mile from here another trail bisects this one. We'll head right; that'll take us to our campsite."

"Where does this 'road' lead?"

"It winds around for another twenty miles, then ends at state route Seventy-seven. Sixty miles south is Tucson, go forty miles north and you'll come out in Globe." After a moment Anna pointed ahead to a huge, decaying saguaro. "Slow down. Our exit is just on the other side of that old cactus."

Dan surveyed the barren landscape. "No roads, utilities, or shade." He chuckled. "No nothin.' In Texas, this meets the criteria for a mobile home subdivision. Trailer-park paradise." Dan hooked a thumb to the window. "Wrecking yard there. Next to it would be a scrap metal dealer." He pointed across the road. "And over there you'll have a video-slash-convenience store. They'll mostly stock beer, ice, ammo, dog food, and sell buckets-full of lottery tickets. Yeah," he sighed, "welcome to Redneckopolis— Rolling Oaks West."

Both laughed, Anna shaking her head. She touched his arm as they passed the decaying, pockmarked cactus. "There's our turn-off." She pointed to a faint trail that led toward the plateau, a mile away.

Downshifting, Dan slowed, easing the Jeep to the right. The CJ-7 crawled onto rocky hardpan with two narrow ruts that passed for a trail. The going was slow, arduous. Sand blew in open windows, smothering them. After what seemed an eternity, the trail petered out at a T. Straight ahead was a sheer rock wall that formed the base of the plateau. Halting in a cloud of dust, Dan turned off the engine. They climbed out and stared in awe at the granite wall before them. High and foreboding, it rose like a monolith, towering several hundred feet.

Dan gave a broken whistle through dry lips. "Good, God." He picked his way over sharp rocks and touched the cliff face. To Dan, the stone wall was an act of finality, thrust up by an angry god from the hell below. Piles of rocks littered the base. He looked at Anna skeptically. "And you say there's a way up?"

"It's on the other side." Anna pointed to twin ruts that paralleled the steep cliff. "That trail will take us there. We'll spend the night at the base. But we need to stop and gather firewood."

"A campfire? Anna, I don't think that's wise."

"Where we'll be staying, it won't be seen or smelled. And you know how chilly it gets at night."

Thirty minutes later they were parked at a blow-down. The couple stood at the bottom of a large shale hill. The ground was littered with timber and debris. Up slope were large tree trunks that hadn't yet tumbled down. The shale continued for 1000-feet, where it met a shelf. All along the shelf were trees in various stages of decay, waiting their inevitable fate. A few feet above the shelf was a steep, tree-covered hill, which was the beginning of the mountain itself. Dan spread a plastic tarp over their gear in the back seat. They gathered wood, laying it on the tarp. Pausing, he stared up to the mountain. "It's been years since I've seen anything like that. As I recall, it was on Mount Charleston, just the two of us."

"And I suppose you expect it to end the same way now, do you?"

"Would that be such a bad thing?" It was sunset when Dan, Anna guiding, drove up a hill and into a large grove of cedars. Two mule deer bounded into brush. The Jeep crept slowly between several large boulders. They found themselves in a narrow cleft in the wall of the plateau. There was only a foot of clearance on both sides and darkness ahead. Dan was about to protest when suddenly the walls dropped away. They were in a shallow cave with just enough room to swing the Jeep around.

"Neat place, baby," Dan said, surveying their surroundings.

"It's getting dark and cooling off," Anna said, climbing out. She brushed herself off. "Why don't you build a fire?" Unplugging the mobile phone from the dash, Anna headed toward the entrance with it. "I'll call Mom, tell her we're okay."

Dan nodded, stepping to the back of the Jeep. "Good luck trying to get out on that thing. We're too remote." Within minutes, he had a small fire crackling. Anna returned to the cave.

"Well?" he said, breaking up small sticks and tossing them in the campfire.

"I got through. But the roaming charge will be horrific. I told mother we might be a day longer and not to worry."

"Those cellular phones are the coming thing." He continued breaking up twigs. "Never used one myself. Never had a need. Besides, I understand they're expensive to use." Anna dropped an armload of wood near the campfire. "It's expensive now, but one day in the near future, cellular phones will be everywhere. Rates will drop; everybody will have one."

"Just another toy for those who fancy themselves important."

"Listen to you! Aren't you just high and mighty? Three years from now I'll remind you of what you just said when you start crying about having to use a landline." Dan grinned. "I hope so."

The two chuckled and unloaded more gear. Dan tugged out a small, portable gas grill from under the back seat, then grabbed a small ice chest. Opening the cooler, he reached for a beer, popped the top and took a quick swig. Sighing, he set the can on the Jeep, then dug around in the ice chest. "Come to papa." He tugged out a large, sealed freezer bag full of meat. "How would you like your ribeye, Annie?"

"Cooked."

After they'd finished eating, both washed as best they could. By now, darkness had settled. Grabbing a flashlight, Anna walked to the rear of the Jeep, leaned through the open window and snaked out the shotgun. She stuffed shells into the magazine.

Dan stood by the flickering campfire, noticing she

handled the weapon like a pro.

Racking the gun with one hand, Anna pushed in a final shell. "Here," she said, tossing it to him. "It pays to be prudent."

Dan caught it, wondering what her rich, glitzy friends would think of her now. He gazed in fascination as she leaned in the passenger door, retrieving his 9mm pistol from the center console; Anna handled the pistol as if she were born with it. Moving the action back and forth, she pushed the magazine eject button. An empty ammo clip fell in her hand. Raising an eyebrow, she held it up to him.

"Box of ammo was next to the 'nine."

"The only other thing I found was a letter from one of your little girl friends," she said, eyes narrowing.

"It's got to be in there," Dan said, ignoring the remark. "I put the ammunition on the kitchen bar at home so I wouldn't forget it." Moving past Anna to search the Jeep, he stopped. "That box of ammo is—"

"On your kitchen bar, collecting dust."

"How could I have forgotten?"

Anna sighed, shaking her head. Slapping the pistol and empty ammo clip in his palm, she grabbed the shotgun from him and headed for the campfire.

He stood there, stupidly, watching her walk away.

Dan leaned against a large boulder by the cave entrance, peering into a placid night. Coyotes yapped in the distance. The scent of cedar and pine wafted in the night air. Except for the campfire's crackling, all was eerily still.

Dan didn't for once believe that whoever was following them had given up. For all he knew, someone could be waiting for them on the plateau. Yet Anna assured him the only ones who knew what was up there were her family and the local Apaches. And few of the latter were inclined to investigate. The Apaches had a healthy respect—and fear—of the place.

Dan looked up to locate Orion, but the sky had clouded over. He sighed.

Circumstance now dictated that he deal with his and Anna's alien heritage, as if he had a choice. Circumstances… what was it he had read somewhere about circumstances? *Circumstances don't break a man; they just reveal him to himself.*

Dan shivered. The knife wounds in his back and arm ached from the beating he took in the Jeep. He dug a booted-toe in the gravel.

"Danny, you okay?" Anna called.

He headed inside. "Yeah, just thinking."

A tarp with a large air mattress on it lay to one side of the cave floor. Anna had unrolled a double sleeping bag over the mattress. Her boots off, she sat cross-legged on the sleeping bag with a blanket over her shoulders. Running a brush through thick hair, Anna glanced at Dan and patted the mattress.

Dan plopped down with a groan.

Anna threw her blanket over her husband's

shoulders, snuggling. He winced.

"I'm sorry. Did I hurt you?"

"No."

"How thoughtless of me. I bet you're sore as hell. Let me take a look."

After a few minutes the two sat quietly cuddled under a blanket, staring at the campfire. Because of the elevation and dry air, the temperature could plunge at night, even in the summer. Reaching for a nearby log, Dan tossed it on the fire, then settled back into his wife's arms.

Anna curled closer.

"Annie, exactly how did you come by that journal?"

There was a long pause. "As I said earlier, my grandfather gave it to me. Three years ago, along with the pendant."

Dan's brow furrowed. "Your grandfather would be kind of old wouldn't he—like a hundred and something? And how did he receive it?"

"He received it in the mail," Anna said. "Postmarked, New York City."

"Why wasn't it sent to me? I was Kalyn's great-grandson. And from what I gather, his only surviving next-of-kin. Why did the journal and pendant go to someone else first?"

"Because, darling, you weren't born yet."

"Oh, Lordy."

"It was mailed by Kalyn," Anna said, hesitating, "postmarked *eighteen fifty-seven*. My grandfather received it in Scotland the following year."

Dan looked into the campfire, swallowing hard. Fearful moments elapsed as he worked up the courage to speak. "Your grandfather gave it to you—personally?"

"Yes."

"You trying to tell me that my great-grandfather mailed this journal to your grandfather in eighteen fifty-seven, and that said grandfather gave it to you *three* years ago?"

Anna nodded.

"You know, Anna, I'm still trying to swallow that crap that we're descended from some space aliens! And now I'm hearing about people who live to be a hundred and—"

"Three hundred and two."

Dan's jaw dropped. He knew deep down that Anna had been hiding something, but hearing her say the words out loud were still too much to take in seriously. "I need to stop listening to late-night AM radio."

"Danny," Anna murmured.

Quiet moments passed. The campfire hissed and crackled. Dan finally broke the silence. "Your grandfather... three-hundred and two?'"

"Was. He died year before last. You met him, Danny. You shook his hand."

"When?"

"The night of my high school graduation," Anna said. "It was late and we were sitting on the trunk of that red hotrod of yours."

"I remember this guy came out and—"

"That was Grandpa Davy."

"As I recall, he stood right next to us and lit that damn pipe of his. Believe me, I got the hint. But the guy didn't seem that old. Maybe in his seventies."

"It's quite common for the Satari to live for over two-hundred years. But the *Mataer* Satari…the *Mataer's* life span is almost double. Grandpa was Mataer, as was *Halaena's* entire crew. The Satari are a hardy species of humans, to say the least. The *Mataer* are even more robust, hence their longer life span. They can physically withstand things, like injuries, that earth humans and even other Satari can't. We also heal quicker, if you haven't noticed." Anna paused. "Your knee is an example. If you had been an earth human, your knee would've been blown out and you would've been forced out of the army. And your back and shoulder? You should've needed surgery and a hospital stay. And look at you now. A week later and your wounds are almost healed." Anna spoke slowly, precisely. "We, Daniel, are *Mataer* Satari."

Dan stared silently at the cave wall. He swallowed, nauseous. "Does this mean you and I will live—"

"Over three centuries. According to grandfather, some Mataer have even reached four-hundred years."

Dan said a silent prayer. Thank God Anna was at his side. He couldn't imagine watching a mate shrivel and die while he looked on in the helplessness of eternal youth. Unblinking, Dan stared straight ahead. He forced himself to speak, to calm himself before his sanity was ripped from his guts. "What side of the family was your grandfather on?"

"My mother's." Anna's eyes took on a silver hue.

"My grandfather's name was Sila tTaeln. Commander Sila tTaeln. He was the oldest, and Second Officer on the *Halaena*. His youngest sister was married to a Lieutenant Commander Kalyn mMyre—Jason McKntyre—your great-grandfather."

Dan eyed her. "So, his sister—"

"Her name was Alisa," Anna interrupted. "Alisa was Kalyn's wife on Serena. She was my great aunt and her living memory—her *ishara*—dwells in me. Ishara can only be willed to one individual. Why I was chosen, I have no idea." Anna sighed. "She was pregnant when Kalyn left. But I know she is now nothing but dust. I sense she died long ago."

Dan sighed, confused. "My great-grandmother was from here. An Earth woman?"

"Your great-grandmother was a female crewmember. Her name was La sShane. She was the communications officer."

"Never heard of her."

"Two years after the crash, after no hope of ever returning to Serena, she and Kalyn married, according to the customs of this world. A year later La sShane died shortly after giving birth to a son—your grandfather. Your grandfather married the daughter of another crew-member and so on."

"Sounds like the gene pool was shrinking awfully fast."

Anna nodded. "You, Mother, Amy, and I are the last of the true Satari on Earth. Our blood is not mixed with the people here." Laying a hand on her belly, she spoke solemnly. "Our children will be the last generation. There will be no 'pure' Satari after they're gone. As you said, the gene pool has bottomed out."

"What about your father, Ben?"

Anna hesitated, clearing her throat. "He's…he's my stepfather. He has Satari blood, but his mother was from an old Scottish family."

"What happened to your real father, Anna?"

Anna fidgeted with a blanket corner. "My biological father was arrested by Czar Nicholas' secret police in nineteen fifteen. He was a British spy and held in a Moscow prison until the Bolsheviks took control two years later. The Bolsheviks accused him of being a czarist sympathizer and terrorist." She looked away. "He was dragged out of jail, thrown against a wall and shot."

Dan stared in disbelief, wondering if he could've laid it all on the line as Anna just had. "I…I'm sorry." Leaning over, he kissed her. "I don't care if you're sixty, seventy or two hundred seventy—I'm still in love with you, Annie girl. I'll never leave you. Ever."

Anna stared at the cave floor. "I wouldn't blame you if you did."

"Shh," Dan whispered, squeezing her. He stretched out from the blanket, tossing a small log on the fire. Sparks circled. The fire hissed. Anna held onto him.

"So, the survivors of the crash made their way to Scotland. Why Scotland?"

"Because that's where descendants of a previous

Satarian visit lived."

"Seems that we're starting in the middle and working our way out."

Anna swallowed. "About a thousand years ago, Serena was at war with a neighboring planet they had colonized. It was a holocaust. Over half the population of both worlds—hundreds of millions—were annihilated. Their technology and modern society was all but wiped out, records lost, destroyed. They were set back several hundred years."

"Anna, how did the Satari arrive?"

"Faster than light travel was still experimental. A starship, their first one ever, had been constructed but not yet tested when war broke out. It was commandeered by a small group of scientists and their families. Two years later they landed on Earth, where they found a simple, agrarian society populated by humans like themselves. Seeking only to escape war and anarchy, they assimilated into Earth's primitive culture."

"What happened to their ship?"

"Legend has it they sent it plunging into the sun."

Dan sighed. "So, there are people who know about us?"

"Yes, but they're few in number, and getting fewer. No one speaks of it anymore; it's taboo." Anna paused, gazing at him. "I shouldn't have to tell you why."

"How many other Satarian ships have been here?"

"Just that one, and then the Halaena. The Brazaryans—mortal enemies of humans—may have sniffed around, but that's doubtful. Brazaryans would come to conquer. Let's pray we never meet them. We would be lambs at a slaughter." Pausing, she took Dan's hand. "Eventually someone will come calling. Let's hope it's the *right* ones."

"What was *Halaena's* mission, Anna?"

"They were to retrieve a satellite. For several hundred years the Satarian government had suspected that some of their people had escaped here and possibly influenced the culture."

Dan sighed skeptically. "How did the *Halaena* end up on a mountain in Arizona?"

"When the *Halaena* arrived, the satellite was gone," Anna began. "They dropped into low Earth orbit attempting a trace when the captain sabotaged the ship. *Halaena* crash-landed here. Out of a crew of thirty-seven, only eighteen survived."

"What happened to their captain?"

"He didn't make it."

"Didn't the crew try to contact home for a rescue?"

"Danny, they were on a covert, top secret mission. You, of all people, should know how that works. It was a time of war; this world was behind enemy lines. They couldn't take a chance on sending a signal. Not only was their own safety at risk, but also the inhabitants of this planet. If their enemy, those…those Brazaryan things intercepted a signal…" Anna shook her head. "Danny, the crew was marooned. After a year or so they made their way to Scotland and were taken in by descendants."

Several quiet moments passed, both lost in their own

thoughts.

"I sense my great-grandfather returned here," Dan said.

"I studied Kalyn from his journal. He was a complicated individual who kept pain to himself. Losing two wives in such a short period was probably more than he could bear." Anna paused. "He's in you. What would you do?"

Caught off guard, Dan blinked slowly. "I wouldn't abandon my only way home. But in eighteen fifties Arizona, the Apache ruled. I'm sure they or the elements did him in."

"According to his journal," Anna said, "he planned on building a communications device undetectable by the Brazaryans."

"Did he succeed?"

Anna shrugged. "Who knows? If anyone out there heard it, they haven't replied."

"Maybe they have, Anna. Maybe that's how the government got wind of you. They intercepted some kind of message."

"That reply would've been years ago, before radio. Besides," Anna glanced at him, "I don't think we could detect a Satarian message. Their technology is far more advanced than anything on Earth." Anna paused. "I don't think we yet have the technology of sending or receiving what Kalyn called, *t-mag* transmissions, whatever that is. Serena may have replied, but if Kalyn were already dead, who would answer?"

"Suppose the Satari heard Kalyn's signal and

rescued him?"

"And leave a starship?" Anna replied. She edged closer to her husband, gently pushing him down. Crawling up against him, Anna propped herself on an elbow. "That technology is laying there for the taking. We can't allow that."

"I was afraid of this part."

"Not to worry," she said. "I'm confident that if we can enter the craft, that you, calling on your *ishara*, will know exactly what to do."

"You've got to be shitting me."

Anna eyed Dan, silent.

"*Ishara*," Dan breathed. "Exactly what is this *Ishara*?"

"It's what you used against my ex last month," Anna said. "It's what makes us Satari."

Dan tossed another small log onto the fire. The crackle and hiss compounded the surrealness enveloping them. Too frightened of what Anna implied about ishara, he forced his thoughts elsewhere.

"I just can't stop thinking about what would happen if the wreckage of the *Halaena* were discovered," Dan began. "Weighing that with the technological gains we could make—"

"Don't even go there," Anna interrupted, her jaw tightening. "We both know the scenario if this country got its hands on Satarian technology."

Dan sighed. "Within a generation, or less, the America I love, that I put my life on the line for, would transform itself into an Orwellian nightmare."

Yapping coyotes shattered the calm.

Anna jerked around, staring in panic at the cave entrance. "They smelled the food!"

"It's okay. They're just coyotes."

"Make them go away!" Anna screamed.

Loud barks came from near the Jeep.

Anna clutched at him, terrified. "Make them stop!"

Shocked at Anna's reaction, Dan pried her arms away and tried to rise, but she tore at him. "Don't leave me alone!"

"Anna, chill! It's only coyotes." Tugging on boots, he grabbed the shotgun, a flashlight, and walked outside. The scurry of padded feet on sand died away. He clicked on the flashlight. Several pairs of eyes reflected back. Luminous yellow embers followed him as he leaned the shotgun against a boulder. He stooped to pick up a couple of rocks, tossed one in his palm, and let it fly. It smacked a coyote between the eyes like a bullet, dropping the animal instantly. The others scattered.

Dan grabbed the shotgun and walked to where it laid. Touching a boot to its head, it lolled loosely around. Grabbing the dead animal by the tail, he dragged it into the brush, feeling no remorse or animosity. The coyotes were only acting on instinct—but so was he. A lethal predator comes in many forms.

"They're gone," Dan announced, stepping back into the cave. He stood in front of Anna. "Mind telling me what that was all about?"

"When I was a little girl," Anna began, "mother and I were on a picnic. I got separated from her and became lost in the forest. I still have nightmares about the wolves howling and growling as they chased me. I climbed a tree but they found it and circled all night long. I spent the night on a limb." She shivered. "I'll never forget the sound of their snarling and snapping. I knew if I fell, the wolves would tear into me."

Leaning the shotgun against the cave wall, he tossed the flashlight near the mattress and knelt. "I'm sorry, Annie." He hugged her. "Seems there's a lot I don't know." Dan rocked her. "I wouldn't let anything happen to you," he whispered. His strong arms and reassuring touch comforted her. He soon had her smiling.

"It's getting late," she said, slowly pulling him down to the sleeping bag.

The fire died to a few glowing embers. Suddenly there was a flash near the entrance, then another. A low, distant rumble shook the ground.

Dan lay on his side, cradling his wife, her warm, bare back pressing against his chest. He moved a leg and she snuggled deeper. Daniel McKntyre, without seeing the flashes, sensed a change, the damp smell of rain thickening the air. He blinked, but the darkness was so complete he wasn't sure his eyes were even open. There was a flash, a pause, then the tearing sound of thunder shattered the stillness, shaking the cave.

Anna quivered. Dan's arms tightened and he buried his face in her thick, curly hair. "Shh, baby," he whispered, "it's only a storm. Don't be so skittish." His lips slowly, sensuously, moved down her neck.

Slowly relaxing, Anna sighed deeply as she responded to his kisses. "Danny, don't stop."
Dan's hands moved over her breasts, gently caressing them, his lips brushing over her bare shoulders. His hand inched down, his touch lingering over her gentle curves. Dan reveled at the sensual feeling and beauty of his wife's body and how she responded. His fingers continued over her hips. Anna sighed.

Outside, lightening flashed and thunder echoed. The sky opened, rain driving down in great drenching sheets. But inside the cave it was dry. Remote and alone, the lovers tore at each other.

19

"It seems the former captain of this ship, a privateer, had the good fortune of always staying one step ahead of the authorities," Ason mMyre said, glancing to the young woman seated next to him at the helm. "May this vessel bring us the same luck."

"I still cannot believe you procured a vessel such as the *Elytra*," Tyona Faelian said, her fingers working over the controls. "I know several worlds that would consider this ship a coup. You must have high connections, indeed."

Ason rose, gazing out a nearby window. A million pinpoints of light hung motionless in the dark infinity of space. "Actually," Ason began, "I was just in the right place at the right time. The *Elytra's* former captain had a pressing need to arrange his own death." Ason gave a wily smile. "The *Elytra* was too conspicuous, and he needed to relinquish it. I acquired this ship at a fraction of its value."

"Sir, possessing obsolete military vessels by civilians is a violation of the Interstellar Arms Agreement of—"

"You are right, Tyona," Ason interrupted. "But you are forgetting this was a *Talarian* ship. Talarians will do anything to undermine their agreements with Serena. If that means selling an old—but heavily armed—starcruiser to the highest bidder, well, so be it."

A particularly obstinate race of humans, Talarians routinely thumbed their noses at Satarian agreements and treaties. Talaria, once a Satarian colony, had gained its independence through a violent revolution. Even after 800 years, Talaria still blamed Serena for the planetary war that ensued, a war that nearly destroyed both civilizations. Then last century the Brazaryans appeared and began terrorizing the quadrant. Serena and Talaria allied against a common foe, beating back the Brazaryans and forcing a truce. An uneasy peace now existed with the Brazaryans, yet Serena and Talaria still suffered strained relations. Talarians prided themselves on being a constant thorn in the side of the Satarian government. The *Elytra* falling into civilian hands was just another jab.

Five hundred meters in length, the *Elytra* could quarter fifty passengers comfortably while holding vast amounts of cargo. But most importantly, it only required a skeleton crew of three—two if they were highly experienced. Two gargantuan engine nacelles attached to the top of the triangular fuselage symbolized speed. Only the new Satarian "Quasar" Class-IV starships could match her swiftness.

"Approaching Outpost Rieling, Lord Captain."

Ason heard the concern in Tyona's voice as he slid into the seat next to her. "Stay out of scanner range, Tyona.

We are not supposed to be here."

"Sir, they have recently installed the new *rt-six-twenty*. I am sure it is too late."

"Whatever happened to my sense of timing?"

"Sir?"

"Stop calling me 'sir'—and 'Lord Captain.'" He smiled at the young woman. "We are both civilians now. 'Ason' will do."

"Yes my—" Tyona caught herself, bowing her head. "Yes, Ason."

The former lord captain had followed through on his plans for retirement. When he spent most of his life's savings to purchase the vessel he and Tyona were now on, his family shook their heads, saying he was going through a mid-life crisis. "No," he told them, "I am just in a transitional period, from what I was doing, to what I am going to do." Ason deliberately avoided telling his family about the signal from the Soladine System. Now his single-minded purpose in life was learning the fate of his father.

"Ason, we are being scanned," Tyona said, looking down to her instruments. "Should I deploy the—"

"Do nothing," the older man interrupted. "We will play their little game, for now."

Beeping pierced the air. "They hail us," Tyona said. "Should I put it on visual?"

"By all means. I know the captain of this outpost. His name is Dnas wWhael. He is a friend, but I would have chosen a better locale for a reunion. Place us in high orbit, Tyona."

A small video screen atop the instrument panel filled with the face of a sullen looking man. To Ason's dismay, it was not his old friend. Dressed in a Fleet officer's uniform, the man appeared to be in his forties.

"I am Commander Scola of Fleet Outpost Rieling," he said harshly. "I request to speak with the captain of your vessel."

"Then speak. Name is Ason mMyre."

The man gave a start. Indecision swept over the commander's face, his tone less hostile. "Sir, may I ask what the Lord Captain of the *Mnaerias* is doing out here in a civilian cargo ship—and one of Talarian registry?"

"I wish to speak to Captain wWhael. We are old friends."

"Captain wWhael retired last month. I am now in charge." He paused. "Please answer my question. You, being a Fleet captain—a *Lord Captain*—should know that you violate restricted space. This region of the quadrant is off limits to all vessels except those specifically authorized by the High Council."

Ason smiled innocently. "Like your former boss, I have also retired. I was unaware this was restricted space. Those *restricted* areas seem to move with no rhyme or reason. Before you know it, the whole galaxy will be restricted."

The commander's features grew taut. "Please state the nature of your business."

"Commander, you have already scanned us and know our destination. It's Mega-five. You see, my hobby is archeology, and I understand that a—"

"Lord Captain," the commander interrupted, "you need to check your navigational guidance; your heading is faulty." His eyes shifted to Tyona. "Who is that seated next to you?"

"Commander, with all due respect, it is none of your business."

"My name is Tyona Faelian," Tyona blurted. "I am the ship's navigator."

The commander frowned. "Are you not the chief science officer on the *Mnaerias*?"

"Was. I resigned my commission two weeks ago."

"I see." The commander's gaze returned to Ason. "So, you hijacked a former crew member."

"Not at all. We are only saving our families from shame."

He paused for a moment. "Excuse me, Lord Captain, but is she not a bit young for you?"

"We need not explain things, Commander Scola," Ason said, giving him a shrewd smile. "If we had remained on Serena, well, you can imagine the embarrassment it would have brought to our respective families, not to mention the Fleet."

The commander nodded. Suddenly his eyes narrowed. "Good try, Lord Captain. If it were anyone but you, I might have believed it." The commander paused. "We have been waiting for you. Were told you may attempt something stupid." He smiled with satisfaction. "Frankly, I am disappointed. Your reputation led me to believe you would be a challenge to catch." His smile disappeared. "Prepare for boarding. And do not try running. The *Antaries* is patrolling a half-light year away. You would not have a chance."

"Computer," Ason barked, "close com-link." The screen went black.

"Shall I give them our teleport coordinates?" Tyona asked gloomily.

"No." Rising, the older man paced around the small bridge. He stopped, then faced the woman seated at the helm. "I will wipe that gloating look off his face."

"Ason, you are not thinking of—"

"Tyona, I am ordering you down to the surface. It is me they want. I am sure no charges will be brought against you. I apologize for exposing you to this. I was crazy letting you come along. You are still so young. You can start over."

Tyona jumped up, livid. "I *am* starting over!" Her fist struck the back of the chair, spinning it around. "I am not leaving—at least not alone. We surrender together, fight together, run together—"

"Or die together."

"I shall not leave."

Ason studied her, gauging her strength. Suddenly the teleporter control beeped. The outpost was attempting to tie in a link. Ason's eyes narrowed, the whiskers on his bushy gray mustache bristling. "Man your station, Lieutenant."

The two slid behind the main control panel. Ason's fingers worked feverishly on the controls as he shouted orders. "Deflector aegis up. Power up the plus-light drives."

Tyona's fingers moved expertly over the many color-coded control interfaces. A low hum vibrated throughout the ship as the massive proton-driven, plus-light engines came alive. The com-link beeped frantically. The two looked at one another. Ason touched a button, manually opening the com-channel.

The enraged face of commander Scola appeared on the monitor. "I cannot believe you are doing this, mMyre! Power down your engines and drop deflectors immediately! Have you taken leave of your senses?"

"Yes, and now I take leave of you."

"One last time, lower your deflectors and let us board. Escape is hopeless."

"Ason," Tyona said, "a Fleet cruiser approaches off our starboard." She looked up from a monitor. "It is the *S'Pamaes*; they have charged weapons."

Ason glanced at the com-monitor. The commander wore a satisfying sneer.

"So, what is it going to be, mMyre? We scanned your ship. You have no weapons systems—"

"That you could detect," Ason interrupt. "Seems you still have a few bugs to work out of your new equipment." Ason glanced to Tyona. "Power up weapons."

Tyona's fingers moved over another console. "Weapons on-line."

Another Fleet officer whispered something to Scola. The commander's eyes widened. Subtle caution replaced scorn.

"mMyre, your weapons array—it is an outlawed

system. That, alone, could get you life on a penal colony. If you surrender now, we will consider not pressing charges for its possession."

"How thoughtful," Ason replied. "Commander, this conversation is over. I am leaving town. Do not try to follow."

The commander began protesting.

"Close com-link," Ason said. The com-monitor went black.

"Ason, the *S'Pamaes* is still closing. We will be in their weapons range in thirty seconds."

"Lay a course for the Soladine System."

"Already done."

"Then take us out of orbit, Tyona. Let us vacate the area—maximum speed."

The *Elytra* streaked away. The Fleet cruiser gave chase, but to Ason's surprise, it never fired. No match in speed for the fast Talarian-built ship, it was soon left far behind.

Talarian vessels enjoyed a huge power-to-mass advantage over Satarian ships. However, the proton-driven, plus-light engines, while more powerful than their Satarian counterparts, were also very temperamental. They had a nasty habit of suddenly exploding, ruining the day for anyone within 1000 kilometers.

Sighing, Ason turned back to his instruments. Tyona and he were lucky. If the *Antaries* happened upon them, the situation would be a quagmire: the captain of the *Antaries* was a close personal friend, and like Ason, was from the old school. He stared blankly at the instruments, jaw tightening.

Tyona felt a void as bleak and empty as the stars they sailed among. She touched the environmental controls. "Ason, what is known of the Illysians? Why the security surrounding that star system?"

Dressed in a gray, loose fitting, hooded tunic, Ason turned to the young woman. "Illysia is something the mighty High Council cannot wish away," he scoffed. He paused, studying Tyona. "I recently uncovered *Halaena's* real mission. If it went public, Satarian beliefs could be shaken to their core."

"What did you learn?"

About to speak, he was cut short by a piercing alarm.

Tyona glanced at a read-out. "A Fleet vessel is approaching. It is the *Antaries*. She is advancing fast on our port flank. Intercept time: two minutes." The com-link flashed and Tyona leaned over a control panel. "We are being hailed." She paused. "They demand we heave-to. Their weapons are charged."

Ason took a seat behind the main control panel and Tyona slid into the chair next to him. He gave her a hard glance. "This seems a re-occurring theme. Power up weapons. Let them contemplate." He touched a symbol and the com-screen lit-up.

A man of Ason's age materialized on the view-screen. His neatly trimmed beard was streaked with gray, his thick, silver hair held in a bushy ponytail. A *Mataer* warrior, his uniform bore the rank of Lord Captain.

The *Antaries* was not an obsolete battlewagon converted to hauling cargo. She was a Quasar class-IV starship—a battle-interceptor—and the pride of Her Majesty's Fleet. *Antaries'* job was to protect Serena, the Fleet, and enforce Satarian foreign—and domestic—policy.

Her captain was one of the most competent in the Fleet. Lord Captain sShaen and Ason mMyre had gone through The Academy together and were close friends. They had served on the same starship during the Brazaryan war. Ason was best man at Celes sShaen's wedding 110 years earlier. The two had faced death, laughed, fought, and gotten drunk together. Pain now shadowed both men's brows.

Ason focused on the com-screen. "Well, well, Celes, need I ask what brings an old friend out to the hinterlands?"

"It should not end this way, Ason," Celes said solemnly. "*You* know my orders."

"And *you* know what I am after."

"Ason, you are foolish. The High Council knows your destination. We—I, was sent to preclude that, to convince you of the folly of your intentions."

"Are you not curious," Ason said, "why the High Council quarantined the Soladine System?"

"It is not for me to question, only to carry out orders. If you—"

"The quarantine began after you intercepted that Illysian probe last year," Ason interrupted. "I saw the probe's data-file."

Celes stared in astonishment. "That probe's recovery was highly classified. So, we now deal with spies."

"The truth must be exposed."

"Speak no more of it, Ason. I remind you of your life-long oath as a Fleet Officer."

"The Illysians even named the probe," Ason continued. "They christened it *Voyager One*. It contained a small collection of tokens, images and recordings that represented their civilization." Ason paused. "Their similarity to Serena's past is not coincidental. The Council knows that. But there are other reasons for secrecy surrounding the Illysians." Ason's eyes narrowed. "Do you not agree?"

Tyona suddenly spoke. "The probe's name sounds so strange. What does it mean?"

"It means, 'One who journeys,'" Ason said. "The Illysian probe was designed for first contact. They seek an answer to the age-old question every intelligent civilization asks: are there others out there? If so, are they like us? The answer to the Illysians' questions are yes and yes."

"And you intend to prove it to them," Celes said.

"No, Celes, you know what I seek. We will never be detected."

"Arriving in a Talarian Warbird is your idea of subtlety?" He paused. "You face two options: accompany me back to Outpost Rieling, or…" Celes hesitated.

"Or you will be forced to destroy me."

The man in the com-screen nodded somberly.

"I have orders from the High Council to use any means necessary—and you know their preference." He paused. "Ason, be reasonable. You can still save face. Just surrender. You will be examined and—"

"And have my memory erased then substituted with a bastardized, sanitized version of what *they* think I should recall? Celes, you disappoint me. We have broken bread for over a century. You know I would never submit to something so heinous."

"I know. That is why my weapons are charged and targeted." His jaw set, Celes glanced to Tyona. "What is your part in this, Faelian?"

"Your tone is that of an accuser," Tyona replied.

"At the moment, you are accused of nothing but youthful indiscretion."

"Youthful indiscretion!" Tyona flew out of her chair, glaring into the com-screen. "With all due respect, Lord Captain, Satarian society needs an infusion of 'youthful indiscretion.' People have forgotten how to live. There are no longer any challenges. Our civilization has become boring, stagnant. I will not return to that cyber-cesspool known as Serena."

Celes glanced at Ason. "She is opinionated."

"Very."

Celes sShaen gazed thoughtfully at Tyona. "Well, young lady, maybe you are the one to 'infuse' us. The bell has not rung. Return with me. I shall schedule a hearing; maybe even get your commission back. We do indeed need fresh thinkers like you." His eyes narrowed. "Please do not throw away your life."

"Lord Captain, my returning to the Fleet, or Serena, will never happen."

Celes studied the young woman. "So be it."

"I am sure you have scanned us," Ason said. "You know our weaponry."

"And you know your Anti-matter Displacer is an unstable weapons system. Possessing such a device is a very serious offense. I have witnessed executions for less. It seems, Ason, you have thrown all caution to the wind."

"No, only being judicious." Ason signaled to Tyona, who was re-seated at the helm. Her fingers danced over the controls. Ason turned back to the com-screen. "We will take our leave now. You may follow if you wish, though I would not recommend it."

"A foolish, inane path you choose, Ason. You leave me no choice."

"Your confidence is premature." Ason glanced out a window, his jaw set. "Good-bye, Celes. Computer, close com-link." The com-screen went black. He turned to Tyona. "I am going to squeeze everything I can from those Talarian engines. You know what may happen." He paused. "Tyona, the *Antaries* is a formidable opponent. There is still time for you to reconsider."

She swiveled around, her gaze fiery. "Thank you, but do not ever ask me again."

Silence enveloped the two. Shaking his head, Ason moved to the engineering controls. "I am entering the modifications to the proton drives. We shall give the crew of the *Antaries* the run—or fight—of their lives. Monitor readings while I operate the weapons station."

"Yes, sir."

The older man ran his fingers over a control panel and the ship hummed from the added power to the plus-light engines. He touched a control surface. With a flash *Elytra* streaked away.

Another flash and *Antaries* charged in pursuit.

Moving to a third seat, Ason touched a control interface. After several long moments he glanced at Tyona. "Our status?"

"*Antaries* matches our speed and heading."

A loud beeping pierced the air. "They just fired a type-two plasma torpedo," Tyona shouted.

"They have reached critical speed," Ason said. "They must finish us before their engines fry."

Suddenly the *Elytra* shook violently. Ason grabbed the control panel and held on. Tyona was thrown to the floor. Warning lights blinked, alarms sounding. Tyona rose slowly, limping back to the helm.

"Ason, our deflectors are down fifty percent; power to the helm and engines unaffected."

The hailing frequency beeped. Ason glanced at Tyona. "Ignore it."

A red warning light flashed just as an energy burst came hurling at them.

"Damn you, Celes," Ason said, "you force me to—" The bridge shook again. Sparks spewed from a wall panel. A warning klaxon blared with an ear-splitting wail.

"Deflectors down point ten," Tyona shouted over the alarm. "Neutronic fluctuation in the port nacelle."

"Take it off-line," Ason barked.

Tyona's fingers flew over a control interface and the warning klaxon ceased.

"Speed is down fifty percent." She cast a nervous glance to the older man. "They are locking a tractor-beam."

"This has gone far enough!" Ason shouted. "Weapons are on line. Computer, port screen on."

The white, sleek shape of the *Antaries* suddenly loomed large in the viewer.

Ason ran his fingers over a small panel. "Targeting their engines." He touched a small red panel.

The *Elytra* surged. A flash and the view-screen brightened. The *Antaries* was engulfed in blue light. The light soon dissipated. The huge starship appeared unscathed. Tyona scanned readouts. "Tractor beam released. Their deflectors are down, their plasma torpedoes are off line— they are at our mercy." Tyona gave the older man a puzzled look. "Ason, they just sit there—"

"Hard to starboard!"

Tyona punched at a panel, and the two were hurled to the right just as a sphere of light left the bow of the *Antaries* and streaked past them.

The *Antaries* peppered the area with deadly disrupter charges. Ason jumped to the helm, maneuvering the *Elytra* around the glowing balls of energy. "Take over weapons control," he barked.

Tyona swiftly crossed the bridge, seating herself at

the weapons station.

"Target their starboard nacelle."

"Ason," Tyona said hesitantly, "their deflectors are down. Our AMD could cascade the *Antaries'* plus-light coils." She paused. "There are two hundred crewman on board."

"You prefer the alternative?"

The ship rumbled. The bridge lights flickered then darkened. Within seconds the lights and power returned. Tyona glanced at several readouts. "We are hit—deflectors off line. Explosive decompression in aft cargo holds four, five and seven. Emergency pressure fields are holding. Anti-grav shows a fluctuation in the inertial drive."

Both eyed the com-screen. Debris from their own vessel drifted into view as a continuous salvo of disrupter charges flashed from *Antaries'* bow.

"Ready weapons," Ason shouted. "Steady—fire!"

A blue beam shot from the *Elytra*. A bright flash lit the windows and com-screen. The *Antaries* vanished.

"They dropped from plus-light," Tyona said. "Ason, now is our chance. Let us run for it—we can get away!"

The former starship captain chewed a lip, letting several moments lapse. "I cannot leave them like that. Reversing engines." His fingers danced over a control panel. "Exiting plus-light. All engines stopped."

The *Antaries* filled the screen. Her starboard engine nacelle had disintegrated, along with most of the pylon that held it. In its place was burned and tangled debris. The starboard side of the hull was blackened. A blue light spiraled from the scorched area like a spider web, quickly engulfing the entire ship.

"It cascaded," Tyona murmured.

The *Antaries* began listing, occasional plasma streamers arcing from her hull. A lone strobe light on her stern flashed. The vessel drifted, lifeless.

"Computer," Ason said, "hail the *Antaries*. Put them on visual."

The screen filled with haunting, chaotic images in the infrared light of *general-quarters*. Commands barked, a warning klaxon wailed. Flames silhouetted the background. Part of the bridge bulkhead had collapsed, crushing two crewmen. Another crewman sprawled on the floor, groaning, smoke rolling from his uniform. Suddenly Celes' bloodied, blackened face filled the com-screen

"So, you returned to pick over the carcass. Take a good look, Ason. I lost fifty-eight crewmen with casualties mounting. I cannot believe you, *YOU*, would ever fire on a Fleet ship! We have been friends for well over a century," Celes shook his head, "but I will never forget this."

Ason's eyes narrowed. "You drew first blood." He paused. "I return to offer aid."

"And tow us back to Outpost Rieling?"

"I will call for assistance," Ason said.

Celes coughed, grimacing with pain. Leaning on an exposed beam, he stared into the com-screen. "I got a message off. Half the fleet is on the way." Wobbling, he steadied himself. "Ason, you have just signed your death warrant—and the young lady's. You are now a fugitive from justice. This is exactly what the High Council wanted. They will come after you with a vengeance...*buzz*...an example out of you—"

The image in the com-screen became digital locked, the audio garbled. The screen went black.

"Lost the com-link," Tyona said, touching a panel. "Attempting to reestablish communications, but—"

"No. It is over." Ason rose and gazed out the star-filled window. The *Antaries* drifted a thousand meters off their port bow. He watched as translucent streamers arced off the damaged ship. "Farewell, old friend." Ason's jaw tightened and he glanced at Tyona. "Get us the hell out of here. Restore our previous heading."

"Ason, we can only limp at quarter-speed."

"I know. I will coax as much as I can from the plus-light drives." He slid into the seat next to her. "It could be a long journey, maybe a month or more."

Tyona blinked nervously. "Will they pursue us?"

Ason stared at the control panel, his gaze unfocused. "They most certainly shall—but not today. The remaining class-four starships are patrolling the DMZ. There is nothing within a week of here that could catch us, even in our present state."

"We will always be looking over our shoulder," Tyona murmured. "Like the lord captain said, we are now fugitives." She gazed at Ason for a moment. "Would they dare jeopardize the Primary Order and pursue us to *Illysia*? That could lead to cultural interference, and disaster."

"That interference, at least on a small scale, has

already happened. I think it will show itself soon, whether we are there or not."

Tyona set the auto-guidance and monitored the long-range scanners. Unnerved from their encounter with the *Antaries*, she was unable to concentrate. That could have been them drifting in space. "I always imagined battle to be enthralling and glorious. But it was neither. I found it terrifying and repulsive. And it was against our own people."

"*We* were also *their* people." Ason glanced at her, his face expressionless. "It is different when your enemy is shooting back, trying desperately to do to you what you so dearly want to do to him."

His words did not comfort Tyona, nor were they meant to. The ramifications of what happened stunned her. She never experienced such desperation. It was no game or bluff, but horrifyingly real. And it all held such an act of finality. Tyona's hands trembled.

For the first time in her young life, Tyona felt real fear. Dread of the unknown clung like a morbid shadow. She had never realized until now what an insulated, secure life she had led.

Tyona took a deep breath. She had better resign herself, and quickly, that there was no going back. Knowing the High Council, there would soon be a bounty on them.

"Tyona."

Startled, she jumped. Her eyes slowly met Ason's.

"Yes?"

"What we just experienced will happen again. And the outcome may be different. If time escapes us, I want you to know that you acted as a professional. I am very lucky, and proud, to have served with you on board the *Mnaerias*, and to have you here now."

"Are you trying to say, 'it's been nice knowing you'?"

"Indulge an old warrior, please."

The shaking in Tyona's hands eased and she bowed shyly. "Thank you, my lord." Her gaze met his. "You are a very kind man. I am indeed honored to be here to help you accomplish your goal."

"What of your goal, Tyona? You must now ask yourself that. Be honest. What are *you* searching for?" He glanced at the view-screen, which held the blackness of plus-light speed. "Do you recall my saying, 'be careful of what you wish for?'"

Tyona nodded.

Ason smiled. "Well, I believe you shall receive it." He nodded towards the view-screen. "Out there are answers. But they may not be the ones we are seeking."

In mid-morning Arizona sun, the blue-and-white Jeep crawled over the plateau's rim and stopped. Dan and Anna emerged, heading to the precipice's steep edge. A strong, steady breeze fluttered their loose-fitting clothes. Only dust devils swirled on the desert floor.

Dan shuddered. "I feel like we're being watched."

"I sense it every time I'm up here," Anna said, "but this time it's stronger."

Over a mile away, the reddish, rocky knees of Sentinel Peak rose from the desert terrain of the plateau. It seemed as if the mountain itself were judging them. The two returned to the Jeep and drove across the windswept, hardpan of the plateau, heading for the mountain.
They quickly crossed the plateau and Dan backed the Jeep behind a large rocky outcropping at the mountain's base. The two climbed out and began unloading gear. Anna pulled a backpack from the open rear window. "Just over the rise is a small meadow, then a heavy forested slope. That's where I saw the wreckage. We'll have to hike maybe a couple of

miles to get there."

Shouldering their backpacks, Dan gazed at Anna, shaking his head.

Anna yanked a strap. "Now what?"

"I can't believe I let you talk me into this."

"Too late now, McKntyre. Let's go."

Dan slung two canteens over one shoulder and the shotgun over the other. The web belt around his waist was stuffed full of shotgun shells, another canteen hanging from it. A bush hat covered his head. Dan followed Anna up the low, rock-covered rise.

"If the wreckage is invisible," Dan said, working around a boulder, "how will you know where to look? Do you have a landmark picked out or something?"

"Don't worry," Anna said, puffing, "when we get to the other side, you'll know where it is."

"*Me?*"

Anna smiled and kept climbing.

Dan reached the top first. He scrambled over the crest, then pulled Anna up. The hilltop was 500 feet across, bare, except for a few scattered boulders at the other end.

He looked at Anna with concern; the short climb was not that strenuous, yet she was pale and drawn. She paused, leaning against him, trembling. Dan ran a hand over her clammy cheek.

"Just a touch of morning sickness," Anna said. "It's not nearly as bad as it used to be."

"Do you want to take a break?"

"Not here. We'll cool off in the shade of those

boulders at the other end." She took a step and stumbled.

Dan caught her. "Easy, Annie. You have nothing to prove. There aren't many women who could do what you do, much less while pregnant." He eyed her. "Let me have some of your gear."

"No, I'm fine."

Dan shook his head, chuckling.

"Are you laughing at me?"

"No."

"Yes, you are—you're making fun of me!"

Sighing, Dan removed his sunglasses, wiping the lenses with a shirttail. "Here we go again." He shoved the sunglasses back on. "Must be a hormonal thing."

"What's that supposed to mean?"

"Can't we go at least one day without us getting into it over petty shit? I just don't want you to overdo yourself, okay? Jesus, Annie, I was just trying to help."

Anna touched his hand. "I'm sorry."

The two turned and, holding hands, headed for the other side of the hill.

"You know," Dan began, "it's beautiful up here, but what I wouldn't give to be back home now. I wished we were sitting on our patio, listening to the wind in the treetops." He glanced at Anna. "Or, the kids and their friends would be outside, Charlie and his family would be over and…well, you get the picture."

Anna squeezed his hand. "When this is over, what are you going to do? I mean about work and all? We haven't talked much about it. I trust you have a plan—and it better not include trucking."

"I have a little money saved," Dan began. "Finances will get better once I sell that friggin' truck. But first I'll focus on building our house. I'll hire a crew to frame and such, but I intend to supervise and do a lot of the work myself."

"A contractor's nightmare."

"Whatever," Dan said dryly. "The important thing is, it'll be paid for. And after that…" He shrugged. "You know I've mentioned returning to the army. I can get my commission back. Annie, civilian life isn't for me. Your father was right; I should never have left the army. I'm a soldier."

"And a husband and a father. And once again, when will we ever see you?" She paused. "Danny, forget that, forget money. If you could, what would you *really* like to do?"

"Finish grad school. If I'm going to make the army a career, I need that Masters."

Anna glanced at him as they stepped around a lone creosote. "How would you like to worry about nothing but school?"

Dan halted. "What do you mean?"

Ignoring his question, Anna stepped in front of him and caught his hands. "Will our home be completed by Christmas?"

"Why do you ask?"

Anna pulled off her sunglasses, letting them hang from her neck. "How would you like to spend Christmas on the sunny beaches of Belize? Just you and me."

"Belize?"

"Danny, I own beach-front property there. It's not much really, just several tracks of land with a few bungalows. It's beautiful, very tropical. An older couple lives there full time, taking care of things for me. I visited last year; it's been well maintained."

Dan stared in disbelief. "Sounds like a resort to me."

"It is," Anna said, squeezing his hand. "We could have a delayed honeymoon on the warm, sandy beaches of the Caribbean—just the two of us."

"I thought you lost that property in the divorce?"

"You're thinking of the property we—Jeffery and I—had in Costa Rica. This place in Belize is mine. Jeffery never had a clue. The income it generates goes into local and other foreign banks—and away from the prying eyes of Uncle Sam. I've made a few coins. Most of the profit is invested in other Central American real estate. That'll be the hot item early next century." Anna paused, hesitating. "Danny, I've lots of overseas investments, and they've all come to fruition. I never needed Jeffrey's money. I could have bought and sold the twit."

Dan stood dumbfounded.

Anna's eyes hinted a silver hue. "You knew I had seen more life than you, even in Satarian terms. To the *Mataer*, I'd be considered young." She paused, her eyes searching his, gauging his reaction.

Dan stood, stoic.

"I've had other identities." She swallowed. "In a few short years you'll understand. People will begin talking.

273

Then one day we will have to bug out. We'll have to change our name, lifestyle, and move on. But we'll do it *together*. And that takes money."

Dan looked away, shaking his head.

"I've amassed quite a fortune," Anna continued. "I have money scattered in banks throughout the world. Dozens of investments in different names. Most are very profitable."

"So, exactly what are you saying?"

"You and I will never have to work again. When we get back, we'll build the house of our dreams—cost is no factor. Forget the army. You can attend grad school full-time. But, I will stand by whatever decision you make."

"Even if it meant returning to the army?"

Anna nodded. "I know you'd do the same for me."

"Anna, how much are you worth?"

"Does it really matter?"

"Hell, yes. I need to know who'll come calling."

"Maybe a few hundred million?" she said meekly.

"A few hundred million! Jesus Christ, Anna, no wonder you're being watched!"

"You know that's not the reason."

Dan eyed her, speechless.

"I wasn't born into wealth, Danny. I know what real poverty is. I lived it. During the war there was hunger. Mother and I would listen for the rat-traps." Anna's gaze leveled on her husband. "We didn't want the meat to spoil."

"Which war, Anna?"

"That's not fair."

Dan's jaw tightened. "God dammit. God dammit

all to hell!" He threw his hat then turned, marching off, swearing and kicking the ground. Chunks of earth went sailing.

Anna stood by, silent.

He charged back, facing her. "God, this is like pulling teeth—what else are you hiding, Anna? Please tell me how to go about prying this stuff out—"

"I've been married before," Anna said, focusing on her boots. "I had another husband before Jeffery. But it was long ago. I was very young." She glanced up. "Danny, he meant nothing to me, really. You're the only one. I've never loved anyone as much as I love you. Please, believe me."

"Is that what you're going to say to the next guy? 'He meant nothing to me, really,'" Dan mocked. "How many other children do you have, 'Anna,' or whoever you are? I bet you have kids older than me. Some maybe even old enough to be my—"

Anna slapped him.

Dan stood, shocked, feeling the prickly sting crawl across his cheek. Anna's hand came up again and he caught it.

"Let go of me."

Dan released her wrist. Blood trickled from his nose. His eyes blazed white.

"Don't do something you'll regret," Anna said, her voice wavering.

Dan spun around, covering his face with his hands.

Anna's shoulders sagged, her breathing ragged. She staggered then caught herself. Turning, she shoved her sunglasses on, cinched up her backpack and trudged away in silence, heading toward the far end of the hill.

Dan stood for several minutes with his back to Anna as she receded into the distance. Taking a bandanna from his back pocket, he wiped the blood from his nose, then turned. His wife had disappeared.

"Shit!" Stomping to where his hat lay, he snatched it up and slapped it on a thigh. "God damn women!" he yelled, yanking the hat down to his ears. He studied the ground in front of him. Anna's boot prints headed in a northerly direction, toward the boulders. Tightening his backpack and shotgun, he started for the rocks. "And I have to fall for a woman with the tenacity of Hannibal and his elephants." He kicked the ground again, swearing.

Hiking across the hillcrest, he rounded the largest boulder at the far end. "Anna?" The place was empty. "Annie," he called, his voice echoing. Peeking around several boulders, Dan saw no sign of her. The feeling of being watched returned. Taking a deep breath, he cleared his thoughts, then searched the ground for boot prints. It was useless. He'd tromped over everything. Cursing again, he turned back to where he'd last seen her tracks, then stopped. Surely Anna wouldn't go to the wreckage by herself?

Dan dashed to the edge of the hill. Below was a small mountain meadow, but what caught his attention was at the far end: giant ponderosas, their tops skewed at odd angles. A hundred-yard area of terrain at the far end of the meadow seemed fuzzy, blurred.

Familiarity spread through him. He tensed, an

alien consciousness speaking to him, stirring his memory. Suddenly, with the clarity of an open book, Dan knew where he was.

Shifting his gaze to the meadow, he spotted Anna making her way through knee-high brush, heading to the distortion. Dan bolted after her. With backpack, shotgun and canteens slapping, he knew she heard him, yet she never turned. "Anna, stop! Please, you don't know what it will do!"

She continued marching.

"Damnit, Anna," he pleaded, "would you at least wait for me?"

Anna took another step and vanished.

"Holy shit!" Dan charged through the brush. Suddenly there was a white flash and he ran headlong into her. She was kneeling, mouth agape, eyes transfixed on an object in front of her. She jumped up, catching him.

"Danny."

About to speak, he did a double take, his gaze following Anna's. "Dear, God."

Not twenty yards away was the end of a massive, gray fuselage. The scorched hull stretched into the forest, seemingly forever.

Dan grabbed Anna's hand. The two took a few tentative steps forward then halted, staring.

Dan was reminded of the time he stood by the massive Saturn V rocket boosters at the Johnson Space Center in Houston. What he and Anna were looking at was twice as large. It arched as high as a seven-story building; its length could only be guessed. Dan searched for the end, but only two hundred yards of the vessel were visible, the rest hidden by trees and brush. Briars covered a good portion of the fuselage, which had burrowed into the hillside. Several mountain jays squawked at the two intruders. They probably had never seen a human. After a few moments they gave up and flew away.

"Look." Anna pointed to lettering near the top of the hull.

The characters were strange and unearthly, yet both recognized the word: *HALAENA*. Underneath was a large white inverted triangle with blue borders. It enclosed a sword with a lightning bolt on each side.

Dan approached the wreckage. Stopping a few paces from the hull, he reached out, hesitantly touching it. Not quite like metal, it reminded him of kevlar. Dan knew he was the first earth-born human to ever lay hands on it.

"I'm back," he whispered. Walking along its side, he trailed fingers along the hull, almost caressing it. "Anna, something's happening to me. It's as if I'm two people in one."

"It's your *ishara*. Stay with me, baby."

Dan's eyes glowed and he spoke in an alien language, the words flowing from him as if it were his native tongue. "Old friend, you will never again glide by the familiar spaceport of your homeland," he said, his voice resonating. "But our fate is shared, for I shall never again see the banners, the streamers flying proudly above the battlements of Home Port, or see Alisa rushing into my arms." Dan paused, gazing around in wonder. He felt more than saw smoke rising from the wreckage, the air filled with dust and the acrid scent of burning conduits. "We who survive are now marooned on this alien world. Anything remotely civilized is far away. The humans here are extremely primitive and use animals for transportation. How are we to survive in such a culture?"

Something gently touched his arm. "Danny?"

He remained silent, his trance-like gaze fixed on the hull. A voice called to him. A woman. "Alisa?"

"Danny," the voice repeated, echoing oddly, "snap out of it!"

He stared at the hull. "Alisa—how can you be here? I must have indeed passed on."

Something shook him frantically. "Danny, can you hear me? Let it go!"

He staggered.

Arms wrapped around him, holding him tightly.

Snapping out of whatever seized him, he put an arm around her, gazing back the way they'd come. The countryside appeared normal. There was no distortion from inside the shield of invisibility.

Anna ran her fingers over a small red welt on his cheek. "I don't know what came over me."

"It's okay," he whispered, catching her fingers and kissing them, "I deserved it." Dan turned his attention back to the vessel. "This is just un-frigging-real."

"Do you know what to do?"

"Yes," Dan's eyes narrowed, "and we haven't much

time."

They followed the hull into the brush. It had broken into three sections, but was still intact at ground level.

"How do we get inside?" Anna asked.

"There's an airlock at the far end, I think." Dan touched the hull again. "You know, Annie, until I saw this, I never really believed you." He glanced at her as they picked their way through thick undergrowth. "I can recall bits and pieces of Kalyn's memory of Serena. It has two suns and two moons, yet it is not unlike our own world. Their air is the same as ours, but cleaner. Serena has trees, mountains with snow-capped peaks, clouds in the sky, but their skies are green, like their seas."

"'Singing seas,'" Anna added. "Sometimes in my dreams I hear their melodious sound. Nothing on Earth can compare."

He halted. "What I wouldn't give to visit there."

"We'd never be able to."

"Anna," Dan began, "one just does not *lose* a starship. Surely the civilization that built it has the technology to know its whereabouts." He paused. "Yes, I know there was a war going on when it crashed, but that was over one hundred years ago. I can't believe things have remained static. Eventually someone from Serena, or whoever won the war, will make a house call, if they haven't already."

"So, we just hang around until someone from Serena shows up, then hitch a ride?" She shook her head. "You're funny."

"Sooner or later someone will come." Dan glanced at the massive fuselage. "It's too bad the *Halaena* won't be here to greet them."

"Maybe they know its location, but don't care," Anna said. "Maybe the decision was made to just leave it. I mean, why waste resources on an old hulk? To an advanced civilization like the Satari, I'm sure that's all the *Halaena* is to them now." She paused, eyeing the vessel. "Danny, it would be like our government losing a jet-fighter in the Brazilian jungle. We'd be concerned for the pilot, but the least of our worries would be that the Yanomami would converge on it to steal its advanced avionics. Carting off metal to be used as a roof for their huts would be the likelier scenario."

"So, now we're Yanomami."

"If that."

"Still," Dan continued, "it's hard to believe the Satari haven't visited here since the crash. The risk of something like the *Halaena* lying around…you said it yourself." He paused. "This ship represented their technology at its pinnacle."

"How do you know that?"

Dan's brow furrowed. "The same way I know that there's an airlock at the far end of the ship."

The two continued through the tangled mass of brush. Dan constantly glanced at the hull as they walked. Here and there was strange writing, followed by small red and yellow squares. Huge, black, scorch marks streaked the sides. The bottom of the hull was totally black and heavily pitted.

Dan nodded at the scorch marks. "She must have come in at the wrong angle of reentry. It's amazing it's still in one piece. If this had been one of our shuttles, there wouldn't be enough left to fill a shoe box."

They began heading uphill. After a few yards Anna dropped back. Dan halted, waiting. "You okay?"

"Yeah. I just wish we'd get to that damn air-lock," Anna puffed, catching up to him. "It's just the altitude."

"Would you like to rest?"

"No, let's get this over with."

The two walked a few more yards when Dan pointed to a spot on the vessel. "We can get in right here." Anna looked skeptically at the pitted hull. No door, seam, nothing.

Dan laid his hand flat on the skin of the ship. A large, square opening materialized two feet from the ground. Anna jumped back. "How did you do that?"

Dan shrugged.

Removing their sunglasses, both cautiously approached the opening.

Hesitating, Dan stuck his head in the dark interior. On one side of a wall was a small, red flashing light. Dan flicked on a flashlight. Part of him knew there was nothing to fear; part of him was terrified. Climbing tentatively into the opening, he turned and reached for Anna.

The two stood back to back, flashlights shining. They were in some kind of chamber. The flashing red light reflected eerily off smooth polished walls. Underneath the light was a panel. A cool breeze stirred Dan's hair and he glanced around. Seeing nothing but darkness, he focused on the chest high panel, holding the light to it. Several small colored squares reflected back.

"Did you find something?" Anna whispered.

"I'm not sure."

"Please don't touch anything."

He reached out and tapped a small square. The entrance suddenly disappeared, replaced by a solid, shiny wall. The red light ceased flashing.

"Shit, Danny, now you've done it!"

Dan touched another square. The red light flashed. The entrance reappeared.

"Feel better now?"

"Quit jerking around."

Another breeze came from the ship's interior. Along with it was a familiar smell that he couldn't quite place. He pushed another square. The entrance once again disappeared.

Dan clicked off his flashlight. "Anna," he said in a low voice, "turn off your light."

"Why?"

"Just turn it off."

Click. The two were thrown into total darkness. A dim light grew behind him, coming from the same direction as the breeze. "Over here."

"Where's the light coming from?"

"From an opening behind me. I think it's a corridor." His brow furrowed. "The device we're looking for was left on the bridge." He looked toward the dim light.

"This is crazy, but I almost feel as if *I* had lived here."

"You have," Anna murmured.

He took his wife's hand. "I know where to go."

They walked through a narrow opening.

Crewmen scrambled about in organized chaos. The red glow of *General Quarters* engulfed the entire craft.

"*We are going in!*" someone shouted.

Dan shook his head and the images vanished.

Anna touched his arm. "You okay?"

Dan took a deep breath. "Yeah."

Dan and Anna followed the corridor a few feet then suddenly halted, finding themselves on a balcony-like catwalk. The railing in front of them was covered with a heavy layer of dust and bird droppings. Shafts of light poured through holes in the high ceiling, creating a dim, surreal scene. Some of the decks had given way. Walls and bulkheads lay scattered. Dan aimed the flashlight down, exposing twisted support-beams. Equipment and debris littered the bottom. The equipment, even in its damaged state, was priceless. A pair of crows, cawing, glided across the wide void, then disappeared through one of the many holes above. The far end, the part protruding from the forest, was lost in dusty darkness.

A similar catwalk to theirs protruded from the far side. In between was the cargo bay. Both catwalks converged at a bulkhead with multiple dark, eerie openings.

Sweeping the light, Dan swallowed. "This is a ghost ship. I hear their whispers."

"I feel it too," Anna murmured. "This ship is not

supposed to be here. We're seeing the forbidden."

"No. We're part of it, Annie." Turning away, Dan halted, surveying the area. "I feel another presence."

Anna eyed her husband. "Someone beat us here."

"Uh-uh. It's an entity. Kalyn, I think. Or the others."

Woosh. Anna screamed. They ducked, a rush of wind blowing past. Dan swung the shotgun around. In the dim light he made out the large gray wings of an owl.

"There's your entity," Anna said.

Dan slung the shotgun back over a shoulder. "I still feel a presence. It's on the ship's bridge, along with what we're after."

"I hope you know where this 'bridge' is."

"Annie, it's incredible. It's like I've walked this place a thousand times." Taking Anna's hand, he started toward the bulkhead. "The bridge is this way."

The couple headed toward the nearest of the openings. "That distress beacon that Kalyn wrote about in his journal," Anna began. "You know how it works?"

Dan shot her a glance.

The two paused in front of the first open doorway. Anna looked at Dan expectantly. "Well?"

He hesitated. "I think we need to go through here."

"You *think*? Oh, God, I thought you knew where—"

"Yes, this is it." Dan stepped through the dark opening, Anna close behind.

They were met with closed double doors. Dan pulled on them. No good. Anna spotted a ladder attached to a nearby wall.

"Where do you suppose that goes?" she asked.

Dan walked over. The ladder appeared from an opening in the floor, then disappeared into a hole in the ceiling. "My guess is it goes through every deck on the ship." He grabbed a ladder rung. "My dear, I'm afraid we'll have to do a little climbing."

"How far up?"

"Probably all the way. That's usually where control bridges are."

"We have to climb this thing all the way to the top?"

"It couldn't be more than seven or eight floors. We'll leave the backpacks here."

"You better be right, McKntyre."

"This was all your idea, Annie. I was dragged, kicking and screaming."

Sighing, Anna shrugged off her pack. Dan did likewise. Stuffing spare batteries and shells in a vest pocket, he slung the short twelve-gauge back over his shoulder. Dan leading, the two scrambled up the ladder. A small landing was on every deck. They took a breather on the fifth. Unhooking the canteen from his belt, Dan passed it to Anna. "Nothing to it, huh?"

Anna shook her head, unscrewing the cap. She took a drink, then passed the canteen back to her husband. "I hope they have a bathroom on this bridge."

Dan chuckled, taking a swallow. "I'm curious to know what their bathrooms look like."

"You're kidding, right?"

"I'm serious, baby. I mean, what if they found

a better way to use the bathroom—some kind of new, revolutionary device. Forget the 'warp-drive' engines, or that invisible screen out there." Dan chuckled. "One can read a culture by its bathrooms."

"Leave it to you, McKntyre, to think of the small and the silly. Here we are, inside one of the most significant finds of Earth's history, and you want to see their bathrooms."

"Well, you brought it up. Aren't you just a little curious? Come on, Annie girl, aren't you?"

Anna chuckled.

Dan winked. Considering what they hoped to accomplish, one had to either laugh or cry. Doomsday loomed large.

They climbed in silence. At the tenth level Dan jumped onto the landing then helped Anna up. "We're here."

"Are you sure this is it?"

"Yes. Look." Dan pointed to an area behind her.

An open set of double doors greeted them, a metal bar on the floor jammed between. Eerie blue light lit the haze.

Dan, flashlight gleaming, stepped toward the entrance. Anna grabbed his hand, following close behind. The two stepped over the metal bar and onto *Halaena's* bridge.

The ceiling immediately brightened bathing the entire bridge in blue dust. Instruments, some still functioning, covered the walls. Dan recognized Satarian numbers scrolling across a nearby monitor. There were several workstations, each with its own set of instruments.

"Un-friggin-believable," Dan murmured. "What a gold mine."

The two walked slowly around, gazing at the endless number of colored control surfaces. Cobwebs draped eerily.

Anna stiffened and squeezed Dan's hand, pointing to a high-backed chair across the bridge. The seat faced a workstation. Long gray hair, fastened in a ponytail, streamed down the seat back.

Taking a deep breath, Dan cautiously crept to the chair. An elbow covered by a dirty white shirt rested on the chair's arm.

"Be careful," Anna whispered.

Dan put a hand on the chair back. Nothing. Why was *he* always the one to find these things? Holding his breath, he spun the chair around.

"Oh my God!" Anna shouted.

A human skull grinned back at them; its parched tight skin covered in cobwebs.

Dan stared in part horror, part fascination at the human remains. A bony hand protruded from a long sleeve, fingers resting on its lap. The skeleton was clothed in a uniform identical to the one worn by the man he'd seen in the dust devils.

Anna tiptoed to Dan. "Is it who I think it is?"

Dan nodded. "Now we know what happened to Kalyn."

"Are you sure it's him?"

"It's him."

"How do you think he died?" Anna asked.

Dan shrugged. "Hell, it could've been anything."

Anna eyed the remains. "Do you suppose he was murdered?"

"No. The *Halaena* was abandoned by the very civilization that sent it. All the losses he suffered killed him inside." Dan paused, listening to the subtle whir of the ship's instruments accomplishing unknown tasks. "Anna, did he write about his plans for the *Halaena*?"

"No, he only mentioned he would try to return here to contact Serena."

About to speak, Dan halted, focused on something in the skeleton's lap.

Anna's gaze followed Dan's. "What's that?"

He brushed away cobwebs. Bony fingers rattled as he gently worked a book from underneath the hand. At least two inches thick, it was surprisingly light. The slate-black cover felt like plastic. Symbols patterned the front cover. Dan traced his fingertips over the words, leaving small tracks in the grimy dust. He handed the book to Anna.

Anna eyed the characters, then gently opened the book. The pages, wafer thin, were made of the same material as the cover. Anna poured over the text. After a moment she looked up, wide-eyed, fingers trailing over the words on the cover. "*Holy Book*," she read out loud. "Danny, this is a Satarian Bible. And except for names and places, this could be our bible." Anna opened the book again, thumbing through back pages. "But I don't think it has a *New Testament*, or even the equivalent of one."

"Maybe that's the key to it all."

Anna closed the text, holding it reverently. "If there really isn't a *New Testament* in *their* version of The Bible, but their *Old Testament* is identical to the Torah?"

Dan rubbed a hand over his unshaven chin; he had expected anything but this. "The Satari discover an alien race that worships the same God they do, only the promised Messiah has visited that world, if one's of the Christian faith. But their promised Messiah—*the* Messiah—is a no-show on Serena." Dan sighed, trying to unravel his thoughts. "If the people of Serena learned of the Judeo-Christian faith on Earth, and their *Old Testament* is similar to ours, our New Testament could've thrown their religious beliefs into chaos. That may be one reason they haven't contacted us: fear of what exposure could do to *their* society."

"Or theirs to ours," Anna added. "The same could hold true for our society. Who is to say *their* bible, their scriptures, are not the true words of God?" She paused. "Can you imagine what would happen if the Catholic Church, the Baptists, or any Christian faith found the words of God written for an alien civilization, maybe thousands of years older than our own, but with no mention of Jesus of Nazareth?"

"Or the Christians of Earth," Dan began, "could simply point to themselves and say 'see, we are the chosen.'"

"But the Satari could do the same," Anna said. "They'd have a valid point. By all appearances, their civilization is much older than Earth's."

"Yeah," Dan added, "but playing devil's advocate, I

can hear Christians singing that God chose to start over with *Earth* as His new playing field."

"Danny, that would imply that God is fallible."

Dan sighed. "The Satari, religious zealots? Surely not. That sounds like the medieval church when confronted with the fact that Earth was not the center of the physical universe."

"But the truth eventually came out, as it will here," Anna said. She handed Dan the book.

Dan reached for it. A folded piece of paper slipped out, drifting to the floor. Both exchanged glances. Anna reached down, carefully unfolding yellowed sheets.

"It's in English."

"What does it say? Is it from Kalyn?"

"Just hold on. The writing is faded. I can hardly read it. It's dated February, *Eighteen fifty-six*. Anna cleared her throat:

I am Lieutenant Commander Kalyn mMyre, Halaena's chief navigator. My Illysian name is Jason McKntyre. I am stricken with a disease called tuberculosis. Our medical supplies are depleted. I drift in and out of consciousness. If an envoy from the High Council of Serena has not yet contacted this world by the time you read this, you must destroy this vessel lest the Brazaryans detect it.

In addition, Halaena could be ruinous to this culture. I do not factor in the present, largely agrigarian society of this planet. But Illysians are extremely intelligent. In another hundred years...?

Another grave concern is theology. Of all

*civilizations encountered, none had common religious
beliefs. Each religion is unique to its own world, until now.
This world, Illysia, for the most part, worships the same God
as the Satari. That, in itself, could imply that Satari and Illysi
may have common ancestry.*

*The Satari see themselves as unique. Discovery of
a world almost identical to Serena, even to worshipping
the same God...the High Council could implode. They
would never allow the discovery to go public. In addition,
the Illysians are the first race of humans discovered to be
biologically compatible with the Satari. The Satari are very
proud; they may fear a bastardization of their race. Yet that
bastardization has already taken place on our own world, by
our own hands. May it never happen here.*

"Bastardization on his home world?" Dan
murmured. Anna ignored him and continued.

*Serena will never willingly contact this world under
its present leadership. I believe the ultimate goal of the High
Council of Serena was to deny the existence of this world
and its inhabitants. The Halaena was sacrificed.*

*This vessel must be destroyed to maintain the status
quo of both worlds. Yet I find I cannot bring myself to do it.
Instead, I am attempting to contact Fleet Control to let them
know there are survivors. I may be naïve, but I pray the High
Council will have a change of heart and send out a rescue
mission.*

How I miss Alisa...

Anna glanced up, hands quivering.

"Is there anymore?" Dan asked.

Anna gently shuffled the pages. "There's one more page, but it's stuck to the last one. The paper is very brittle. I'm afraid it'll tear." After a moment she freed the page and continued reading:

Nearby you will find a distress beacon stuffed into a large knapsack...instructions...implode...

Anna glanced up. "He's writing about the very thing we're looking for, but the paper is too faded." She handed Dan the yellowed letter.

He sighed and stuffed it back in the bible. Dan surveyed the bridge, his gaze coming to rest on Anna. The two neither moved nor spoke.

Fear and anxiety now fueled Earth's modern societies. And governments fanned the flames. Dan knew the American public was, incrementally, trading freedom for security, yet would attain neither. Knowledge was the real freedom. Yet that craving for enlightenment was now strewn along the roadside of history, replaced by a teddy bear and flowers mentality. Dan knew his government preferred it that way. Satarian technology, if discovered, would be used to strip away any remaining freedoms in America.

Placing the book in a nearby seat, Dan spied something wedged under the control station. He bent down, clearing cobweb, and found a cloth military backpack. He had seen similar packs in Civil War exhibits. Dan gently worked it free. The knapsack was in remarkably good shape, thanks to the dry, Arizona climate.

The couple knelt over the navy-blue pack. Anna nervously touched Dan as he fumbled with buckles, finally throwing open the top flap. The two stared at a small gold cylinder. Hesitating, Dan lifted it. Made of alloy, it was two feet long, maybe a foot wide and surprisingly light. One side was flat, the other side held a large silver lens. Underneath the lens were several multi-colored squares. Slowly turning the cylinder, Dan wondered how something so innocuous could cause so much devastation.

"Doesn't look very impressive, does it?" Anna said, reading his thoughts. He laid it on its flat side. "Not by our standards."

"Is it the beacon we're looking for?"

"Yes."

Dan ran a finger over the colored markings underneath the lens. He hesitated over an orange square. His vision blurred then cleared. A voice whispered through his ear. "It's this one," he said, pressing it.

"Danny, wait—"

A tiny red light flickered above the lens.

"Scanner on," Dan said in Satarian.

A red beam flashed from the lens, covering Dan's eyes.

Anna jumped back. "Danny?"

"I'm okay."

Click. The light vanished, the lens pulsating with green luminosity. Unscathed, Dan stared in fascination at

294

small, flashing squares on the control interface. A metallic, feminine voice spoke from the cylinder. *Nine-zero-zero-six-three activated.*

"God, I hope you know what you're doing," Anna breathed.

Dan's brow furrowed in confusion.

"You told the damn thing to scan," Anna said, rising. "You spoke in Satarian. Don't you remember?"

"No. I mean," Dan stammered, "I remember getting scanned." He glanced to the cylinder. "What do I do next? The beacon looks familiar but—"

The bridge lights flickered then went out. A warning klaxon sounded. Several lights on a control panel across the bridge flashed. A nearby video monitor came alive and small colored patterns began scrolling across the screen.

Dan rose, Anna clutching him. He reached for his flashlight when the overhead lights returned. The klaxon ceased. The patterns on the monitors continued scrolling.

"Mister, you better have a goddamn brainstorm."

He pointed to the nearby monitor. "Why is that still on?" Dan chewed a lip. "Something's changed. I think we're visible."

Anna pointed to the gold cylinder. "Can't you turn that thing on or something so we can get out and be done with this? We've been in here too long."

Ignoring her, Dan knelt by the alien device. "I must be an exact match to Kalyn."

"You saw Kalyn in the dust devils. You said you two could pass for twins."

Mumbling something about needing a miracle, Dan focused on the beacon. The lens pulsated. He touched another square, several lights changing color. "Authorization code two-two-five-zero-alpha-three," he blurted in Satarian.

Authorization code accepted, came the reply. *Standard parameter guidelines responding, transmission guidelines responding. Distress Beacon series six-three activated.* The lens' soft green glow transformed into a flashing red strobe light, each flash followed by a low ping. A small display appeared under the lens, characters scrolling across it.

Dan eyed the device. "We just shot up a flare."

"Can our government detect it?"

"I doubt it. The signal's traveling faster than light."

Anna knelt by her husband, touching his arm. "You hope the Satari hear it before…"

He glanced at her then looked away.

"Don't give in," Anna whispered.

"It's like I was part of the crew," Dan choked.

Anna gave Dan's arm a reassuring squeeze. "It'll all be over soon, baby. Then we can go home and forget this ever happened."

"I can't, Annie! I feel what I'm doing is wrong. We've too much to offer humanity! It carried us—"

"Damnit, McKntyre. Don't do this. That's Kalyn talking!" Anna touched Dan's chin, turning his face toward hers. Her gaze softened. "I need Dan McKntyre back."

*Ping…ping…ping…*the alien signal pounded into Dan like a hammer. "Anna." The two embraced, clinging to one another, hearts pounding.

Ping...ping...ping...

"What's this?" Anna said, running her hand over his right vest pocket.

Dan fished out a small black-and-gray stone. "It's a lucky rock."

"A lucky rock?" Anna said, reaching for it. "Did you pick this up out here?"

"No. A little girl gave it to me. Why?"

"This isn't a rock," Anna said, examining the object. "It's fused composite material, just like what's scattered on the ground around this ship. This so-called 'rock' came from the *Halaena*."

"That's impossible. This twelve-year-old girl gave it to me last month."

"I'm telling you, Danny," Anna said, "this is part of the Halaena's hull!" She eyed Dan. "Who is this girl? What's her name?"

"Elizabeth." He paused. "She never gave me her last name. She was at Charlie's the day of the cookout."

"What was she doing there?"

"She was a friend of Charlie's grandkids. What is this, the Inquisition?" Dan eyed Anna. "Charlie said she was from South Africa and was being treated here in the States for leukemia." Dan looked away, recalling that stormy evening. "She gave me the strangest look. It was as if she recognized me, yet I don't recall ever meeting her."

Anna silently put the rock in Dan's left vest pocket. Snapping the pocket shut, she patted his chest. "Well, maybe she knows something you don't? When we get to Texas, I *definitely* want to meet her. Either she's been up here, or somebody who has, gave it to her."

Ping...ping...ping...

"Gather our things," Dan said, pointing to the blue knapsack, "and put that 'bible' in there."

Anna rose, stuffing the book in the musty backpack. "You know this book's existence is dangerous."

"So is what we're standing in," Dan said. "In a few minutes, there'll be nothing left to trace the book to." He turned his attention back to the beacon. Opening a panel on the side he found a small compartment with a tiny video screen. It flashed four symbols in sequential order. Clipped to the bottom of the panel were instruments that looked like tools. He gave a dry chuckle: one of the tools was nothing but a simple screwdriver. The others were small stainless-steel tubes. The tubes, transparent in the middle, were about four inches long with flat ends.

Dan stared at the compartment in sudden recognition. Removing one of the small tubes, he grabbed the beacon from the floor and stood up, cradling it in his arm.

"Danny, what are you doing?" Anna asked, slinging the shotgun over a shoulder.

"I need another power source." He glanced around, panicked. "There," and he stepped toward the control panel where the remains of Kalyn sat. "I can transfer power from the helm, if there's any left, to the beacon."

Anna gave a puzzled look. "The helm?"

"Never mind, Anna," Dan said, sliding the flashing

beacon under a control station. Clearing away cobwebs, he crawled in after it. "I need to get this finished," he pointed to his head, "before *it* leaves me." Lying on his back, Dan jerked on a bottom panel. It swung away. His hands disappeared inside the compartment. "Hell, I have no idea what I'm doing."

Anna stood nearby, rummaging through the backpack. Closing the flap, she slung if over a shoulder then slung the shotgun over the other. "Danny, look what else I found in the backpack." She held out a small wafer-thin square.

Dan glanced up. "I think it's the ship's log. Whatever it is, it's important. Put it back in the pack and get ready to run like hell."

Anna stared first at the wafers then at Dan with mixed worry and fascination.

"There," Dan said, "that should do it." Sliding out from under the table, he positioned the beacon so the flashing red lens was directly under the open maintenance panel. "Annie girl, get ready."

Dan twisted, feeling the nearness of the skeleton; a twinge of guilt moved through him. He glanced to Anna. "You go now. Head to the bottom of the ship. I'll—"

"No!" Anna snapped. "I'm not leaving you. No argument. End of discussion."

"Jesus, Anna."

Anna stood; arms folded.

"Okay, okay. Would you at least stand by the door and wait for me?"

Sighing, Anna marched to the opening.

Dan worked feverishly. He held the small stainless-steel tube between the lens of the beacon and a power conduit in the control panel. He glanced inside the panel, positioning the lens on the small tube so that it aligned with the power conduit.

Anna paced impatiently. "How much longer?"

"Not now, baby." He worked furiously, sweat forming on his brow and dripping onto the beacon. Pausing, praying, he held the end of the tube with one hand, twisting the other end.

A bright blue laser shot from the upper portion of the tube into the open service panel. Bridge lights flickered. Dan moved the tube slightly and another laser beamed from the bottom into the beacon. A light flashed briefly, then plunged them into darkness.

"Danny?" Anna's flashlight clicked on, illuminating his prone form.

"It's okay," Dan shouted. "Gt ready." He let go of the tube; it remained suspended. Dan's finger hesitated over a control button on the beacon. "Oh, Jesus. Oh, Jesus, please." He paused, then pushed a small colored square. The pinging stopped. The screen under the lens cleared, different symbols appearing.

Dan scrutinized the tiny screen in the blue laser light. The symbols were in threes. Only the middle set was changing. A chill shook him; he was looking at a timer. Dan squirmed out. "Let's go, Annie! Go! Go! Go!"

Anna bolted for the ladder, disappearing below.

Dan tripped over the bar wedged between the bridge doors. His head bounced off the metal floor. Everything momentarily went black.

Warning, came a metallic voice, *overload in the t-mag spiral has occurred. Implosion is imminent* Dan rose, groaning, a wave of nausea hitting him. He hobbled to the ladder. His head throbbed. He grabbed a rung, descending. Anna was already out of sight.

The voice he'd heard on the bridge echoed through the decks: *Warning. An overload in the t-mag spiral has occurred. Implosion is imminent.*

Dan found Anna two decks from the bottom, waiting. He jumped down beside her. He grabbed his temples and groaned.

She touched his arm. "You okay?"

A muffled explosion shook the landing. He shoved Anna to the ladder. "The ship's power converters just failed. It won't be long."

A klaxon shrieked.

Security protocols violated. Termination of systems initiated. Self-destruct sequence initiated.

"What?" Anna screamed as she neared the bottom. "What the hell did you do?"

"What you wanted me to do."

"You set off the self-destruct!"

"The ship will implode first."

Shaking her head, Anna jumped over the last few rungs, landing hard. Dan dropped down beside her.

Anna threw off her knapsack and shouldered her

other gear. Dan followed suit, then slung the shotgun over his shoulder, handing Anna the old pack. They bolted toward the airlock.

Security protocols violated. Termination of all systems initiated. Self-destruct sequence initiated.

The couple was almost to the airlock when the warning changed. *Self-destruct will occur in twenty nikos.* The voice began speaking in monosyllables.

The two rushed into the dark airlock. Throwing herself against a wall, Anna breathed in tearing gasps. Clicking on a flashlight, Dan shot to the control panel. Hand shaking, he located the blue button and mashed it.

Nothing.

"Do something!" Anna shrieked.

"I'm trying!"

The synthesized voice reverberated around them like a death knell.

Dan pounded the control panel in frustration. "Shit!"

Suddenly the red light on the wall flashed and the entrance materialized.

"Sweet Jesus, thank you," Dan breathed, running for Anna. He jerked her toward the exit. His throat tightened; the fear in her eyes unnerved him.

He leapt from the airlock, helping Anna down. She fell into his arms, quivering. She needed rest, yet time was a commodity they could ill afford. Why had he let her talk him into this? They could all be sitting comfortably at home in Texas by now.

The alien voice blared. Anna leaned against Dan, her

breath easing. "We need to go straight up the hill," Dan said, pointing to the woods. "That's the quickest way to safety."

"I'll never make it. Besides, there is no safety if the ship self-destructs first. Let's go back the way we came. At least it's easier."

Dan nodded. The two moved to the spot where the *Halaena* should be invisible. It remained stark, ominous. Dan swore; Anna shoulders sagged. They turned, heading downhill.

"How much time do we have?" Anna asked.

"Hell if I know, Annie." He reached back, helping her through the brush. "Let's pray the beacon implodes before the ship self-destructs."

Anna took his hand as she crawled over a boulder. "What was it you said yesterday? Flat, glassy, and glowing in the dark?"

"I didn't say that. You did." Yesterday seemed a lifetime ago. The couple picked up the pace as they approached the ship's end. Suddenly they were down the hill, open meadow in front of them.

Shrugging off her backpack, Anna tossed Dan the old knapsack and darted for the meadow.

"Run, Annie!" Dan shouted.

Anna sprinted through tall weeds, Dan behind her. They were just clearing the tail-end of the wreckage when a man jumped from behind it, blocking their path. In his hand was .357 Python. Benjamin Morgan appeared beside him. "Today is not a good day for running," Jeffery Albright said, smiling.

21

The white, four-wheel drive pickup whipped behind the rock outcropping and parked next to the jeep. Agent Simon Terrell holstered his .45, grabbed binoculars, then walked to the Jeep. Inside was mostly camping gear. About to search the vehicle, he paused. Leave it to McKntyre to have a surprise waiting. Besides, there would be time for that later. Turning, the agent hiked up the short, steep hill.

He heaved himself over the top, sweat dripping, winded. He yanked out a handkerchief from a back pocket, wiping his forehead.

Terrell scanned the hilltop; only russet-colored boulders jutted from the far end. Two sets of boot prints headed toward the outcropping. He lifted his binoculars, concentrating on the boulders. Nothing. The agent headed for the rocks. Terrell cautiously approached the first large boulder, noticing the ground around it was trampled. He thought of drawing his gun but squashed it; he was not the McKntyres' enemy.

The agent inched around the boulder. As suspected,

the place was empty. A few yards away a small outcropping of rocks marked the hill's edge. Making his way to the outcropping, he knelt, peeking over a small boulder to what lay below. His breath left him as if slugged in the gut.

Across the wide meadow, jutting from a forest of tall pines, was a giant vessel, larger than the largest aircraft carrier. He didn't have to see the inverted triangle and alien characters to know what he was looking at. "Well, now," he said outloud, thinking of the dossiers. "Now things are beginning to make sense. The Wildaers aren't *human*."

How could the government have missed locating something so large? *Why* haven't satellites detected it?

He spotted two people near the vessel's end. They were dwarfed by its massive size. Thinking it was McKntyre and his wife, he focused his binoculars on them, then swore.

"So, Albright and his goon are loose," Terrell murmured. "How the hell did they get out here?" Guns were in their hands. A distant shout came from the wreckage.

Terrell lowered the binoculars to get a broader view. McKntyre and his wife sprinted into sight.

Albright and Morgan crept near the edge of the wreckage. Terrell was about to rise and warn the couple but was too late. The lawyer and Morgan, with guns drawn, bounded into the McKntyres' path.

The agent raised binoculars. Both men trained guns on McKntyre. Albright spoke; Terrell couldn't make out the words.

Moving to get a better view, he heard a murmur in the distance: a helicopter, and getting closer. A *whumpta-*

whumpta echoed off nearby hills, making the helicopter hard to pinpoint. Lying where he was, he'd be spotted from above. He threw himself under a nearby rocky overhang just as a white Jet Ranger shot over at ground level, heading toward the open meadow.

Straining to see, Terrell's foot slipped. He tumbled into a cleft under the overhang. His head struck a rock, and his senses faded.

Tyona Faelian hunched over the edge of her bunk. She stared morosely into darkness, confused by the dissolving mental images. It was still at least two hours before her shift on the bridge. Sleeping fitfully, she had fought her pillow all night.

Sighing, she waved a hand over a small panel near her head, her quarters brightening. Tyona closed her eyes, strange images still fresh in her mind. She dreamt she was on Illysia, a breath of rain in her nostrils. She had never *smelled* rain, but recognized it for what it was: the seeds of change. She stood, arms outstretched, enjoying the pelting of cool drops on flesh. Tyona still saw the lightning flashes, heard the ear-splitting thunder. The wind stirred her hair as she turned, facing the dark, water-laden clouds. Tyona had never experienced a thunderstorm; it had been over a century since one occurred on Serena.

Tyona shivered. Seared in her mind was the tall man standing next to her. He was Illysian. A strange anticipation ripped her as she recalled the haunting look in his gray eyes. He spoke in a strange tongue, yet she understood him, answering him. She laughed and melted into his arms. He kissed her. Heart thumping, Tyona touched her lips. With a disappointed sigh, she hopped off the bed, quickly dressed, and headed for the bridge.

Ason mMyre turned in his seat as the door slid open. "Cannot sleep?"

Tyona stepped through the doorway, somber and forlorn. She was dressed in loose-fitting, dark pants that were tucked into the standard pull-on boots worn by space-crews. A hooded, fireproof tunic and waist sash typified the look of a veteran interstellar traveler.

Tyona silently trudged past Ason, flopping in the chair next to him.

"Want to talk about it?"

Tyona sighed. "The past month I have immersed myself so much in Illysian culture that I feel as if I am one of them."

"Are you dreaming about them yet?"

Tyona shot him an embarrassed look. "I understand and speak their language in my dreams, yet when I wake, I know not what I have said." The memory of the man returned and Tyona eyed her boots, hoping her flushed face did not show.

"Dreaming about it. Indeed, a good sign." Ason glanced at a reading on the control panel then gave her a fatherly smile. "When I was a boy, my grandfather told me the first step in learning another culture was when you dreamt in their language."

"You never used the phonic implants?" Tyona asked, astonished.

"No. I acquired foreign language the hard way, the way we are doing now. But do not misunderstand me. If one has a pressing need to quickly learn another language—as we do—then the implants have their place. I never had that need until now." He paused. "The implants may teach you a language, but they don't teach you the culture that's behind it. And that, young lady, is as important as the words themselves."

"But, Ason, Illysia has so many different cultures and languages, how do we know which one to learn?"

"I selected the language of the makers of the Illysian probe. They're probably the most advanced, at least technologically, of any on the planet. Their language is probably the dominant one."

"And I have barely learned a few phrases." Tyona sighed with worry. "It is so intimidating."

"Get used to it."

Rising, she walked to a nearby window, staring into blackness. "We are less than a day away from our destination, and there is still no sign of the Fleet. It has been over a month and *still* no pursuit." She faced the older man. "Will a Fleet ship greet us at Illysia?"

His face shadowed, he returned to the instruments.

"Ason?"

"That is the most likely scenario." He swiveled around, facing her. "The Fleet will not give up. They must make us an example." He paused. "They cannot let us reach the surface of Illysia because then their job is infinitely more difficult."

Rising, she stepped toward Ason, halting in front of him. Inching up a sleeve, she gingerly touched a tiny red scar on her forearm. For the past one hundred years, all citizens born on Serena or its territories were implanted at birth with a bio-transponder. The reason given by the government was that it would help stave off sickness by boosting the immune system. In addition, it insured that every citizen was accounted for, which, according to the High Council, guaranteed the population's safety.

The small device was implanted just under the skin, containing the entire genetic code of its host. Most knew it was nothing but a sophisticated tracking device, but the penalty for removing it was severe.

Before leaving Serena, Ason used a bio-traser to cut the device from his arm. No sooner had Tyona come aboard than she shoved a forearm in his face. "Get this thing out of me."

She eyed the thin red scar. "If the transponder is removed, how can they still track us?"

"Residual biotons. We've had the devices in for so long that it's affected our blood cells. I'm not sure how, but when pursuing fugitives on other worlds, I was told they could be tracked up to a year after the transponder's removal."

Tyona sighed with disgust.

"There's a positive," Ason said. "We will at least have resistance to Illysian viruses, toxins, and other microbes. By the time the residuals dissipate, we will have developed a natural immunity to their environment." Ason paused. "Tyona, have you any idea the type of world we launch into?"

"Aggressive, hostile?"

"And scared of its own shadow. From what I have studied, they seem almost neurotic. The Illysians are so self-absorbed that they are at the point of becoming stagnant. However, it has been over two hundred years since the last extensive observation was taken. Their 'deep-space' probe is—"

"So," Tyona interrupted, "the only thing we have to go on is the scant information from their probe, *Voyager*?" She enunciated the name slowly.

"Yes—and at least you have the pronunciation correct."

"I'm still skeptical on how one learns another language by your method."

"At the moment, I would entertain other ideas."

They both laughed. It was not because what Ason said was humorous. Actually, Tyona shuddered inside. Their long-term survival was doubtful. If they did not assimilate, or their origin was discovered and they were imprisoned, there would be no rescue. She sighed heavily; they had only their wits, and each other.

A pensive silence ensued. Tyona flopped into a seat. "Ason," she said, hesitating, "I have never questioned your motives, actions, or abilities."

"But?"

"But, have you any idea to the exact location of the *Halaena*?"

"Not in the least."

"Pray tell, you *do* have a plan on how to locate her?"

"I am still working on it."

"You are still working on it?"

Ason began chuckling.

"You find this humorous? I certainly do not!"

"Tyona," Ason said, "I think I know how to locate the ship, or what is left of it."

The young woman gazed at him expectantly.

"The *Halaena's* hull is cobalt-belaium. Those materials are only produced on Serena. We shall simply scan the planet's surface and—"

"That could take forever."

"We are not going anywhere."

"And that is another thing, *Lord Captain*. Suppose we find nothing on the surface; no wreckage, no beacon, no survivors. What then? Return to Serena, pleading for mercy? Or do we just abandon ship, setting up a nice, comfortable home in a world where people *still* use fire, rely on internal combustion machines and the air is choked with filth? Or, maybe we can find an uncomplicated, little world where we are looked upon as gods." She paused. "By now, a huge bounty is on our heads."

"There is another option you failed to mention," Ason replied with irritating cheeriness. Tyona gave a vexed stare.

"We land near their center of government and ask

for political asylum," Ason said. "The dominant government on that world is a republic based on democratic principles, as ours once was. They would understand our request. We could offer the *Elytra* as a token of good faith."

"I can picture the Fleet allowing that to happen," Tyona replied dryly.

The two grew silent.

"From what I have learned of their world," Tyona began, "if the Illysians had stumbled onto any Satarian wreckage, we would be answering to *them*."

Ason nodded. "And do not think that has not crossed the High Council's collective minds. They are mortified that distant cousins may one day challenge them. A technologically advanced, free society of humans could threaten the so-called order the High Council surreptitiously created."

Tyona frowned. "Why do you refer to the Illysians as cousins?"

Before Ason could answer, a piercing beep shattered the calm.

The two scrambled to the master control station. Tyona arrived first and slid into a seat, her fingers playing over an interface. "A Fleet distress signal." She glanced at Ason, hovering over her. "It is from the *Halaena*!"

Ason blinked, momentarily stunned. Dashing back to the helm, he shouted orders. "Lock on to that signal. I want a triangulation emitter on it!"

"Ason, that could damage any nearby Illysian satellites. Remember, we want to be discrete."

"Just do it!" Ason's fingers played over an interface. "I will tweak these engines a bit more. We cannot afford to waste the gift given us."

Interminable minutes passed. The signal from the distress beacon continued beeping. The two worked feverishly to locate its exact origin, praying silently.

"Scans for graviton residue are negative," Ason said. He glanced to Tyona, unable to hide relief. "No sign of a Fleet vessel. Maybe we arrived first." Ason touched a green control surface. "I am taking us out of plus-light. Computer, view-screen on."

The screen suddenly filled with stars. Ason pointed to a bluish marble, brighter than the others. "There it is."

A bright, blue twinkle in the center of the sea of stars began growing, soon recognizable as a planet.

"I am placing us in low orbit," Ason said. "Our sub-light shields are still operable. We should be invisible to their instruments."

"But visually…" Tyona said.

"Only if someone were out here, and the chances of that—"

"Are excellent," Tyona said, studying an instrument. "A manned vehicle is inside our orbit. Detecting five humanoids."

"What is their trajectory?"

"Twelve degrees at eight-one kilometers."

Ason nodded. "Our paths will not cross. Unless they know exactly where to look—with their crude instruments blinded that will not happen—we should not be discovered."

He turned his attention to the planet in the view-screen. "So, that is the mysterious Illysia."

Rising, Tyona looked out the nearby window. "It is beautiful."

A large, blue ball, punctuated with brown and green, filled the window. Here and there white clouds, in long, spiraling wisps, hung above the surface. Tyona stared at a deck of clouds clinging to a large landmass, wondering if the people on the surface felt as she did when the suns were obscured. Then she remembered; there was only one sun here. How strange it would feel to live on a world with only one shadow. Tyona shook inside from fear of the unknown. Taking a deep breath, she calmed. "Do they have climate management?"

"No," Ason replied, "they are years away from weather control. The Illysians are very primitive." Ason chuckled. "I scanned their orbiter. It is very similar to a picture I once saw of one of our early space vessels in a museum on Serena. It was a great loss when that museum was destroyed during The Colonial War." He paused. "Their craft is so cumbersome, crude and fragile it is amazing it does not fall apart. And, they still use chemical rockets for propulsion—chemical rockets!"

"Their crew must indeed be brave," Tyona added. "They pilot a flying coffin."

"But what I would not give to pilot one," Ason said. "That vessel has no anti-grav oscillator. Now that would be *real* flying!"

"So the crew of that orbiter is just floating around

inside? I cannot imagine."

"There will be infinite things, Tyona, that we shall witness but could not imagine. Picture going back several centuries on Serena."

"The cultural similarities to our past is an unbelievable coincidence."

Ason raised a brow. "Coincidence?"

Tyona frowned, about to comment, but decided the discussion was best left for later.

"Have you pin-pointed the source of the distress beacon?" Ason asked.

"Yes." She strode to a large wall-monitor, touching a small colored panel beneath. A blue holographic sphere filled the screen, a light flashing in the upper portion. "The signal originates from the planet's northern hemisphere."

Ason rose, studying the projection.

Tyona touched another colored symbol and the picture zoomed in on a topographic map, a cross-hair in the middle. At its center was a flashing light. "The signal is coming from this continent." She looked at a nearby computer display. "We are fortunate. Even though the continent has a large, industrialized population, the signal emanates from a remote desert region."

"Is it detectable by the inhabitants?"

"Doubtful; there is no indication they posses *t-mag* technology."

Ason stepped back to the helm. "I shall place us in geostationary orbit over the signal. I want a complete scan of the area."

"Yes, sir."

"Are our food and medical inventories geared?"

"Yes." Tyona hesitated. "Our plans for the *Elytra*… are you sure you will not change your mind?"

"We have few options." Ason studied the Illysian orbiter though his instruments. "It is much too risky to allow our technology to fall into hands not prepared to receive it." He paused, chewing a lip. "Rest assured that the Fleet will track the *Elytra*. We must be prepared to follow through with our plan."

The two decided that once they removed what was needed, they would send the Elytra plunging into the nearby sun, fully severing ties with their society, and leaving no trace for the Fleet.

"When we arrive over the signal," Tyona asked. "What then?"

"I will teleport down, survey the area. Something must be left. At the very least, we must retrieve the beacon." Tyona began protesting when the older man held up a hand. "I need you up here, Tyona, if things go wrong."

"But—"

Ason stared, jaw set.

Tyona's eyes lowered. "I understand."

The two fell quiet. Tyona glanced at the control panel. "Instruments detect belaium near the signal's source. Ason, the *Halaena*!" Her excitement was short-lived. "Oh, my," she breathed, glancing at her instruments. "There are five life forms in the area. Human. Four are located near the belaium, the fifth is two hundred twenty meters to the east."

She looked nervously at Ason.

"Teleport me several hundred meters away."

"Suppose you are seen?"

"I will take precautions."

"Ason, wait." Tyona's fingers touched a control. "Our current orbit brought us close to the Illysian vessel."

"Proximity."

"Our orbits are parallel; they will pass within ten kilometers off our starboard. We will be as visible as a *Krauthian* batfish."

Ason sighed, rising. "Time to their approach?"

"Twelve minutes."

"The teleporter is damaged. If we orbit higher it is of no use," Ason said. "If we lower orbit, we will be too close to the atmosphere. Deflectors will drain reserves."

"And no teleporter," Tyona added.

Ason headed for the door. "After I arrive on the surface, move *Elytra* to a higher orbit and stay there until I say otherwise."

"Ason, I have a bad feeling about this. So, what if the Illysians in the vessel see us? What can they do? Their instruments will register nothing." Tyona chewed a lip. "Please do not go down there. Wait until the area is clear."

"I must learn who activated the beacon. The possibility of survivors cannot be discounted." The exit opened. Ason paused in the doorway. "If I am spotted, I will signal for retrieval. If that risks *Elytra's* detection, then so be it." He turned, the door closing silently behind him.

Tyona slammed a small fist on a panel. Shaking her

head, she reluctantly returned to the controls.

Within minutes the ship-to-surface com-channel flashed.

"*Tyona, can you hear me?*" Ason said, voice hushed.

"Yes," she replied, "but your signal is weak."

"*Tyona, my dear, I am lying in tall grass, and looking at the **Halaena**! Her plus-light nacelles are missing, but otherwise, she appears intact.*"

"Ason, your signal is degrading." Tyona touched another instrument. "Interference originates one hundred meters north of your position."

"*The **Halaena's** location.*"

"Ason, distance yourself from the wreckage. You are phasing in and out of teleporter lock."

"*I cannot. There are four Illysians, three men and a woman, near the stern of the ship. If I move, I will be discovered.*"

"But the fifth person, Ason? I still read a fifth human, two-hundred-twenty meters southwest from your position. The reading has not changed in several minutes. Perhaps a sentry."

"*I see no one. Nothing but low hills. Hold while I scan.*"

Tyona shook her head; the interference was growing. She stepped to another workstation.

Ason's quiet, calm voice returned. "*I also have too much interference for accurate readings. As you said, **Halaena**, for some reason, is obstructing the signal.*"

Tyona's hands slid over the controls. Her fingers froze, her gaze riveted on an instrument. She dashed back to the communications station. "Ason, I found the source of interference. A graviton spiral wave is building. The beacon is about to implode!"

"*Tyona, the security procedures to enact a—*"

"Do not argue. Vacate the area!" Another instrument flashed. "Ason, Halaena's self-destruct system just armed!" Silence.

"Ason," she shouted, "if you can hear me, the self-destruct system on the *Halaena* has armed!"

"*Maybe I should warn the Illysians?*" Ason said suddenly. "*Termination time?*"

"Eighteen minutes. And do nothing of the kind. It could make matters worse. I am retrieving you." She touched a small panel, holding her breath.

Nothing happened. No conformation signal, nothing.

"*Tyona, why am I still here?*" came Ason's quiet voice. "*Young lady, you may retrieve whenever you are ready. Please act in haste.*"

"Your signal is degrading. I am recycling the particle rods." Tyona's fingers raced over the teleporter controls. "Standby." She again touched the teleporter control.

Nothing.

"*I am still waiting.*"

Fighting panic, Tyona's fingers played over the controls. "Ason, the gravity displacement in the Halaena casts out a distortion field. It corrupts your teleporter signal. I cannot lock. Move away!"

"*I cannot believe my eyes!*" he said suddenly. "*It is impossible, but there they are.*"

"Ason, what is it?" Tyona said, her fingers moving over various control interfaces. "What do you see?"

"*A young man and woman who look amazingly like my parents. I know that is preposterous, but there they are, not a hundred meters from me. Two men are aiming what appear to be weapons at them.*"

"Ason, you are seeing what you want to see." Tyona replied. Swallowing hard, she concentrated on the task at hand. As her fingers worked expertly over the different control surfaces, she talked, trying to calm them both. "Maybe it is your father's ishara?"

"***Isharas*** *do not converse with strangers.*"

Before Tyona could reply, an instrument flashed on the far end of her console. Glancing at the reading, her shoulders sagged. She leaned toward the communications console. "For what it is worth, the Illysian orbiter is approaching. Within visual any moment."

"*Wave to them. That will give them pause.*"

"Ason, this is no time for joking."

"*Suggestions?*"

She returned to her instruments. "I know you cannot escape the self-destruct blast, but if you distance yourself from the graviton wave interference, I believe I can retrieve you. I almost have a lock—wait—I have you!" She touched an icon. There was a flash and the teleporter controls went dead.

"Ason?"

Silence.

"Ason!"

Buzz…

"No, no." Tyona choked. She scanned the instruments for life signs or radiation in the vicinity of the Halaena. The instruments failed to respond. Although activated, they were frozen. Her first thought was that the Illysians had sabotaged the ship's sensors. Maybe they were more advanced than first believed? She hung a head, stifling tears. Now everything depended on her.

Composing herself, Tyona rose, peering out a window. To one side was the planet's surface. She glanced left and spotted it: a tiny delta-wing craft converging on the *Elytra*. "Brave fools," she murmured. "The proton fields around our engines, alone, will shatter your fragile little vessel."

Yet she understood their curiosity; in their place she would do the same. Tyona prepared to move *Elytra* to higher orbit.

All five astronauts, three on the lower deck and two on the upper, stared out the starboard windows of the United States space shuttle *Orion*.

"What-the-fuck. Look at the size of that mother!"

"That thing's as long as three football fields."

"It can't be Soviet."

"If it is, we're in deep doo-doo."

"We're already in neck-deep."

"Johnny, get the—"

"I'm right behind you and it's rolling." Johnny bobbed up and down in weightlessness, aiming a video camera. Grabbing a hand-hold, he steadied himself. "Man, oh, man, wait until my old lady sees this."

Strapped into the captain's chair on the flight deck, Colonel Brian Chandler's gaze shifted from a control panel to the window. "Houston," he shouted into a headset, "I don't care what your friggin' instruments show. I'm looking at the biggest goddamn spacecraft I've ever seen, and it's not ten klics off our starboard." He punched several buttons, then flipped a toggle switch. "I just completed computer diagnostics. Everything checks out, yet there's nothing on radar. According to onboard systems, it's not there, but we all have a visual."

"*Brian*," said the voice in his headset, "*we show nothing in your vicinity. Can you describe it?*"

The colonel tore his gaze from the window and glanced to his co-pilot, Major Curtis Linsky. "How long would you say it is, Link? A thousand feet?"

"Hell yeah, at least," the major said, gawking.

"Houston, did you copy that? Four, maybe five hundred meters in length and it's triangular shaped."

"*A quarter mile long?*"

The colonel adjusted his mike. "Roger that, Houston. The fuselage alone is over four hundred meters. On one end are two large nacelles. There's a kind of luminosity to them, probably its power source. The craft is just sitting there, like it's waiting on us."

"*We copy, **Orion**. Are your cameras zeroed in?*"

"Affirmative, Houston," the colonel said, "and Johnny's down below with his video camera rolling."

"*Orion, we calculate you have enough fuel to return for a closer look. Download these figures and—*" Crackle...

"Houston? Come in, Houston." The colonel glanced to the co-pilot. "Link, we lost them. Check the antenna-gain and I'll—" Chandler's words died.

A huge shadow crept over the flight deck, blocking the sun. The two astronauts simultaneously looked through overhead windows, jaws dropping.

Overhead, a massive white object, lights blinking, slid eerily by.

"Sweet mother of Jesus," Link breathed, crossing himself.

An ear-splitting buzz shot through the intercom and both men yanked off headsets. Sparks spewed from control panels; warning lights flashed and alarms shrieked. The crew was slammed down by instant gravity. The shuttle spun wildly.

Chandler regained control of the orbiter. The crew was bruised and frightened, but unhurt. Even though the shuttle was knocked several miles away, the astronauts still had both vessels in sight.

The major laughed nervously. "A raft hitting an aircraft carrier." He pointed out the window to the long, rectangular vessel in the distance. "That one must be two miles long. Where the hell did these things come from, Brian?"

"The question is: what are they doing *here*? God,

let's hope we didn't piss'em off." The colonel flipped a toggle switch. "Houston. Come in Houston."

Buzz.

The shuttle crew watched helplessly as the larger ship crept toward the smaller, triangular-shaped vessel. Suddenly stars disappeared on the other side of the smaller vessel and the blackness behind it blurred. The ghostly outline of another spacecraft began materializing.

The colonel stared dumbly. "Jesus Christ. It just came out of nowhere!"

Tyona touched the controls to move *Elytra* out of orbit when another instrument flashed. She froze. "How can that be? Computer, port screen on."

A monstrous, rectangular vessel filled the monitor. Identical to the *Antaries*, it lay thirty kilometers off her port, gliding her way.

"A shrouding system!"

The same instrument flashed again. Tyona ignored it. Swallowing hard, she glanced into the view-screen just as a large shadow appeared in the window. A huge vessel was now parked between her and the planet below. Tyona choked as she watched an identical vessel suddenly materialize off her starboard, effectively surrounding the *Elytra*.

Tyona chewed her lip. Perspiration beaded her brow. She bolted to the weapons station. Fingers danced across the control interface. A warning light flashed. She looked up just in time to see a burst of light coming at her.

She unconsciously ducked as her instrument console exploded, slamming her into a wall. Stunned, she fell to the deck and rolled over, groaning. A warning klaxon screamed and she grabbed the console edge, struggling. Tyona gasped, her chest throbbing. Her right side seared.

Her training and experience took over. Ignoring the pain, Tyona surveyed the smoke-filled bridge, bathed in infrared light. The weapons station was on fire, sparks cascading from a wall panel. The warning klaxon, along with other alarms, continued wailing.

A strong voice boomed through confusion. *"Tyona!"*

She limped to the com-link. "Ason! I am under attack!"

"There are two bright specks in the sky. The Fleet?"

"Yes—I am surrounded! They neutralized our weapons, and power converters are off-line. I am on auxiliary power."

"Tyona, abandon ship! They will give no quarter."

"The teleporters are down. I must reroute power from the engines to teleporter relays."

"Do what you must, just get out—" Communications became garbled, *"dangerous...must help them—"* Buzz...

Tyona staggered to the helm, working feverishly. The teleporter controls came alive. "Yes!" Shaking, she forced herself to focus. Lesser individuals would be curled on the floor in a fetal position, awaiting the inevitable, but not Tyona Faelian. Her will to live was potent. She wondered if the Fleet thought of that. Her throat tightened; the two

Quasar Class starships surrounding *Elytra* were her answer.

A plan flashed as she worked on the teleporter controls. It would be so easy to overload those high-strung, Talarian engines. She could take out at least one Fleet ship, maybe both. By the time the overload was detected—*boom*. Sighing, Tyona dismissed the thought. *She* would not be the cause of death for the innocent crewman aboard the Illysian orbiter.

Tyona was almost complete with the power transfer when the *Elytra* shook. She did not have to look at her instruments to know they had locked on tractor-beams. Tyona knew the scenario: the *Elytra* would be towed away from the planet, then vaporized

Warning lights flashed chaotically through the choking smoke. The *Elytra* had represented freedom, home and security. Glancing around, Tyona swallowed; sentimentality was a luxury she could not afford.

Tyona prepared to abandon ship. If she used the escape pod, they would grab her. The teleporter was her only hope. She programmed final commands, then bolted for the exit. The door and part of the bulkhead was now a pile of smoldering junk. Tyona squeezed through a narrow, jagged opening. The teleporter station was one deck below. Not risking the elevator, she grabbed the nearby ladder and hopped down the rungs. Landing on her feet, she doubled over with pain, trying to catch her breath. An explosion tossed her against a wall. Another bulkhead gave way and metal beams crashed behind her. Roaring flames swept her way. She yanked a hood over her head and fell. Flames jetted within inches, showering her with hot debris. They retreated. She jumped up, knocked fire from her tunic and raced for dear life toward the teleport chamber. A choking, toxic cloud blanketed the deck.

Coughing uncontrollably, Tyona stumbled onto a teleporter pad, then touched the controls near her shoulder.

Nothing happened.

Tears streaked her cheeks as she punched on the controls again.

Nothing.

Noxious smoke began filling the chamber and she gagged. The vessel swayed and the deck began collapsing. *"Fatal decompression, abandon ship,"* blared a synthesized voice. *"Fatal decompression, abandon ship."*

She gulped air. Refusing to give up, she weakly punched on the controls, smoke and heat filling her lungs. Fighting to remain conscious, her eyes slowly rolled back in her head. Tyona clawed feebly at the console, fingers sliding off. Leaning against the chamber wall, she collapsed.

The crew of *Orion* gawked as another gigantic vessel suddenly materialized opposite the triangular craft. The two starships, as birds of prey, were poised ominously above the smaller vessel. A ball of light left the bow of the larger ship. It exploded into the smaller vessel's hull, chunks of debris spiraling away.

"Jesus! They're taking pot-shots at it!" Linsky

shouted

The entire crew crammed onto the small flight deck, faces glued to windows. One astronaut held a video camera.

Colonel Chandler continued trying futilely to contact Houston. "Those things out there have jammed communications." He glanced at the crew; jaw tight. "Let's pray we're not even a flea on a gnat's ass."

Grim silence fell. All knew the vessels were extraterrestrial, probably from some distant star system. What was more disturbing was the aliens' propensity toward force. The foremost question in their minds was: would the aliens contact Earth, or attack it? If they chose the latter, Earth wouldn't stand a chance.

"Son-of-a-bitch! Would you look at that!" someone cried.

Bright yellow beams shot from underneath the two larger vessels, engulfing the smaller craft. Both vessels moved away, their prize in tow. After several seconds the alien ships were out of sight, bright yellow beams receding in the distance.

Major Linsky turned to the rest of the crew, breathing a sigh of relief. "I guess that's that."
The whole crew began speaking at once. Suddenly there was a flash in the direction of the vessels. A long second passed, then a blazing orange fireball as bright as the sun bathed the small shuttle cabin. The astronauts held up arms, shielding themselves from the intense glare. After several seconds, the light faded. The crew of *Orion* gazed into the black emptiness of space, and they were silent.

23

"Well, if it's not the Off Brothers, Jack and Jerk," Dan said. "You two make losing a virtue."

"But look who's holding the gun," Albright replied. "I apologize," Dan said. "Next time I kick your ass I'll try not to hurt your feelings."

"Your 'ass-kicking' days are over, buddy." Turning to Anna, Albright pointed his gun to the wreckage. "Why didn't you tell me about this?"

Dan noticed how the lawyer treated the weapon; a novice. He prayed Albright repeated the gesture.
The pistol in Morgan's hand never budged, his eyes never leaving Dan. The Apache was an experienced killer, and the one that McKntyre *should* be concerned with. Morgan was cold and calculating, contrasted to Albright, who was wrapped in an orgy of passion and self-glorification. Morgan never killed from emotion; emotion got in the way. Profit was his game.

"I'll ask you again, bitch," Albright snarled, "why didn't you—"

"Fuck you."

"I'll fix that attitude," Albright said, moving where he could keep both the couple and the wreckage in sight. He glanced to Dan. "Why were you running?"

"Today is not a good day for explosions either," Dan said. "That thing is about to go up."

"Oh, really?" Albright replied. "No, I think you two found something inside and are trying to cover it so you can return later."

"Then why would we run right into an ambush?" Albright hesitated and glanced sidelong at the wreckage. Morgan fidgeted, eyes darting to the spacecraft.

"I've got a better idea," Albright began. "We'll *all* take a walk inside. Obviously, you two found a way in," he glanced to the jagged top, "other than going in from up there."

Morgan said, "Boss, maybe the guy's right. *Why* were they running?"

"It's nothing but a ruse." His eyes returned to Dan. "I need to be here when the others arrive, to protect my interest." He smiled. "After all, *I* am the first one to discover this wreckage."

Dan's shotgun bumped his back. They hadn't spotted the riot gun slung upside down behind the old knapsack on his shoulder. Could he get to it in time? He had to try.

Eyeing Dan, Albright spoke into a hand-held radio. "Everything's secure."

"How do you know there's no one else around?" Dan asked.

"Because I know her," Albright said, nodding to Anna. "She works alone. *Doctor* Wildaer needed you for something, otherwise—"

Anna cut him off. "It's Doctor *McKntyre* now."

Albright's mouth tightened. He waved his gun at Dan. "Off with the packs. We're taking a little walk. You're going to show me the way in."

The *whump-whump* of a helicopter echoed in the distance.

Dan glanced at Anna; his eyes narrowed and he gave her a subtle nod.

"Mr. Albright," the Indian said, "maybe we ought to let the ones in the chopper go in first. These two were running from *something*." He paused. "I've got bad vibes."

"I want my piece of the pie," Albright snapped at the big man. The lawyer turned back to Dan. "I said off with the gear."

Dan began shrugging off the pack.

"We're going in there," he waved the gun at the wreckage, "and—"

In the blink of an eye, Dan had the shotgun in hand and aimed at Albright. As he squeezed the trigger, Morgan shot him.

Dan staggered backwards from the bullet's impact but managed a shot in the lawyer's direction. Albright jerked back, his right shoulder crimson.

Dan felt the hot smack of led hit him. He twisted, caught himself, then fell, face down.

"Danny!" Anna screamed, running to her husband.

Albright leveled his gun and fired.

Anna stumbled, but kept running.

The lawyer shot her again and she fell. After a moment she began crawling towards Dan. Albright fired at the prone, moving figure in the grass, but missed. Swearing, he moved closer, firing a fourth time.

Anna stopped moving.

Morgan ran to Albright, who was holding a hand to his shoulder. "You okay, boss?"

"Yeah, most of it missed me."

A white helicopter appeared over a low hill and circled the area. Albright fished out a handkerchief. "Make sure she's dead. I'm going to meet the others."

"What about him?" the big man said, nodding to the fallen body of Dan.

"He's had it," Albright said, pressing the handkerchief against his shoulder, "but check him anyway. And grab their packs."

Morgan nodded and stepped to the fallen body of Anna, Albright hurrying to the landing helicopter.

Gun trained on her, Morgan approached Anna's body. She lay on her side, eyes closed, facing him. A crimson stain pooled on the ground near her breasts. Morgan halted a few feet from her, shaking his head and sighing. "What a waste." He shoved the gun in his waistband.

Anna's eye flew open, two silver orbs blazing.

Morgan froze, a giant statue, his will suddenly snatched away. Try as he might, he couldn't tear his black eyes from her piercing gaze.

"Today, you heard the crow cry, did you not, *Big Tree*?" Anna said, speaking in perfect Athabaskan.

Big Tree was Morgan's Apache name.

"I have heard his cry before," Morgan replied in his native tongue. "The crow's message rings hollow."

"Tell me, Big Tree, what does he say? What does the crow tell you?"

"Death. The crow speaks of death."

"And you heard many crows today, all crying of death! The death of *Big Tree* the coward, the murderer of women and children. You are not a warrior. You are a dog. You dishonor your people! Soon, you will be nothing but carrion."

Instantly Morgan's vision faded into black. He cried out. The darkness cleared and he was gazing at a blue sky, black spots floating in the clear air. He tried averting his eyes but couldn't. Without warning, the spots dived at him.

The crows cawed his name. A huge black beak filled his vision, then another, and another. A hard beak, like a steel rod, jabbed at one of his eyes. He tried to move an arm to swat it away. Nothing. Claws dug into the flesh on his head and shoulders. He screamed. A crow flew away with one of his eyes in its beak.

Something exploded. The crows vanished. Morgan found himself on his knees, shaking and sweating. Glancing up, he saw the lawyer standing over Anna, his gun pointed at her. She was on her back, eyes closed, another dark stain swelling the sand.

"You fool!" Albright yelled. "What did I tell you about their eyes? You're lucky you're still alive and not a quivering pile of shit."

Morgan slowly rose.

Their attention shifted to the chopping sound overhead. Both watched a helicopter descend in an open area near the huge spacecraft.

Albright pointed with his pistol to the nearby body of Dan. "Check him out while I take care of business. Be careful this time, and don't forget about their packs. No one sees them, got it?"

Morgan nodded feebly, still feeling the effects of the "vision." He avoided looking at Anna while working his way to the other body. Dan lay sprawled in a puddle of blood, red blotches smearing the tall brush around him. Morgan's pistol was aimed at Dan's prone form as he jabbed him with a booted toe.

Nothing.

Satisfied Dan was dead, Morgan shoved his pistol back in his waistband and began gathering the couple's gear.

On a nearby hill a man crawled up a crevice at the base of a large boulder, his boots digging into loose gravel. Groaning, Simon Terrell rose and a wave of nausea hit him. Sliding a hand from his temple, he stared at the red streaks on his fingers. He wiped them on his pants and checked his holster. His pistol was still there, and he could feel the binoculars hanging from his neck. The agent looked around for his sunglasses and found what was left of them at the bottom of the crevice. Retrieving his squashed cap from the ground, he punched a fist in it, then gingerly worked it on. The nausea easing, he staggered to the hill's edge.

The last thing Terrell recalled was the chopper flying over. He glanced at his watch; he'd been out only ten minutes, yet it seemed much longer. He vaguely recalled hearing gunshots.

Terrell reached the last rock. A white Jet Ranger sat in an open area near the wreckage. Two figures emerged from the helicopter's front door while four men in black SWAT gear piled out the back. They fanned out, combing the area.

Another figure caught Terrell's attention. He raised binoculars: Albright, running toward the helicopter. Terrell looked around for Morgan and spotted him on the other side of the wreckage. He appeared to be searching the ground. Where were the McKntyres?

The agent focused on the two men approaching Albright. Suddenly Terrell dropped the binoculars and stared blankly, not wanting to believe what he'd just seen. Swallowing hard, Terrell forced the binoculars up again. Senator George Perryman shook Albright's hand. FBI Director Harlan Fairchild stood next to him. So, the Chief was in on it.

Terrell lowered the binoculars. But shouldn't he be?

That wreckage jeopardized national security. But what was Albright's part? And why was the Senator here? Perryman *did* oversee the FBI budget appropriations committee. Maybe, Terrell mused, Perryman's appearance was designed to loosen congressional purse strings.

Terrell recalled rumors about the Senator. It was said he could be bought. Yet when news of the Senator's behavior was brought to the Bureau's attention, it was always quashed.

Terrell assumed the Director knew the score. Surely there were ethical reasons for the Director to look the other way. But now, with both the Senator and the Director embracing a scoundrel like Albright… The agent gave a disgusted laugh, tapping a finger to cracked lips.

Terrell's eyes pressed against the binoculars again. Director Fairchild shook Albright's hand while pointing to the attorney's shoulder. Albright gestured behind him, waving off Fairchild.

Terrell focused on the red smear on the lawyer's right shoulder. The agent made a quick scan for the McKntyres. Did they get away? Yet Terrell knew if McKntyre had escaped, Albright and Morgan would be dead. Terrell fought to steady the binoculars as he scanned the area.

24

Albright, Perryman and Fairchild stood outside the helicopter rotor wash. Albright said, "We were ambushed. They were waiting for us."

"They?" the Director replied. Harlan Fairchild, a distinguished looking man of fifty, was medium height and slightly overweight. Clean-shaven, his short, dark hair was shiny and combed straight back. His piercing blue eyes scrutinized Albright. "I thought your ex was the only person who knew about this place?"

"Her new husband was with her," the lawyer said. "But don't worry, they're both out of the picture—permanently."

Senator Perryman turned to Fairchild. "Her husband was that McKntyre fellow I told you about, the one that killed my son." Glancing back at Albright, Perryman gave a satisfied smile. "Good job."

At sixty-one years of age, Senator George Perryman could easily pass for a man in his early forties. Possessing that charismatic personality that is so often found in people of his ilk, Perryman was the consummate politician. Trustworthiness oozed from every pore. And the public bought it.

Perryman was never disappointed in the general public's irrefutable stupidity. Keeping in tune with his constituents' shallowness, he was careful to present himself as a champion of the little people. Naturally the public loved him; he was in his third term.

The senator was handsome, especially considering his age. He was tall with a trim build. Carefully groomed gray-blond hair just touched his ears and collar. He had a gray-streaked, neatly trimmed goatee that stood out starkly in his narrow, tanned face. His deep-set, piercing green eyes could bore through a person.

The senator *always* got what he wanted. Anyone in his way suddenly found him or herself having a run of bad luck. The "lucky" ones only suffered financial ruin. The less fortunate suddenly had an "accident". Perryman chose his allies carefully. Jeffery Albright was an example. The attorney was an excellent spin-doctor and insulated Perryman from the unsavory.

Perryman had made powerful connections over the years and wasn't afraid to use them. When he got wind of an FBI investigation into a possible extraterrestrial visit, he was at first leery. But the Bureau was treating *this* investigation differently, with utmost secrecy.

The Senator soon learned Albright's ex-wife, already linked to his adopted son's death, was at the center of the extraterrestrial inquest. That was too close. His son's demise already brought unwanted attention to his personal life. Perryman could ill afford further shenanigans.

Very subtly, he began scrutinizing Anna Wildaer. He learned that her age—or lack thereof—along with possible extraterrestrial contacts, was the target of the investigation. Then when he came across those top-secret NASA photos, he smelled a gold mine.

Perryman learned about Wildaer's mysterious visits to Sentinel Peak. Growing up in Arizona, he'd heard rumors about the mountain, but discounted them. Yet Wildaer was a professional and wouldn't waste time in a remote area unless there was reason. Last week he decided to check it out. Perryman took a plane over the mountain; nothing.

A relative's recent death broke things open. A few days earlier, Perryman's grandfather, at 104, lie gasping on his deathbed, claiming he was from a planet eighty-eight light years away. He said he was ordered to sabotage his vessel. It crashed on Sentinel Peak around *140* years ago and he was one of only eighteen survivors, but there were four direct descendants still alive. Humoring him, the Senator asked if he, George, was a direct descendant. "No," the old man croaked, "your blood is mixed with *Illysian.*" Perryman asked who or what was "Illysian." His grandfather only waved a frail hand. The Senator asked about the direct descendants and the old man became tight-lipped. Moments before passing away, his grandfather claimed he was *358* years old, then asked forgiveness for his crewmates' deaths and the anguish he caused the survivors. Perryman would have thought the old man senile and blown it off if it wasn't for the FBI investigation. The Senator was still skeptical; the whole story was absurd.

Yet, what if there was something up on that plateau? Why else would the Wildaer girl go up there? Maybe his grandfather and her had met? If the FBI files were correct, Wildaer was descended from a long-lived race of people.

In less than thirty minutes Perryman was on a secure line to Fairchild. The Director owed him several favors; Perryman would collect. The Senator wanted the Wildaer case closed ASAP. He told Fairchild there was a potential for billions to be made. His next call went to Albright.

Now here they all stood. Perryman glanced to the giant spacecraft more in worry than awe. His concern was not with who built it, but what he and the others would do with it. Why wasn't it spotted before? He saw it plainly from the helicopter as they came in. Why was it suddenly visible?

He was expecting only a few bits of twisted metal, not the Empire State Building. The place would soon be crawling with government agents. "We're wasting time, gentleman," Perryman said, wiping sunglasses with a handkerchief. "I don't have to tell you why."

"If we can locate its control center," Fairchild said, "we'll have the meat of the technology that kept it invisible, maybe even find a living being. At the very least, something is still intact." He looked at the others. "You know the government will end up with this thing, and it'll be squelched. The meter's ticking. Let's make our risks worthwhile."

Albright curled a lip at the two men. "This is asinine.

This spaceship can't be kept a secret!" He pointed to the wreckage, sneering. "When the media gets wind of this—and they will—there'll be news choppers, mini-cams and anorexic women holding microphones, rushing all over the frigging place."

"Could we claim 'salvage rights?'" Perryman asked.

"I can't believe I heard that," Fairchild said. "What do you think this is? Fucking finder's-keepers? When my guys locate this, even a grasshopper won't get within twenty miles. Nobody in, nobody out—that includes airspace. And if you don't think they wouldn't shoot down civilian aircraft," he gave them a hard glance, "think again."

"The public would demand answers," Albright said.

Perryman laughed. "The public is stupid. Give them a video and liquor store, cheap rent, cheap cable TV, cheap gas, and promise the lottery winnings will be increased, and they'll believe any damn thing you say."

After a momentary silence, Fairchild nodded toward the bodies of Dan and Anna. "Were those two inside?" Albright shrugged. "Like I said, we had little time for conversation. Morgan and I were looking for a way into this thing, when McKntyre surprised us and opened fire."

Silent, Fairchild eyed Albright.

"We need to find a way inside," Perryman said. "Grab what we can and go. I know some software firms that would piss all over themselves at the sight of this."

"I think we can get in from up there," Fairchild said, pointing toward the top. "I saw cracks in the hull as we flew over. I'm sure there's room to land." The others nodded.

Fairchild signaled to his men and everyone headed to the helicopter.

Albright shouted for Morgan to get the McKntyres' bodies ready for transport.

Nodding, Morgan headed for where Dan McKntyre had fallen, giving the area one last inspection.

The chopper lifted off, flying to the top of the huge starship. Always cautious, Fairchild left one man on the ground.

The helicopter hovered over the top-rear of the vessel long enough to disgorge a black-clad man. He darted for the edge of the wreckage and knelt, sniper rifle in his arms.

The chopper skirted the top of the hull and landed near a gaping fissure, scattering loose pieces of the ship's skin. With the exception of the pilot, everyone climbed out, sprinting to the jagged tear in the fuselage. The opening was at least twenty feet long and two yards wide. Naked superstructure was exposed like rib bones on a giant, beached sea creature. What looked like a catwalk was visible fifteen feet inside the vessel.

Perryman cocked his head. "What the hell is that racket?"

Fairchild gazed into the dark interior. "Sounds like someone speaking over an intercom." He paused, jaw tightening. "It doesn't matter. We've come too far to back out now. Let's get this over with."

The Director spoke into a hand-held radio. The chopper lifted, then came to rest nearby, straddling part of the opening. Two black-uniformed men hooked a chain ladder to a landing skid. Tossing the other end into the fissure, they shimmied down into the dim, cavernous interior. After securing the ladder to the catwalk, they turned, Uzis in hand, and cautiously crept toward the front of the ship.

Fairchild was next down the ladder. Perryman stepped down then halted just inside the opening, glancing at Albright. "You coming?"

Albright hesitated, glancing to the chopper. "Yeah, I'll be right behind."

Perryman paused, his gaze following Albright's. Rotor blades spun lazily, the pilot preoccupied with a chart. He glanced back to the lawyer. "Make it quick." The senator disappeared inside the spacecraft.

Perryman and Fairchild surveyed the gloom, pausing with each tentative step as if in rhythm to the feminine voice reverberating around them. The alien words echoed in monosyllabic cadence, slicing through shadows like a scythe.

Perryman frowned. "What's she saying?"

"Who knows? Probably an automated alarm that Wildaer and her husband triggered." Fairchild chuckled. Perryman nodded. Craning, he peered down the catwalk, hoping to glimpse Fairchild's men, but they had disappeared into the gloom.

Stepping lightly, Fairchild seemed to focus on the strange, feminine voice. His gait slowed. "That rhythmic tone is familiar...the words distinctly paced." Fairchild halted.

The Senator glanced at him nervously. "What is it?"

Fairchild jerked around, face ashen.

"What's wrong?" Perryman shrieked.

"It's a countdown."

A muffled explosion came from the front of the craft. A cry was drowned by the torturous sound of twisting metal. Another explosion and the catwalk vibrated. The two turned, bolting back to the ladder.

Outside, Morgan looked up at the sound of the blast. Wafts of gray smoke began drifting from the top of the wreckage. He'd had enough. Turning to run, Morgan suddenly spotted a blue knapsack lying near McKntyre's body. He hesitated, than ran for it. Licking lips, he reached down. The Indian froze. Where was McKntyre's shotgun? "Oh, shit!" He fumbled for his pistol just as Dan rolled over. Morgan stared blankly into the cannon barrel of the twelve-gauge.

"Bubba, you're outta' chips." The shotgun jumped in Dan's hand. A heavy boom echoed across the plateau.

The charge of buckshot hit Morgan in the face point-blank. Blood, teeth, bone and brain-matter fanned across weeds as Morgan's head, from the mouth up, vanished in red mist. Blown backwards, the almost headless body hit the ground like a sack of potatoes.

Dan's first thoughts were of Anna. He struggled to rise. Pain split his side. Using the shotgun as a crutch and bleeding profusely, he stumbled toward Anna's prone form.

At that moment a black-clad man ran from around the corner of the wreckage. He raised his Uzi.

A beam of light streaked from the brush near Anna, striking the man in the chest. The man was hurled backwards, coming down hard several yards away. Blue light engulfed the lifeless body then dissipated.

Almost blind with pain, Dan ignored the display. Blood sloshed in his boot; his left leg dragged as he limped toward Anna's still form. "I'm coming, baby," he gasped hoarsely. "I'm almost there." He glanced to the top the wreckage. A man kneeled, aimed a rifle, then lowered it and glanced back, distracted. Dan hurried, stumbling.

A tall man appeared from the grass near Anna. He faced Dan and held up his right hand, palm out. "I am friend," he said in broken English.

Dan swayed. "Then help me." He pushed past the older man. "My wife's been shot. We need to get her to a hospital."

The man stepped aside, staring after Dan. After a moment he dashed past Dan to where Anna lay. Kneeling beside her, he quickly pulled a small metal disk from a pouch and scanned it over her chest, then over the wounds in her shoulder and stomach.

Dan approached the still form of his wife. He dropped the shotgun and knelt next to her. "Annie, baby," he whispered. He touched her neck, feeling only a faint pulse. He ran a hand over her blood-caked hair, casting a tearful glance at the man next to him.

The man continued moving the metallic disk over her wounds.

Anna coughed once and her eyes fluttered open. "Danny," she rasped.

"Shh, baby, we'll get you help."

Her gaze moved to the strange man next to Dan. About to speak, she began coughing.

"Anna," Dan held her in his arms, "just hang on, baby, just hang on."

Dan turned to the man next to him. "We've got to get away from here." He nodded toward the wreckage. "That thing is going up any second. I don't think I can carry her. Can you help me? Please?" For the first time, Dan studied the stranger's face. Recognition dawned on him and he stared in disbelief. "My God."

The stranger returned Dan's gaze then took Anna from him, lifting her.

Dan rose, fell to a knee, then rolled on his side. "Go on—keep going!" he waved. "Get her out of here! Save yourself!"

The man hesitated. He eased Anna back to the ground and ran over to Dan. Pulling the silver disk from a pouch, he moved it over Dan's wounds.

Dan's pain lessened. His breathing eased. "You are from Serena," Dan said in Satarian.

The man gave a start. "My name is Ason mMyre,"

he said. "I am looking for Kalyn mMyre. Are you him?"

"No. He was my great-grandfather," Dan said, struggling with pain.

"Was?"

"He died over a century ago," Dan nodded toward the wreckage. "What is left of him is in there." Dan winced. "I cannot believe you came all the way from Serena to—"

"He was my father. Does your world not value family?"

Dan glanced at Anna, then back to Ason. "I do." Dan knew there was no time to savor the moment of "first contact." Distancing themselves from the wreckage was the priority. "Do you understand our danger? We have little time."

Ason stared wide-eyed. "You speak my language?"

"Your father's *ishara*." He looked over his shoulder to the wreckage, then back to Ason. "We will answer each other's questions later. Right now we need your help." Dan paused, his strength draining. "Do you have a ship nearby? You must take us with you. Surely you can do more for Anna than we can do here."

"Anna?"

"Anna is my wife." Crawling to where she lay, he cradled her in his arms, kissing her bloodstained cheek. "She is your mother's niece, or great niece or something—good God, man—cannot this wait? Look at her!" Anna coughed blood and Dan squeezed her tighter.

"You were right, my love," Anna whispered, her arm draped loosely around Dan. "They came back." She glanced at Ason. "We are family," she said in Satarian. "You must take us with you."

Ason blinked as if coming out of a trance. "Alas, no. I—we—have nowhere to go. We are fugitives from our own world. Our capture will result in our execution. We seek freedom. We had hoped to quietly assimilate, but now…" Ason paused, eyeing Dan. "We offer technology for asylum."

Dan stared in disbelief. "This cannot be happening." His head sagged. "This isn't happening," he repeated in English.

"Your world is our home now." Ason surveyed the carnage, his eyes narrowing. "The irony of it all. I should have known this is what fate had in store for me. But Tyona—"

"Tyona?" Dan asked in Satarian. "What is Tyona?"

"Not what, but who," he said. "She is my navigator, and like a daughter to me." He paused. "I pray she can cope with your hostile culture." Ason glanced to the sky. "Our vessel is—" Horror swept over his face. "No!"
Dan and Anna followed his gaze, their eyes widening in wonder.

High up were two silver specks. So huge were they that even in Earth orbit, their rectangular shapes were identifiable. A flash came from one of them.

Ason glanced at the couple then stepped away. Touching something on his waist, he spoke into the collar of the hooded tunic. A female voice replied.

Dan couldn't make out what was said, but there was

no mistaking the panic in the woman's voice.

"Danny," Anna said, squinting in pain, "are those Satarian ships?" She glanced toward the stranger. "That man over there seems afraid of them."

"No telling who intercepted the beacon's signal," Dan said. "Besides, you heard him. He's on the run. Could be a criminal for all we know."

Ason dashed back to the couple. Reaching down, he gently lifted Anna. "I will help all I can, but escape from this world, for now, is impossible." Ason shifted Anna in his arms and glanced at Dan. "*We*—you and I—need each other. I shall return for you. We need not go far. We have almost cleared the implosion radius." Turning, Ason carried Anna toward a low, nearby hill.

Dan studied the wreckage behind him, knowing the implosion had begun. Black smoke poured from openings in the hull and a tearing, rending sound echoed across the meadow as though a tornado churned inside it. Dan tried rising, but fell back to a knee, twisting in pain.

Whispering reached his ears. It took a moment for him to recognize Anna's voice, weak from her injuries, and probably asking questions he wasn't meant to hear. "Who will care for my husband after I am gone?" Anna sobbed. "He and Amy will be so alone."

"Do not speak of such things," Ason replied. "You will survive, and so will your man." He glanced at her then looked Dan's way.

Dan shooed Ason on as he struggled to rise. Ason, carrying Anna, reached the edge of the meadow.

Gently easing Anna to the ground, he ran back for Dan. Throwing an arm around him, he half-dragged, half-carried Dan to where Anna lay, easing him down next to her.

"The backpacks!" Dan yelled in English. "You must go back for our things. Your father's mission logs are there!" Dan pointed near the body of Morgan. "Your answers are over there."

Ason wrinkled a brow and glanced to where Dan was pointing.

Suddenly there was a loud thump, followed by the crack of a rifle. Ason staggered backwards, his chest spurting crimson. He collapsed.

Dan glanced to the sound of the shot. A man on top the wreckage dashed out of sight.

Anna cried out, crawling to him, screaming. "God, no!" She shook him.

Flat on his back, Ason blinked slowly. "It appears, young lady, you and I now languish in the same predicament." He coughed. "I pray you and your family will watch over Tyona. She will be even more alone." His gaze remained skyward. The two crafts had disappeared. "Please, Tyona," Ason breathed, "abandon ship. Teleport anywhere. Live another day." A wracking cough tore through him and he rolled over, groaning.

Dan rose. Limping to the fallen Satarian warrior, he dropped by his side. "It can't end this way!" Dan pounded a fist in the ground, screaming. "Damn you all to hell—I'll live only for revenge! I'll hunt every goddamn one of you down, I swear it!"

Suddenly the ground shook as if from an earthquake.

"A graviton wave," Ason whispered. "It appears the beacon won the race—at least we will not be incinerated." Ason glanced at the couple. "Inside *Halaena* is the cauldron of hell. The flow of space and time has turned in on itself. Within moments the starship will cease to exist—as will anything caught in the spiral wave." His gaze met Dan's. "Young man, I recognized the word 'revenge.' Indeed, you may have it sooner than you hoped." His eyes flicked to the wreckage. "The deserving are inside." Ason winced, scrutinizing Dan. "Revenge is whispered sweetly by the unknowing...poisonous for the unforgiving...let it go."

Metallic ringing filled the air, as though a giant slammed a huge hammer against an anvil. Anna covered her ears; Dan and Ason gazed in awe. Huge pieces of the wreckage bent inwards, disintegrating. The craft folded in on itself, creating a gigantic vacuum. Gale force winds whipped weeds around, the wreckage sucking in everything. Tumbleweeds skidded by as Dan crawled to Anna, sheltering her body with his own. Sand and gravel stung them; the wind tugged their clothes.

Dan raised his head, struggling to see. The giant ponderosas that flanked *Halaena's* sides were gone, pulled into the gaping vortex that had once been a starship. A roar thundered across the meadow. All three clung to the ground, a black, horizontal tornado swirling towards them.

Albright kneeled, peering down the chain ladder the two men had descended. The alien voice chilled him.

Suddenly the craft vibrated. The vessel swayed and he grabbed the chopper's landing skid, steadying himself. Men screamed. Gray smoke drifted from several holes in the top.

The lawyer had seen enough. Rising, he collected several pieces of composite material that were scattered about—he would not leave empty-handed. Stepping back to the helicopter, Albright jerked open the right-door, tossed in the chunks of wreckage, then scrambled in.

The pilot turned in confusion. "What the hell?" He froze, staring down the barrel of a .357.

"Get this thing in the air, now!" Albright shouted, pointing the gun at the pilot's head.

The pilot reluctantly obeyed, turning knobs and toggling switches. Rotor-blades rotated sluggishly as the jet engine spooled up. Within moments, the blades were at a rapid whirl. "Where are the others?" he shouted. "We can't leave—"

"Fuck them. We don't have time."

"Have you unhooked the ladder?" he shouted over the roar of the jet turbine. "It'll hold us like an anchor."

"Shit!" Eyeing the pilot, Albright climbed out of the chopper and stepped to where the ladder was attached. He glanced down the hole just in time to see the Senator climbing up. Fairchild was struggling behind.

"Let's get the hell out of here!" Perryman yelled, extending a hand.

Laughing, Albright slapped his hand away. "Us?"
He viciously kicked Perryman in the face.

The Senator screamed and fell back into Fairchild.
The two crashed onto the catwalk below.

Albright unlatched the ladder, tossing it in the hole
after them.

"Albright, you son of a bitch, get us out of here!"
came a muffled shout. Several shots rang from the jagged
opening but the lawyer had already vanished.

"*C'est la vie*," Albright yelled, climbing back into
the chopper. The helicopter precariously lifted.

The sniper on top the wreckage watched events
unfolding. He glanced back to the meadow, then did a double
take. A strangely-dressed man was standing at the far end. In
frustration, the sniper kneeled and fired. He jumped up and
ran toward the moving chopper. It moved out of range before
he reached it. The sniper aimed his rifle at the Jet Ranger
as it sailed over. Just as he squeezed the trigger, the roof he
stood on collapsed. He found himself flying through the air
toward the front of the vessel, debris swirling around him as
he was sucked into the immense gaping maw of a temporal
displacement. A scream died on his lips as he was stretched
then flattened into nothingness.

Lying in the meadow, Dan cradled Anna. Both watched in fascinated horror as the giant vessel disintegrated. Through billowing smoke, Dan caught sight of a helicopter lifting off the wreckage. It rose, then hovered motionless in mid-air. Gradually it was pulled back toward the fiery hell of the alien starship. Yet, even as Dan watched, the chopper's reverse motion stopped and it slowly gained the advantage, pulling away again. Dan's pain was replaced by rage; whoever was in the chopper was escaping.

Flames shot from the engine cowling and the entire helicopter seemed to stretch. All at once it exploded in a giant fireball that was sucked into the wreckage. Large chunks of debris escaped the graviton field and sailed into the air, raining down onto the surrounding countryside.

The concussion from the explosion boomed through the meadow, rolling across the three in the grass. "Jesus Christ!" Dan shouted, ducking as pieces of fiery, twisted metal flew past. In nightmarish slow motion, the large tail section of the Jet Ranger spun crazily in their direction, tumbling end over end. Suddenly picking up speed, it took aim at them as if a parting shot from Albright.

Dan threw himself over his wife. *Woosh*. The tail-boom shot over, showering them with scalding hydraulic fluid. With a loud *thud* it imbedded itself in the ground ten feet away. The tail jutted in the air at an odd angle, the small rotor still attached and spinning wildly.

"What happened?" Anna whispered.

"Paybacks are mother-fuckers," Dan croaked.

The gale force wind had eased. Anna stirred and

Dan moved off of her. "I need…to see," she whispered, struggling to an elbow.

Light flashed overhead. Dan and Anna shielded their faces. After a few moments the light dimmed, then went out.

"The *Elytra*," Ason murmured, "our vessel, is no more." Groaning, Ason sat up. "Tyona," he whispered, his breath coming in ragged gasps, "my dear, sweet Tyona." With superhuman effort, he forced himself to his feet. Staggering, he surveyed their surroundings. "Tyona!" The word came out more whisper than scream. He took a deep breath, winced, then managed something louder. "Tyona!" He scanned the horizon vaguely, as if hoping for a response. His legs quaked. Slowly his gaze came to rest on Dan. Nodding once, he collapsed.

Dan crawled over to the prone form. The Satarian had fallen on his stomach, his head turned to one side. Dan didn't check the older man's pulse; he knew the look of death. Dan touched Ason's long hair. "To think you came all this way, through dangers we could never imagine. You won't be forgotten, my friend." Dan gazed at the fallen *Matair* warrior. "That family reunion will have to wait," he whispered, head bowed.

Anna wept. Her crying grew to a tearing cough. Dragging himself back to Anna, Dan held her as both looked on the holocaust behind them.

The *Halaena* folded in on itself. A cracking, tearing sound rolled across the meadow, echoing off nearby hills. Then, as if someone had flipped a switch, what remained of the *Halaena* vanished. The only trace of her was a deep furrow that retreated into the forest.

Sparks arced from the scorched earth where the vessel had lain. The wind calmed, now blowing gently, stirring their hair. He surveyed their surroundings. Jutting nearby was the giant tombstone of the chopper's tail-boom, the rotor still spinning eerily in the otherwise silent meadow.

"Danny, I'm cold."

Cradling his wife, Dan pressed his face against hers. A wracking pain shot through him and he almost lost consciousness.

"Are we the only ones left?" Anna asked, her voice faint.

"Yeah," Dan gasped. His embrace tightened. "As soon as I get my strength back, I'll get us out of here."

"We're going nowhere," Anna replied. She forced a smile. "I love you, Danny, forever and always." Anna ran a hand feebly over his chin. "You need to shave." Her eyes fluttered closed.

His grip on her loosened. His arms slipped away. The sound of helicopters filled Dan's ears as blackness finally overtook him.

Terrell stared in shock. Rising, he scrambled down the hill to where the McKntyres and the stranger lay. Wading through knee-high weeds, Terrell looked up as three helicopters shot overhead. The white letters FBI were stark against the dark-blue underbelly. One peeled off and circled back to Terrell, the pilot searching for a place to land. The other two continued to where the wreckage had been.

The agent drew up, staring at the prone forms of Dan and Anna. A dark stain grew under them. McKntyre's body lay over his wife's. Blood was everywhere; it reminded Terrell of Vietnam. Kneeling, the agent touched behind Dan's ear, then Anna's. "My God, they're still alive." The agent laid a hand on Dan's bloody shoulder. "Hang on, man. Help's on the way." Rising, his eyes searched for the stranger's body. Discovering it twenty feet off in high weeds, Terrell started for it, then hesitated. A chopper had landed fifty yards away and two men were already out and running toward him. He recognized a tall, slender man: Deputy Director William Heath.

Glancing once more at Ason's nearly-hidden corpse, Terrell reluctantly turned and ran to meet the men. "We need a medivac," Terrell shouted to Heath. "There's two down over there." He pointed in the direction of Dan and Anna. "I don't know if they're going to make it."

"*Careflight* is on the way," Heath said. "What the hell happened here, Terrell?"

"I wish I knew." Turning away, Terrell pretended to search the area, casually meandering to where Ason had fallen. Agents in SWAT gear were already combing the meadow.

"Looks like a goddamn war zone," Heath commented. "I want this place secured. No media, nothing. After *Careflight* departs, I want no one in or out without my approval. Got it?"

"Yes, sir."

"What a clusterfuck," Heath said, stepping to the McKntyres.

Terrell stood over the stranger's body, his heart pounding. The man was on his stomach, an arm outstretched. The agent hesitated then rolled him over. He was dead. The agent sighed, his jaw tightening. A small metal pouch hung from a strap across the man's shoulder.

Terrell glanced around nervously. The Deputy Director and his assistant were occupied with the McKntyres. The other agents were combing a different area and not looking his way. Terrell grabbed the small case, shaking it. Something rattled inside. He searched for a way to open it but found none. Yet he had seen the man pull something from it and treat McKntyre and his wife.

Terrell nervously groped the pouch, finding a tiny black spot near the bottom. He touched it and the top evaporated. Inside were two, silver-colored devices. He snatched them out, jamming them in a back-jean pocket where they barely fit. Terrell quickly searched the body of the strange, longhaired man. The only other thing found was a gold-looking button attached to the collar of the man's tunic. Terrell tried to remove it but it wouldn't come off. He reached for his pocketknife and cut the tiny device from the man's collar, then shoved the device in a jean pocket.

"Who the hell is that?" Heath said.

Rising, Terrell swore under his breath, a forefinger discreetly pushing the knife back in a pocket. "I don't know. I just stumbled on him. Whoever it is, he's had it."

Heath was about to speak when a red-and-white *Careflight* chopper shot over, circling the McKntyres. Another agent stood near the fallen two, radio in hand, directing the helicopter.

Suddenly shouts rang out from the far end of the meadow. Several agents gathered around a wisp of smoke rising from weeds.

Heath lifted the two-way. "What do you have?"

"*It's another body, sir. This one's intact—and alive!*"

"We're on our way. Don't touch a thing!" Heath and Terrell exchanged glances, then broke into a run toward the smoke.

Terrell was first on the scene, Heath trotting breathlessly behind. Other agents crowded in as the two knelt.

The body lay face down, coughing, a hood pulled over its head.

Terrell turned the person over. The woman gasped, gulping air, her hair singed, and her face soot-coated. Smoke rolled off her. Fair skin shone through rips in her scorched clothing. Slowly catching her breath, she looked first at one man then the other, brown eyes wide. Terrell reached for her and she shrank back. Her pensive gaze moved here and there, surveying the surroundings.

"It's okay," Terrell said. "Other than burns, are you injured?"

She stared, trembling.

"She's in shock," Heath said.

A paramedic pushed through the crowd, kneeling in front of the woman.

Glancing at his helmet, she drew back.

"We're here to help you," he said softly. "We're your *friends*."

She gave a start at the word "friend." About to speak, she grabbed her side, wincing in pain.

The paramedic reached down, gently examining her. She remained still as the medic slipped a respirator over her face. "She's suffered smoke inhalation, probably toxic, burns and possible rib fractures." The medic eyed a nearby chunk of metal from the chopper. "I don't see how she's even in one piece, much less alive."

Heath and Terrell rose, stepping aside as another paramedic rushed up.

Heath stared silently at the woman on the ground, then to the tail-boom off in the distance. "Just a friggin' miracle, I guess." Sighing, he glanced to Terrell, then to the men around him. "I want her 'IDed' and a twenty-four-seven guard on her. That goes for those two over there," he pointed to where Dan and Anna lay, "providing they make it." He stepped away, nodding for Terrell to follow. The two men headed toward the blackened area where the spacecraft had lain.

"Miracle my ass," Heath snorted. "That girl wasn't on that chopper. What's going on, Terrell?" He gestured around. "Did you see what happened?"

The veteran agent's pace slowed. Casting a glance in the direction of the McKntyres, Terrell halted, eyeing Heath. "Didn't see a thing. I was tailing the McKntyres when I took a bad fall on the hill behind us. Came down on my head." He pointed to the red gash on his temple. "I was out cold. I came to with this bright light in the sky." Terrell glanced back to where the strange, young woman lay. Two agents were helping paramedics put her on a stretcher. "By the time I got down here, everything is as you see it." He shrugged, glancing at his superior. "I know nothing more than you." Heath scrutinized Terrell, silent.

Terrell's cold, hard eyes returned the Deputy Director's gaze.

"Weren't you taken off the Wildaer case?"

"Yeah."

"Well, now you're back on it—or what's left of it."

Ten minutes later, rotor wash swept over the still bodies of Anna and Ason as the *Careflight* helicopter lifted off, speeding southwest toward Tucson.

Dan groaned, eyes fluttering open, the whine of the helicopter engine filling his ears. He reached for the respirator over his nose and mouth but his arm dropped away. An IV was in his other arm, the end attached to a bottle of plasma hanging from a rack. He spotted a paramedic kneeling over someone in a nearby stretcher. "Anna," Dan said through the respirator.

The paramedic moved to him. "You're going to be all right, just lie still."

Dan focused his attention to the stretcher across from him. A strange young woman, also wearing a respirator, gazed back at him. Her large brown eyes held fear and recognition.

"Where's Anna?"

Within seconds two medics were at his side. One restrained Dan while the other injected him. Dan's struggles weakened, arms dropping. His vision became blurred, and darkness closed in.

The woman hesitantly reached out, touching him.

Unable to focus, he nonetheless felt her caress. He blinked, trying to fight off the darkness overtaking him. Suddenly everything went black, and he knew no more.

"Cardiac arrest!" a paramedic screamed.

26

The man jogged on the shoulder of a quiet country road, small puffs of dust rising with every footfall. Sweat rolled and dripped off his nose. He felt he'd been running on the rough, potholed road forever. Just a little farther, he thought, then he could stop and catch his breath.

He heard a vehicle coming up behind. By the creaking of springs he knew it was a pickup truck. Bouncing along the rough road, it eased up beside him. The man stared straight-ahead, trying to ignore the old pickup keeping pace with him.

"Hey, stranger," shouted a woman's voice from the open window, "don't you think it's time you came back home? Everyone's worried."

"Worried? About me?" the man puffed, picking up speed. "Surely, you jest."

"Do I look like I'm kidding? Amy and the others are waiting for you to make up your damn mind. They can't wait forever."

Drawing up, the man bent over and the pickup halted

next him. Panting, he glanced at the truck. "Jesus, Annie," Dan McKntyre said between breaths, "why did you ruin my day by bringing me back to reality?"

"Come here," Anna said.

Straightening, Dan stepped to the driver's window and gazed silently into Anna's hazel eyes. Shoving his head through the open window, he kissed his wife gently on the lips.

Their kiss lingered, Anna stroking his unshaven chin. "Get in," she whispered, "I'm taking you back home."

He climbed in on the passenger side. As they took off down the road, Dan eyed his wife.

"What are you looking at?"

"When was the last time I told you how beautiful you are, and how much I love you?" Dan said.

"Around eight o'clock this morning."

"Eight o'clock?" Dan shook his head, chuckling. "I guess you wrote that down in your journal then circled it on the calendar, huh?"

Both laughed.

Minutes later the pickup pulled into a long cement circle drive and stopped. In the middle of the drive was a huge magnolia tree in full bloom. Dan climbed out, staring in awe.

His travel-trailer was gone. In its place was an enormous two-story log home. "Baby," he said in a low voice, "you pulled into the wrong driveway. I think—" Turning to Anna, he halted.

Anna had vanished. There was no trace of her or the

old truck. It was as if they'd never existed. He took a step toward the road then halted. A familiar scent hung in the air. Lilacs. Anna's fragrance.

"Annie girl," he whispered. Eyes watering, he swallowed hard. Plopping down where he stood, his head drooped to his chest. "Damn, I need a beer."

Sitting in front of the third story window of Saint Mary's Convalescent Center, Daniel McKntyre stared unblinking into the cool, gray winter day. The skyline of downtown Phoenix filled the horizon. Yet he saw nothing, his once piercing gaze now blank, expressionless.

An older Hispanic woman in a white nurse's uniform grabbed the back of his wheelchair and moved him away.

Suddenly Dan stirred, his eyes focusing. "I need a beer, and in the worst way," he said in a gravely voice.

The woman screamed, letting go of the wheelchair as if it burned. Backing up slowly, chattering in Spanish, she crossed herself.

Dan looked at her, furrowing a brow. "*No habla Ingles?*"

The woman grew silent, quivering.

"*Necesito una cerveza fria,*" Dan said casually.

"A miracle has happened," she whispered in English.

"What miracle?" Dan said innocently. Perplexed, he glanced down. A robe draped loosely over him. He touched the sash. "What's this crap?" Dan found it took concentrated effort to move. His arm suddenly dropped, eyes widening in shock and confusion. "What the hell am I doing in a wheel chair? Those are for cripples." Attempting to rise, he felt like he was glued to the seat. Jaw tightening in determination, Dan grabbed the arms of the wheelchair and pushed.

"No, you're much too weak!" she shouted, backing across the room. Mashing a button on the wall, she darted back to Dan.

Panting with fatigue, Dan managed to push himself up. Wobbly but erect, he took a step and collapsed, flipping the wheelchair on top of him.

"Mr. McKntyre!" the aide screamed, kneeling over him. "Please do not move until help arrives! Someone is on the way."

"This is un-frigging-real!" Dan cursed, lying on his side. "What the hell happened to me? Where am I? I...I should be at home, in Texas." He paused, coughing, trying to clear his throat. "What the fuck?" He coughed again, laying his head on the carpeted floor, his heart thundering. "What's happened to me?"

A pretty nurse in her late twenties walked casually through the door. "So, what is it, Carol? Did you forget to—" The nurse stopped mid-sentence, mouth agape.

"What are you staring at?" Dan said from under the wheelchair.

"My, God!" Turning, she shouted to someone in the hall, then dashed over to Dan. "You're awake!" She touched his arm. "I can't believe you're awake! How do you feel? Are you okay?"

"Do I look like I'm okay? Where the hell am I at?"

Within seconds a male nurse entered and between the three, they worked the wheelchair off of Dan and got him into bed. Propping him up with pillows, they made him as comfortable as possible but refused to answer the myriad of questions Dan shot at them.

"A doctor will be here any second," the male nurse said. "He'll answer everything."

"We know you're confused, maybe even a little scared," the female nurse said while preparing to check his blood pressure, "but everything will be fine. The doctor has been notified. He's on his way."

"Notified?" Dan said suspiciously, trying to clear his throat. "Notified of what?"

The nurse simply smiled, continuing to work.

Dan noticed his arms for the first time. Gone was their tan, muscular definition. They were now as thin and frail as an old man's, and his skin was so pale as to be almost translucent. With his free arm, he felt his shoulders. They were bony, scrawny. Hair brushed his hand as he moved it over his neck.

"What the?" His long hair was in a thick ponytail that trailed down his back. "What is this?" he said, holding the ponytail out.

"It's called hair," the nurse said, pumping up the cuff on his arm. After a few seconds she wrote down the readings and unwrapped his arm. "Your mother-in-law said long hair looks good on you."

"My mother-in-law? I don't have a mother-in-law.

At least not yet."

The nurse shot him a confused glance.

Dan started to press her when a crowd gathered outside his room. They tried entering but the male nurse shoved them out. Several white-uniformed people hovered just outside the door, constantly peeking in at him. Soon the crowd grew to several dozen. The nurse attending Dan picked up a phone, calling for Security. She replaced the receiver. Dan glanced her. She stared.

He returned her gaze, silent. She was very pretty with her long, red, braided hair. Instinctively he glanced at her left hand. Naturally, there was a wedding ring. Dan sighed; the bright, pretty ones were always taken. He turned his attention back to the circus outside his door. "I have right to know what that's about," Dan said. His voice was gravelly from disuse, and he paused, clearing it. "What did you mean when you said, 'you're awake'?"

"I'll probably get written up for this," she said, hesitating. "You must forgive them. It's been years since there's been any excitement around here. It's not everyday that someone comes out of a *three-year coma*. And as coherent as you are. It's like you just woke from a nap."

Dan nodded, struggling to comprehend. He tried to talk but his throat was sore. He felt like a child abandoned in a crowd of strangers.

A man wearing a white coat rushed in. Slamming the door shut, he shook his head in disbelief. "Hell, even the newspapers are here." Walking over to Dan's prone form, he stopped and peered down at him. "How is he?"

"Why don't you ask him?"

The man studied Dan for a long moment, then extended his hand. "I'm Preston Roberts, physician on duty."

Still trying to digest everything, Dan slowly extended his hand, gazing at the man in silence.

In his early thirties, the doctor was medium height with a slender build. He had short blond hair and was clean-shaven. "Squeeze, as tight as you can," he said, holding Dan's hand.

"I'm in pitiful shape, Doc," Dan said, feebly gripping the doctor's hand.

The doctor smiled, releasing Dan's hand. "You did fine, considering." He hesitated, casting a glance at the nurse.

"I told him, Doctor, but only how long he'd been in a coma. I'm sorry but—"

"I had to pry it out of her," Dan said. "I told her she was going to hell wearing gasoline-soaked pantyhose if she didn't tell me how long I'd been out."

The nurse blushed. The doctor chuckled, shaking his head.

"That must've been one hell of a truck wreck that put me out that long," Dan said. "Three years, you say? Jesus. I'm sure Anna is out of my life by now."

The nurse and doctor exchanged glances.

Dan sighed, looking out the window. "Yeah, I bet Anna—that's my fiancée—dropped me like a bastard step-child, and I wouldn't blame her." Fingering the ponytail on his shoulder, he suddenly eyed the nurse. She turned away.

"Excuse us for a moment," Doctor Roberts said to Dan as he led the nurse to the far end of the room. Once out of earshot, the doctor turned, facing the young woman.

"I'm sorry, Preston," the nurse began before the doctor could speak.

"I have no problem with what you told him, Jamie," he said in a hushed tone, "but we can't slip again. Temporary amnesia is common in these situations. What must be determined is if his memory loss is due to emotional trauma. He may be traumatized to the point that he's deliberately suppressing everything."

Nodding, the nurse glanced at Dan, who watched them.

The doctor ran a hand over slicked-back hair. "I've never dealt with someone coming out of a long coma. For him to be so alert is remarkable." The doctor glanced at Dan then turned back to the nurse. "I'm going to check him over while finding out how much he remembers. But I won't tell him *everything*, even if he asks. For now, the less he knows…"

"Yes, doctor." The nurse bowed. "I understand."

"Yes, doctor." The nurse bowed. "I understand." "Jamie, I know you've been tending him the last six months. Don't let that get in the way." Glancing in Dan's direction, the doctor lowered his voice even more. "I've contacted his in-laws. They've been raising his daughter. They should be here in a couple of hours. Apparently, they, and a friend in Texas, are the only family the guy has." He paused, swallowing. "I've also contacted the FBI."

The nurse, Jamie Moreland, gave a start. "Preston, couldn't you have waited on the FBI? It's not like the guy is going anywhere soon."

"The physician over McKntyre was instructed to notify the FBI *immediately* if there was any change in his status. I'm only covering our butts. However, I won't let anyone see him until he's had time with family."

Dan glanced at the two murmuring in the corner. Red flags were everywhere. Something tragic happened; he could read it in their faces. Sighing, he stared at the ceiling. The last thing he remembered was pulling away from the weigh-station in New Mexico on his way back home. He and Charlie had stopped at Anna's. He remembered proposing to her and she had accepted. He would sell his truck and return to her.

Suddenly he recalled the cookout with Charlie and the strange little girl giving him that rock. Dan shook his head. Things were returning, but only in frustrating bits and pieces.

The doctor returned to Dan, the nurse at his side. He began a routine, cursory exam of Dan, telling him there would be a more thorough physical the following day. Dan glanced down to his pale stomach, watching the doctor move the stethoscope across his chest. His ribs jutted out; he looked like a refugee from Dachau. Suddenly his eyes widened as he stared at his left side. "What the? I've been shot."

"How do you know that?" the doctor asked.

"I know what bullet holes look like. I've seen enough of them." On Dan's left side, just above the waist, were three quarter-sized dimples.

"It was a miracle that no internal organs were permanently damaged. You had another wound up here," Jamie added, tapping Dan's right shoulder. Her hand moved down to Dan's left knee. "And another one here. As you can see, they've long since healed."

"Reconstructive surgery was done on your knee," the doctor said. "You should be able to walk, but don't plan on any wind sprints."

At a loss for words, Dan stared straight ahead. "What the hell happened to me?"

"We were kind of hoping you could tell us," Doctor Roberts replied.

"I must've really pissed someone off." Dan gave a bewildered nod. "The last thing I remember was loading my Jeep for Stanton." Suddenly his head jerked around. "What am I doing here in Phoenix? Why aren't I in Texas?"

"What makes you think you're in Phoenix?" Dr. Roberts asked.

Dan nodded to the window. "I recognized the skyline."

The doctor asked Dan to state his full name, address,

phone number, and next of kin. Dan paused at the last request.

"I have no next of kin yet—except my daughter, Amy. She lives with her mother in Stanton. At least they used to live there." He looked at the two. "That's not far from here, you know."

Jamie glanced at the doctor.

"Can you bring me a phone?" Dan continued. "I'd love to talk to them. Let them know I'm okay."

Jamie turned, darting for the door. "I need to check on other patients."

"Was it something I said?"

Dr. Roberts forced a smile. "She's just had a rough day."

Dan started to speak when the doctor interrupted. "I know you have a lot of questions; a lot of catching up to do. Someone will be here this afternoon to talk to you, bring you up to speed."

"A shrink?"

"No, it's someone close."

"Who? Anna?"

"I can't say," the doctor smiled. "We want it to be a surprise."

The doctor left, but not after posting another nurse in Dan's room. She was a middle-aged woman with short, gray hair. To Dan, she seemed more a guard. He tried engaging her in conversation but she only looked over her glasses at him, not even telling him who was president.

Sighing, Dan placed his hands behind his head,

examining the ceiling. Feeling his long hair, he thought about what the young nurse had said earlier, that the long hair was his mother-in-law's idea. Who was his mother-in-law? Could it be Anna's mother, Joan? Why had the doctor asked for next of kin? If Dan were married, wouldn't his wife be next of kin? Yet a wife was never mentioned. Icy dread crept over him. He forced his thoughts elsewhere. He was resolved to do whatever it took to get out of this damn place and back home.

Two hours later Dr. Roberts returned. The commotion outside had subsided. The doctor scrutinized him. "Do you feel like having a couple of visitors?"

"Who are they?"

"You'll see." The doctor nodded for the gray-haired nurse to open the door.

Within seconds, a woman and a teenage girl stepped through the doorway.

"Dad!" Amy shouted, bolting toward him. "You're awake!"

"Careful," the doctor cautioned, "he's still very weak."

Ignoring the doctor, Amy vaulted onto the bed, flying into her father's arms.

Dan held her tightly.

Amy pulled away. Dan couldn't believe what he saw: a beautiful young lady had replaced the gangly girl he remembered. Stammering, he gazed at her; she was almost a mirror image of Anna. "Amy, you've grown," was all he could manage.

"I'm fourteen now," she said, smiling.

"What grade are you in?"

"Freshman." Amy eyed him. "So, when are you getting out of here and coming home? Do you still plan on moving to Texas?"

Dan smiled; she even had Anna's mannerisms. "I hope to be out of here in a few days. Then we'll see about Texas." He glanced at Joan, then looked expectantly to the door.

Joan turned to her granddaughter. "Amy, would you step outside for a few minutes, please? All of you." She turned to the doctor and nurse. "Would you please give us a few minutes alone?"

"I don't think that's advisable," Dr. Roberts said. "I'd prefer a specialist check him."

"If you'll excuse us?"

Sighing, the doctor motioned for the nurse and Amy. All three headed for the door.

"I'll be right outside, Dad," Amy said.

Dan watched as the trio left the room. "Where's Anna?"

"Anna's not here."

"Where is she?"

Joan swallowed. "She's dead, Dan."

Dan's throat tightened. "Dead?"

"I'm sorry."

"She can't be dead. I mean, we were planning a wedding and, and—"

"That wedding took place. But it was over three

years ago."

Blackness closed in. Dan gripped the bed rail, fighting to remain coherent. A kaleidoscope of memories popped into his conscious bit-by-bit; he chewed a lip, trying to focus. "Gone," he repeated.

Joan stepped closer. "Anna and your unborn children died the afternoon they *Careflighted* you to the hospital." The older woman looked away, a tear streaking her cheek. "As I said, that was a little over three years ago. It happened in September of Nineteen Eighty-Six. It's now January, Nineteen Ninety." Her voice wavered. "We thought we'd lost you, too. You died on the operating table, were brought back, but never regained consciousness."

"I—gone?" he repeated. He took a deep breath. "Oh, Jesus." He buried his head in his hands, still trying to process everything. After a few moments he murmured. "You should've let me die."

"Don't say such nonsense." Joan reached out, embracing him. "You have family who care."

"So did Anna." A lump rose and Dan swallowed hard, his voice gravely. "It's not fair that she…" Dan shook his head. "It's just not fair, Joan." His eyes welled. He brushed an arm over them, forcing calm. "I, I don't know what to do. I think I caused this." He fixed her with a wide-eyed look and asked, "Gone?" again, as if it would eventually change the answer.

"*You* didn't 'cause this.'" Joan patted his back. "The main thing now is for you to heal—both inside and out. Anna would want that. She'd want you to celebrate life, raise Amy.

And of course, you have us."

Joan released Dan and he sat straight in bed. His jaw tightened.

Joan eyed Dan. "Anything coming back to you?"

Dan nodded, silent. Inside, he held Anna, shaking her. Blood coated everything. *Anna—wake up! Oh God—no!*

"Can you talk about it?"

He shook his head.

"I understand your grief," Joan began. "We all felt it—still do." Joan touched his hand, concern in her eyes. "We want you whole again, Dan. You may not think so now, but you have a *lot* to live for."

He swallowed hard, fighting for words. "It doesn't matter. Nothing matters anymore. Not without Anna."

Joan's chin tightened and her eyes flashed. "And you think we don't hurt? You better learn to deal with it—and quick. Don't tarnish my daughter's judgment."

Tense silence hung in the air.

Joan suddenly reached for his hand. "When you get healthy, we want you to be the person you really are. Don't harden your heart. It won't bring her back."

"I watched Anna die." He hadn't expected the words to sound so final. "To you, it happened three years ago." Dan's voice wavered. "To me, it was yesterday."

"It's okay," Joan whispered, giving him a motherly hug. "I know this sounds cliché, but time will mend your pain."

As if a veil were lifted, everything hit Dan at once. He recalled his marriage to Anna and their sensual dancing on their wedding night, their drive to Sentinel Peak, the wonder of the starship…getting ambushed by Albright. Assailed with an onslaught of emotion, Dan choked. He wanted to scream. He turned away, silent.

After several moments, he faced Joan. "The *Halaena*. Did we—"

"It's gone," Joan murmured. "There's not a trace of it."

"What about our backpacks? Inside were artifacts, evidence—"

"They no longer exist, Dan. There was no trace of *anything*, no backpacks, no bodies, nothing. You and Anna accomplished your goal. But please, don't ever, ever mention that vessel again. The government has a mystery on its hands; let's leave it at that." She paused, lowering her voice. "From today forward, you must choose your words carefully. Government agencies will hound you from now on unless you convince them you're not worth it. And the media wants answers. But we can use them as a shield. The last thing the government wants is publicity while investigating a case so bizarre." Joan paused, glancing around. "We're probably being watched now."

Thirty minutes later Amy, the doctor, and the young nurse named Jamie came back into the room. Dan asked how long before he could go home.

Doctor Roberts pointed to the bathroom. "As soon as you can use that by yourself." The doctor also informed Dan that the state police, along with the National Transportation Safety Board—NTSB—had already requested an interview, as had several newspapers, and local TV stations. Waking from such a long coma had thrown him into unwanted celebrity status.

"It must be a slow news day," Dan sighed. "I have nothing to say to anyone." The doctor had wisely postponed all interviews for a few days. Dan needed time for readjustment, which would be difficult with microphones and minicams shoved in his face.

The next day Dan climbed out of bed and, with Jamie at his side, he hobbled to the bathroom. The nurse hovered by the closed door while he took care of business. Tying his robe sash, Dan forced himself to look into the full-length door mirror. He choked with horror.

The reflection staring back at him was nothing but a wraith. His athletic build was gone, replaced by something pale and gaunt. He was amazed how anyone could look at him. His jaw jutted out and dark circles were under his eyes. He was a walking skeleton, a Holocaust survivor. His hair caught his eye. So dark to be almost black, it was extremely long and wavy, draping over his shoulders and down his back. His eyes focused on a huge shock of gray in the center. At least an inch wide, it was stark against the dark hair around it.

Without warning, he was again on the bridge of the *Halaena*. The grinning skull of his great-grandfather, Kalyn, stared back at him. "No!"

Jamie jerked opened the door. "Mister McKntyre, everything all right?"

Dan stared at her, trembling. "No, everything isn't

'all right.' Thanks for asking." He shuffled through the open doorway. "And it's Dan. Call me Dan."

Rushing to his side, she took his arm, guiding him to a chair by the window.

"I just want to get out of here," Dan said tiredly. "I just want to go home." Dan's eyes watered and he looked away.

The next few days flew by for Dan. In between physicals, psychological exams, and rehab sessions, what he had for family was always around him. Amy, Joan, and Ben were constantly at his side. Charlie and Carolyn even managed a visit. They assured him that his home in Texas was cared for and not to worry. When he was ready to return, they expected him and Amy to live with them while his house was under construction.

"But you can only stay with us on one condition," Charlie said, grinning. "I don't want to be embarrassed when I introduce you to company."

"You mean that *prozac* bunch from the state hospital that you call friends?" Dan said, sitting on the edge of the bed. "Hell, Charlie, they're the only ones who'd think I was normal."

"The hairs gotta go," Charlie said. "Someone get me some scissors."

"What? You don't like my hair?"

"Hell no!" He pointed to Dan's head. "And get rid

of that gray. You're too young for it." He paused, grinning. *"Lilly Munster."*

"Well," Dan said slowly, "if you don't like it, I guess you'll just have to kiss my ass because now I'll keep it—the long hair, the gray, everything."

Carolyn ran to Dan's rescue. Draping an arm around him, she looked smugly at her husband. "Charlie, you have no taste. I think it gives him—"

"Let me guess," Dan interrupted, "'character.'"

"I know you have a job to do. You've examined the NTSB's interrogation of me. I have nothing new for you." Dan sat in a padded chair, gazing out a window at the Phoenix skyline. "Ankle-biters, all of you. Every friggin' alphabet agency, except the FBI, has been here. And I'm sure they'll show anytime. This is your second visit, Detective— what did you say your name was?"

"Carter. Detective James Carter," the policeman said.

"My story hasn't changed, Detective Carter. That should tell you something."

The two plain-clothed state troopers sitting across from Dan glanced impatiently at each other. "There's only one witness to the death of a United States Senator and the Director of the FBI—and we're looking at him," Carter said.

"*Alleged* deaths," Dan said, facing them. Both detectives were in their mid-thirties. One, an Hispanic, took notes. The other, Carter, had blond-hair and sharp features. Dan addressed him. "No bodies were ever recovered."

"Mr. McKntyre, this isn't going away," Carter said. "DNA blood samples from three different individuals were recovered from your clothing. Two have been identified: your wife's and ex-felon Benjamin Morgan's. The third is unidentified. Mind telling us who that third belonged to?" Carter eyed Dan. "Your wife's body was the only one recovered. What happened to the others?"

Dan's throat tightened. "I have no idea. You have my written statements. I was out-of-it. Unconscious. I saw nothing after I was shot."

"You have no idea who this third party could be?"

"None."

"And another thing," the Hispanic detective said. "The motive. You expect us to buy the revenge story? Come on, Mr. McKntyre. A U.S. Senator and the Director of the FBI both coming after you and your wife? There's more than 'revenge' here."

"You know about the run-in I had with the Senator's son," Dan said.

"Yes. How unfortunate for the young Mr. Perryman," Carter said. "But where does the FBI figure in?"

"I haven't a clue."

"I'm sure you knew the FBI had your wife under surveillance."

Dan acted shocked. "No, I wasn't aware. Why?"

"They won't say," Carter said. "But it doesn't matter. We clean our own house first."

"You mean your agencies don't communicate?" Dan said, chuckling. "Perhaps there's yet hope for this country."

"What's that supposed to mean?" the Hispanic detective shot back.

"It means," Dan said, "that I've told you all I know." He paused, sighing. "I'm getting tired. Unless you have more questions of substance?"

As they rose to leave, Carter gave Dan a hard glance. "Don't leave the state."

"Let me lay a little something on those earlobes, Detective. I'll go where I damn well please, when I damn well please."

Carter's face turned red. "I wouldn't get an attitude if I were you, Mr. McKntyre. Things could get very difficult for you."

"*Attitude*? Mister, you ain't seen 'attitude!' Either you charge me or subpoena me, but don't threaten me. You must've flunked 'intimidation one-o-one' in junior college. You guys are amateurs."

Stepping away, the detectives spoke quietly among themselves. After a moment, Carter stepped to Dan, flipping a business card onto a nearby end-table. "We'll be in touch." The two turned, leaving the room.

From then on, Dan had an attorney present during questioning. Joan hired a friend of Anna's to represent Dan. Within the next two days the NTSB, the reservation police and the dreaded FBI all made appearances. The FBI's visit was the briefest, and, Dan thought, most strange. Only one agent dropped by the hospital. His name was Michael Jennings. Around forty and dressed casually, he presented an innocuous image. Yet Dan knew it for what it was—an image. The agent's job was to derail Dan.

Jennings went over information given to other agencies, then asked a few personal questions about Anna, for which Dan was prepared. Dan's story never wavered. The agent seemed satisfied with his answers, which increased Dan's suspicions.

"What do you plan on doing with your new life, Mr. McKntyre?" Jennings asked innocently.

Almost caught off-guard, Dan studied the agent for a moment. About to speak, he felt a hand on his: his attorney, Jennifer Castleberry, was shaking her head for him to be silent. She turned to the agent.

"Not to be rude, but it's not yours or anyone else's business what my client's future plans are." She glanced at Dan. "You don't have to answer that question."

"It's okay," Dan said, raising a hand. He turned to the agent. "I really don't know what I'm going to do. So there. For now, I'll just take it one day at a time."

The agent eyed Dan. "Well, you better give it some thought, because I'm sure you're going to live a long, colorful life now that you've inherited your deceased wife's vast fortunes. Don't spend it all in one place."

"What?"

Seated next to Dan, Jennifer rose. "That statement is out of line and has absolutely nothing to do with business at hand. My client is not required to, nor shall he respond to, such an offhand remark. He just woke from a three-year coma. Doctors say he's still traumatized." She gave the agent a hard look. "Have you no decency?"

The agent seemed unfazed by Jennifer's outburst. He asked a few more general questions, then abruptly left. Dan stared out a window. He'd honestly forgotten about Anna's wealth. Their argument on the plateau haunted him. What he wouldn't give to have that day back.

Jennifer turned to Dan. "Next time, he'll be back with the whole damn posse."

Dan ignored her comment, continuing to stare out the window. "I have a warehouse full of regrets. I can't sell them. Hell, I can't even give them away. And the inventory keeps growing." He faced Jennifer. "They treat Anna as if she were only a number."

"They're only doing their job." Jennifer paused. "I'm sorry for your loss, Dan. We all miss her."

Dan nodded. "Half of me is gone." He rose, stepped toward the window and paused. "Going through the motions. Coldly, methodically, I breath in and I breath out, but I only go through the motions."

The attorney stared in awkward silence.

"Where are those friggin' truck keys?" Dan said, rummaging through a kitchen drawer, where he knew a spare set was kept. He slammed the drawer shut. "Damn—nothing!"

"Did you lose your keys again?" Joan stood in the doorway, gazing at him. "Hard to keep up with things when you're drunk."

"Don't start in on me again."

Joan stepped to Dan, who was leaning against a counter top. "Amy's worried sick about her father."

"Where did you hide the keys?"

Joan paused, arms folded. "Do you know Amy was awake when you rolled in at three this morning?"

"What was she doing up that late?"

Joan pointed toward the other side of the house. "She was in her bedroom, agonizing over what you two are going to do with your lives."

"Where are the extra set of keys, Joan?"

"Last night you came home drunk. Again. God only knows where you left yours. Ben and I will not contribute to your disgusting behavior." Joan paused. "You're pushing it, Dan. You're already banned from the local pubs. That should be a hint. And don't go to the reservation. The police are watching. You'll get a DUI, if you aren't thrown in jail for assault first. You're still on probation from last time."

"I know where I left them," Dan said, ignoring her. "They're still in the truck." Dan turned to leave.

Joan blocked his path. "You haven't heard a word I said."

"I heard."

"Dan," Joan pleaded, "let me call someone, a doctor, someone you can talk to. You haven't talked to a psychologist since you've been home."

"A psychologist?" Dan sneered. "What the fuck more could I say to a shrink? 'Umm, gee, Doc, you should've seen this cool starship that my grandparents crashed in. Alas, we had to destroy it lest it corrupt Earth. My wife was killed while we saved humanity from—"

"Stop it!" Joan eyed Dan. "You should've taken care of Albright when you had the chance."

Dan's jaw clinched. "Yeah, shoulda, woulda, coulda."

"We see how you protected our daughter. Can we expect the same for our granddaughter?"

Dan stared at Joan.

Joan's gaze met Dan's, their eyes locking. "You know who we are. You are the same. You, Dan, hold our lives hostage as well."

Dan's stomach knotted. He wanted to vomit. He swallowed, regaining control. "Outta my way. I need—"

"You need help."

Dan stopped. "Joan—I…let me deal with this in my own way."

"If you leave now, your clothes will be piled in the driveway when you return. And we'll file for custody of Amy."

Hesitating, Dan turned, storming out of the kitchen.

"I mean it, Dan McKntyre!" Joan screamed. "Turn around and be a man!"

Dan slammed the front door, heading for Anna's pickup.

Reeking of alcohol, it was well after midnight when Dan pulled into the Wildaers' driveway. He did a double take at the boxes stacked to one side. Climbing out of the truck, Dan limped to his belongings. Sighing, he glanced to the house. A lone kitchen light burned. Walking back to the pickup, he eased the tailgate down and began tossing his things into the bed.

"Never thought I'd see the day you would cut and run."

Dan turned, making out Ben Wildaer's silhouette in the soft darkness near the corner of the garage.

"What's got into you, boy?" Ben said. "This isn't you."

Ignoring the older man, Dan returned to loading the pick-up.

Ben sauntered over and stopped a few feet from the truck. He watched Dan in silence.

Dan shoved a box in the truck bed. "If you came out here to lecture me, save your breath."

"What are your plans?"

Dan reached for a box and shoved it in the bed. "Start life over where I left off, back before Anna."

Ben chuckled, handing Dan a box full of clothes. "Ah, the alcohol speaks. Confidence from a bottle. What's going to happen when you sober up?"

Dan reached for the box, shoving it next to other and paused. "I smell a lecture coming. It won't work, Ben."

"Well, son, you've got that last part right. Your plan won't work. It's shot full of holes." Ben dropped a box on the tailgate, pausing. "In case you forgot, you're a millionaire now. Several times over. And, of course, there's your teenage daughter, who may have a few things to say about your 'plan.' But then again, who cares about her, right?"

Dan shook his head and resumed loading.

"Do you think you've cornered the market on suffering?" Ben continued. "There are a hell of a lot who hurt worse than you. And they deal with it—in an adult way."

"We've already had this discussion."

"Let him go, Ben," Joan said, walking up next to her husband. In her hand was a small shoebox, which she handed to Dan. "Inside you'll find a few personal items from your 'previous' life."

The box contained a small ring box, along with a few letters and postcards. Setting the items on the hood, he pulled out the ring box, staring at it in silence.

"Yours and Anna's wedding rings are inside, along with your class ring. You'd lost so much weight they kept falling off. We waited to see if you were going to ask for them." Joan paused. "Do you know how painful it was to pack Anna's things after her death, then have to go through them again?" A tear left a wet trail down her cheek. "That was your job. Yet you never asked about her belongings, where they were, or anything."

Dan looked away. He fidgeted, the chirping of crickets reaching an annoying crescendo.

Joan made a move to strike him but caught herself. Ben stepped over, draping an arm around her. Joan said, "When you came out of the coma, we relived her death all over again. We could live with that. But you seemed to disregard her memory. Pain turned to insult." She buried her face in Ben's shoulder.

Ben gave Dan a hard glance. "You need to go."

He knew all he had to do was apologize and they would take him back. It would take just a small show of concern on his part. Turning away in silence, Dan glanced at the ring box in his hand. Without opening it, he placed it back in the shoebox, then replaced the shoebox on the hood of the truck. Ignoring the couple across from him, he stepped back over to his belongings and resumed tossing them into the truck bed.

Sniffing, Joan stepped to the shoebox on the hood, lifting the lid. Retrieving what look like a small rock, she stomped over to Dan with it. "You could've saved everyone a lot of pain," she said, shoving it in his face, "if you had left this in Texas."

"Joanie!" Ben shouted. "Don't say such things!"

Joan remained silent, her eyes glowing silver.

Dan's eyes took on the same hue as he recalled that moment up on the bridge of the *Halaena* when Anna had pulled the "rock" out of his vest pocket. It seemed like a lifetime ago. "Your daughter took it out of my right pocket and put it in my left," Dan murmured. "Annie put it in my left vest pocket."

"That 'rock' stopped a bullet meant for your heart. Anna wanted you to live, be a father to your daughter."

Dan silently took the fragment of the *Halaena's* hull from her hand. Staring at it, he wondered why fate brought it to him. Dan tried contacting the little girl who gave it to him, but she had moved. Somehow, he wasn't surprised. Charlie said the girl, along with her entire family, had vanished, leaving no forwarding address. It was as if they had never existed.

Sighing, Dan placed the rock-like object reverently back in the shoebox. Replacing the lid, he set the small box in the cab of the truck. Reaching behind the bench seat, he retrieved a folded tarp. Stepping to the rear of the pickup, he shook the tarp open, flinging it over the bed.

Joan trailed after him. "So, you're going through with this? You're *really* going to just walk away from your daughter?"

"Actually," Dan said, yanking a tie-down, "I'm going to drive away. Besides, weren't you going to take her?"

"What should we tell her?"

"I'm sure you'll think of something."

"You bastard."

Yanking on a rope, Dan looked up. "Yeah, reckon so." He looped the rope over a hook and jerked. It burned his hand. Silence filled the air like rotting flesh.

"What about Amy?" Joan shouted. "You're her father. You can't just go off and pretend she doesn't exist. You two *need* each other. Soon, she'll be asking questions you must answer."

"Amy's better off with you and Ben. I have no business raising a child. What could she learn from me?" Joan grabbed Dan's arm, spinning him around. "It's not our job to tell her who she is or who her ancestors were. It's *yours*. For once in your life, show some goddamn responsibility!"

"Amy is yours. I'm outta here." Glancing once more at the couple, Dan straightened his shirt, then climbed into the truck. He backed out and drove off.

Dan drove aimlessly. His thoughts were jumbled. He glanced at his shaking hands, a slow resolve creeping in.

Without realizing it, he'd driven to the cemetery. Parking outside the gate, he killed the engine, glancing at his watch; 2:45 A.M. Head against the steering wheel, he sighed. After several seconds, Dan climbed from the truck. Reaching back under the seat, he pulled out a .45 auto, shoving it in his waistband. With flashlight in hand, he staggered across the graveyard. He stumbled, catching himself, unsure which way to go.

Several minutes later, Dan's light shone on the headstone he was looking for.

Anna Lynn McKntyre and children
Anna: August 2, 1954 September 2, 1986
"Forever and Always"

Dropping the flashlight, Dan knelt down in front of the grave, jaw quivering. "Annie, baby, I…I can't go on without you. I'm all alone, and used up." Dan began sobbing. "You left me when I needed you most." He rose and stumbled, swinging a fist. "I'll live for three-goddamn-hundred years—all alone? You have got to be shitting me!

What kind of sick joke is that?"

Reaching into his waistband, he slowly withdrew the pistol. "I hate what I've become. I've hurt so many."
He fumbled with the pistol, finally chambering a round. He shoved the barrel of the gun against his temple, feeling the cold steel.

Dan's hands shook. His finger tightened on the trigger. Tears streaked his cheeks as he held the gun to his head. "Jesus, forgive me."

"Now you know how I felt."

"What?" Dan jerked around, aiming the pistol at the voice. "Who's there?"

He was no longer standing. He sat at a control station in the wreckage of the *Haleana*. His fingers played over several interfaces. *I must get back to Serena. Alicia is alone and needs me.* Dan coughed and blood droplets hit the control surface. *No! I must live long enough to see Alicia and our child. My duty is to Serena and Alicia. I must survive!* He touched an icon and a nearby instrument panel came to life. He coughed and more blood splattered. His body racked in a coughing fit. Dan fell back into the chair, hacking, struggling to breathe. *I-must-live*, he choked out.

Suddenly he was back in the darkness, standing over Anna's grave. The vision faded. "What the… I'm either too drunk or it's—what did Anna call it? God, I can't think straight." He retrieved the flashlight from the ground and staggered.

"Is there no fight in you, lad?"

Dan turned, waving the flashlight. "Who the hell is

disturbing my misery?"

"Let us pray you never have to suffer mine." A man stepped into the flashlight's beam. "Daniel."

Dan stared. He was looking at a twin of himself. The man was clothed in a strange, military-style uniform. "You're nothing but a ghost. You don't exist."

"At this moment, I'm as real as you are, even down to the hell you are experiencing now."

Dan caught the strange accent. It was similar to Ason's but with a hint of Scottish brogue. Comprehension drifted through the fog of alcohol and Dan swallowed. "Why are you here?"

"You know the answer to that. Store the weapon. Now is not your time."

Dan stepped closer, but the man never wavered. "You're trying to save *me* today? *Me*? Where the hell were you when we were on that friggin' mountain?"

"I was there with you. You and I were one. *We* did all that we could do."

Dan waved the pistol. "That's it?"

"Everything has its price. And everything has its time. You—we—prevented a disaster of epochal proportions. The status quo has been reestablished—for now."

"For now? You mean all this shit's gonna happen again?" Dan's chin quivered, tears welling. "So, Anna's death was pointless."

"I said those exact words as I witnessed most of my crew die a needless death. And then my second wife, your great-grandmother, taking her last breath in my arms shortly after giving birth to our son."

Dan wiped his eyes on a sleeve. "You're the reason for the all this. If it hadn't been for you—"

"All that you know, all those that you love, would be gone." Kalyn paused. "If it hadn't been for my *ishara*, this world would have been unrecognizable by the time your daughter reached adulthood. By then, death would be welcomed. A monstrous race of beings lurks just over the horizon. Thanks to Anna, and *you*, Daniel, for now, there they shall stay. I remind you that *you* are Satari. Your task is only beginning. This current status quo must last for generations. This world is still not prepared for what *our* world brought…and what awaits the inhabitants here."

Dan blinked. "No. I, I can't."

"Yes, you can—and you will." Kalyn gazed at Dan for several quiet moments. "My ishara's task is complete, Daniel. I shall visit you no more." Kalyn turned, disappearing into the darkness.

"Kalyn, wait! Kalyn!"

Dan stumbled after the man, but he was gone. Dan paused, waving the flashlight. "I can't do this alone! I don't know what to do!" Only headstones and tree branches reflected back. It was as if Kalyn never existed.

Dan returned to Anna's grave. Pistol in hand, he chambered a round. "Real kind of bastard, isn't it? Just appears to give cryptic advice and leaves." He paced, staggered and caught himself. "He just flicked me away like I was a goddamn fly." Dan paused, staring at the headstone. His chin quivered. "Kind of like you, right? What the hell am

I supposed to do, now that you're gone?"

Everything has its time.

He couldn't be sure, but he thought he heard Kalyn's words spoken with Anna's voice.

"Fuck! But it wasn't your time!" He lifted the shaking gun to his head.

It's not yours, either.

Dan screamed. He threw the gun, and fell, a disconsolate mess, against her grave.

It was the quiet gray before dawn. An occasional bird fluttered and chirped as it prepared to welcome another day. The invigorating scent of ponderosa pine hung in cool, morning stillness.

At 5:30 A.M., traffic was light in front of the cemetery. A green Nissan swept past. Brake lights flashed and it screeched to a halt. Suddenly reverse lights lit and it shot backwards, pulling even with Anna's old pickup parked outside the cemetery gate. After a moment it whipped in next to the truck and parked. Jamie Moreland, the nurse who had attended Dan while he was in a coma, emerged from the driver's side. Passing the cemetery on her way to work, she recognized the pickup parked near the gate. Jamie knew Dan McKntyre drove it.

It had been over two months since she last saw Dan, but she heard what he had been up to. In a small town like Stanton, there were few secrets.

Jamie tiptoed to the driver's side of the truck, not knowing what to expect. The cab was empty. Walking around to the back, she stared at the tarp-covered bed, shaking her head.

It was really none of her business. Glancing at her watch, she told herself she needed to leave or face being late.

Oh well, Jamie thought, Dan was no concern of hers. From what she'd heard about the guy, she needed to steer clear of him, especially now. Her marriage was teetering. If a man like McKntyre entered her life…

Sighing, Jamie turned, traipsing back to her car. Walking, she thought back to the conversations she had with Dan back at the Phoenix convalescent home. He'd made her laugh, and her heart raced when she recalled his gray eyes. Yet she sensed a grim, frightening side to the man. He was stalked by more than his wife's death. Something happened to him up on that mountain that was so tragic, he could never share it. Even the authorities squeezed little from him. Jamie glanced to the cemetery. Without realizing it, she had stopped. Hesitating a moment longer, she turned and ran back.

Squeezing through the partially open gate, Jamie glanced around at the huge, cooling oaks and cottonwoods. He would be at Anna's grave, but where was it? The cemetery, while not large, was nonetheless scattered over a wide area. She would try the newest part first.

Jamie trotted through the center of the graveyard. Almost to the new section, she spotted something lying on the ground. Choking back a cry, she dashed towards it.

Dan was face down on Anna's grave, arms under him.

"Oh, dear, Lord," Jamie whispered, running up to him. Kneeling, she gingerly touched his shoulder. "Dan?" No response. She felt his neck. His skin was warm, his pulse strong.

"Dan, can you hear me? Are you all right?"

"Yeah," he groaned, rolling over.

Her breath caught at his ragged appearance. Dan's long hair and week-old beard were matted with grass and dirt. He reeked from alcohol and sweat.

With Jamie's help, Dan slowly sat up and looked around, bleary-eyed.

"You look like you've been living in a Dumpster," she said, wincing. Then she caught sight of the gun on the ground. "You were going to—"

"But I didn't," Dan said. "I have a beautiful daughter who needs a father. I couldn't put her through the stigma of her father blowing his own brains out." Glancing at the pistol on the ground, Dan shook. "I can't believe I was...was..."

Jamie stared at him. "Neither can I. Are things that bad?"

"They were."

"Good thing I found you before the police did. This is something you definitely don't need right now."

"So, you've heard?" Dan snorted. "What are you doing here anyway, Jamie—it is Jamie, isn't it?"

"You remember me?"

Dan nodded.

"I live in Stanton now and work at the local hospital," she said. "I saw your pickup parked out front.

Seemed like a strange time to visit."

"Thanks," Dan stammered. "Thanks for stopping."
He ran a hand through his hair, picking out grass and leaves.

"I feel like the wreck of the *Edmund Fitzgerald*."

"You look it." Jamie eyed him. "I'm taking you to
work with me and—"

"No, no hospitals!"

"If you'll shut up and let me finish?"

He stared at her, silent.

"As I was saying, I'll take you to work with me
and you can use the employee shower to clean up. Then, at
lunch, I'll take you back home. You don't need to be driving
in the shape you're in."

"Better make it a long lunch. My home is a thousand
miles away."

"Daniel McKntyre, must you be so difficult? Weren't
you living with someone here in town?"

"Yeah. I was living with my in-laws, Ben and Joan
Wildaer."

Jamie smiled. "Good people. I'll take you back
there."

"I can't go back there. They…they, uh…I was sorta
thrown out."

"I wonder why? No doubt you deserved it."

"Like I said, I managed to screw things up pretty
good."

"Yes, you did, and you'll find no sympathy here."
Jamie paused. "But you look like you could use a friend right
now. I'd like to be that friend, if you'll let me."

"I've used up my allotment of friends."

"I'm willing to take a chance," Jamie said, blue eyes sparkling.

Dan studied the young woman. "Why are you doing this, Jamie? You don't even know me."

"I have no idea," she said, averting her eyes. "Maybe there's just too much in you to let go to waste. I think you have a lot to offer the world." She glanced at Anna's headstone. "If you'll just let her go." As soon as she said it she regretted it. "I'm sorry, Dan. I had no right to—"

"It's okay. It's true." He paused, staring at the headstone. "She's gone, and no matter what happens to me, Anna is not coming back." He sighed, looking up to the young woman next to him. "I had to let her go, and she understood. Others depend on me now. I can't let them down."

Jamie gazed at Dan, a smile spreading across full lips. "I bet there are people who would give anything to hear you say that." She reached down, offering her hand. "Come on, old man, let's go."

With a groan, Dan rose. Picking up the pistol, he shoved it in his waistband, took a step and staggered.

"Careful," Jamie said, reaching for him. She held him as he limped alongside her. "You're still not completely healed. How's that knee anyway? We put the best hardware in it."

"We?" Dan said, hobbling beside her.

"Yes, 'we.' I assisted in its rebuilding."

"What I want to know is, where are the grease

fittings? It's got to be greased, right?" He grabbed his left knee. "I mean, this bad boy is so stiff in the mornings."

Both laughed as they walked out of the cemetery. Dan never looked back.

Jamie suggested Dan leave his truck. Her husband was off that day and would see that it got back to the Wildaers. She insisted that Dan still come with her to the hospital, promising him everything would be okay.

Walking to the truck, he grabbed his overnight bag and shoved the pistol in it, then glanced at the shoebox on the front seat. He gently removed the contents, stuffing them in the bag. Placing truck keys under the floor mat, he limped to Jamie's car.

She stood outside the driver's door, a cell phone to her ear. Seeing him walk up, she smiled. Smiling weakly, Dan tossed his bag in the back seat and climbed in.

Jamie slid in behind the steering wheel. "My husband and my brother will be here in an hour or so to get your truck. They'll park it at the Wildaers. In a few hours, you'll be there with it." Putting the transmission in gear, she glanced over her left shoulder then stepped on it. "The rest is up to you."

It was a little after noon and Dan stood alone in the Wildaer's driveway, watching the small green car back out. The woman driver waved, put the car in gear and sped away.

Dan's appearance had transformed since earlier in

the morning. His dark hair, although still long, was washed, neatly trimmed and worn in a loose ponytail. The large streak of gray hair only enhanced his rugged looks. He was now clean-shaven. A light-blue golf shirt was tucked into cleaned and pressed Wranglers. Not given to wearing jewelry, Dan nonetheless had suffered himself—at Jamie's urgings—to at least wear his watch and class ring. Jamie made the comment that he reminded her of one of her college professors.

"I don't know if that's a compliment or not. Do I look that old, thin and geeky?"

"No, not at all!" she had said. "Take it as a compliment, please. That professor was sharp. I admired him a lot." Her comments made Dan blush.

Dan stood alone in the driveway, gym bag over a shoulder. Off to one side was Anna's truck, his things still covered in the back. Unable to avoid it any longer, he finally glanced to the house. All was quiet. Sighing, Dan started up the long path. The closer he got to the house, the more he shook. He was almost to the front steps when the screen door opened and Joan stepped out. Dan looked past her, watching for Ben or Amy. Then he realized Amy was at school. The John Deere was gone, Ben out in the field.

Joan slowly marched down the steps. Reaching the bottom, she stood rigid, staring coldly at Dan. Dan halted a few feet from the older woman, his gaze focusing on an ant mound. Taking a deep breath, he finally looked up. "I'm sorry for being such a selfish SOB—"

"I think I used the word 'bastard.'"

"My behavior the past month was unconscionable.

I'm sorry. I beg yours and Ben's forgiveness. Is there anything I can do to set things right?"

Several long, tense moments passed. Joan eyed him, gauging his sincerity. "Yes; you can start by being a father to Amy. And that means apologizing to her. Amy couldn't understand why you didn't want to be with her."

"I can be a good father," Dan said, "if she'll just give me another chance."

"You need to ask her for that chance."

Dan paused. "How about you and Ben? Can you ever forgive me?"

Joan sighed, her eyes growing soft. "Of course." She stepped forward, hugging him.

Dan returned her embrace.

"You look good, Dan," Joan said, leading him into the house. "It's a miracle what a good night's rest can do."

Dan stopped and stared.

Joan looked back innocently.

He didn't know whether to laugh or cry.

28

Another two months passed. The vision Dan had at Anna's grave ate at him. Had he passed out from drunkenness, or was it real? Regardless, he knew that there were challenges ahead concerning his race. Lately, Dan had forced things to the back burner, struggling to get on with his and Amy's life. Yet sooner or later, he knew the shit was going to hit the proverbial fan.

Today Dan sat on the outside steps of the Wildaers,' enjoying the warm spring day, waiting for the school bus to arrive. The leaves on the giant cottonwoods near the driveway shimmered. Feeling the breeze move through his hair, he allowed a smile inside. Even though he'd seen a therapist a few times, there were still good days and bad days. Today was not the latter. It was early May and Dan was anxious to return to Texas. When school was out, he and Amy would move. He thought of how Anna should be with them, and forced his thoughts elsewhere.

There were still loose ends concerning his inheritance. Four days earlier he and Joan returned from

New York City, where they had met with the attorneys who were Anna's financial advisors. A week before her death, Anna had changed the account numbers on all her domestic bank accounts to read McKntyre. Unbeknownst to Dan, she had also made out a will, leaving Dan her possessions in the United States. In the event neither she nor Dan were around, everything would go to Amy, Joan as trustee.

When all was said and done, Dan ended up with 10.7 million dollars in assets. Two million was immediately transferred to a bank in Dallas. The rest was left where Anna had put it. Her real wealth lay in overseas holdings, most of which were in Central America. It was those holdings for which Joan was left as sole proprietor. Anna had four resorts, two of which were in Honduras—one on each coast. The other resorts were in Belize and Costa Rica. In addition, she had several hundred acres of choice property in Honduras and Costa Rica. Dan learned that in Costa Rica alone, land values had gone up over 300% in the last year. Anna also had controlling interests in several banana plantations in Guatemala. Anna's Central American holdings alone were now worth over a half billion dollars, and still growing. Her Central American assets were kept in local financial institutions and out of reach from the U.S. government. The downside was the unstableness of the governments in the surrounding countries, especially in Nicaragua. Yet, with the possible exception of Honduras, the countries she had investments in were comparatively secure. The governments welcomed the desperately needed capital and offered huge incentives, such as high interest rates if the money was invested locally. Dan learned that all of Anna's foreign business ventures were done through an anonymous International Business Corporation—IBC—making it difficult to track down the real owner.

Until Dan could learn the ropes of the business world, Joan would retain control of Anna's foreign investments. His hands full with his newfound wealth at home, he never complained.

Something nagged him. The reporters had disappeared. Even the authorities no longer called, apparently knowing they would get nothing further from Dan and were forced to settle for his version of what happened on Sentinel Peak. The silence from the *Federal* government was the most disturbing. The FBI had not contacted him in months. After transferring two million dollars to a Dallas bank, he was sure the *$10,000 currency transaction requirement* would trigger alarms with the Treasury Department. But as of yet, he'd heard nothing. Maybe it was simply too soon for them to notice.

Dan rose as the school bus approached, shoving hands in back pockets. He found himself, again, waiting for the other shoe to drop.

Dan turned the wheel of the riding mower and made another pass across the lawn. It was a bright Saturday morning and Ben normally would be doing the mowing, but Dan insisted on pulling his own weight. The old man told him to have at it.

Glancing toward the house, he spotted Amy walking toward him, a glass of iced-tea in her hand. He did a double take; she looked so much like Anna that at times, it took his breath away. At five-seven, she was already as tall as her mother. Yet it was her dark, waist-length hair that really caught one's eye. That particular day she wore it in a thick braid that trailed down her back. As Amy approached, Dan noticed she wore eyeliner—something that was still forbidden. He chuckled inside. Her grandparents had commented that she had her mother's looks but, unfortunately, her father's stubbornness.

She held the glass out as the mower crept passed.

Stopping the mower, Dan reached for it, winking. "Thanks. I bet Grandma put you up to this."

"No, she didn't," Amy replied defensively. "You looked hot. Thought this might cool you off."

He took a long swallow, sighing. "It's good—but the answer is still no."

Amy stomped a foot. "Like, why do you always think I want something when I do something nice for you?"

"Do teenagers do anything nice for anyone unless they want something?"

"Dad! That was mean!"

Dan smiled and drained his glass. "I'm just covering my bases. So, when you ask me something that you know better than to ask, you already have your answer."

"Oh!" She grabbed her father's shoulder, playfully shaking him. "You're doing this on purpose. You enjoy aggravating me, don't you?"

"Uh, huh."

Both laughed.

Handing the empty glass back to his daughter, Dan shoved the mower in gear.

Turning to leave, Amy stopped, her gaze riveted in the direction of the driveway. "Who's that?"

Dan turned just as a white Thunderbird swung into the Wildaers' drive.

Killing the mower, Dan sat watching as the soul occupant, a middle-aged man in a gray business suit, stepped out and walked toward them. A military bearing in his gait, he paused, glancing around.

"I know him," Amy said. "He's that FBI guy from the hospital."

"What FBI guy? What are you talking about?"

Amy shot her father a worried glance. "He was at the hospital the day they brought you and this other person in," Amy whispered. "He and Grandma got into it. They don't like each other. He hung around the hospital for a long time, waiting for you to wake up." Amy paused. "I don't like this, Dad."

"Daniel McKntyre?" the man called out.

Dan climbed off the mower, stepping over to him, Amy close behind. "And you are?"

The man held out his hand. "Simon Terrell. Special Agent Simon Terrell with the FBI." He quickly flashed a badge.

Dan shook the man's hand, glanced at the badge,

then back to the agent. He instantly recognized him. He was the man on Sentinel Peak kneeling over Ason's body, covertly stripping what he could. "I'm Dan McKntyre, and I think you know my daughter, Amy."

"Yes, we've met." He gazed at her. "Hello, Amy. You've grown quite a bit. You're a young woman now."

Amy's eyes narrowed, flashed silver, then returned to the same gray as her father's. Nodding, she smiled politely. "Thank you."

"Daughter," Dan said slowly, "tell your grandparents we have a visitor, but I'll see to him."

"Yes, sir."

The agent watched Amy walk away. "A lovely young lady, Mr. McKntyre. Be a shame if anything happened to her."

Dan gave the agent a hard look. "I'll take that as a show of concern."

A moment of silence ensued as the two veteran warriors scrutinized one another.

"Mr. McKntyre," Terrell began, "I know I'm the last person you want to see, but we need to talk—in private."

"We certainly do." He motioned toward the house. "How about the front porch?"

"What's wrong with inside?"

"I don't think that would be wise. I understand that you and my mother-in-law had a few words."

"She accused me of having you and your wife set-up," Terrell said. "You're right—outside would be more judicious. Besides, my visit won't take long. You strike me as a reasonable man."

"I've been called a lot of things," Dan replied, signaling for Terrell to take a seat at the patio table, "but reasonable was never one of them."

Removing his coat, the agent laid it across the back of a chair and sat down. The gun in his shoulder holster shone starkly against the light-blue dress shirt.

Tossing his floppy-hat on the table, Dan pulled out a chair, easing down across from the agent. He winced, straightening his left leg with his hands.

Terrell eyed Dan. "You're lucky to be alive, man. I understand you still carry a bullet in your shoulder."

"Yeah," Dan continued pushing on his leg. "It's a bitch. I set off metal-detectors at every airport." He paused, looking up. "I was told you were the first one to find us."

"I'm sorry about your wife, Mr. McKntyre. There was nothing I could do."

Tense moments passed, Dan eyeing the agent. "Something's been bugging the hell out of me ever since I woke. Actually, several 'somethings' are eating at me." He paused. "Were you the one following us in that white truck that day?"

"That was me," Terrell said. "Now that I've confessed to something, it's your turn."

Dan gazed cautiously at the agent.

"Where was the *extraterrestrial from*? You know to whom I refer. The deceased individual laying a little ways from you in the weeds?"

Dan cleared his throat. "Don't know what you're talking about."

"Come off it, McKntyre," Terrell continued. "Stop feigning ignorance. We *both* know what *really* happened that day, don't we?"

Terrell seemed too eager, Dan mused. He had a gut feeling that the agent and his employer weren't on the same page.

"You haven't answered my question," Terrell continued. "Where was that guy from? Did you, your late wife, and them," Terrell nodded toward the house, "come from the same place as the *alien*?"

"What do you want from me?" Dan said, eyes narrowing.

The agent, elbows on the table, clasped and unclasped his hands. "I was up in those rocks on top of the hill, just to the east. I saw that giant spacecraft, or whatever it was, disintegrate, witnessed those cretins ambush you and—"

"And you didn't try to stop them?" Dan snapped. "So, we *were* set-up."

"If you were 'setup,' we wouldn't be having this conversation." Terrell paused. "I was too far away and alone. There was nothing I could do. McKntyre, you and I are the only ones left that know what really happened."

"What about your employer?"

"They have a dead alien in cold storage, a video taken by a space shuttle crew, and they have you."

Dan sighed, wishing he could go back to his old life in East Texas; things were unpretentious and defined then.

"Look, McKntyre," Terrell continued, "I saved your

ass—and I'm not talking about up on the mountain. If it weren't for me, you would've wakened in an eight-by-eight laboratory room with nothing but sagebrush and scorpions for company. And those people in there, including your daughter, would be wishing they were dead."

"If I talk to you?"

"You get your life back, McKntyre. Talk to me—and don't blow smoke up my ass. Tell me your connection to all this, and I'll try to keep the hounds at bay."

"Agent Terrell," Dan chuckled dryly, "at the risk of sounding cliché: don't piss on my head and tell me it's raining."

"We know the alien was a relative of yours."

Dan ceased laughing. So, the ruse was up. Still, they couldn't know *everything*. Terrell sitting across from him proved that. "Look, Terrell, I don't know what you or your *compadres* think you know or found, and I don't care. All I want is to be left alone."

"Won't happen, unless you cooperate with me. Now, will you deny that you and your late wife belonged to the same race of beings as the alien?"

Dan's jaw flexed. "No, Terrell, I won't deny it."

"Where are you people from?"

"'You people?'" Dan cocked a brow. "Terrell, you know where I was born—Lackland Air Force Base, San Antonio. Anna was born in Utah, and our daughter, in Scottsdale."

"McKntyre, cut the crap; you know what I want. Where were they—"

"From a binary star system in the Constellation of Orion."

Terrell's eyes widened. He swallowed, hesitating. "Did the alien come down in that wrecked ship?"

"No, he had just arrived."

"How do you know?"

"Because he told me."

"He told you?" Terrell scoffed. "You actually talked to him? In what language?"

"English."

"How the…?" Terrell rubbed a hand behind his neck. "Why were they here?"

"I might just tell the press first. Then you can read about it in the papers."

"McKntyre, you're not that stupid." Terrell smiled. "I hope you have good life insurance."

"I'm not the one who will need it," Dan replied. "But to your question: my wife and I stumbled onto an extraterrestrial salvage operation. The alien man was trying to get us out of the area when he was shot and killed. You know the rest." Dan eyed Terrell. "They're not our enemies. They're human, like us."

"Us?" Terrell said. "Speak for yourself."

"Fuck you."

The agent fished out three Polaroids from a shirt pocket. He tossed them on the table in front of the younger man. "Who's that?"

Frowning, Dan picked up the photos. He glanced at the first one and stiffened. A chopping sound or rotor blades hammered his memory; he was in a helicopter, on a stretcher. An IV hung from an arm and a respirator fitted his face. Dan had wrenched that moment from his mind, hoping to salvage remnants of his sanity.

Dan gazed with uncertainty at the Polaroid. He believed it the strange woman he now recalled seeing in the helicopter. Her eyes were large and brown, her gaze haunting, but he couldn't quite recall her face.

The first photo was of her lying in the weeds in the mountain meadow. Her clothes were similar to the male Satarian's, but torn and scorched. The next photo was a close-up of her, still in the meadow. Pale skin shone through ash and soot. Laying the two photos aside, Dan picked up the third. She lay in a hospital bed. He could now pick out details: what was left of her hair was dark. Her face, now clean of grime, revealed youth and beauty. Dan stared at the photo, mesmerized.

The agent noticed Dan's reaction. "So, you know her?"

"Who is she?"

"We were hoping you could tell us." Terrell eyed Dan. "But you do recognize her?"

"Yeah," Dan tossed the photo on the table with the other two, "she was in that Careflight chopper with me—you know that. But I don't know her identity."

"Think hard, because if you're lying—"

"Bullying, Agent Terrell, is what really pisses me off. Sometimes, when I'm angry, well, I snap. It's ugly." Dan paused, scrutinizing the agent. "You referred to only *one* extraterrestrial—a male. Don't tell me you've misplaced a female alien?"

"Never said she was alien, nor did I say she wasn't in custody."

"She's dressed like the other. And as for her being 'in custody'…" Dan chuckled. "Your eagerness betrays you, Agent Terrell. I'll sleep better knowing we have such competent shepherds guarding the flock."

"McKntyre, she's dead."

"She looks fine in the photo." Dan lowered his eyes, recalling her soft touch. "Dead, huh? I bet she escaped and you guys are ashamed to admit another botch-job. You're hoping I can lead you to her."

"I wish that were the case, McKntyre. She died from her injuries a few days after those photos were taken. After an autopsy, she was mistakenly cremated. But, like I said, we still have the other one on ice. All we know is, she's extraterrestrial like the other." Terrell paused. "Info, Mr. McKntyre. All we want is info. Any information you have about either of them, or their intentions—"

"I told you what the alien told me. I have nothing more to say."

Terrell sighed, frustrated. "McKntyre, what were you and your wife really doing on Sentinel Peak? And don't feed me that crap about finding ancient Indian ruins or some alien salvage operation. That's bullshit. The only thing up there was that gold-mine of an alien spacecraft. And both you and your wife knew that. What were your *real* intentions?"

Dan grew even colder. This had to end. If he could

use the agent's eagerness against him, maybe he could shed Terrell, and the government, forever. But if it backfired, and it very well could, he *and* the Wildaers would go down in flames. "We found the wreckage and planned to explore it."

"You just *stumbled* on it?" Terrell growled skeptically. "Come on, man, don't jack with me. You knew it was there because you and that bunch in the house were its crew, right?"

"No, Terrell. I told you where we were from."

"Then what happened to the crew?"

"I don't know," Dan shrugged. "The wreckage showed signs of weathering. It'd been there for decades. I'm sure the crew was rescued, or is dead."

"McKntyre, you're not even a good liar. Explain how you found it before us. Were you two in contact with those aliens?"

"No, I told you why they were here." Dan forced a smile. "Everyone knowing about the wreckage but you. Blow to the old ego, huh?"

Terrell's lips tightened. "Why wasn't it detected by satellites?"

Dan shrugged. "I'm not an aeronautical engineer."

"I want to know how you guys knew where to look."

"Rumors. Legends from the local Apaches."

"Again, bullshit."

"Some legends are based on facts," Dan said. "Anna's archeological instincts took over and she decided to investigate. And lo and behold, an old legend comes alive." Terrell paused, studying the younger man. "You and Wildaer were running away. You and your alien cousins sabotaged it. Nothing to trace back to you, or them. And you guys almost pulled it off."

Dan's throat tightened; Terrell was uncanny. Yet he knew the agent was still fishing. "As Anna and I neared the ship we heard a lot of racket coming from it."

"'Racket.' What kind?"

"A voice that sounded computer generated. We thought we'd set off an alarm, and took-off."

"You never got inside?"

"No."

Leaning back, Terrell gave a long sigh, eyeing Dan. "What would you say if I told you your wife was seventy years old when she died, or your mother-in-law is around one hundred nine?"

Dan's heart almost stopped; he forced calm. "I'd say both held their age well. Wouldn't you agree?"

"How old are you, McKntyre? A hundred and something?"

"Not yet." Dan rubbed his chin. "I want to say that I'm thirty-three, but that would be wrong."

Terrell moved closer.

"I keep forgetting about those lost years. So, I guess I'm, what, thirty-six?"

Terrell flopped heavily back in the chair. He hooked a thumb to the house. "I still have Joan Wildaer."

"Yeah, the dragon-lady." Dan chuckled. "You haven't seen her really pissed yet. I won't tell her how old you think she is. I'll leave that to you. Menopausal women are vicious."

"I don't care. I have proof. Birth certificates, passports; it's all documented."

"I'm sure it is, Agent Terrell. But even if it were true, one has to ask themselves, 'so what?'" Dan stared back at the agent. "I think your records are flawed. Just look at Joan Wildaer. Does she look like someone who is 'one hundred nine?'"

"Might be normal for your kind to live for a century or more, McKntyre. And you may be right. Not all of you are from another world, but…" Terrell eyed Dan. "But what if the crew of that crashed spaceship had children? Or maybe they found they could breed with humans? Can the half-breeds live that long, too?"

Dan winced at the word *half-breed*. His stomach knotted. Fighting down panic, Dan shook his head, smiling innocently.

"McKntyre, you and your late wife's blood have the same peculiarities as the aliens; *your* DNA matches the male's."

"The only explanation I can offer is that your blood tests gave your bosses the results they wanted. We were convenient. It seems that I'm the scapegoat for the ineptness of the Federal government. They need an out. I'm their 'warm body.'"

"How about submitting to another DNA test?"

"Why? The results wouldn't change. We both know that. Terrell, if they prove I was extraterrestrial, what would the government do to me, or my daughter?"

Terrell licked his lips and looked away.

"That's what I thought."

"So, you're admitting it. You're alien?"

"I admit to nothing."

"I think that spacecraft came down a long, long time ago," Terrell began. "I think there were survivors. And you know what else? I think you, your late wife, and the Wildaers are the crews' descendants, still hanging around the crash scene waiting for rescue. Those aliens weren't on a 'salvage' mission. They were on a rescue mission."

"That's ludicrous. But I'll give you this, Terrell, you do have one hell of an imagination. You ought to sell the friggin' rights to MGM."

The older man scratched the underside of his chin, smiling. "It's true, isn't it? Alien blood flows through your veins. You all aren't human, at least not like us."

Dan's heart pounded in his ears. He studied the older man for a moment. Terrell was smug, confident. Dan recognized the look; the agent wore it while rifling through Ason's belongings.

"Tell me," Dan began, "what did the government ever do with those gadgets you lifted from the alien male?" Terrell stiffened. He stared, blinking dumbly.

"You know which devices I'm referring to—the ones you shoved in your pants pockets? Did anyone figure out what those things were?" Dan repressed a smile. "You did turn them in, didn't you?"

Terrell studied the screendoor behind Dan.

"You were caught shoplifting, Agent Terrell. What

happened to your oath? And to think because of selfishness on your part—"

"That's enough."

Dan's gaze leveled. "In my neck of the woods, we'd call this a Mexican Standoff."

Sparrows chirped under house eaves.

Terrell swallowed; his throat suddenly dry. He looked to the younger man. "What do you propose?"

"I won't tell if you won't."

"Just like that?"

"Just like that."

Terrell eyed the younger man. "How do you know that my people haven't reached the same conclusion as I have?"

"Because I'm still here. I'm confident you'll see that it stays that way." Dan nodded toward the house. "And that includes them; they're to be left alone. All any of us want is to be left alone."

"I can't guarantee that and you know it."

Dan's eyes flashed. "Mister, if I go down, you're going with me."

"That's blackmail."

"That's survival."

"I just have to know," Terrell murmured.

"I'm flesh and blood," Dan rose, stepping toward Terrell, "just like you. I have the same desires and weaknesses as anyone." Dan's eyes glowed, two silver embers, his gaze freezing the agent in place. "Leave-it-alone."

Without warning, Terrell fell out of his chair, eyes still locked with Dan's. He cringed.

Dan's eyes dimmed, returning to somber gray. "You seem to have slipped, Agent Terrell." He helped the older man up.

Terrell jerked away, grabbing for his gun.

"Wouldn't do that if I were you."

Terrell swallowed hard, hesitating. He lowered his hand. "What did you do to me? What kind of monster are you?"

"Like you, the human kind."

Terrell brushed himself off. He yanked his coat off the chair and reached for the Polaroids on the table.

Dan slapped a hand over the pictures. "I appreciate these. Kind of a show of good faith."

"As you wish. But McKntyre, those photos are cancer. I thought you wanted this behind you."

Dan moved to shove the photos in his jeans but stopped. Blinking slowly, his gazed moved to the Polaroids in his hand. Terrell's words stung. The last thing he needed was another ghost. Reluctantly, he handed the photos to the agent. "Pretend we don't exist—*quid pro quo*."

"I can't promise anything."

"I understand, but I trust you'll do your best, for both our sakes."

Giving Dan a last glance, the agent turned and headed for the door.

"Goodbye, Agent Terrell."

The agent ignored Dan. *Whack*! The screen door

slammed behind him.

Dan watched the white Thunderbird shoot backwards, then speed up the road. His hands shook.

He turned to the house at the sound of the opening door. Amy rushed out, throwing herself into her father's arms.

"Dad, what was that all about?" she sobbed.

"Just a misunderstanding. Everything will be fine, now."

"I'll be so glad to get away from here," Amy said, fighting back tears. "People are beginning to treat us different. Why?"

Holding his daughter tightly, Dan remained silent. Sooner or later he had to tell her. Glancing at Anna's old pick-up in the driveway, he bit a lip, hesitating. That talk would be later. "We'll move soon, Amy. Start a new life. Everything will be okay."

Amy pulled away, about to speak when Dan touched a dark streak on her cheek. "What's this?"

"You know what it is." Blushing, she wiped her eyes with a finger. The black smeared even more. "Dad, please. I'm fourteen!"

"And when you're fifteen, you can wear it— maybe—but not until then. Now go wash it off."

"It's not fair!"

"Life's not fair. Get used to it. And don't whine. You know what I think of whiners."

Turning, she stomped back into the house. Dan followed.

The phone rang.

"I'll get it!" she yelled.

"I'm sure it's for you anyway," Dan muttered. "And don't get that black junk all over the phone," he shouted. Pausing, he looked up. "Why a teenage daughter, Lord? Haven't I done enough penance?"

Summer, 2024.

Sweat rolled from the man's forehead, dripping off his nose as he ran down the quiet country road. The air was so thick from humidity it could be sliced, diced and quartered. All in all, it was a typical East Texas summer day; warm and humid in the morning, hot and sweltering in the afternoon. Sticky moisture hung in the air like a fog. The runner loved it.

The man eyed the large old oak up ahead; the road split, curling around it. The tree was a local landmark, and his turn-around point. He would circle the oak then head the mile and a half back home.

Suddenly the rattle of a vehicle drifted through warm air. Without looking back, he moved further to the left shoulder. The noise gained. "Damn, she found me."

The maroon Escalade pulled up alongside him, keeping pace. The driver's window slid down. "Dad! What're you doing?" screamed an annoyed female voice.

"What's it look like?" Daniel McKntyre shouted,

puffing.

"We have a fund-raiser to attend. You promised me you'd make this one!"

He kept running.

Amy McKntyre eyed her father. She whipped the vehicle in his path and halted. Amy jumped out of the SUV, a towel in her hand.

Laughing, Dan crossed the road, running past her.

"Oh, no, you don't!" she shouted, bolting after him.

He broke into a sprint.

"Damn you!"

Dan suddenly stopped, grabbing his left knee.

"Serves you right," Amy said, reaching him. She dabbed her forehead with the towel. "Now look, you've got me sweating." She threw the towel at her father. "Dry off good. You're coming back home. I don't want you dripping everywhere."

"Yes, ma'am," he grumbled. He ran the towel over his face then through short, dark hair. He glanced at his daughter, dressed in baggy shorts and a loose-fitting T-shirt. "You know you're wasting your time."

In her forties, Amy was a strikingly beautiful woman, looking fifteen years younger. Except for extremely long, dark hair, she was almost a twin of her late mother, Anna. Glaring at Dan, she pointed to the Escalade. The two, Dan limping, trudged back to the SUV.

"I can't believe you'd do this again," she said, sliding behind the wheel. "You were going to skip out on another one, weren't you?"

"Amy, you know I hate those things." Dan climbed in the passenger side. "Besides, I wanted to stay home this evening, watch the *Artemis* moon-landing from my own couch. It's been fifty-five years since man last set foot on the moon." Dan slammed his door shut. "And by God, I've missed it."

"It'll be even better on the giant screen at the hotel though, don't you think?"

"I don't like crowds."

Putting the Escalade in gear, Amy swung it around. Head shaking, she glanced at her father.

Dan eyed her. "What the hell's wrong now?"

"Are you ever going to marry again?"

"Hold on. I think I'm having a déjà vu." He placed fingertips to his temples. "Yes, I seem to recall us having this conversation before."

"Dad," Amy said, sighing, "you're not getting any younger. If you haven't noticed, you're in your sixties. Lord knows you don't look it, but sooner or later you'll—"

"So?" Dan interrupted. "They say life begins at sixty."

"And at forty, and at thirty," Amy continued, "and I'm sure they'll say 'at seventy.' I worry about you, Dad. Don't you want someone to grow old with?"

"If you're trying to hook me up with someone again, forget it. It ain't gonna happen, little girl."

"Why? Won't you even consider another relationship?"

He stared out the window. He never gave—couldn't

give—his real age to those he had dated and it tore him up. He allowed most to believe he was around forty, but held his age well. Thank God Amy never knew that he had dated several women younger than herself. They were mere girls, though, and he had little in common with them. Yes, sex drove him and it was good, but he needed more. He had dated a few women nearer his age, and the sex was even better, but he was never sure if he was being manipulated. The higher the stakes, the better the actresses. His near-fatal mistake was thinking he knew the opposite sex. Dan was embarrassed at how naïve he'd been when dealing with women, especially of the so-called "high society," Hollywood-type crowd.

A few years ago Dan donated several million dollars to the State University's new School of Astronomy. Asked to say a few words, Dan rose and asked the president of the university why a course on, "How to deal with the rich without sinking to their level," was not offered. He thought he'd have to call 911 to resuscitate everyone.

Generally speaking, and there were exceptions, he'd never met such a phony, self-aggrandizing group of people as the uber-wealthy. Most were out of touch with reality. Dan's view echoed what F. Scott Fitzgerald wrote about the rich: t*hat they smashed up things…then retreated back into their money or their vast carelessness…and let other people clean up the mess they had made.* Those words, although written in the 1920s, were just as true 100 years later.

He recalled his last disastrous relationship. Her name was Melissa Whitely. A very attractive woman who came from a wealthy, influential family, she had said all the right things. Yet money throws only a temporary front on character. They had dated for two years and it was getting serious. Then he caught her cheating on him. And she had the gall to flaunt it, believing he couldn't do without her. He sent her shit packing in a hurry. Dan sighed. To his chagrin, he had learned that one could have all the money in the world and still be the world's loneliest person. And lately, he seemed to have a knack for attracting the mentally deranged. Was it desperation on his part? Probably so, he mused. Now, he chose to play it safe.

"They're not all like Melissa," Amy said, reading his thoughts. "There are some very decent, classy women out there who'd give anything for a man like you." She glanced at him. "You, father, are the one letting money get in the way."

He sighed, shaking his head. Last decade, the great sadness of his marooned ancestors began setting in. Except for Amy, he was alone. His only child, Amy, was also alone, and worse yet, she didn't even know it. She didn't yet know about their ancestry, although he knew she suspected there was something *different* about her grandparents and themselves. Eternal youth can only last so long before it, too, grows old.

"What I am is friggin' flypaper for freaks."

Chuckling, Amy drove through an open gate and into the large circle drive. Jose, the grounds-keeper, rode a lawn tractor across the well-manicured turf. A huge magnolia tree stretched its limbs in the center of the lawn. Turning off the circle drive, Amy pulled through an open garage door and stopped. Tarped in the garage corner was the old 1979 blue-and-white Jeep—the CJ-7. It was an ornament from the past, but still drivable. The passenger seat was still inclined exactly as Anna had set it thirty-six years earlier, and Dan refused to let anyone adjust it.

Because of remodeling, access to the house from the garage was temporarily blocked, so Dan and Amy were obliged to use the outside entry. After a moment, the two emerged from the open garage door and headed up a small path toward an enormous two-story log cabin home.

Somewhere a mourning dove called, its haunting sound echoing through the nearby forest. Dan glanced at his daughter. Amy had not dodged life's blows either. While in graduate school, she "fell in love" and married. The guy turned out to be a flake and the marriage ended in divorce. Thankfully, there were no children.

Dan smiled. Now, things could not be better for her. Amy had returned to school to pursue a Doctorate in graphic arts. Buying a house in a north Dallas suburb, she worked as a graphic arts designer part-time while attending school full time. Her future was secure financially, but it worried him.

The Wildaers recently told Dan time had run-out for them and they were *disappearing* within the year, leaving everything to their granddaughter. Dan was happy for Amy, but again was torn because he knew he must tell his only child of her heritage. And, that, in the not-too-distant future, they both would face the same fate: they would uproot and leave all behind to start a new life. Perhaps Dan was wealthy enough, eccentric enough, to escape the fate of displacement, but what of his daughter?

How do you tell someone they're descended from extraterrestrial beings who had a life span of over 300 years? Dan recalled the hard time *he* had accepting it. He prayed his daughter would be spared the same trauma. How would she handle marriage and children once she learned the truth? As far as Dan knew, Amy and he were the last of the "pure" Satari on Earth. Barring an accident, Amy would outlive any husband and children several times over.

Living for three centuries wasn't going to be all it was cracked up to be—not if you're the only one left. Amy had to be told soon. Putting it off longer only jeopardized both their futures. The truth had to come from him.

Dan walked up the long path in silence. Pausing, he glanced to the huge log home and shook his head. There were times he felt guilty. *Anna earned this type of life, not me.*

Twenty years ago, Dan gained control of Anna's Central American holdings. Surrounding himself with competent people was a challenge that had paid off: he was now a billionaire times two. The resorts, along with the foreign construction companies he owned, were making money hand-over-fist. He was paid to build his own resorts. And there was no end to the line of people willing to spend money in them.

The sound of Jose's mowing drifted across the lawn. Smiling, Dan recalled when the only mower he had was a push-mower, and mowing was a major weekend chore.'

Amy turned, hands on her hips, exasperated at her father's lagging. "Hurry-up, slow-poke, or we'll miss the big moon-landing tonight."

Jose's wife, Maria, greeted them as they entered the foyer. Dan had met the couple eighteen years earlier while in Honduras. Jose and Maria Garcia managed one of Anna's resorts, and at first, were suspicious of him. Dan's genuine character soon won them over; he and the older couple became fast friends. Within a year they were U.S. citizens and worked for Dan personally at his home in Texas. Since Charlie Fulton's death two years ago, and the Wildaer's upcoming "disappearance," the Garcias and Amy were his only family.

Maria smiled at Amy, who turned and headed upstairs. As Dan walked by, the older woman's gaze fell on him. "Go with your daughter this evening, *Senor* Daniel," she said. "She is so looking forward to it. You two have not been together much lately. Amy would like her father with her."

"I know," he sighed, "but I just hate those functions. It's always the same boring stuff."

"Stop giving money and you will not have to go."

"I can't do that. Not if I want to sleep at night."

Maria smiled warmly. "You are very generous and a good man, Daniel. Your heart is pure. You will be rewarded for that in ways you cannot yet see. I do not know what troubles you, but I pray every night for peace in your heart." She raised a brow. "Maybe tonight will be different? Your presence may bring unforeseen benefits to you and others."

"I doubt it. I hope to die at a fund-raiser; the transition to death is so subtle." He pecked the older woman lightly on the cheek. "You, Maria, are the mother I never had." Smiling, he turned and headed upstairs to shower and change.

30

It was almost dark when the brown, King Ranch Ford truck stopped in front of the hotel entrance. The pick-up would've been out of place, except in Texas. There were just as many high-dollar trucks and SUVs at the hotel as there were high-dollar cars.

A valet opened the driver's door. Dan stepped to the curb where a doorman held open the passenger door. Amy exited, wearing a long evening gown.

Dan extended an elbow, Amy hooking an arm through it. She glanced up to her father, now dressed formally. "You clean up good. Very handsome."

Dan blushed, grinning. "And you, as usual, will break a lot of hearts this evening."

The two walked toward the entrance, Dan chuckling.

"I'm almost afraid to ask," Amy said, "but what are you snickering about?"

"I'll bet you a pizza tomorrow that at least twice tonight someone will mistake you for my wife."

"Don't flatter yourself—and you're on." She looked

around. "Most everyone here knows us." She smiled at the doorman, then turned back to her father. "You know how I like mine—extra sauce and cheese."

They both laughed while walking through the metal detector just inside the door. It went off and Dan stopped, pointing to his shoulder and knee. Smiling, the security guard waved them through.

Dan kept informed with advances in the science community when it came to space travel. He especially took note of the periphery areas, the fringes of modern science, those who claimed travel to the stars was feasible. He recently donated five million to a research institute that had, in the laboratory, successfully challenged Einstein's Theory of Relativity. However, tonight, all that took a back-burner to the up-coming moon-landing.

Back in 2022, what appeared to be several man-made objects were discovered in Ukert crater. Skeptics believed it simply satellite debris. Possibly not wanting to admit another failure, NASA was silent. However, because of increased UFO sightings, accompanied by a growing awareness that intelligent life may exist in newly-discovered solar systems, the U.S. government bowed to public pressure and forced NASA to act. Investigating the anomaly was deemed too important for robotic vehicles. For the first time in fifty-five years, humans would walk on the moon.

The lunar project, christened *Artemis* after the

ancient Greek god and twin sister of the god *Apollo*, was
a joint venture between U.S. and Russia. The Mars project
was put on hold as resources were funneled into the *Artemis*
program. The one-piece lunar vehicle was assembled at the
International Space Station and had a crew of four. Minus
landing struts, it had made one trip to the moon, where it was
placed in a stationary orbit over the crater. High-resolution
photos showed a large debris field—definitely manmade.
The charred region was intriguing, as only something with
great energy far beyond Earth's means could create that in
a vacuum. Naysayers still believed it a downed lunar probe,
yet most credible scientists knew better.

  Artemis I then slightly altered its orbit, sending back
live video feeds of the Apollo 16 landing sight. For the first
time ever, in high resolution, the base of a lunar-lander was
accurately identified. Conspiracy theorists who said man
never set foot on the moon claimed the video feeds were
faked. Then there were the few who asked when did humans
first walk on the moon?

  Dan, with drink in hand, mingled with guests in
the hotel commons where huge, wide *Monstertrons* were
installed. Everyone talked excitedly while glancing at the
screens.

  Glancing around nonchalantly, Dan spotted a dark-
haired, attractive woman across the room. Perhaps in her
thirties, she was talking to an older couple. A man of about
her age was at her side. She laughed at something he said
and glanced Dan's way.

  Their gazes locked for an instant and Dan's breath

caught. Laughing again, she quickly turned away. The man threw an arm around her and smiled. He gestured in an animated fashion. The woman continued laughing.

"Who is that?" Dan asked.

Standing at Dan's side was Jonathan Stiles, a thirty-eight-year-old investment researcher who worked at Dan's firm. Stiles was shorter than Dan and heavy set, with a large, pudgy face. His brow furrowed. "Who's who?"

"That dark-haired woman in the corner. She's wearing a cream-colored dress and talking to an older couple." Dan sipped port. "Who is she? Do you know her?"

"She's the organizer of this little event," Stiles said. "I'm not sure of her name; I think it's Fisher." He sipped from his glass. "Lovely piece of womanhood, isn't she?"

"Very much so."

A waiter passed. Dan set his empty glass on the tray. "I've seen her before. Just don't know where."

"Yeah, yeah, we all say that." Stiles glanced at Dan, seeing he was serious. "Maybe you met her at another fund-raiser. She does it for a living. I hear she's good. Manages to bring in lots of dough for all sorts of bizarre projects, like this one."

"I don't know," Dan murmured. "I would've remembered *that* meeting."

Stiles laughed, nodding.

Amy touched his arm. "Dad, there's—"

"Amy," Dan interrupted, "who's that woman over there?"

Amy's jaw dropped.

"What's wrong?"

"Uh, what's going on here?" she said. "You two setting me up for something?" She stared at her father. "That's so weird that you would ask about her. I was about to say that *that* woman singled me out then asked about *you*."

"She did?"

"Yes, and I told her I would introduce the two of you. Dad, she's very nice."

Dan glanced first at Stiles, then to Amy. "Well, I am the king of weirdness."

Stiles laughed. "Yes, you are. Nothing like having a daughter to set you up, huh? Of course, being a billionaire helps."

Before Dan could reply, Amy grabbed her father's arm. "Come on." She tugged him across the room.

Dan glanced in the woman's direction. She spoke to the couple in front of her. "She probably just wants to thank me for my donation," Dan whispered.

"I doubt it," Amy whispered back. "For your sake, and hers, I hope she's older than she looks."

"What do you mean by that?"

"You know exactly what I mean."

Her comment set off alarms. After a moment, he glanced across the room. The woman's back was to them; she was now alone. Dan couldn't help but notice how feminine and graceful her bare shoulders were.

For the first time in years, Dan got butterflies. Feeling like a star-struck teenager, he pulled away. "Amy, I don't think this is a good idea."

"You're not going to wimp out! Can't you see she's waiting for you?" Amy paused, lowering her voice. "I've heard of her. She's of impeccable character. Okay—forget what I said about age. Are you scared to meet someone decent? Now let's go before she gives up."

The two worked their way through the crowd and approached the woman.

"Excuse me, Ms. Fisher," Amy said. "I'd like you to meet my father."

The woman turned. Dan's heart almost stopped. Her brown eyes were captivating. There was a complexity in them that startled him.

"Dad," Amy said, "this is Beth Fisher, the benefit organizer. Ms. Fisher, this is my father, Daniel McKntyre."

The two shook hands.

Amy leaned to her father. "You're on your own," she whispered.

"But," Dan stammered, watching Amy walk away. "God, I feel like a retard."

"Excuse me?" the woman said, a smile hinting full lips.

"Uh, nothing," Dan replied, his face crimson.

"I want to personally thank you, Mr. McKntyre, for your contribution. You're very generous."

"Thank you, but others might argue that point."

"It doesn't matter what others think, Mr. McKntyre. It's what is in your heart."

At a loss for words, Dan looked away. The woman spoke with a distinct accent that he couldn't quite place.

"Those are very kind words. And it's Dan—call me Dan."

"And I'm Beth."

Beth Fisher was of average height. She was somewhat slender, her evening gown enhancing her curves. Skin creamy white, she had delicate, feminine features, with a small nose and full lips. Dan took in the gracefulness of her bare arms and shoulders. Her dark auburn hair was short, exposing an elegant neck. She wore an expensive necklace with matching earrings.

But it was her eyes that took Dan's breath away. Doe-like and brown, they held a haunting triangle of light. He instinctively knew she had experienced more life than her soft, outward appearance belied.

The two held each other's gaze longer than normal for strangers. Suddenly Dan blinked, feeling like a high-school kid seeing his prom date for the first time.

"Love the accent," he finally choked out. "Dutch?"

"Afrikaans. I'm originally from Cape Town. I became an American citizen seven years ago." She smiled, revealing perfect white teeth. "I love it here."

"And where is 'home' now?"

"New York City."

"Of course," Dan said, "and I am sorry."

Beth laughed. "I find that so strange! What do people in this part of the country have against New York City?"

"It's a cultural thing. We have it and they don't. Not everyone who lives west of the Hudson is a rogue. Here, some folks call the North, 'wimpy Yankee do-nothings.' I wouldn't dare. Yet one must admit, even terrorists steer clear of the South."

Beth laughed. "I could say terrorists see no significant targets in 'The South.' They feel at home here, smell and all. Who wants to blow up 'Bubba'?"

Both laughed, the ice broken.

Dan's eyes flashed to her bare ring finger. *Oh shit…I'm going to blow this. God, why am I even thinking about that?*

"Is this your first trip to Texas?" Dan asked.

Beth's eyes widened. "Oh, no! My line of work takes me all over the country. Although this is only my second time in Dallas."

"Of course," Dan said, "how stupid of me to think—"

"Stop trying so hard to keep the conversation going."

Both laughed again. They began walking to the far end, where it was quieter.

"So," Beth began, "I'm sure your daughter told you that I asked about you?"

"Yes, but it seems I'm at a disadvantage."

"How so?"

"You seem to know more about me than I—"

"What do you want to know?"

"Have we met before?"

"I don't think so." Beth averted her eyes. "Isn't it fascinating that we're finally returning to the moon?"

"It's about time," Dan said, noticing how quick she changed the subject. "I was in high school when the last

Apollo mission landed and—" Dan stopped, realizing what he had revealed. Jesus, he just shot himself in the foot—again.

"*High school*?"

"Yeah. I actually went to high school, even graduated." But he knew that's not what her look was about.

"Dan, the last moon landing was in nineteen seventy-two."

Swallowing hard, Dan shoved a hand in a pocket, looking away. So this is how it would be. Beth was probably history now.

"You ought to bottle and sell that stuff," Beth said under her breath. She paused. "Please forgive me. I meant it as a compliment. I never would've guessed. I thought you were closer to my age."

"Thanks."

"Not that it makes any difference," she quickly added.

The din of the crowd drifted from the commons. Dan waited, anticipating what would follow.

"That means your daughter is…?"

Dan nodded.

Beth stared. "I don't believe it. How can you two…?"

"Let's just say, it runs in the family. You know, good genes and all that stuff."

"I like older men," Beth blurted. "I mean—" she stammered, blushing. "How did we get on this subject? I'm sorry, I didn't mean for it to sound—"

"Don't worry about it," he said, grinning. "Amy is my part-time guardian. She picks me up from the nursing home every weekend. She doesn't let me get far out of sight, though. Thinks I'll wonder off. My advanced age and all."

"Stop it," Beth laughed, touching his arm. The two continued walking until they found a quiet spot away from the crowd. Stopping, Beth leaned against the wall and glanced shyly at Dan.

"Beth," Dan began, studying the young woman's face, "I know this sounds cliché, but I swear we've met before."

"We probably crossed paths at other fund raisers," she said. "But I know we've never been introduced." She paused, looking into his eyes. "I think I would have remembered that moment."

"And I, also."

Amy came around the corner. "There you are!"

"Like I said," Dan glanced at Beth, winking, "she's like a mother hen."

Beth laughed.

"Okay, okay," Amy said, "I'm missing something here." She glanced first at Beth, then to her father. "Oh, forget it." Turning, she disappeared into the commons.

"So," Beth began, "do you believe the rumor that those are alien artifacts in that moon crater?"

Dan wondered that himself, but for different reasons. He was as worried as he was curious. He couldn't recall the mention of the Satari having anything to do with the moon. But then again, it didn't have to be Satari. He visibly shook.

"Dan, what was that all about?"

"Just wondering," he paused, "just wondering if we'll ever learn the truth about what's *really* up there."

"You're not one of those conspiracy whackos are you?"

"No, just a realist."

"The government is spending too much tax-payer money to chase after phantoms," Beth said. "I think they're convinced it's extraterrestrial."

"How about you, Beth? Do you think it's alien?"

Beth hesitated. "Wouldn't it be the find of history if it was?"

Beth's eager expression belied a cautious tone. Was that a flash of fear in her eyes or was it just his imagination? "If it is alien," he offered, "I just hope the religious nuts don't go crazy. They would deny the existence of extraterrestrials even if aliens landed on the Whitehouse lawn."

Their conversation turned to other things. Witty and with a dry sense of humor, Dan found Beth fascinating. He enjoyed making her laugh, watching her eyes sparkle. "Have you ever had Texas barbecue?" Dan asked suddenly.

"When I was in Houston a few months ago. It was catered."

"Catered?" Dan chuckled. "There's this unusual place I have in mind. That is, if you're interested."

"I have a nine-thirty flight to Atlanta in the morning," Beth said. "I'll be there for two days, then I'm flying back home for much needed rest." She gazed at Dan for a moment. "What did you have in mind?"

"My place, when you get the chance? I'll smoke a brisket."

"You, as in yourself?"

Dan nodded.

"A billionaire who cooks?" Beth laughed. "No caterers or chefs?"

"None," Dan said sheepishly. "I smoke briskets for my hired help. I'm really just a regular guy. I didn't always have money. I haven't forgotten what it's like to *work* for a living. Believe me, I come from very humble beginnings— and I can cook one helluva brisket."

"You know, when I first heard about you, I feared you might be one of those overnight, rags to riches 'Silicone Valley-Wall Street' guys. Stuffed-shirt, here today, gone tomorrow."

"And?"

"No way. Anyone who would mistake you for that needs a blood-alcohol test."

"I take that as a compliment."

"As it was meant." She paused, gazing at him. "Did you notice the guy with me a few minutes ago?"
Dan nodded.

"Well," she continued, "all he talked about was the sport franchise he was purchasing. He bragged about how much money he would make when he added on to the current sports arena, using taxpayer money. Then he said he was going to build a gym or something at his home—his mansion—for his players. It went on and on." Beth laughed. "He just couldn't understand why I wasn't impressed. I guess he got bored with me."

Dan smiled. "It was probably the other way around." He glanced toward the commons. "He does sound like a good businessman. But, I know what you're talking about."

"Would you do that, Dan? Would you use taxpayers' money for your own benefit?"

"If I could get away with it, hell yes."

"Talk about a 'realist.' At least you're honest."

"Some accuse me of doing that already." Dan looked past Beth. "I've never taken, without giving more than equal back. I'll never backup to a mirror. Of course, that's easy to say, now that I have money. Some find it hard to believe there was a time when I didn't have two nickels to rub together, living paycheck to paycheck, wondering how I was going to pay the electric bill. But it was my own fault." He chuckled. "There were even times when I had to make a choice between food or beer. I couldn't afford both."
Beth stared at Dan, then burst into laughter. "My, now that's what I call monumental decisions!"

Dan mimicked popping a top. "I wish all my decisions had been that easy."

Beth's laughter subsiding, she gazed at Dan. "But even back then I'll wager you never compromised your beliefs, did you?"

"I compromise with every breath."

"I'm sorry. I didn't mean to—"

"It's okay. You haven't said anything to apologize for."

Beth touched his hand. "*You* know the real rewards

in life. I think what you do is very admirable—and I've probably said too much."

"I see my off-kilter reputation proceeds me."

"'Unique' is a better word."

A quiet moment passed. Dan twisted the toe of his shoe on the floor. "You never answered my question about visiting. If you don't trust my cooking I'll have Jose, our maintenance man, whip up a batch of *fajitas* instead. And Maria, his wife, can make the best *chili rellenos* you've ever sunk your teeth into. Or if you like, we can go out to *The Mansion* and—"

"Okay."

Dan halted. "You said 'okay.' Okay to what?"

"I said 'okay' to any or all of it."

"You'll have dinner with me next time you're in?"

"Why wouldn't I? Dan, you're a perfect gentleman. Maybe I'm old fashioned, but the world needs more gentlemen. I sense a fascinating man behind that façade of shyness, if I may be so bold."

Dan was about to reply when Amy rushed up to them. "Come on, you guys, the moon landing's started!"

Holding each other's gaze a moment longer, they turned, heading for the commons. The couple squeezed into a spot with a good view of a *Monstertron* screen. Dan felt Beth's closeness as she stood by his side, the intoxicating scent of her perfume enveloping him.

Live coverage of the lunar mission began five hours earlier. A window-mounted camera in *Artemis II* gave the world a live shot as the ship descended to the lunar surface.

The vessel would set down two miles from the target crater to avoid contamination of the sight. "Oohs" and "ahhs" echoed, features on the gray moonscape sliding eerily past. Suddenly the landscape stilled. All grew silent.

"*Houston, we're down*," crackled through speakers. A cheer, then clapping, moved through the crowd.

A piercing scream froze everyone. "My God. He has a gun!"

Dan and Beth turned in time to see a man jump on a chair not ten feet away, a 9-millimeter in his hand.

"It's Satan's work!" he screamed in an Arab accent. "Your technology cannot help you now!" Pointing the gun at a *Monstertron*, he pulled the trigger. The shot exploded in the cramped hall. The bullet smacked into the screen with a loud *pop*, showering those under it with glass. There were more screams and everyone fell to the floor. "You, you and you," he shouted, pointing with the gun, "all of you are responsible. Infidels, all of you!"

"How did he get past Security?" someone shouted.

Dan instinctively threw Beth to the floor, shielding her.

Shivering, she looked up. "Dan."

The horror in Beth's eyes triggered something. He shook with an anger and rage he hadn't felt in decades. He rose. "I've had enough of this shit!"

"Dan, don't!" Beth pleaded, clutching his arm. "He's crazy!"

"So am I."

Still perched on the chair, the gunman turned at

the sound of Dan's voice. The man was perhaps thirty and Middle-Eastern. With short, neatly groomed hair, clean-shaven face and formal attire, he could pass for a CEO. But his bulging eyes held the look of a rabid animal. Leveling the gun on Dan like an accusing finger, he spoke with venom. "So, there is a wolf among the sheep? Come, my friend, we will die together, brave souls that we are." His eyes narrowed. "Praise Allah!" Ripping open his coat, he revealed a bandoleer loaded with plastic explosives. His left hand held a small detonator.

Dan was nearly within reach of the gunman. "Praise Allah my ass," Dan replied. "You're outta chips, buddy." The man hesitated, puzzled. A long moment passed. The hammer on the gun clicked back. He smiled. "On second thought, you will see the virgins first, 'Mr. Wolf.' Save a few for me." He shook the detonator at the crowd on the floor. "I have unfinished business here."

Dan's eye's blazed silver. The gunman's hands wavered, then slowly lowered. His face became tortured, twisted. He let out an animal scream, fighting to regain control of the will that was snatched from him.

Someone kicked the chair out from under the gunman and he hit the floor with a loud *thud*. Dan was on him like a panther and the two grappled on the floor. There was a gunshot; a ceiling light shattered. The pistol slid across the floor. The man struggled violently. Dan snatched the detonator from the gunman and tossed it away. With one swift move, he yanked the man's arm behind his back. A sickening crack and the arm broke, dislocating the shoulder.

The man yelled and tried rolling away but Dan caught him and jerked him back. Grabbing an ear, Dan banged the gunman's head on the floor. He repeatedly slammed the guy's head into now blood-spattered tile. Dan continued pounding the bloody mass into the floor even after the man went limp.

"Mr. McKntyre," a hand was on his shoulder, "ease-up. He's had it!"

Suddenly several arms gently held Dan, pulling him off the sprawled, motionless body. One of the arms belonged to Beth.

"It's okay, Dan," she said, tentatively moving her hands over his shoulders, "it's okay, it's over. Calm down." Beth nodded to the others and they let go. She touched his cheek. "Are you hurt?"

The iron-scent of blood in his nostrils, Dan stood silently in front of her, quivering. Gasping, he blinked rapidly, trying to compose himself. "I'll be fine," he croaked, "some day."

Beth quickly helped him out of his blood-soaked coat. Napkin in hand, she gently dabbed at a cut on his chin, her eyes meeting his. "I've seen a lot of things, but nothing like..." her voice trailed off. "Before we go out on a date, let me know if helmets and Kevlar-vests are optional. You seem to bring out the best in people."

How could she joke after what just happened? Dan sighed, shoulders sagging. Beth's comment had its effect and he shook his head, managing a weak smile. "Christ, why am I always around when shit happens?"

"Thank God *you* are," Beth replied. "I bet you don't even realize what you did."

Within seconds Security arrived and the building was evacuated. Soon came the police, followed by paramedics, then the media. The only casualty was the gunman. Dan swallowed hard. The rage he held inside was more frightening to him than any terrorist.

Two hours later the building was declared safe and they were allowed back into the hotel. Everyone agreed, including the authorities, that if Dan had not acted, more bloodshed would've resulted. It was found that the dead gunman was part of a radical Islamic sect the FBI had been monitoring for years. Privately, Dan was told he did the world a favor.

Finally getting rid of the police and media, Dan and Beth stood alone near an elevator just off the hotel commons. Amy had already retired for the evening, the stress evident on her worried features. It was well after midnight. "I wish the guy had waited until after the moon landing," Beth began. "I was really looking forward to seeing all of it live. Now we'll have to settle for a replay."

Dan glanced at the dispersing crowd, knowing Beth was trying to lighten things. "Yeah, me to," he murmured, enthusiasm for the moon landing shot. Disgusted, he sighed, looking away.

Beth touched his hand. "You did the right thing. If you hadn't acted, a lot of us would've died. The cretin got what he deserved." She kissed him lightly on the cheek then straightened his collar.

Turning crimson, Dan shifted, his torn coat in his arms. A small gray object fell from a coat-pocket.

"You dropped something," Beth said, reaching for it. She suddenly cried out, wincing.

"Beth?" Dan said, touching her shoulder.

"Whew," she straightened, catching her breath. "I'm fine. Just an old injury. I broke several ribs years ago. If I turn the wrong way, sometimes they remind me."

"How did you break them?"

Ignoring Dan's question, she examined the gray rock-like object in her hand. "Unbelievable," she murmured.

Dan gave a start. "What's unbelievable?"

"Oh, uh," Beth stammered. "Uh, nothing." She held the rock to Dan. "What is this?"

Dan scrutinized her. "You tell me."

"Looks like a generic rock."

Dan reached for it. Old memories from his previous life rushed back. Was *Beth* the adult *Elizabeth*, the little girl who gave him that chunk of the *Halaena*, decades ago? And *how* did that girl come by that artifact to begin with? He recalled Charlie saying the girl was from South Africa and that the family had mysteriously disappeared. Is this woman standing in front of him and that little girl from his distant past one and the same? The coincidence of that would be astronomical. So astronomical that it was unthinkable. Yet he had found, sometimes to his dismay, that not only can the unthinkable become the thinkable, it has a habit of becoming reality.

"Dan?" Beth touched his arm. "You okay?"

"Yes." He decided not to press the issue. "It's my 'lucky rock.'" Dan shoved it back in a coat pocket, again eyeing Beth. "I've had it for years. There's a lot of history behind it."

"I bet there is," Beth replied. "It certainly worked its magic this evening." She wrinkled her nose. "It's getting late. I wish we had more time this evening, but I think we'll be seeing each other again."

"Count on it."

The two exchanged phone numbers. Dan promised to call her the next day. They said goodnight and Dan watched Beth walk to the elevator. He swallowed, noticing how her hips swayed. Dan waved at Beth as she disappeared behind the closing door. Staring at closed double doors for quiet seconds, he collapsed against a wall, rubbing his forehead in mixed exhaustion and confusion. If Beth was the little girl from the past, why didn't she reveal herself? He swallowed, sighing. Seems the past just wouldn't stay dead.

After a brief moonwalk, the four astronauts, three Americans and a Russian, called it a "day." The real excitement, they told the world, would come tomorrow when they explored the crater. Saying "goodnight" to the world, the crew turned off the cameras.

An hour later, a lunar rover crawled to a soundless stop fifteen meters from the rim of the Ukert crater. Bright lunar sun glistened off white spacesuits as three Earthmen trudged up ancient ejecta, halting at the edge of a twenty-three kilometer-wide depression. Bleak, gray walls reflected off gold visors. Their gazes moved slowly down, taking in the entire crater. They finally found their target: a blackened area on the crater floor. Within minutes the rover, all three spacemen on board, eased over the crater rim. Huge balloon tires threw out puffs of sand as the rover silently glided down a smooth, gentle slope.

Mission Commander Brian Chandler stepped tentatively through the scorched debris field. The place held a macabre beauty. Kicking the black ground, he swore softly.

The sand was fused, hard as granite. He spoke into the helmet mike. "What do you make of it, Carla?"

Dr. Carla Espanoza, an astrophysicist, glanced at an instrument in her suit. "Radiation's normal, for the moon." Reaching down, she pulled up a charred, half-meter-long piece of composite material. "This must've been one helluva spacecraft." She turned it slowly. "Now, it's one helluva souvenir."

"This hell wasn't caused by anything from Earth." An excited voice with a distinct Russian accent crackled in their helmets: Sasha Norvo, structural engineer and co-pilot. "Hey, guys, I found something!"

Chandler and Espanoza turned to see Norvo standing 200 meters away, frantically waving. The two bounded to the cosmonaut. Norvo was on his knees just outside the scorched area, brushing sand from something. "My God."

All three stared at a partially buried transparent girder. Its length they couldn't guess, but every three meters another girder intercepted it perpendicularly.

Standing, Norvo gazed at his reflection in Chandler's visor. "Brian, this was a substructure for some kind of base. An outpost."

Chandler was about to speak when a flash caught his eyes. Something glistened brightly in the sun a few meters away. Shaking with anticipation, Chandler quickly bounded to it.

"A base you say?" Espanoza looked doubtfully at the Russian. "That's impossible! Who could build a base up here without us knowing about it?"

"These guys could." Chandler stared at an emblem of an inverted triangle.

"Brian, what did you find?" Norvo shouted in his helmet.

Chandler trudged over, handing the piece of "metal" to the astrophysicist. "Check it out, Carla." He pointed to the triangle. "I've seen that before."

The cosmonaut stared at the jagged piece of debris in Espanoza's hand, eyes focusing on the emblem. "Where?"

Chandler hesitated. To hell with it. The bickering of nations on Earth was now petty, insignificant. Chandler tapped the triangle with a gloved finger. "I saw it on a UFO thirty-seven years ago, during my first shuttle mission."

"I heard the rumors," Espanoza said. "So, it was true? There really was some kind of giant spaceship?"

"Three of them." Chandler swallowed. "It was a humbling experience."

All three astronauts stared solemnly at the charred moonscape, overwhelmed by the implications. Chandler finally broke the silence. "We need to prep for live TV. As much as I hate it, you know what must be done." He glanced at the Russian. "We flipped a coin. Whoever was first down the lander's ladder gets other honors as well."

Espanoza glanced at the other two then stepped away. She stooped, collecting charred pieces of debris, stuffing them in a pouch hanging from a shoulder.

Chandler stared at the unmoving cosmonaut. "Sasha."

"Yeah, yeah, I know," Norvo said, waving him off.

Chandler joined Espanoza in collecting samples and taking photos while Norvo trudged to the rover. Within minutes the cosmonaut returned, lugging a large white trunk. In the slight moon gravity it weighed next to nothing. He dumped out the contents. Norvo kicked, scattering the debris around. On one large piece were the Cyrillic letters *CCCP*.

It was a cool, gray winter morning, five months after the moon landing. Thunder rumbled, its echo dying slowly away. It was not the angry, splitting sound one hears in spring or summer. The low thunder was almost tranquil, giving one the feeling of anticipation. Soon gentle rain pattered the window, followed by the soothing drip of water from nearby pines. It was the type of morning meant for staying in bed, lying in that state of half-dream, half-wake.

Dan opened a blurry eye, focusing on fuzzy red numbers glowing from a nightstand. It was a little after six on a Sunday morning. Beth Fisher's bare breasts pressed against his back. He shifted and she stirred, tightening her arms around his waist. Her soft, steady breath moved feather-like over his neck. Closing his eyes, he settled deeper into Beth's soft arms, her warmth enveloping him.

It was ten days after Christmas and Dan had the house to himself. Maria and Jose were spending the holidays with family in Honduras. Normally this time of year Dan would also be traipsing around somewhere in Central

America. But now, life had changed. Things were anything but "normal" for him and he couldn't get enough of it.

Beth reached up, pulling a quilt over them. Dan rolled onto his back and she snuggled into his arms. "When did you say the Garcia's are due back?" she murmured.

"This evening," Dan said groggily. "No one will bother us today. Go back to sleep."

Several still moments passed. Beth worked her fingers up his side, her touch lingering over several quarter-sized dimples. "Daniel," she whispered, "you never told me exactly why you were used for target practice. You needn't keep it in anymore."

Half asleep, Dan gave a slight smile. "That part of my life is dead and buried."

Beth crawled on top of him, her nude body pressing tightly against his. "Anna left you in good hands," she murmured against his chest. "Now it's my turn." Sliding up, she gently kissed him. "I love you, Daniel McKntyre, but sometimes you scare me."

"I love you, Beth Fisher," he whispered, "and sometimes, I scare myself."

Beth was slight of build; Dan scarcely noticed her weight. The two were soon fast asleep.

Dan was roused by a gentle shaking.

"Daniel, wake up. Someone just pulled into your drive."

"Huh, what?" Yawning, he glanced at the clock. 9:30. Draped in his robe, Beth sat on the edge of the bed, concern furrowing her brow.

"You said someone's here?"

"Yes. The slamming of a car door woke me." She rose, quickly making her way to a window.

Dan couldn't pull his eyes from her; even his large robe couldn't conceal her curves.

She peeked through the curtains. "There's a gray Lexus in the driveway, but no one's around."

Dan sat on the edge of the bed. "How the hell did someone get in here? The gate was supposed to be locked." Rising, he reached for his jeans, then abruptly collapsed.

"Daniel!" Beth bounded over to him. "Are you okay?"

With Beth's help, Dan pulled himself up and sat down on the bed. "Just my knee," he said nonchalantly, rubbing a hand over it. "It's like an old car: needs to be warmed up first." He pointed to a nearby chair. "Would you toss me my jeans, please?" Slipping into Wranglers, Dan limped over to the window, sweatshirt in hand.

Beth eyed him. Even though he had an excellent physique, Dan seldom went without a shirt. It caused people to gawk. Then he would look at them in that easy way of his, asking, "What's wrong? Haven't you ever seen anyone that's been stabbed and shot?"

Dan stood by the window, about to pull on the sweatshirt when he caught Beth staring. Tugging the sweatshirt over his shoulders, he glanced at her. "Having second thoughts?"

"Should I?"

The two gazed silently at one another. Dan turned

back to the curtain. The rain had stopped, but dreary fog shrouded the countryside. "I don't recognize the car," Dan said. "Not a soul around either. I wonder…wait. There's a man. He's just standing around near the south side of the house, looking toward the garage."

"Do you know him?"

The stranger was dressed in a light winter coat, jeans, and work boots. Glancing around nervously, he looked to Dan's bedroom window.

"It can't be."

"Dan?"

Seconds ticked. The doorbell rang. Beth jumped. The two stared at one another. Dan stepped into boots.

Beth moved in front of him. "Don't answer it," she pleaded. "Ignore it. Whoever it is will go away."

"No, *he* won't," Dan said. "It's begun again." He rose, gauging the woman in front of him, seeing the fright in her eyes. He pulled Beth to him. "Everything will be okay."

"What are you involved in?"

Dan shook his head, the doorbell singing. He turned, limping down the hall to the stairway.

Beth ran after him, grabbing his arm. "What's going on?"

"Just stay here until I say otherwise."

"Daniel, don't go down there."

The doorbell chimed frantically. Gazing at her a moment longer, Dan turned and hobbled down the steps, Beth close behind. As he strode across the foyer, someone banged on the door.

"McKntyre, I know you're in there," shouted a male voice. "We need to talk. We're running out of time!" A pause. "Damnit, open up!"

Dan hesitated, then jerked open the door.

An aged Simon Terrell rushed in. Slamming the door shut, he fell back against it, panting. "Things are collapsing. I can't hold the wolves off much longer. We have twenty-four hours, tops."

Dan stepped toward the agent. "What the hell are you talking about?"

Terrell ignored Dan's question, his gaze on the woman at Dan's side. "Hello, *Beth*."

She turned away.

"So, that's the way it is, huh?" Terrell chuckled. "Well, after all these years, I don't blame you."

Dan grabbed Terrell by the collar, slamming him against the wall. "What the hell are you doing here?"

"Today, I come as an ally," Terrell began. "Tomorrow, I'll come to arrest you—and her. You'll never make it without me. If you care about the girl, you'll listen."

Dan released the agent, scrutinizing him. Terrell had to be in his eighties and looked it. His crew-cut hair was white, his features more hard-bitten than ever, yet he was far from a frail old man. "How do you know Beth? And why haven't you been put out to pasture?"

"I retired twenty years ago. Then I received a call after the moon landing. Seems the FBI once again needed my expertise." He eyed Dan. "You're a wanted man, McKntyre."

A wave of nausea gripped Dan. He took a deep breath. "There's nothing I can give you or them."

"We'll see," Terrell replied, brushing past the younger man. Stepping out of the foyer, he flopped in a nearby Victorian chair. Unzipping his coat, he made himself at home. "I'm here to offer my services. I suggest you take them."

Dan, Beth at his side, followed the agent into the house. "Don't get too comfortable, Terrell. You're about to limp back into the hole you crawled out of." The couple sat down on a sofa opposite the older man. Beth grabbed Dan's hand.

Terrell eyed her, indicating the robe. "Seems I interrupted something."

Dan's eyes narrowed. "Get on with it."

Tension filled the room, gasoline, waiting for a match.

Terrell sighed. "Alien artifacts were discovered on the moon."

"Then why haven't we heard about it? Everyone saw the broadcast. It was just an old Soviet lunar probe that crashed."

"McKntyre, you know how things work. They found evidence of an extraterrestrial base there. The government believes it belonged to your cousins. Remember them?"

"Daniel," Beth said, wary, "what's he talking about?"

Dan squeezed her hand. "It's extortion. Don't listen to him, baby. He's full of lies. He's just a senile old man—

and he's about to leave."

"You've got balls, McKntyre, talking about 'lies.'"
Terrell gestured at Dan. "Have you looked in the mirror
lately? The eternal spring chicken. So don't tell me about
lies. You live one everyday."

"Am I mistaken, or do I hear jealousy?"

"Stop it—both of you!"

Both men grew quiet, staring at her.

Beth faced Dan. "Why is an FBI agent here?"

Dan gazed at Beth in silence.

Beth turned to Terrell. "Perhaps I can get an answer
from you?"

Terrell glanced first at Dan then to Beth, and shook
his head.

Beth sighed and turned back to Dan. "Okay, fine."

"Beth, wait." Dan rose, reaching for her.

She darted up the stairs.

Dan stared after her in shocked silence.

Terrell rose, stepping toward the younger man. "It
had to be done, McKntyre. It's for the best, for both of you."
He nodded toward the stairway. "She can't leave. They'll
nab her."

Dan turned to Terrell, about to unload, but the look
on the older man's face caught him cold. Dan swallowed.
"She's too damn headstrong. Beth Fisher will do whatever
the hell she wants." He looked hard at the agent. "Why your
sudden concern for our well being? What did you have, an
epiphany?"

Ignoring Dan's question, Terrell reached inside his

coat pocket. Working out a small manila envelope, he tossed it to Dan. "They're yours, for a price."

Quickly opening it, he peered inside. His heart stopped. He looked up in disbelief.

"I see you recognize them," Terrell said, stepping toward the younger man. "It's what I took off that—"

"I know where you got them," Dan said coldly. "It's Satarian."

"Is that what *your* race is called?"

Dan eye him, silent.

"Make sure Beth sees them."

"Beth? Why Beth?"

"We're wasting time, McKntyre."

Dan closed the envelope, eyeing the agent at length. "You mentioned a 'price?'"

Terrell nodded, "I'll get you two to safety—but I'm coming with you." The agent gave a calculated smile. "We'll *all* just 'disappear.'"

"Isn't it a bit early to hit the bottle? What about my daughter, Amy?"

"She's waiting for us, but they really don't care about her, at least not for now. *You* are the prize."

Dan tossed the envelope on the couch and grabbed Terrell by the coat, jerking him up. "So help me, if you're—"

"You'll have to trust me, McKntyre."

"Why are you doing this?"

"Let's just say, it's getting harder to sleep."

"Bullshit."

They both turned at the sound of Beth rushing down

the stairs. Dressed in jeans, sweatshirt, hiking boots and with an overnight bag slung over a shoulder, she hurried toward the foyer.

Releasing Terrell, Dan stepped to her. "So, just like that, you're gone?"

She brushed past, silent.

Dan hurried after her. "Beth." He grabbed her arm.

She jerked free. "If you're not going to explain to me why you're about to be arrested, then I'll not gamble my future by getting arrested with you."

"Beth, I…don't leave—please."

Nearing the foyer, she slowed, eyes wet.

"Listen to him, dear," Terrell said. "You two need each other."

Dan spun around to Terrell.

Reaching the door, Beth hesitated then yanked it open. Stepping out, she left the door swinging. A cold wind whipped through the foyer, blowing drapes about.

Dan glared at Terrell. "If you hadn't opened your mouth—"

"Later, McKntyre. We have to stop her."

Dan swung at the air in disgust. "Shit!" He bolted after her, Terrell close behind. Beth was halfway to her car when Dan caught up to her, blocking her path. "Beth, can't we talk? We've always been able to talk."

Beth's chin quivered. "Daniel, I can't live like this. I have a life of my own. I need to get back to it."

"I thought I was part of that life, Beth." Dan's eyes pleaded. "How can you just…?" He glanced at Terrell, standing a respectful distance away. He returned to the woman in front of him. "I'm flesh and blood, just like you."

"You're not like anyone I know, Daniel." Beth turned, brushing away tears. "I need my old life back—and time to think. I love you, Daniel, but, this is goodbye."

Dan sighed, head hanging. Soft rain began falling.

Beth walked away, leaving Dan standing alone. She neared the front of her Jaguar, hesitating.

"Beth," Dan called out.

She turned, facing him, shaking her head in confusion. "Oh, Dan."

Terrell took a step toward the couple and the air exploded from the crack of a high-powered rifle. The agent collapsed backwards, his chest crimson.

"Simon!" Beth screamed. Ripping the bag from her shoulder, she sprinted over to his fallen body. Dan was already there, kneeling over him.

"God damnit!" she screamed. "This is what I was talking about!"

"Beth, knock it off! Let's get him inside. Help me!"

Dan lifted Terrell's shoulders as Beth grabbed his legs. They half-dragged, half-carried the agent back to the house. Bullets whizzed around them, kicking dirt in their faces.

"They're trying to kill us!" Beth shouted, almost hysterical.

Terrell's eyes fluttered. "*Elizabeth*," he rasped, "they won't kill you. Not yet. They need you two alive."

Struggling backwards, gripping Terrell, Dan stared at Beth.

Beth gave him a hard glance but remained silent.

The gunfire ceased. "*This is the FBI,*" barked a voice over a bullhorn. It came from nearby woods. "*Drop him and stand away with your hands up. You're surrounded. You can't get away. Surrender and you won't be harmed.*"

Terrell flicked a bloody hand in the air, giving the voice the finger. "Keep going," he croaked.

Again the sharp crack of rifle-fire split the air. Bullets thumped around them. "We're almost there," Dan shouted. They dragged Terrell onto the porch. A volley of gunfire flashed from the forest. Bullets spat into a wooden post inches from Dan's face, showering him with stinging splinters. Automatic weapons fired just as they hauled Terrell through the open door. *Ping-ping-ping-ping…* Dan dropped Terrell, slamming the door shut. Bullets smacked angrily into solid oak with a dusty *whop*, but none penetrated. They shattered windows, cutting drapes to ribbons. Glass and debris showered the three as they lay flattened.

Beth crawled to Terrell, throwing herself on top the older man. "Simon, I never meant for it to come to this."

Terrell dragged bloody fingers over her chin. "Elizabeth. Go with McKntyre. He'll protect you. He's kind. Strong." Terrell groaned, coughing. "You and McKntyre are one and the same."

The gunfire ceased. A bullhorn echoed through shattered windows. "*McKntyre, you have ten minutes. Don't make us come in after you. Surrender while you're still ahead. You know what we want. We promise not to hurt you or the woman. Just come out with your hands up.*" There was a pause. "*Ten minutes, beginning NOW.*"

Beth wept softly. His face grave, Dan leaned over the fallen agent. "Where were we supposed to go, Terrell? Where is Amy? Do you understand me?" Dan shook him gently. "We need your help."

Terrell groaned. He winced. "Forget the municipal airfield. They're waiting. Caldwell. Caldwell farm." His eyes rolled back and Dan shook him again. "Seven in the morning," Terrell gasped. "A chopper…take you to Piedras Negras. John will, will…" he paused, catching his breath. "If Ifs and buts were candy and nuts… we'd all have a Merry Christmas." Terrell suddenly gripped Dan's arm. "Elizabeth…like you, McKntyre…take care of her." Arm falling away, his head lolled over, eyes glazing.

Dan sighed, jaw tightening. He closed Terrell's eyes then touched Beth. "We've gotta' go."

Beth wiped her eyes on a sleeve. "Are we surrendering?"

"Hell no!" Crouching, Dan headed for the stairwell. Beth moved to follow when Dan held up a hand. "Stay there," he whispered. Setting the stairwell door ajar, he crawled around to the other side, then signaled to her.

Beth crawled over. "A way out down there?"

"That stairwell leads to an alligator-infested bayou." Grabbing Beth's hand, he pulled her down the hall with him, heading for his study.

"*You have nine minutes, McKntyre,*" shouted the voice. "*Don't do something stupid. You can't get away.*"

The couple burst into the study. Dan flipped over a chair and tossed aside a small piece of carpet, exposing a metal ring. Yanking on it, a trap door swung up from the center of the floor. A dank, musty smell filled the room. A ladder disappeared into gaping darkness.

"Inside, quick," Dan said, shoving Beth down the steps. "It's only ten feet down. I'll be right behind you." Dan quickly straightened the carpet, up-righting the chair over it. Running to his desk, he jerked open a drawer and pulled out a web belt. A .45 auto was tucked into the holster, several ammo magazines attached. He strapped on the belt and grabbed a nearby winter coat. Dan climbed into the opening, pulling the top down as he descended. Fastening a dead-bolt, he clicked on a flashlight and joined Beth at the bottom of the stairs. A backpack and Dan's old shotgun lay nearby, covered with a tarp. Shoving himself into the coat, he tossed the tarp away, shouldering the backpack.

"I can't believe this is happening," Beth said. "An hour ago we were lying quietly in bed, our whole future in front of us."

"Our future is *still* in front of us." Racking the shotgun, he thrust it to her. "Just not here."

Beth slung the shotgun over a shoulder. "My life is gone. Like Simon's. Just like that." She paused. Something flashed across her face. "I'm so tired of running. I say we stay and fight. We have a right to be left alone."

Dan stared. "What do you mean 'tired of running?'"

Beth eyed Dan in silence.

Dan shook his head; there was no time to digest

her words. "Yeah, we have a right to privacy, darlin.' And the gendarmes would like nothing more than for us to hang around and try to prove it."

Beth turned away in disgust.

Chambering a round in the .45, Dan shoved it back in its holster, snapping the flap. Swallowing, he looked past her. A dark, seven-foot diameter tunnel yawned behind them. "Listen carefully: we'll head down this culvert about a mile. It empties near a creek. I have a small boat waiting. Hopefully it's still there. We'll head downstream a few miles then ditch the boat. There's a place we can stay the night. It's only five miles from the old Caldwell farm. Terrell said a helicopter would be there in the morning."

"What if the helicopter doesn't show?"

Suddenly there was a dull *thump*, followed by several more.

"What was that?" Beth whispered.

"Their answer to privacy rights: tear gas. Let's move." They fled down the culvert. As they ran, Dan's mind flashed to thirty-eight years ago, Sentinel Peak. Today he would not falter. God help anyone who got in his way.

The large culvert sloped downward and they made good time. Dan picked up the pace, but after a few minutes Beth began lagging. "Baby," he tugged on her arm, "we have to keep moving. We'll rest later."

"I must stop," Beth panted. She staggered, leaning on the culvert wall. She bent over and threw up.

Dan caressed her back. "It's just nerves. We'll make it." Yanking a bandanna from his pocket, he handed it to her.

Leaning on him, Beth dabbed around her mouth,

eyes softly glowing in the dim light. "I feel better now."

Her gaze made him uneasy and he deliberately turned away. Dan took her hand. "Let's go."

Several minutes later Dan unlocked the fenced gate at the end of the tunnel. Brush fell away. He stepped warily into driving rain. Beth, wearing his rain-slicker, followed Except for the sound of rain and rushing water, all was quiet.

Dan locked the gate behind them, the two-piling back brush. The smell of damp earth filled their nostrils. A swollen creek, now more a river, moved swiftly through a heavy forest of mixed pines and hardwoods. Beth stepped closer to Dan, touching his hand.

He pointed to a brush pile, fifty feet away. "There it is." They hurried to a capsized boat, half submerged in the flooded creek. Dan, Beth helping, pulled the twelve-foot boat further up the bank then flipped it over. Underneath were two paddles and several large coffee cans. "This boat was twenty-feet above the creek bank," he said, gently pushing it into swirling water. "A few more minutes and it would've been gone."

Beth handed Dan the shotgun and, with him holding the boat steady, she carefully climbed in. "No life vests?"

"Life vests?" Dan chuckled dryly, tossing her the coffee cans. "I'll paddle, you bail."

Rain-soaked and shouldering the backpack and shotgun, Dan climbed aboard. Working out his cellphone, he tossed it in the rushing water. He caught Beth watching him.

"You need to do the same."

"But—"she sputtered.

"You know they can track us."

Beth pulled her phone from a back pocket, and, with reluctance, dropped it in the swirling water. "I can't believe this is happening."

Dan shook his head. Shoving off with a paddle, the swift current quickly caught the boat, sweeping it downstream. Dan fought to keep them in the center of the creek and away from debris. After a few minutes the creek widened.

Taking a break from bailing, Beth moved up front with Dan. "Scoot over."

Sliding over, he handed her a paddle. "Just keep us away from the bank."

Drifting with the current, rain pelting, they sat in silence, each anticipating—fearing—the other's questions.

"I can't believe I left it," Dan half-whispered, breaking the stillness.

"Left what?"

Dan stopped paddling. "The envelope that Terrell gave me. I left it sitting on the sofa."

Resting her paddle on the gunwale, she gazed at him. "What are you talking about? What envelope?"

"You were upstairs when Terrell handed me this manila envelope and—"

"So, what was in it? Secret documents or something? What the hell are you involved in, Dan?"

"What am I involved in?" Dan asked. "Terrell wanted you to see what was in that envelope. Why? What the hell are you involved in? You knew Terrell. How?"

"What was in that envelope?"

"Extraterrestrial technology that's centuries beyond ours," Dan blurted. He stared blankly into swirling water. "My, God. What have I done?"

Despair seized him, strangling his insides with an iron grip. He had lived in mortal fear knowing those devices were out there. Then like a miracle, his destiny was suddenly in his own hands—and he blew it. He flat out blew it. Now, he might as well display a neon sign, flashing arrows pointing directly at himself. *Alien, Alien*, the words would beam, *Freak, Bizarre* they would blink. If the government ever had any doubts about his involvement with extraterrestrials, they were now erased.

"You mean that stuff Simon mentioned is true?"

"Do you think those guys were there for a traffic warrant? Girl, I'm right in the cross-hairs."

Both grew silent, the boat drifting lazily downstream.

Dan glanced to Beth. "You and Terrell knew each other."

"I've known Simon for years."

"Unfortunately, so have I." Dan paused, hesitating. "Did you know about the extraterrestrial items?"

Beth returned his gaze. "No."

Did he catch a moment of indecision in her reply?

"And, if they are what you say they are," Beth continued, "why would he give them to you?"

Dan cursed himself for telling Beth about them. Yet, she must be prepared for the government's onslaught. He thought it doubtful the government knew about the items, but they definitely knew about his heritage. Did Beth know his ancestry, he wondered? Still, even if Beth didn't know his family secret, or know about the devices, she wasn't coming clean with everything. Terrell insisting that Beth see the alien devices proved that.

Beth stilled her paddle. "You never answered my question."

Dan studied the dark, rain-laden clouds. "I guess Terrell thought that with my money and interest in interstellar travel, I could unlock a few secrets, use the knowledge constructively." Dan gave a disgusted sigh. "Now, because of my own stupidity, God only knows what I unleashed."

"Honey, it's not your fault. Bullets were flying. Your first instinct was the right one: saving lives." She resumed paddling. "There's nothing we can do about it now."

Silence fell between them. Using the paddle, Dan pushed away from a log. "He called you 'Elizabeth.'"

"You know 'Elizabeth' is my given name. I don't see the big deal."

"It's not *what* Terrell called you, it's the way he spoke your name. Like a father." Shoving his paddle back in the water, Dan gave a determined stroke. "I met an 'Elizabeth' once, but that was decades ago."

"And what was this 'Elizabeth' to you?"

Dan stopped paddling. "If it wasn't for her, I wouldn't be here now."

Beth gazed at him from under her hood, eyes

haunting.

"Are you the little girl who was at Charlie's, the one who gave me that rock that day?"

"I don't know 'Charlie.'" Beth averted her eyes. "And I'm not sure what 'Elizabeth' you refer to."

"The Elizabeth I refer to is the little girl that gave me that rock. She was from South Africa, like you. And then when that rock fell from my coat the night you and I first met, you seemed to recognize it." Dan paused, continuing. "I'll never forget the way that girl looked at me that night at Charlie's, or the next morning when she handed it to me. It was like she recognized me from somewhere. There was a weird connection between us that I couldn't explain."

"Then why haven't you said something to me?"

"Beth, I could ask the same of you. You knew all about my past. Why didn't *you* confront *me*?"

Beth bit a lip, looking away. "I knew what had happened to you and your first wife. I didn't want…" She glanced at Dan. "I wanted something new. What about you, Dan? If you were suspicious, why didn't you bring it up? Was it for the same reason as me?"

Dan paddled slowly, deliberately. "Actually, it was just the opposite. I had this fantasy about you, Beth. This fantasy that part of my past had come back to save me. That little girl, who saved me, now all grown up and coming back into my life, was all just too incredible." He glanced at Beth. "I didn't want that fantasy to end. I wanted to ride that horse as long as I could." Dan paused. "The truth, Beth. Are you the Elizabeth who gave me that rock?"

"No."

The boat drifted. Quiet, contemplative seconds passing. Dan finally broke the silence. "Something just doesn't jive here."

Beth reached for a paddle. Dipping it in the water, she took a long stroke and sighed. "I knew her." Beth paused. "She told me about meeting you."

Dan stared.

"Let's just say, I'm here because Simon grew a conscious."

Tentative moments passed. Dan swallowed. "Was Terrell your father?"

Beth looked away.

"Well screw me with a rusty totem pole," Dan murmured, shoving a paddle back into the swirling water. He gave it several rigorous strokes. "Where's your mother?"

"Decades ago I lost contact with my biological mother. I was young and homeless. I met Simon and I guess I tugged at his heart strings. He was a widower. He had a mistress in South Africa. He and his mistress took me in."

"What happened to the little girl, Elizabeth?"

"She succumbed to what you call leukemia. She was only fifteen."

What **you** *call leukemia? Why did she use the word 'you'? Who the hell is sitting in this boat with me?* Dan rested his paddle against the gunwale, scrutinizing Beth. His thoughts were jumbled. "You two having the same name: must've been confusing—and convenient."

Beth shot him a quick glance, then looked away.

"We worked it out."

"Apparently." Dan catalogued Beth's words and tone. Now wasn't the time to pursue that topic. "Do you know where that 'rock' came from?"

Beth avoided his gaze. "Simon's mistress, whom I called 'mother,' only said it was very rare, worth more than gold. She told me it had special power—that is, would bring good luck and to keep knowledge of it secret." Beth's eyes met Dan's. "Seems it's found a good home."

"Un-f'n-real." Dan murmured, thrusting a paddle back into murky water. "What did Terrell mean when he said you were 'like me?'"

Beth blinked, hesitating a fraction of a second. "I never heard him say *that*."

"Well, he did." Dan shot her a quick glance. "What else are you hiding?"

"What?" Beth glared at Dan. "I can't believe you, of all people, would accuse me of 'hiding' something." Beth gave the water a disgusted jab with her paddle. "And why do you seem so caviler about alien technology? What about that, huh? Jesus, Daniel."

Dan sighed and returned to paddling, occasionally eyeing her, expecting Beth to press him. She remained stubbornly quiet, which ate at him even more.

An hour passed, the creek widening with the rising water. Huge cypress limbs draped with Spanish moss arched over the small boat, creating a dense canopy. Gnarled branches, with splotches of gray, drooping algae cast an unearthly pall over them.

"Daniel, how much longer before we get out of this crap?"

"Right now." He paddled toward the opposite bank. "We're here."

The boat dug into soft earth. Drenched and cold, the couple climbed into knee-deep water. Struggling up the slippery bank, they hauled the boat up as high as they could, flipping it over.

Pulling her collar tight, Beth shivered, staring into the driving rain. "If I keep praying, perhaps I'll wake up." Reaching for her hand, he turned. They slogged through a marsh, their boots oozing into ankle-deep muck. After several miserable minutes, they reached higher ground. Walking near a grove of trees, Dan drew up. "This is it," he said, nodding to a dim path that led into a gloomy, dank forest.

"What about snakes?"

"You're right. This place is crawling with moccasins and copperheads."

"Dan." She pulled away.

"Have you seen any?" he said with a faint smile.

"Well, no. But—"

"It's winter, darlin'; they've all gone beddy-by. Now let's go. My deer-lease isn't far."

Beth stepped past.

Dan caught her arm. Beth's short, auburn hair was pasted to her face, her delicate, porcelain features glistening with rain. She gazed back silently from under her hood.

"Beth, will you marry me?"

"Huh?" Jerking away, she gawked in disbelief. "Are you feeling sorry for me or what? This is a hell of a time to ask!" Beth stomped away, hands on hips. Pausing, she turned fiery eyes on him. "McKntyre, you should come with a warning label! You act like this is 'business as usual,' living on the edge. Yes, I've shared your bed, but sharing this type of world? You can't be serious?" She slapped her thighs. "You're the last type of guy I would ever marry!" Turning, she trudged into the forest.

"Just thought I'd ask," Dan murmured.

Within an hour, the two were standing in front of a small, four-room cabin. Finding no tracks in the muddy road in front, they dashed for the covered porch. Beth looked around anxiously while Dan fumbled with the keys. Seconds later they were inside.

Beth threw off her hood. "Shelter at last. Thank God we don't have to sleep in the woods."

Dan locked the door. Unslinging the shotgun, he leaned it against a chair. "We probably will before it's all over." He paused. "This is probably our last night at 'home' for a long, long time." He sighed, looking away.

"Daniel," Beth said, her gaze softening, "I'm sorry I blew-up out there." She eased her head on his wet shoulder. Dan held her tightly.

The couple settled in. Beth checked the cabinets. They were well stocked with canned and dry goods. Reaching for a light switch, she flicked it up and down. Nothing. "No electricity?"

"Only if I fire-up the generator," Dan shouted from

the living room. "But it's diesel and makes a hell of a racket. I don't think it's wise."

"How about heat?"

"I'll turn on the propane," Dan said. "We can run the stove for heat and cooking. No fireplace tonight. The smoke could give us away."

Beth noticed a washer and dryer in the corner of the small kitchen. She turned and ran into the living room. "Dan, please—the generator?" She touched her damp sweatshirt. "I have nothing but these soggy things. I feel like a prune."

"I've got a closet full of clothes. You can wear some of mine until—"

"It won't hurt to run the generator for a few hours," Beth pleaded. "No telling when we'll have clean clothes again."

Dan sighed, then stepped outside, turned on the propane, and started the generator. He came back and lit the water-heater. "We'll have hot water in thirty minutes. Enjoy."

It was after dark when he shut off the generator. Beth lit an oil lamp, placing it on the kitchen table. Taking a seat, Dan opened a half-warm beer, trying to collect his thoughts. Beth glanced at him strangely, then walked to the dryer. She began quietly folding clothes. Dan eyed her. She wore baggy sweat pants and one of his flannel shirts, which hung over her like a burlap sack. When she moved a certain way, the shirt highlighted her curves. He tried not to stare, still feeling the sting from her words earlier in the day.

As if reading his thoughts, Beth turned from her task,

gazing at him. "Dan, I don't know what you want from me. It's just…" She shrugged. "This isn't how I envisioned our future."

"*Our* future?"

"Yes."

"What about your life, Beth? Your business, condo, friends—they're all gone. This is some serious shit. I'm sure you know there's no going back for either of us." He paused. "It's gone."

Beth plopped down across from him. Taking a sip of his beer, she gazed at him. "What about you? You've got a helluva lot more to lose than I."

Dan remained silent. She took another sip. "Hello, Daniel? You're a billionaire! What about *your* loss? Can't you buy our way out of this?"

"Money will get us away," he said, reaching for the beer can. He took a quick swallow. "But ghosts have no use for money. They'll always be there, hovering around me." He downed the beer and fidgeted. He reached for Beth's hand. "This morning, when Terrell was there, you were going to walk out on me."

"But I left the door open, didn't I?"

"You mean…?"

Beth snickered and Dan jumped for her. Ducking, she rose, sprinting across the kitchen, playfully screaming. Dan cornered her near the dryer. Beth spun around as Dan's arms slid around her soft, supple form. She never struggled.

Their lips parted as Beth lifted up from Dan. Breasts jutting out, perspiration dripped from her face, mingling with the sweat on his chest. Her eyes were closed, her breath ragged. Suddenly stiffening, she convulsed, nails raking across his chest. She collapsed, her teeth sinking gently into his shoulder.

Beth's heart pounded against his. His fingers traced over delicate shoulders.

Their breathing settled to a steady cadence. After a moment, Beth rolled off him.

"Dan?" Beth whispered.

"Yes, baby?"

"What *did* Simon mean when he said 'some of your kind?'"

"I, uh, I'm not sure."

"No mind games, Daniel," Beth said. "It's like you knew all this was coming down. The tunnel, the boat, this place. You had everything planned."

"Just friggin' ESP."

"Cut the crap." Beth turned her head on the pillow, gazing at him. "Why are they after you?"

"Because," Dan rolled over, facing her, "I know too much. Terrell and my late wife uncovered evidence of an extraterrestrial visit. Only five people on Earth—that I know of—knew the truth about it. Two are dead and two won't talk."

"That's only four."

"You're looking at the fifth."

Beth frowned. "Other than being Anna's husband,

how did *you* get involved? Were you a government agent?"

"No."

"Then what are you?" A quiet moment lapsed. "Answer me, Daniel." Beth shifted, facing him. "If there's something you haven't told me about yourself, you better speak now." Her eyes searched his in the gloom. "You asked me to marry you today."

"And you said, 'no.'"

"I didn't say 'no.'"

"Christ, you were just so subtle. What do you say when you really mean 'no?'"

"If you want us to share a life," Beth said, "we start with honesty."

Swallowing, he took a deep breath. "Those extraterrestrials I mentioned? They were Anna's grandparents. And mine."

Beth rose on an elbow and her eyes widened. "You're lying!"

Dan shook his head.

She abruptly turned her back to him. "I never believed—Why didn't you *tell me*?"

"Beth?"

She never answered.

Dan lay as if paralyzed. After several agonizing seconds he touched her bare shoulder. "Beth, talk to me."

She remained silent.

Dan gently caressed her back. He was in uncharted territory. He had never spoken his secret out loud in over thirty years. What is the proper way of telling someone that your ancestors came from another world? Not only would you lose all credibility but they would think you were a couple of french fries short of a *Happy Meal*. Dan swallowed, sighing. "Damn, girl, it's not like I commit ritualistic animal sacrifices or something."

Beth remained silent.

He let his hand drop.

"To borrow one of your sayings, 'I don't know whether to laugh or cry.'"

"Beth?"

She spun around and buried herself in his arms. "I, I just need time to digest all this. Give me time. Please."

Dan held her tightly. They clung to one another as the terror of the day's episode finally played out.

"What was that?" Dan shot up in the darkness, the bed creaking loudly. He glanced at the battery-powered clock: 3:25 A.M. "I heard something!"

"You're dreaming again, baby," Beth murmured. Laying a warm arm on his shoulder, she curled up to him. "Go back to sleep."

A car door slammed and Dan bolted. Jumping into Wranglers, he grabbed the .45 hanging from the bedpost, chambering a round. Holding the pistol low, he crept into the living room. Beth scampered out of bed, throwing a blanket over her shoulders. Snatching the nearby shotgun and flashlight, she followed Dan.

Keys rattled and the front doorknob twisted. Dan waved Beth back as he snuck behind the door. It creaked. Someone slowly stole through. Dan aimed the pistol at his head. "Freeze."

The guy froze.

Another person stepped through the door. Beth racked the shotgun. The person in the doorway halted mid-stride.

"*Senor* Daniel, it's me!" said the terrified man Dan held at gunpoint.

"Jose?"

"Si—yes!"

Beth clicked on the flashlight, illuminating a frightened Amy, Maria behind her.

"Dad, it's us! Thank God you're alive!"

Beth lowered the shotgun, visibly shaken. "We could've killed you."

"Jose!" Dan embraced the older man by the shoulders. "Man, are we ever glad to see you!" He glanced to the others. "Hope none of you have a phone on you."

"I pushed the 'fry' button on mine" Amy said, "and tossed it out the car window back in Dallas." She nodded to Maria. "They didn't like it, but I made sure they did the same."

Beth sighed. "Well, everyone, don't just stand there."

Minutes later, all five sat hunched around the kitchen table in the faint light of an oil lamp, catching up on events. Shadows played large on the walls.

"So," Dan glanced at Amy, "how did you know where to find us?"

"I know you," Amy replied, a strange edge in her voice. In the flickering light, she stared at her father. "That's why I'm shocked. How could you keep this from me?"

Beth and the Garcia's heads snapped around.

"Agent Terrell stopped by my home late day-before-yesterday," Amy continued. "He told me not to contact you

that evening. He warned me that this was going to happen—
and why." Amy twisted uneasily. "Tell me it's not true."

Dan averted his eyes. "Amy, forgive me. I was going
to tell you. I just didn't know how."

"Damnit, Father!" Amy screamed, slamming an
angry fist on the table. "Why didn't you tell me about our
ancestors?" She aimed an accusing finger at him. "How
could you keep something like this from me?"

Feeling their worried glances, Dan's head sagged.
They all trusted him; now that trust wavered.

"Amy, was that necessary?" Beth said, breaking the
stillness.

"Who are *you* to ask that?"

Beth turned red, biting a lip. Tense seconds passed.
She suddenly jumped up, knocking over her chair, and darted
for the bedroom.

Dan sighed. "Here we go again." He buried his face
in his hands. "That's all I need—two pissed-off females!
Find the FBI. I'm surrendering." He dashed after Beth.
Taking three steps, he pulled up, grabbing his left knee.
Cursing, he hobbled to the bedroom.

Beth lay face down on the bed, gripping a pillow. "I
just want to wake up."

"I know you do, honey." Dan limped over to her.
"I too felt I was in a nightmare that wasn't my making." He
paused. "I came clean. Now it's your turn."

She hugged a pillow, silent.

"Let me guess," Dan began. "I think you became
'orphaned' around, let's say, nineteen eighty-six?"

Beth sniffed. "That was a long time ago."

"I never forgot your eyes. The way you looked at me when we were in the helicopter." Dan paused. "You're her, the 'alien girl,' aren't you? The one who Terrell said died."

She nodded against the pillow. "Yes. And I also lost someone close to me that day."

"I know. He was close to both of us." Dan sat down on the edge of the bed, his gaze softening. "My sweet baby," he whispered, gently running a hand through her hair. "Didn't you know that I'd eventually find out?"

"I could say the same," Beth cried. "All I ever wanted was to fit in. And it was working until *you* came along." Rolling over, she cast a challenging glance. "Simon was right: you and I do have something in common—a past. And mine is just as dead as yours."

"Our past isn't 'dead.' It's waiting for us in another time and place. But you're right; not here." Dan hesitated, then rose.

"Daniel."

He paused, gauging her. God, they shared so much! Yet why weren't the words there?

Beth begin to speak, then sighed and fell silent.

Dan shook his head and headed back to the kitchen.

Minutes later, Beth returned to the kitchen table, her eyes on Dan. Maria stepped to her, murmuring.

Dan glanced at Amy. "Did Terrell tell you his plans?"

"Not exactly," Amy replied, an edge still in her voice. "He said Jose and Maria were due in. He wanted me to meet them at the airport and send them back to Honduras.

Said it was too dangerous for them here."

The two elder Hondurans had remained quiet throughout the whole affair. Now Maria spoke. "We will not leave you, Daniel." Holding Beth's hand, Maria reached across the table and placed her other hand on Dan's. "You're like a son to us—*familia*. We will not abandon *familia*." She turned to Beth. "And you, *senorita*, have brought a life to Daniel that we have never seen."

Beth smiled meekly. "As Daniel has done to me."

Dan's gaze caught Beth's. His heart raced. He had a thousand questions. He wanted to give himself up to her—and he sensed she felt the same—but that would open a flood gate of emotions that neither was equipped for. Dan nodded at Beth. Her eyes held a faint shine. It seemed as if he and Beth were looking *into* each other. She smiled, returning his nod.

Everyone grew quiet. Dan scrutinized his daughter with concern. "Amy, did Terrell say what to do once the Garcias were gone?"

"He told me to destroy my cellphone, pack what I could get in one bag, then be at the old Caldwell farm by six this morning. Said he, you, and Beth would be there. A helicopter is supposed to meet us at seven, then fly us all to Piedras Negras, Mexico."

Dan nodded. "Did he mention a final destination, money, or anything else?"

"No, Dad. He did tell me not to contact you—said all communications were monitored." Amy chewed a lip. "Dad, you ought to hear what they're saying about you. The police said you killed him! They said Terrell was serving a warrant for tax-evasion when you blew him away in cold blood."

"Amy," Beth broke in, "Simon's own people killed him and they almost got us."

Amy shook her head. "They said you're desperate. That you'll kill anyone who gets in your way."

"Now I'm a desperado." Dan chuckled. "You know what? They're right." Sighing, he scrutinized them, one at a time. They gazed back, hoping for answers. Dan prayed he had them.

Lifting his backpack from the floor, he dumped the contents on the table. *Thump*. Two million dollars in stacks of twenties, fifties and hundreds hit the table. All eyes widened. No matter how wealthy one is, it still does something to see that much money piled in one spot. Jose whistled; Amy and Maria simply stared.

"Damn," was all Beth managed.

Dan stuffed $600,000 in a money belt, shoving it in his backpack. He spread the remainder among the other four, who put it in overnight bags. "If we're careful, this should get us where we need to be. I have some *real* friends in Nicaragua—ex-*Contras*. They know how to hide, fight—"

"And die," Jose said soberly, shaking his head. "First Cocoa, now opiates."

Dan glanced at him, his jaw tightening.

"Daniel," Maria interrupted. "I also have people there I can trust. My father's Miskito Indian. His family lives in the jungle villages. There, we will all be safe."

"As safe as one can be hanging out with drug-smugglers," Dan added dryly. "The region's infested with them. Even the law shies away, which is a plus for us."

Within minutes they were outside in predawn darkness, loading gear into an old, beat-up Suburban Jose had borrowed from a friend. The rain had ceased, but water dripped incessantly around them. Dan caught Beth and Amy off to one side in an animated, heated exchange. Beth threw up her arms, glanced at Dan, then looked away.

The last bag was tossed in. He called to the two women. "Ladies, it's time."

Amy brushed silently past, Beth following. Dan gave Beth a questioning look. Avoiding his eyes, she followed Amy to the truck.

Jose driving, the Suburban slipped and slid down the muddy road. Amy remained unusually quiet. Whenever Dan glanced at her, she looked away. He cursed himself for not telling her of her heritage. He wondered how much she really knew. In the upcoming days, he would explain all to her. Damn, would he ever get it right?

The Suburban slid to a halt at the highway in the chilly, gray dawn. Foggy, wet mist rolled across the road, shrouding the forest on the other side. Twenty minutes later the Suburban, in thick fog, eased to a stop at the old Caldwell farm.

All climbed out, stretching. Shoving the .45 behind him in his waistband, Dan glanced at his watch: 6:30. He looked around, a cool mist stinging his face. He strained to see. "Damn, this is pea soup."

Beth gave Dan a worried glance. "There's no way a helicopter is coming through this crap."

Amy pointed to a large shadow in the fog. "It's already here."

Nearly obscured in the mist, a huge dark shape, like a giant bovine, sat motionless in the nearby pasture.

Grabbing their bags, they hustled the thirty yards to a blue-and-white Jet-Ranger. All was quiet; there was no sign of anyone.

Dan opened the pilot's door. Without warning, a man bolted out of the back seat, blurry-eyed and holding a gun. Dan's .45 was instantly in his hand.

They stood facing one another other, pistols in each other's face.

"Didn't mean to startle you," Dan said casually.

"Just resting my eyes." The man, who had to be near eighty, lowered his pistol. "You're Bo McKntyre's son. Recognize you anywhere." Pausing, he gave Dan a curious look. "Thought you'd be older."

Dan stuffed his pistol back in his waistband. "You knew my father?"

Donning a baseball cap, the old man climbed out of the cabin and stretched. He was shorter than Dan, rail thin, and spry as a quail. "Flew with him in Plieu Ku back in 'Seventy-two. First Air Cav'." He chuckled. "Hell, I was just a pup back then." The man removed his glasses, wiping them with a handkerchief. "Damndest gunship driver I ever saw." Replacing the glasses on his nose, he thrust out his hand. "John—John Saxon."

As the two shook, the older man looked around. "Where's Simon?"

"He didn't make it," Beth said. "And neither will we if you don't get this thing in the air."

"And who the hell are you?"

"Beth Fisher."

"So, you're his *other* daughter," the older man said, scrutinizing her. "You must favor your mother." Saxon looked past Beth and nodded to the Garcia's. "I don't remember any wet-backs in the deal."

Dan's eyes narrowed. "They're family. If you don't have room, I'll ride on the fucking skid."

"I'm sure you would. Heard about you—Army Ranger and all. Your old man would be proud." His gaze tightened. "Where you're going, you should feel right at home." He turned to Beth. "I'm sorry about your father. We had worked together at the agency. After retirement, we kept in touch. I told him he was stepping on too many toes. He knew this might happen." Striding to the side of the helicopter, Saxon yanked opened the passenger door. "It's all paid for," he said. "Don't just stand there. I'm not your friggin' stewardess."

A few moments later Saxon, in the pilot's seat, began flipping switches and turning knobs as everyone stowed gear. A high-pitched whine filled the air, the turbojet engine spooling-up. Rotor blades turned painfully slow, gradually picking up speed.

"I got here before this shit settled in," Saxon shouted to Dan, who was standing just outside the pilot's open door.

"It's only ground fog. We get a few hundred feet up and it's smooth sailing, trust me." Saxon ducked his head inside and lit a cigar, then gestured to the swirling mist. "This'll keep their puppy-asses on the porch. By the time it lifts, we'll be tilting Sols and doing *la vida loca* in Mexico."

The whirling blades created a horrendous racket, the rotor-wash flattening grass outwards. Dan helped the Garcia's strap in, then turned to help Beth. Amy remained outside. Giving Beth a questioning look, he dropped what he was doing and strode out to his daughter. Beth ran after him.

"Amy, what is it with you?" Dan shouted, approaching her. Something behind her caught his attention and he halted. A black-and-white state trooper's car loomed up out of the fog.

Instinctively Dan reached for his gun. Beth held his hand. "No! It's not what you think!"

"What the hell's going on here?" Dan shouted.

Amy turned to her father. "He's here to pick me up."

Dan stared in shocked silence.

Amy stood in front of her father. The trooper stepped from the cruiser, casually walking up to her. She moved next to him, then looked at Dan. "I love you, Dad, but I'm staying. My home is here," she reached for the trooper's hand, "with him."

Dan felt left out, abandoned. He never had a clue. About to speak, he did a double take at the highway patrolman. "Davy? Davy Fulton?"

Charlie Fulton's grandson smiled. "Hello, Dan. It's been awhile. What was it Grandpa used to call you when he was pissed—'Danny-boy?'" He nodded to Beth. "I see you made it 'Beth.'" The trooper paused. "Got a strange email from a retired FBI agent Simon Terrell last week. Un-freaking-believable."

Dan and Beth exchanged glances; Dan swore under his breath.

Davy eyed Beth. "Take care of him—for Amy and my folks."

"I intend to."

Dan sighed, shaking his head. "I see some of Charlie has rubbed off on you." He stepped toward the younger man. They grabbed one another.

Davy stepped back to Amy. "Dan, you don't have to do this," he said. "Someone on the TAC unit that hit your home spilled his guts. All charges of killing the agent are dropped. Come with me. We can get this straightened out."

"I can't go back," Dan said. "If you heard from Agent Terrell, you know why. Administrations will change. It will happen again."

Amy stepped forward, standing in front of her father. "Dad, listen to him. Don't let it end this way!" Her eyes welled; she stepped closer. "Davy and I are getting married. For Christ's sake, stay here. Watch your grandchildren grow up."

Dan gazed at his daughter. "And their children, and their children."

Davy's brow furrowed. "So it's true? You guys can live—"

Dan moved toward the trooper. "I can give you over

three-hundred reasons why you shouldn't marry Amy."

Beth stepped in front of Dan. "Daniel—no!" Her eyes held a silver hue. "Let Amy have her life; let her be happy."

All four gazed at one another in silence. The rotor wash increased to gale force, scattering dirt and debris around them, pulling at their clothes. Without a word, Dan and Beth turned, heading for the chopper. Dan dragged his feet, then paused and turned back. Amy rushed toward him. "Dad!" She launched herself into his arms. "I feel like a traitor."

Dan embraced her. "No, you have the brains in the family. And congratulations—you couldn't have found a better man. Keep the money I gave you as a wedding gift, as poor as it is."

Amy sobbed. "But, who will walk me down the aisle?"

Dan released her, wiping his eyes on his sleeve.

"This isn't 'goodbye,'" Amy said, "it's 'so long.' We'll do what we can from here to clear your name, but it would be easier if you stayed."

"Ain't gonna' happen, little girl."

Amy's eyes were swollen. "Take care of Beth; she needs you."

"Amy!" Davy shouted over the roar of the turbojet.

"Your man is calling," Dan said. "Go to him."

Amy hesitated, then turned, sprinting back to Davy.

Dan trotted for the helicopter, Beth at his side. They scrambled in, never looking back. Slamming the door shut,

Dan signaled to the pilot. With a jar they lifted off and were swallowed by fog.

Beth reached for Dan's hand. After a moment she handed him a headset. "Amy is grown, Daniel. You must let her go; now you must focus on your new child."

He frowned, headphones dangling. "Say what?"

Beth's eyes searched his. "I'm pregnant."

34

Maria stood inside a doorway. "*Senor* Daniel, the tribe leaders say you are welcome to stay as long as you can supply medicine."

"Thanks, Maria. Just tell them we'll be moving on in a week or so. I'll see that they're well-stocked with the medicines they need." Dan paused. "I'll talk to the chief about it. What did you say his name was?"

"Jorge."

"Jorge," Dan repeated. "Tell Jorge, I'll meet with him when he returns from the fishing trip." Dan sat at an old picnic table inside a room that passed for a kitchen.

"*Si*." Maria nodded, disappearing down the long, rickety steps leading to soggy ground.

Dan rose and strolled to the open window. There were no screens on any of the numerous windows, which were designed to catch the sea breeze coming in from the Caribbean coast, twenty miles away. He glanced across the muddy road to the other ramshackle houses built on stilts. The poverty-stricken Miskito fishing village on Nicaragua's east coast stood in stark contrast to what they had left behind less than two weeks earlier. Dan sighed, reflecting; it seemed like a year had passed since they had lifted off on that foggy morning, escaping from Texas, the United States. Dan winced inside at the word *escape*.

"Daniel."

He turned, eyeing Beth, who sat at the far end of the picnic table. She was scribbling in her journal. "Yes, baby?"

"I feel the same way."

Dan gave a quizzical look.

"That 'not-in-control, out-of-my-hands' feeling I see in you." Beth clicked the pen, set it inside the spiral and closed the notebook. "I felt the same way thirty-nine years ago, and the memory of that nightmare still lingers."

Dan stepped behind Beth and gently rubbed her shoulders. "You're reading my mind—again."

Beth sighed, closing her eyes. After a moment she stilled his hand. "Would you like to know my birth name?"

Dan paused at the suddenness of the subject. "Doesn't matter. You'll always be 'Beth' to me. But, yes, I'd kinda like to know—just curious. But it can wait." Dan seated himself across from her. "If I let it, knowing who or 'what' you actually are would send me screaming into the night."

"'What *you* are?' Honey, *you* and *I* are of the same race."

"From totally different backgrounds." Dan paused. "I didn't fly all over the galaxy or pilot a starship—."

"—Your great-grandfather piloted a starship." Beth

gave an exasperated sigh. "Last week, when I asked you about the *Halaena*, you said you became Kalyn through his ishara and were able to destroy the ship. Kalyn was its pilot. I bet I could put you behind the controls of starcruiser and within a few hours you'd have it down."

It had been over thirty years since the mention of the *Haleana*. Last week, Beth asked if he was responsible for the *Haleana's* destruction. It caught him off-guard. Yet, to his surprise, the opening of old wounds didn't bring on an onslaught of painful memories.

"Tyona Faelian."

Broken from his thoughts, Dan blinked. "What?"

"That was my Satarian name: Tyona Faelian." Beth looked wistfully past Dan.

"Tyona," Dan pronounced slowly, "Faelian?"

Beth nodded. "Yes, Faelian."

Dan recalled Anna having different identities. Would he follow in those tracks, he wondered? He gazed at Beth for long moment. "I hope you don't want me to start calling you Tyona. Don't know if I could do that."

"I'm Beth, Daniel." She touched his hand, caressing him. "I'll always be Beth Fisher."

Dan gripped her fingers. God, they seemed even more slender than before. He smiled and nodded. "So be it."

"While we're on the Satarian subject," Beth began, "those Satarian devices you left lying on the couch back home—they really worry me."

"Me, too." Dan released Beth's fingers. "I'm not sure what Terrell got, but I saw Ason use a weapon. It really did a number on one of those bad guys."

"Ason only took a photon pistol and a traser. They were carried in a pouch-like container—"

"Yep. Terrell got them. I saw him take two devices from this metallic pouch and shove them in his pants. He also cut off some kind of device from Ason's collar."

"The molecular communicator."

"Afraid so."

Beth gave a long sigh. "The communicator scares me the most. It will be the easiest—and most dangerous—to back-engineer."

"It's all dangerous. Our technology compounds monthly. Today's gadgets, six months later, don't even make good doorstops. Satarian technology? A steroid on steroids. In no time we'll be lightyears—literally—ahead of where we should be. Medieval serfs with machine guns." Dan paused, scrutinizing Beth. "But why are you more worried about the communicator? I figured the weapon would be of most concern."

"Back-engineering that weapon will take a while." Beth gazed at Dan. "The communicator, however, might activate during disassembly. It will send out a plus-light pulse, marking earth's spot to anyone out there who's listening."

"The Satarians already know about us." Dan paused, eyeing Beth. "You wouldn't be referring to those lizard creatures, the Brazaryans, would you?"

"I most certainly would." Beth paused. "Daniel, I think they're already sniffing around. All the plus-light transmissions from this world back in the eighties may have piqued their interest."

"Do you think the rash of UFO sightings around the world the past two decades has anything to do with them?"

"Absolutely. It's their calling card. I think those UFOs are nothing but Brazaryan probes. The Braz never take unnecessary risks. Once they realize we can't defend ourselves, then it's all over. Earth will never have witnessed such slaughter; an apocalypse on an unmitigated scale."

Dan sighed, leaning back. "Well, there goes the neighborhood."

Beth reached out, touching his hand. "It could happen anytime, but that's doubtful. More than likely it will be within the next year or two if they follow their past actions. They are predictable." Beth paused. "One thing they won't do is wait around for us to develop a defense. And Daniel, the Braz won't announce their intentions and ask for parley or surrender. They will hit like a salt-water croc. It will be ruthless."

Dan rose, making his way to a window. Two young children were pushing a truck tire down the muddy, rutted road, a small child inside the tire. He thought about the current technology of the U.S. and compared it to what he was gazing at now. Inside, he cringed. He figured Brazaryan technology was on par with Satarian. He shuddered to think of that advanced technology used to enslave and murder.

Without warning, soft arms encircled his waist, warm breath tickling his neck. "Beth?"

Beth snuggled against his back. "What is it, my

love?"

"Do you think the Satarian government still has that death warrant out on you?"

"Now look who's reading the other's thoughts?"

"We, as in Earth, are going to need some help."

Beth sighed, her grip tightening. "I know."

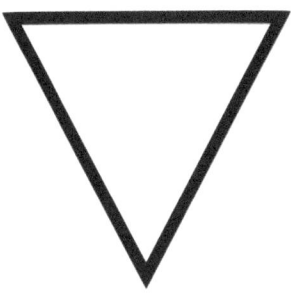

ABOUT THE AUTHOR
JAY CHALK

Jay Chalk is the author the dystopian novel, *Revolution 2050* (Dancing Lemur Press). A long-haul trucker at one time, he now lives in East Texas and is a twenty-two year veteran high school teacher of U.S. Government and History. When he's not teaching, writing, or playing the guitar, he's flying. Currently he's working on a sequel to *Sentinel Peak*.